A YEAR OF FINDING HAPPINESS

LISA HOBMAN's debut novel was shortlisted in the 2014 RNA. Her stories centre around believable, yet down to earth characters and the places in Scotland she has visited and fallen in love with. She is a happily married mum of one with two energetic dogs.

A YEAR OF FINDING HAPPINESS

Lisa Hobman

www.ariafiction.com

First published as *Bridge of Hope* in 2014

First published as *A Year of Finding Happiness* in 2017
by Aria, an imprint of Head of Zeus Ltd

9 7 5 3 1 2 4 6 8

A CIP catalogue record for this book is available from the British Library.

ISBN 9781035903535

Aria c/o Head of Zeus
First Floor East
5–8 Hardwick Street London
EC1R 4RG
www.ariafiction.con

Also by Lisa Hobman

A Seaside Escape

About *A Year of Finding Happiness*

Poignant, heart–warming and gorgeously romantic, this is a love–story with pure, unadulterated happiness at its heart. *A Year of Finding Happiness* shows you that the little things in life can make you smile, even when you think you might never laugh again…

Happiness doesn't factor on the deliciously rugged but utterly heartbroken Greg's radar much these days. Only his beloved Labrador Angus seems to understand his search for a way to make sense of tragedy, until he meets new neighbour Mallory Westerman…

Instantly they know that the other understands how they feel, and over time, as romance blossoms, they dare to wonder if they might, one day, be truly happy again…

There are two sides to every story, and *A Year of Finding Happiness* is Greg's journey back from the darkest depths to happiness…

A Year of Finding Happiness was previously published as *Bridge of Hope*.

Prologue

I watched her falling... down... down... down. I was helpless. I could do nothing, say nothing. The woman I loved more than anything in the world was falling to her death and all I could do was stand there...

*

I sat bolt upright and my eyes sprang open. My chest heaved, desperately trying to pull air into lungs that burned. As usual I was soaked in sweat and my legs were tangled in the sheets whilst the rest of my body shook violently, thanks to the images racing through my mind all too clearly...

Chapter One

Present Day

It had been the same damned nightmare again.

I'd been experiencing what the doctor called *night terrors* ever since receiving the news that Mairi had been declared dead. The love of my fucking life… *dead*. There were no words to describe the physical pain knotting my insides every time I realised it was true and not just a cruel dream.

There had been no body to bury. But apparently that's not uncommon when people are lost up the side of a mountain like K2. People can lie undiscovered for years up there, so I'm told.

Sobering thought.

Over and over I asked myself why she couldn't just be satisfied with bagging Munros here in Scotland. It's not as if there's a shortage. But of course that wasn't enough of a challenge for her. She was a free spirit; an adrenaline junky.

The stupid thing was that I wasn't even there when her accident happened, but for some bizarre reason my psyche had built up its own series of events and insisted on torturing me with the movie of Mairi's death every time I closed my eyes.

What I wouldn't give for a peaceful night's sleep.

I'd taken on extra work whenever I wasn't on the water. The boat was only a seasonal thing anyway. And although tourists loved the area surrounding the bridge over the Atlantic, taking a trip out on *Little Blue* on choppy water wasn't for faint-hearted, unseasoned sailors. So I'd taken on work as a handyman. I was fixing taps, sealing sinks, unblocking drains. Oddly, all the jobs seemed to be water related. Maybe that was because I had a combination of water and single malt running through my veins. Who knows?

Keeping busy was my intention. Being occupied was the only thing stopping me from slipping into a deep depression, and I knew all too well how easy it would've been just to let go and fall into the abyss as Mairi did in my nightmares.

I'd met her when I was out walking. I'd pretty much given up hope of ever falling in love for real. I'd had a shot at it before – Alice was her name, but the less said about her right now, the better. But life likes to throw in curveballs every so often. And so there I was up by the Buachaille, aka the Buckle, Etive Mor in the Highlands, taking in the finest scenery my home country has to offer and the freshest air you could ever wish to breathe, when this fiery-haired girl tripped over her laces and into my arms. She had the most stunning smile I'd ever seen.

And her eyes... Let's just say when she gazed up at me she melted my heart.

We chatted for ages and it was just... so *natural.* It turned out she and I shared a passion for the great outdoors. The rugged expanses of moorland that stretched out around us in their palette of browns, russets and gold were a pull for both of us. Only her sense of adventure outweighed mine ten to one. Where I loved to saunter along appreciating the warm musty smell of the bracken and heather, she loved to climb anything that had stood still for over a hundred years. And here in Scotland there's plenty of that around.

It was clear to me from that first meeting that I was never going to be the same again.

Our relationship progressed quickly and was *very* physical. I was a fair few years older than her but I had no trouble keeping up, if you know what I mean. I loved every inch of her body with a passion I'd never experienced before. It was raw and real. I'd sit watching her as she studied maps and reference books about climbing. Every so often she'd glance up and catch me staring and she'd just smile, climb into my lap, and kiss me.

After Alice and I split – I won't bore you with the details yet, let's just say that she was a nasty piece of work who messed with my head and broke my heart, more than once – I swore off love and all it entailed. I didn't *need* a woman in my life. Or so I thought. But when I lost Mairi, it was as if someone had ripped out my heart and stamped on it whilst I watched. The pain was excruciating.

Physical, gut-twisting pain.

I felt sure they'd got it wrong. She went to K2 with experienced climbers. *She* was an experienced mountaineer too. It'd been her dream for so long. I wasn't about to stand in her way, and the thought that she might not come back never even entered my head.

Not being able to say goodbye was the worst thing. The small memorial service held by her parents was strangely devoid of emotion. It was as if her friends and family were in some kind of denial.

I think I was too.

Thinking back to the morning she left for the trip broke my heart, but I couldn't stop myself. It was just like those recurring nightmares, only more painful.

*

Her long, titian curls fanned out on the pillow beside me and she smiled as she slept. She was exposed to me from the waist up and I lay there on my side, willing her to awaken. I wasn't going to see her for months and I wanted to get my fill whilst I still could. I gently stroked her chin, down between her creamy bare breasts to her navel. It was cruel but I wanted her to open her eyes. Instead she whacked my hand away and muttered expletives. I burst out laughing, trying my best to do it quietly but failing miserably.

She picked up one of the spare pillows and hit me on the head with it, making me chuckle again. 'Gregory McBradden, you're a total shit. I was having a really sexy dream,' she whined, eyes still closed.

I leaned in and, with my mouth next to her ear, I whispered, 'Open your eyes and let's make your dream come true, love.' That got her every time. Goose bumps pricked her skin and she moaned. Her eyes sprang open and she pounced on me, pushing me onto my back and straddling my waist.

God, she was so beautiful.

I gazed up at her. Her pert breasts begging for my touch. I was already hard, but seeing her like this did something to my insides and brought out the animalistic side of me. I gripped her hips as I inhaled a deep breath, trying my best to calm the furnace raging beneath my skin. As she bent to take my mouth in a deep, sensual kiss, her hair cascaded to my chest. Our tongues slipped and slid together in an erotic dance, and every nerve in my body sprang to life just for her. Every fibre of my being was drawn to her; needed her.

I swept the hair back from her face and fixed my eyes on hers.

'Do you know how much I love you, Mairi? Do you know how much I'm going to miss you when you're gone? It doesn't matter how far apart we are. You're still in here,' I said, touching my head. 'And in here.' I touched my chest over my heart. She stared silently at me for a moment and then closed her eyes. A tear slipped down her cheek and I caught it with my thumb. 'Hey, what's wrong?'

She inhaled deeply. 'Nothing. I'm just… really nervous about the whole trip. K2 has been my dream for so long, but now… I'm terrified. What if I'm not fit enough? What if I can't do it, Greg?'

I slid my calloused hands up her smooth, taut thighs where they gripped me, to the dip between her hip and waist as my eyes followed the journey of my fingers. I swallowed hard at the feel of her muscles tightening under my caress, and my breath caught in my throat as I replied, 'Come on, love, you *are* fit enough and strong enough. You've been working towards this for so long, how could you not be? You're bound to be nervous. But you're fulfilling a dream, and there's not many folk can say they've done that. You'll be fine. Absolutely fine. But I might not be.' I stuck out my bottom lip, trying to lighten the mood. 'My heart might break into a million pieces when I'm left here by mysel'. What will I do?'

She bent and kissed my nose. And then, with a sexy smile, she smoothed her hands down my chest and it was my turn to shiver.

'You'll have to dream of me naked on top of you like this, and that'll cheer you up.' She rolled her hips, making me bite my lip.

I inhaled deeply. 'Aye, I suppose it will. But having you back here so I can do this again…' In one sweep of my arms I had her beneath me, my body between her silky thighs. I sank into her, pleasure radiating from where we were joined. '… is what I'll be looking forward to.'

A breathy moan escaped through her full lips. She closed her eyes as she welcomed me in and slipped her arms around my neck. I kissed her everywhere I could reach, taking each nipple into my mouth slowly and nibbling on the little buds as they tightened. Gasping, she fixed her eyes on mine as I moved deep within her.

Overwhelming emotions ripped through me as I made love to her. *My Mairi.* I took in every sensation and every look; my heart aching at the thought of being apart from her for so long. As she pulsed around me and her orgasm took her soaring off into the stratosphere, I kept my gaze locked on hers, hoping I was conveying everything through my eyes that I couldn't put into words, and I followed soon after.

Afterwards, we lay there in each other's arms for what felt like hours. I was unwilling to let her go, telling myself I'd hold her for a few minutes more. When she eventually withdrew from my embrace, I lay back and fought the fears niggling deep within me.

Stupid fears.

What if she meets someone who's more her age? What if she meets someone who loves climbing the way she does? What if she doesn't miss me as much as I miss her? What if she loves it so much out there that she decides to stay? What if? What if? What fucking if?

A couple of hours later we set off to the airport in Glasgow where she would board her flight and leave me behind, and for the first part of the journey we both sat in silent contemplation. Loch Lomond lay beside us, Ben Lomond visible across the water, reaching skyward. I wanted to stop the car and point it out to her. Tell her she could stay here. Climb these mountains again and again if it meant she stayed. But of course I couldn't take her dream away like that.

I could see through the intermittent gaps in the trees that the calm glass-like surface displayed a mirror image of the vivid azure blue above. Only a few wisps of cloud like candy floss hung there to break up the vast expanse of sky and I remember thinking how the cheeriness overhead was the antithesis of the black cloud hanging over my heart.

There were so many things I wanted to say, but the words never came and I cursed myself for being so damned useless at expressing myself.

Luckily, she knew what I was like. I'd spent the day before looking for songs to express how I felt and I'd made a CD. The silence in the car was deafening and so I reached over and hit play. I made eye contact with her for a few moments as the opening chords to 'I Will Remember You' by Ryan Cabrera filled the small space between us. Turning my eyes back to the road, I saw her in my peripheral vision, wiping her eyes as her lip trembled. At least if I couldn't find my own words to tell her how I felt I could use those of the songwriters.

At the airport I pulled her into my arms and held her against my chest. I knew she must have felt the rapid pounding of my heart as we stood inside the terminal. Tears threatened. My eyes were desperate to give them up, but I tried so hard not to make the situation more difficult than it already was. Swallowing the lump in my throat, I pulled away and gazed into her emerald eyes one last time.

My voice wavered as I told her, 'I'm not going to say goodbye because I hate that word and we'll be back together before we know it anyway. So I'm going to say have a great time and stay safe. And know that I'll be thinking of you every moment whilst you're gone.'

Pulling me towards her, she kissed me with a ferocity that took my breath away. I fisted my hands in her hair and returned the kiss with equal passion. When I eventually pulled away, I cupped her face in my hands and stroked the apples of her cheeks with my thumbs. 'It's just a few months, love. Go and show 'em what you're made of, eh?'

She nodded and gripped my hands where they lay on her skin. Relentless tears spilled from her eyes as she let go and turned to walk away. All my fears bubbled to the surface again and I couldn't hold back. 'I love you,

Mairi. And one day I want to marry you!' I shouted.

As soon as the words left my mouth I clamped it shut.

Fuckfuckfuckfuck!

We'd never discussed marriage before. But I have a tendency to say what's on my mind without thinking about the consequences, and this was one of those times. I was filled with dread. Had I just given her a ticket to Get-Out-Ville? *Again, fuck!* My heart hammered as if it were trying to do a runner and my mouth went dry.

The people around us stopped and stared.

Mairi halted in her tracks and I froze. She turned to face me, her mouth open in what I can only describe as utter, mind-frying shock. I swallowed hard, my mind racing to find something to say to take the words back. But a beautiful smile appeared on her face. She ran towards me and flung her arms around my neck, her legs around my waist. Everyone around us applauded as I hugged her into my body before letting her go and setting her down again. With one last heart-melting smile she stroked my cheek, turned, and walked away.

Chapter Two

Present Day

I untangled myself from the sheets and stumbled into the bathroom. I hardly recognised the gaunt man staring back at me. The dark circles around my eyes aged me beyond my thirty-seven years and the smattering of grey in my beard was becoming more obvious.

I turned the shower on and let it run until I was enveloped in a steamy cocoon. Once under the water I closed my eyes and tried to blank out thoughts of Mairi and the times we'd made love in the very same place. As the water tumbled down my tired muscles, I ran through the list of jobs I had planned for the day.

After climbing out of the shower, I dried, dressed, and then called to Angus. The yellow Labrador crossbreed came bounding up to me, and we set out for our morning walk. The air was chilled and my breath vaporised as soon as it left my body, forcing me to pull my zip up as far as it'd go.

We aimed for the main village of Clachan and set off on our favourite route, which included a brief pause on the bridge over the Atlantic. The views of the estuary and out to sea were stunning from there. The water was framed on one side by a row of whitewashed stone cottages and on the other by the trees of mainland Scotland and, in my opinion, it was a tough view to beat. The bridge has been there linking Clachan to mainland since 1793 and these days it's become quite a tourist attraction. I can understand why. It really is beautiful. And people usually think it's a gimmick that we say it crosses the Atlantic. But it really does. Check it out on a map for yourself.

Ron, the old guy from up the road, was walking towards me, his newspaper tucked under his arm. 'Hello there, Gregory. Have you heard the news?'

I stopped in my tracks and waited to hear the latest gossip from the village know-it-all. 'What news would that be?'

'You know James McLaughlan's old place, Sealladh-mara Cottage? It's sold.'

'Really? He *will* be pleased. Any idea who bought it?'

He scowled and shook his head. 'Therein lays the issue, Gregory. Apparently, it's some young executive couple who are using it as a weekend and holiday home.'

I rolled my eyes. 'Oh, great. This place'll have no bloody locals left at this rate.'

Ron wagged a wizened finger. 'Aye. That's exactly what I said. The last thing we need is more damned weekend interlopers who don't contribute to the village.'

'Well, Ron. Not a lot we can do about it really, I suppose. Did you see them?'

'I caught a wee glimpse last week when they were here with the estate agent. He looked all businesslike and she was... well... she was a bonny lass, actually. Lovely long hair and very smiley.' He shook his head as if trying to remind himself how pissed off he was. 'Anyway, I'm not happy.'

I huffed out a breath. 'Well, let's just hope they at least spend *some* of their executive pay-cheque money in the pub when they're here on weekends, eh?'

'Aye, we can hope, young man. We can hope.' He went on his way back home and I smiled to myself and continued walking my dog.

Young man. When you get to thirty-seven you don't think of yourself as particularly *young* anymore; but I supposed to someone Ron's age, however old that might've been, I still was.

James McLaughlan was a nice old guy. He'd moved farther north to be with his family up above Inverness, and he'd been heartbroken when he left the wee cottage down by the bridge. As Angus and I stopped at the centre of the arched stone structure I glanced over to James's old place. Maybe it wasn't such a bad thing really, getting new blood into the village.

Most of the people here had stayed at Clachan Seil all their lives, and when they'd passed away or moved on to be with family, tourists had cottoned on to how beautiful it was. I was an interloper myself. I'd only moved to the village after splitting up with my wife and leaving my old life behind. But I'd felt at home right away. Stella at the pub and Ron, bless his heart, had taken me under their wings. Despite my antisocial nature and lack of people skills, Stella had given me a job in the pub and I became one of the locals.

Standing there on the bridge, I remembered back to when Mairi and I used to stand in the same spot, looking out over the Atlantic, and a lump formed in my throat. I'd considered moving away after she was declared dead in August the previous year – seeing as there was a memory of her around *every* sodding corner – but I'd never belong anywhere like I did in Clachan.

Never.

And so there I was five months on and still grieving.

*

Later on, I made my way down to the pub for the lunchtime shift. Stella was working in the kitchen, thanks to our chef's leaving to go back to Australia. Well, I say chef. He was a bloody good cook, was Chris, but he wasn't qualified. He was a young guy with a passion for food, but somehow he'd landed a job as a bloody underwear model. How to make Greg feel inadequate in one easy step. Anyway, he'd gone back to Oz to start working for some modelling agency even though his ultimate dream was to train at some flashy restaurant in Sydney called Alonzo's. He seemed to think that being back home would improve his chances. Personally, I thought that getting experience actually *cooking* for a living was better, but what the hell did I know? I'd attended university only to end up pouring drinks, fixing taps, and taking tourists on boat trips.

Anyway, I digress. So Stella was in the kitchen preparing her famous steak pie for the evening. There was no doubt about it: it was the best pie I'd *ever* bloody tasted. And the smell emanating from the kitchen was making my mouth water so much, I was on the verge of flooding the place. There was a lull in the lunchtime patronage, and so I picked up my guitar and went to sit by the fireplace. I'd been playing a lot since Mairi died; another method of distraction, I suppose.

The only problem was that everything I ended up learning to play was melancholy, which didn't exactly help me achieve the goal of distraction. A glance around the room assured me that I was alone. After taking in a deep breath I began to strum away the chords to 'Disarm' by Smashing Pumpkins. The lyrics spoke of loneliness and denial and they tugged at my heart, resounding all too much with my situation. A familiar lump lodged in my throat and my voice cracked as I sat there, eyes closed, pouring my heart into the empty room. When the song came to a close, I heard someone clapping. Horrified that my pain had been heard by someone, I snapped my head up in the direction of the applause.

Stella stood there, tears streaming down her face. 'Oh, Gregory, that was so beautiful.'

I cleared my throat and wiped the back of my hand across my damp face. 'Ahem... oh... I had no idea you were listening. I wouldn't have—'

'No, no. I'm glad I heard you. I have a proposition for you.'

I scrunched my brow. *What the hell could she be talking about?* 'Oh?'

She walked carefully towards me as if I were a horse about to bolt. 'I've been thinking about getting some live music in. You know... not every night, but maybe once a month or something? Maybe *you* could be it?'

'Me? Play? Here? To *actual* people?'

She laughed. 'I'm sure Angus is a great audience, but maybe *actual* people would like to hear you play too.'

'In front of... *people*?' The words weren't really registering in my brain. Looking back, I know I sounded like a complete tit.

The smile on her face widened as she stood beside me and shook her head. 'You really have no clue how talented you are, do you, Greg?'

I frowned and cocked my head to one side. 'But I can't play in front of *actual*, *real people*.'

She placed her hands on her hips. 'Well, I don't really fancy filling the place up with mannequins. They don't tend to drink much.'

'But... I don't know many songs. And the ones I do know make you cry, by the look of it. And me? That'd be a great draw for audiences. *Come and see the grumpy-arsed Scotsman cry all over his guitar. It'll be a hoot.*'

She chuckled at me. 'Well, perhaps you can think about it, eh? I haven't seen you smile in the last five months, and it's a shame. You've such a handsome face. Have a go at some other songs that are maybe a bit more... uplifting. It may actually help you, you know.'

She had a point. 'Okay. I'll have a wee think about it. But I'm not promising. And the answer'll probably be no.'

She shrugged. 'Well, like I said, have a think.'

Just then a couple walked in through the door and made their way over to the bar. I stood and carried my beloved Rhiannon round to the back and propped her up against the wall out of the way. By the way, in case you're wondering, Rhiannon is my guitar. And I don't really give a shit if you think I'm a fuckwit for naming her. She is what she is. And right then she was the love of my life.

Chapter Three

I arrived home after my lunchtime shift. It was around five in the evening. Not really caring whether it was too early, I opened the latest bottle of single malt and poured two fingers of the amber liquid into a glass. After lighting the fire I sat there a while, watching the flames dance. Mairi and I used to sit for hours just holding each other and staring into the flames. She always said there was something hypnotic about fire, and I think she was right. Sometimes I'd come in from work and she'd be lying asleep on the rug, her head on Angus's furry body as he slept too. He'd always look up when I walked in and wag his tail a couple of times very gently as if he didn't want to wake her. He's a sweet thing for such a big dog.

As I sat there drinking and reminiscing, I began to think about what Stella had suggested. Could I do it? Could I get up there in front of a live audience and play? What was more, could I *sing*? My voice was okay, I suppose, but I was no Eddie Vedder, that's for sure. I saw Pearl Jam live many years ago and, let me tell you, the way he sang 'Black' sent shivers down my spine and brought tears to my eyes, I don't mind admitting it. Such raw emotion oozed out of every syllable. I could *never* be that good.

Anyway, I picked up Rhiannon and began to think about the stuff I used to listen to with Mairi. Stella wanted uplifting, so I racked my brain for songs that took me back to happier times. I smiled as the perfect song sprang to mind and I began to play Semisonic's 'Closing Time'. Well, I potentially was going to be playing in a pub, so it was probably the most fitting song I could close a night with.

And the song made me think about Mairi.

We'd been at a club in Oban with some of her friends. It was a kind of indie-rock club that had an open mic night every so often. They were a loopy bunch, that's for sure. I was leaving my car at the club, and we were staying with the crazy crowd that thankfully lived within staggering distance. They'd all had a bit to drink, and Mairi had told them that I had Rhiannon in the back of the Landy. So the group encouraged me to get up and sing a number. Luckily I'd had a fair few bevvies too, and so I was relaxed enough to think it was a *great* idea! Anyways, I got up and played 'Closing Time'. The whole place joined in at the chorus, but I was aiming those particular words right at Mairi as she danced with her eyes locked on mine. She was the one I was going home with and home was wherever she happened to be so it all worked out fine. It was such a buzz and I was all hyped up when I got off the stage. My performance had quite an effect on Mairi too, and she dragged me into what turned out to be a broom closet to ravish me. So as you can imagine, the song has a special place in my heart and always brings a smile to my face.

So I had one song.

Great.

But one song does not a performance make. Placing Rhiannon down safely, I decided to go through my CD collection – I'm old school and still like CDs even though I have joined the twenty-first century with my iPod, in case you were wondering – and pick out some more songs that I could play *if* I were to do a gig. Which I *wasn't*, of course. I'd already decided not to. But it wouldn't hurt to listen to some music, would it? And if I happened to learn a few more songs on the guitar, where would be the harm in that, eh?

An hour later I had the makings of a set list. I'd chosen 'Trouble' by Ray Lamontagne, 'Caledonia' by Dougie MacLean because of its connection to my homeland, and 'Chasing Cars' by one of my favourite bands and also Scottish, Snow Patrol. Another hour and I'd found a few more songs that I could play fairly easily without much practising: a bit of Fleetwood Mac, some Oasis, and a few other tracks that made me smile. The more I played, the more I got lost in the music and the poetry of the lyrics. Maybe Stella was right after all. Maybe playing music in front of an audience whilst I was sober wasn't such a bad idea. I resolved to give it some serious thought.

As I restrung the E that had snapped when I got a little overzealous – playing à la Jimmy Page and making rather a poor attempt at an acoustic version of Zeppelin's 'Dazed and Confused' – although I blamed the crap sound on the fact that the tuning was slipping – the landline rang. My brow furrowed in confusion. No one ever rang me. I reluctantly placed Rhiannon down again, deciding that maybe she needed some work and that I'd have to take her in to get her looked at.

'Hello?' I couldn't hide the frustration in my voice at being disturbed on my evening off.

'Gregory?'

'Aye, that's me. Who's this?'

The man at the other end of the line cleared his throat. 'It's Duncan... Mairi's father.'

My stomach dropped. The last time he had called me was to tell me that Mairi wasn't coming home and that they'd called off the search.

I swallowed hard. Five months had passed since he had dropped that bombshell, and I was dreading the reason for his call. I inhaled a deep, cleansing breath as quietly as I could.

'Duncan... hi. What... what can I do for you?'

'I... erm... thought you'd want to know that some of the equipment belonging to Mairi's expedition team has been recovered.'

Fuck! 'I see... I see. Anything else?' My heart was

hammering so hard, I felt sure he could feel the vibration all the way down in Dumfries.

'Nothing else. Just some of their smaller items. Due to the location they were found in, it appears they may have fallen from higher up the mountain. There was no sign of – of bodies.'

The word *bodies* made my head swim, and suddenly I felt overcome with nausea. I had to lean on the windowsill and breathe deeply. 'Okay. Thanks for letting me know, Duncan. I appreciate your call.'

'That's okay. And, Gregory?'

'Yes?'

'I'm… erm… very sorry about what Paula said to you last time we spoke. She knows deep down that none of this was your fault. She was just looking for someone to blame. Mairi was her only daughter and losing her…' he cleared his throat again '… was so very painful for her mother.'

My lower lip began to tremble as Paula's words echoed in my mind and stabbed at my heart all over again. *'If you hadn't encouraged her, she'd still be here. You should've stopped her from going. You obviously didn't love her enough. And now she's dead thanks to you!'* I closed my eyes and chewed the inside of my cheek, fighting the despair tugging at my insides.

'Aye, Duncan. I know that. Thank you.'

'Right… well… if I hear anything else, I'll let you know.'

‘Thanks, Duncan.’ I ended the call and pinched the bridge of my nose between my thumb and forefinger. More shit had been found but still no sign of my Mairi.

The fact that Mairi’s mother had blamed me for the death of her daughter five months ago had saddled me with a heavy weight of guilt that I was struggling to shake. How could I move on with my life when things kept reminding me that I was doing so alone? Without her.

I needed some air.

I grabbed my iPod and my thick jacket. The sky looked heavy with snow, but I needed to get out and clear my head. I pulled on my hat, scarf and gloves and called to Angus. He’d go out whatever the weather.

We walked down the lane from my house towards the main part of the village. I stuck the buds into my ears and hit play. ‘Set Fire to The Third Bar’ by Snow Patrol filled my head as I walked. The lyrics about distance tortured me and visions of Mairi out there in that icy landscape all alone plagued my frontal lobe but still I listened. The words took on their own meaning just for me and I wished more than anything that I could hold Mairi again; be transported to where she was just like the song said.

Huge, glistening flakes of snow began to float to the ground, twisting and turning as they made their descent. Gazing up into the dark sky, I watched their journey. There would’ve been snow at the high altitude of Mairi’s climb. The fact that she would have been so frightened, cold, and maybe even physically hurt twisted at my gut and my eyes began to sting. Was it my fault? Could I have done anything to change her mind?

No.

And if I had stopped her, she'd have resented me, and I would've lost her anyway. It was a lose-lose situation whichever way I looked at it, and I knew I had to work on the blame I was piling onto myself.

Pulling the chilled air into my lungs, I hoped that I could somehow exhale all the anguish that I was holding onto. But instead when I reached the centre of the arched stone bridge, my legs almost gave way as I stopped and listened intently to the heartbreaking lyrics being played directly into my brain. Like a blade the words pierced me to the core, reminding me yet again that I was, in fact, without the woman that I loved and that the situation would never improve. I would *never* see her again.

She was gone forever, and forever was a hell of a long time.

Chapter Four

By the time I arrived back home, there was a thick covering of white over the road. The garden looked like an iced Christmas cake waiting for its holly and berry adornments. A veritable Christmas card scene, in fact. The thought made me snort derisively.

That was another thing that irked me: Christmas had always been my favourite time of year. Mairi was such a kid when it came to gift giving, and she always went over the top. She never spent lots of money or anything, but you could hardly move in the house for bloody paper chains and tinsel. There was always the biggest tree we could find, taking up half the lounge and decorated in such a way that made it look as if we'd hired five-year-olds to do it.

We had every crass singing Santa figure she could find and a life-size inflatable snowman for the front yard. She was so thoughtful when it came to gifts too, and there were always lots of daft things for me. I'd received things like a key ring with a photo of the two of us on it, a guitar-shaped air freshener for the Landy – 'cause she always said it stank of wet dog – charming, eh? There was always a T-shirt of one of my favourite bands and usually some chocolate novelty thing like a Santa or reindeer. One time I got a photo collage she'd made of us in all our favourite places throughout the Highlands – that gift was my favourite. Aye, she never failed to make the festive season special.

We'd usually defy convention and have something completely different from most Scots at Christmas. There was no turkey, no haggis, and no stuffing. Instead we'd have something like curry or kleftiko – just because it was fun and different. My favourite was the Mexican food we had at Christmas one year. She'd put too much chilli in the fajitas and they were almost inedible, but it was hilarious seeing the rainbow of colours our faces turned as we tried to get them down. I think we went through more beer in that one meal than we did the rest of the season put together.

This last Christmas, however, had passed me by in a kind of drunken blur. There had been no tinsel or inflatable snowmen. No tree and no gifts. I'd been holed up in the house, drinking whisky and wallowing in self-pity with no intention of venturing outside at all if I could help it.

Stella and Ron had insisted on making the journey up the icy lane to bring me food and logs, despite my numerous protests. Stella had even warmed up a beef stew and stood over me to make sure I ate it. I had lost all the muscle definition that I'd spent time building up, and I was beginning to look anorexic. As a man who usually ate a tattie more than a pig does, I was very much aware that this was not normal; nor was it healthy.

Since Christmas I'd been lifting the weights again in my spare room. I'd always taken pride in my physique – and let's face it, it was another great way to release some of the tension and anger lodged deep inside me since Mairi disappeared on K2. I was carrying the pain, bottling up so much grief and anger that at the beginning of the December after she died I made a decision that would stay with me permanently.

*

In early January I was sitting in the plush waiting area of the tattoo parlour in Oban, surrounded by black leather and images of the most intricate ink work imaginable, I bounced my knee up and down as my nerves jangled and my heart did its best to vacate my ribcage. Some of those tats must've taken hours upon hours to complete, and I could only imagine the pain that these victims – erm, *clients* – went through. I was no wimp but electing to have someone stab me with a needle a few thousand times was not something that had ever really appealed to me before this shit had happened in my life.

I'd been thinking long and hard about designs throughout the rest of December, and I'd settled on two. If I was going to go through the pain of permanent scarring, I figured, sod it, might as well get it all done at once.

One of the tattoos was to mark the biggest loss of my life. But in complete contrast, the other one was a Gaelic phrase that roughly translated as 'Love Conquers All'. A K2 wrapped in barbed wire would circle my bicep, and the Gaelic phrase would be printed across my chest in the hope that every time I saw it I'd be reminded not to give up on love. I'd had shit luck with women in the past, that was certain. But I was still hopeful that one day, far off in the future – but not so far off that I was an old decrepit fart incapable of getting an erection – I'd meet someone who wouldn't shag my best mate *or* die on a fucking mountain.

One day.

The artist called me over and I sat in the chair, bare-chested and gritting my teeth. We'd discussed the designs and he'd shown me what he was going to do as soon as I arrived. To say I was shitting bricks was a major understatement. And my God did it hurt. But a few hours later – and with my teeth surprisingly intact despite the fact that my jaws had been clenched the entire time – I was lathered in lotion, cling-wrapped, and ready to go.

The tattoos looked *amazing*. It was definitely the right decision.

When I got home I stood in the bathroom, removed my T-shirt and the coverings, and stared in the mirror, focusing on the new ink. I had my permanent reminder. Not that I thought I would ever forget, but the memorial service her friends held had felt inconsequential and so this had felt necessary. It was cathartic somehow. It was my own personal tribute to Mairi and what we'd shared.

After the utter bitch my ex-wife had become, Mairi was the light in the darkness. She was the one person to make me hope again. To love again. I doubted whether I would ever love as strongly again, but… as my tattoo reminded me: *Love conquers all.*

As I stared at my sore and bloody reflection, my lip began to tremble and my eyes stung with tears. Barbed wire was a fitting symbol of the agony I had gone through in the last four and a half months. Barbed wire that sliced into my heart and tore at my insides as I grieved without really knowing the truth and without being able to say goodbye.

I re-covered the newly inked wounds, taking care not to catch the raised lines where it was sorest to the touch. A sob ripped from my chest and I hung my head as I let my grief pour out once again. *How could this have happened? Mairi was an experienced climber. I just don't bloody get it.* I clenched my fist and slammed it onto the tiled surface surrounding the sink. The pain of the impact was a distraction from the aching in my chest, but it was only fleeting. A growl erupted from deep within my body and I smashed both fists down this time as I let a guttural, incoherent roar free from my throat. The noise sounded completely alien to me, and shivers vibrated down my spine.

Why? Why did this happen to Mairi? Where's the justice? She was so young, so beautiful, and so special. And she's fucking gone! Ripped from me far too young and I can't handle it.

I just can't bear it.

I dropped to my knees on the cold, tiled floor and held my head in my hands. My stomach knotted; and as I clenched my eyes closed the dreaded images from my nightmares came back to haunt me yet again, assaulting my frontal lobe with such vividness. The fear in her eyes was more than I could take. Her outstretched hands reached for me as she fell. Was this how it actually happened? Her falling, terrified, to her death? Oh, *God*, I hoped not. Why did my psyche insist on torturing me in this way?

I tried to breathe deeply, and, after eventually gathering myself, I staggered downstairs to grab the half-empty bottle of single malt from the kitchen countertop. I didn't bother with a glass this time. I flicked on the CD player and turned up 'From Where You Are' by Lifehouse as loud as it would go. I kept on torturing myself with music and lyrics that reminded me how much I missed her, but it felt necessary. I felt closer to her when I listened to my innermost feelings expressed in music. The songs became a soundtrack to the less painful memories I held dear.

I needed to get out of my head. I dropped onto the couch as the lyrics seeped into my mind and took hold of my heart, making my chest ache. The harsh sting of the tattoo was nothing compared to the nagging throb of emptiness inside me. I needed to numb the pain, and whisky was the only way I knew how.

Chapter Five

The nightmares continued and I found that whisky helped but it didn't block out the terrors completely. January ran into February and my routine continued. Work, get drunk, sleep, have nightmares, wake, and the whole cycle would start over.

One such morning after, I was woken by an ear-piercing, high-pitched ringing. At first, I presumed it was just my dehydrated brain rattling around in my head on account of the whisky consumption of the night before; but… as it continued, it registered in my foggy consciousness as the telephone.

Oh, fuck. Who the fuck is bothering me at this fucking time? It's the middle of the fucking night. No one ever fucking rings me unless I'm feeling like shit! What the fuck?

I dragged my arse off the sofa where I'd crashed out and rummaged around with my eyes half closed until my hand located the cold plastic casing of the landline phone.

'What?' I barked down the line.

'Gregory? Are you okay?' a worried voice asked.

Shit.

'Oh… erm… hi, Stella. Yeah, yeah, I'm okay. Sorry for snapping at you. What's up?'

'Well, it's just that it's gone twelve and you're supposed to be at the pub for your shift, hon.'

'What? It's gone twelve? Midnight?' Why would she want me in when the pub was *closed*?

'No, hon. Mid*day*. You were supposed to start at half eleven today to stock up the bar.'

Shit. I'd overslept… no… no, hang on… I'd *actually* slept.

No nightmares.

'Oh, fuck. Shit, sorry for swearing, Stella.'

She laughed. 'Don't worry, I've heard much worse from your mouth, Gregory. So, are you coming down?'

'Erm… yeah, sure. I'll have to shower and… I probably shouldn't drive, so I'll walk down. Give me an hour or so and I'll be there. Sorry. I had a really shitty night.'

'So I gather. Don't worry. I was just worried you'd disappeared into your own head again like you did at Christmas.'

'Na'… nothing like that.' My stomach rolled and bile rose in my throat as my mind flicked back to why I had drunk so much the night before. 'Just… thinking too much, that's all.'

'I see. That's what I was worried about. You're not helping yourself, Gregory. You're spending too much time on your own. It's not healthy to do that when you're grieving.'

Grieving. That damned word. 'I'm fine, honestly. I used to spend time alone before… before she—'

'Look, love, I don't mean to interfere, but I really think you need to stay busy and… and be with *people.* I can give you some extra shifts at the pub or… or you could come and play at the pub on an evening like I suggested to you. What do you think?'

'I don't know, Stella. I just don't know if I'm cut out to be a performer, you know?'

'I'm not asking for you to be Freddie Mercury, love. Just sing and play like you did that time I was listening. It was lovely. You're a natural.'

'I'm still thinking on it. I'll let you know, okay? Look, I'd better go get ready before the lunchtime rush, eh?'

'All right, hon. See you in a wee while.'

After I hung up, I rubbed my hands over my face and made my way up the stairs to the bathroom. I downed a couple of painkillers then turned on the shower and waited a few minutes for the water to run hot. After stripping out of my jeans and boxers, I flung them into the laundry basket and climbed under the cascading water. Drained of energy and emotion, I easily could've fallen back to sleep on my feet. My muscles ached as if I'd been fighting, and my head throbbed as if bloody *Riverdance* were going on up there.

*

About an hour and a half later I arrived at the pub. I glanced over at the bridge, where a young couple was standing looking out at the view, arms around each other. For a split second I was filled with envy at how happy they seemed to be. Laughing and pointing out into the distance.

For a split second I *hated* them.

I pushed through the door and made my way through the crowd of tourists to take my place behind the bar. A blonde woman sitting on her own was eyeing me up as I began to take drink orders from the busload of tourists that had descended upon the place. I'd noticed the coach parked over by the little shack across from the pub, and I hoped I'd arrived in time before Stella got pissed off with me for abandoning her on such a busy day. But I mean, come on, who goes on a bloody coach tour in the Highlands in *February*? Apparently Londoners who like to ski do.

The blonde woman was wearing a low-cut sweater despite the winter chill and was eye-shagging me from the far end of the bar. I glanced over to make eye contact. She gave a sultry come-get-me smile and licked her full lips as she held her empty glass aloft. *What the fu-u-u…?* I finished serving the tourists and made my way over to her.

'What can I get you?' I asked in my usual surly manner.

She leaned forward, giving me a full view of her

cleavage.

'What do you recommend?' Her accent wasn't Scottish but I couldn't quite place it.

'Well, that depends on what your tastes are like,' I said, propping myself up on the bar before her.

'Oh, I have very… how should I put it? Hmm… *varied* tastes.' Her eyebrows rose infinitesimally. The innuendo wasn't lost on me.

I swallowed hard. She was an attractive woman, but she was no Mairi. Blonde hair in a flicky kind of style just above her shoulders. Nice figure, if a little too thin for my taste. But as I watched her, I wondered if maybe what I needed was uncomplicated, no-strings sex. Would that help? Probably not in the long run, but it was clearly being offered on a plate – and I am a hot-blooded male after all.

'I can recommend the Oban single malt. It's very smooth going down.' What the hell was I saying?

She bit her lip. 'I like things that are smooth… going down.' I poured her two fingers of the amber liquid and handed her the glass. She pouted. 'And one for yourself. I don't like drinking alone.'

I poured myself the same and took a mouthful, hissing as the warmth coated my throat. 'So, what brings you to Clachan Seil?'

'I'm here with those guys.' She gestured with a nod of her head. Her expression told me she was none too pleased about the fact. 'I live in London. I was supposed to be here with my boyfriend, but he broke up with me two days before the trip so I figured sod it, I'll go anyway. I thought perhaps I might meet someone to help me take my mind off things.' She swirled the liquid in her glass and looked at me from under her long eyelashes.

I dragged my cloth across the bar in front of her. 'You're not a Londoner though, eh? What's that accent?'

'I'm from Adelaide originally. I came to the UK with my family when I was around sixteen. I stayed. Never lost the accent though.' She smiled, revealing perfect white teeth.

'What do you do for a living, then? I'm guessing you're a model.' *Oh, hell, seriously? Now you're trying too hard, pal.*

She laughed. 'Very observant of you. I *am* actually a model.'

I felt my eyes widen. 'Fuck, really? And here was I thinking it was a shitty pickup line.'

She tilted her head. 'And is that what you're aiming for here? To pick me up?'

I stopped wiping the bar in front of her and considered her question. *Was* I trying to pick her up? I'd thought it was the other way around.

Stella came through from the back and made her way over to me. 'Greg, I need you to change the Gairloch Grinder. It's empty.' She scowled at me as if she'd caught me doing something wrong.

I frowned. 'Aye, okay. Be right there,' I told her before turning back to the blonde woman whose name I didn't even know.

She raised her eyebrows at me. 'Someone's a little pissed off that you're chatting to me.'

I cringed. 'Aye, well, she is ma boss so I'd better go and do ma job, eh?'

'Okay, *Greg*.' She said my name as if the feel of it on her lips turned her on. I nodded, at a bit of a loss for words. I was filled with a sense of relief that the conversation had been cut short. To be honest, I had no clue what I'd have done if I'd taken her home. No doubt I would've chickened out at the last minute and made a complete tit of myself.

As I walked through to the back to make my way to the cellar, Stella grabbed my arm.

'Look, Gregory, I know I wasn't meant to interfere, but...' She sighed as if unsure whether to carry on. 'I'm not sure what's going on with you and that blonde girl, but be careful, okay? Tell me to mind my own business, and obviously you do what you want to do. But you're grieving, and I know from personal experience that silly mistakes can be made when you're in the wrong frame of mind.'

I nodded and she released my arm and patted it.

As I changed the beer barrel down in the dimly lit cellar, I thought about what she'd said. She was right. I was a one-woman kind of guy. Sleeping with someone for the gratification of it just wasn't me. I thought maybe I needed to keep that in mind when I went back up to the bar.

The barrel was a tricky sucker, and I was down in the dingy cellar longer than anticipated. When I arrived back up at the bar, I spotted the blonde sitting on the lap of one of the other London tourists. Her tongue was stuck down his throat so I shook my head at my near miss and got back to work. Good to know I was so desirable, eh? Well, at least the experience taught me something. I wasn't a one-night-stand type of guy. Never would be.

Lesson learned. Thanks, blondie.

Chapter Six

February turned into March, and I was astounded at how life was going on as normal around me despite my grief. Stella gave me a weekend off, second weekend in March, and I decided to get out of the village. I packed up my Landy with my sleeping bag and a thick fleece blanket, a little stove, and some tins of crap I wouldn't normally be caught eating. Angus and I got in the car and headed over to Etive Mor. We'd set off when it was still light, but it would be over a two-hour drive.

As the Buckle came into view, my heart leapt at the stunning sight of the snow-capped mountain rising out of the bracken. I turned off down a little side road that I was very familiar with and pulled into my usual lay-by off to the left. Pulling my sleeping bag and other stuff from the car, I made my way down to the water and under the little bridge. Angus followed close behind. He knew the routine. I placed my sleeping bag and my stove on the ledge there and trudged back up to the road again. After gathering a few twigs and branches, Angus and I played for a while. He loved to fetch sticks, but he never brought back the one I'd thrown. Instead he always managed to find one that was far too big for his mouth and weighed far too much, almost toppling him over as he ran back to me. I couldn't help but laugh at the crazy canine.

As night fell, the temperature plummeted, and I sat myself on the little rock facing the craggy mountain where I'd met my true love a few years before. I pulled the flask of whisky from my coat pocket and unscrewed the lid. I took a long pull and gulped it down, appreciating its warmth. The complete disc of the silver moon was clear and bright, and it cast the most wonderful spotlight on my mountain.

Our mountain.

The night was cold but peaceful, and I stared upwards at the starry sky that surrounded the summit like a crown of diamonds. Was she up there, in the heavens, watching me? If she was, that would be the cruellest kind of torture. The familiar lump lodged in my throat, and tears began to trickle down my unshaven cheeks; the moisture left cold trails in its wake, but I didn't much care.

There was a sense of calm around the place. I felt at home despite my melancholy. Mairi and I had camped under the little bridge a couple of times, and it had become a special place for me. I felt her there. It was as if she was some otherworldly presence wrapping herself around me and comforting me.

The trouble was, whenever I came here I didn't want to leave.

Eventually I began to yawn, and so Angus and I made our way under the bridge to shelter. The big ball of fluff snuggled up to me under the blankets as if he understood that I needed him, and I eventually wept myself to sleep.

My dreams weren't as traumatic when I was here. I'd be sitting on the rock, playing Rhiannon as Mairi watched, her head on one side as she swayed to whatever romantic mush I was playing for her. Oftentimes, I'd dream of taking her in my arms after night had fallen, and we'd make love in the car before making our way down to the underside of the bridge to sleep. Those dreams were a double-edged sword. Waking up was a cold slap in the face from reality when I realised I was alone again.

*

Just as the sun was coming up, my eyes fluttered open. My body clock was attuned to this place. Sunrise was by far my favourite time of day here. Angus stood and stretched, and I grabbed the fleece blanket I'd had covering my sleeping bag. We followed the trail back up to the road to my favourite little rock so I could sit and watch the sun come up. Angus sat beside me and laid his head on my fleece-covered legs. The orange and golden hues of the sunrise cast an ethereal glow over the mountain, and I sat in silence as more and more of the jagged rock face became illuminated.

Simply breathtaking.

I was taken back to times when it was Mairi and me sitting here. Me on the rock and her between my legs, head resting on my chest as we watched the changing colours of the morning. Just thinking that I would never do that with her again brought the anger and sadness bubbling to the surface once more. I'd cried so much in the months since she'd gone that it was a wonder there were any tears left.

When the latest stream of tears had subsided and the sun was fully risen, Angus and I enjoyed a tin of some breakfast concoction that didn't taste half bad. We walked for a while and played fetch again. This time Angus's large stick fetish sent him tumbling into the freezing stream that ran towards the river. I laughed loud and unabashed for the first time in a long while, and it felt good.

Mad bloody dog.

Once we were back in the car, however, and all's I could smell was stinky, wet dog, I glanced up at the guitar-shaped air freshener that Mairi had bought me. My laughter dried up. 'Fat lot of bloody use you are now you've lost your smell,' I told the inanimate object and then rapidly questioned my sanity. It was one thing to talk to a dog – but an air freshener? Yep, I was losing the plot!

*

When we arrived back in Clachan Seil and crossed the bridge over the Atlantic, I spotted a removals van down by James McLaughlan's cottage. His furniture was being carried out and loaded into the van. That meant the new folks would be moving in any day now and I had mixed feelings about that. More tourists were good for my boat business and the pub, but if they were only here for weekends, would they take the time to get to know people? Or would they simply use the house as a base to travel from? The village had always been a close-knit community and it saddened me that it could be about to change. Not a lot I could do about it, really.

I pulled up outside the pub and made my way over to see if I could help. James was there directing the younger men, and clearly he was having a hard time watching his Sealladh-mara Cottage become nothing but a shell.

'Now then, James. How's it going, old pal?' I asked as I grasped the old guy's wizened hand in a warm handshake.

His face lit up. 'Gregory, my boy. It's good to see you. How are you keeping?'

I shrugged. 'Oh... you know, getting by.'

His smile disappeared and he shook his head sadly. 'I was so sorry to hear about your wee girl. Such a tragedy. Such a waste of a young life.' He squeezed the hand he held and patted it with his other.

His compassion made my eyes sting.

I cleared my throat in order to speak. 'Aye, James, it certainly was.'

'Are you coping okay? Are you getting any support?'

His concerned gaze made my stomach knot. *Such a nice old guy.*

Nodding in what I hoped was a reassuring manner, I told him, 'I'm… I'll be fine, James. Don't you worry about me, eh? You've spent years doing things for others, so go and be looked after. Enjoy your retirement, my friend.'

The old guy pulled me into a hug. 'You take care, Gregory. And someday, let yourself fall in love again, eh?'

I chewed the inside of my cheek at his earnest words, and I nodded, unable to utter further words of my own.

Seeing the number of helpers around the place, I figured I'd only be in the way, and so I left them to it and made my way back to the Landy.

James's comment about falling in love again rattled around my head. At that moment I felt sure that it just wasn't possible. The tattoo scars had healed, but they were surface wounds I had inflicted upon myself. The real scars – the emotional ones – surely wouldn't be so quick to heal. I shook my head to try and dislodge the thoughts of new love from my mind. It was time I got used to my own company again. I wasn't sure my heart could take any more.

Chapter Seven

April

April saw the beginning of warmer weather, albeit rainy, and the eight and a half months since I'd lost Mairi still seemed like mere days to me. I still thought about her all the time and I was still plagued by the relentless nightmares. It seemed nothing was going to ease the pain except whisky.

There had been comings and goings down at James McLaughlan's old place, and I was intrigued to meet the couple who'd bought it. To get the measure of them, so to speak.

I saw the large van pull up down by the house and watched as the men began to load the furniture in. Classy stuff. The new owners liked their artwork, judging by the wrapped canvasses that were being carefully handled by the removals men. I purposefully walked Angus by the cottage, hoping to get a glimpse of the interlopers, but other than the men in work troos and logo'd T-shirts, I spotted no one.

Typical.

On my way past, Colin, from the shop, called me

over.

I jogged over to where he stood in the doorway of the little grocery store. 'What's up?'

He looked frustrated. 'I thought I could fix it myself, but it turns out the tap is a little more than I can maybe handle. If you get a chance, can you come and take a look?'

'Sure thing, Col. I'm not sure when it'll be. Can you manage for a wee while with it?'

'I can. It's just driving Chrissy mad with its drip-dripping.'

I smiled. 'I can imagine. Hey, do you know anything about the people who've bought James's old place?'

He scratched his head. 'Not a thing. It's all been a bit quiet over there. I see they're moving in. I guess we'll soon find out, eh?'

'True enough. Right, well, I'd better get Angus home. I'm due at the pub in a while.'

I waved and set off back to my house with Angus trotting ahead. After opening the front door and following the dog inside, I checked my appearance in the hall mirror. Faded grey T-shirt and faded jeans to go with my faded mood.

When I arrived at work the pub was quiet, which was a blessing. I wasn't in the mood for being chatty. Not with strangers anyway. Ron and I had been putting the world to rights until he said something that sparked off a memory of Mairi and I sank back into my own head again. All's he'd said was that his granddaughter, who he rarely saw, was coming up twenty-one years old and she had the most beautiful red curly hair and green eyes. That combination brought images of my girl to the forefront of my mind; her curls bouncing and her laughter ringing out through the air as I chased her along the beach before taking her in my arms. I rubbed my hands over my face as I felt the colour drain away.

Oh God, would it ever stop?

Would it ever get any easier?

Ron continued trying to chat to me and show me photos of his family, of whom he was so proud, despite the distance between them; but I had no interest and my ability to converse regressed as the day went by.

The lunchtime rush wasn't really a rush, and I ended up spending most of the day chatting to Ron. Well, I say *chatting*. Grunting as he talked *at* me was more the case. It wasn't his fault that I'd been having a bad couple of days. It happened every so often. Who am I kidding? It was a daily occurrence. Getting Mairi out of my head was something I only managed to do temporarily with the help of whisky; but I always ended up feeling like shit, so I was doing my best to just get on with life lest I stumble into alcoholism.

Getting on with my life. Hmm.

Because that's what you do, isn't it? When you lose someone. You say goodbye. You grieve and then you move on. Except I was having real trouble with that last part on account of the part before that. The fact that I'd never said goodbye. I hadn't been able to. And that unavoidable fact still tore at my heart all these months later. The unknown was such a scary entity.

She'd always tried to get me to go with her on her expeditions. I'd done a few climbs, but I can't say I enjoyed them all that much. I was in no way experienced nor fit enough to go to K2.

If I'd been there I'd be dead now too.

Sobering thought, really.

*

I heard the pub door creak open and slam shut and so I turned, still wiping a glass.

Fuck.

My heart did this funny flip in my chest and I gulped.

She was *gorgeous*. Long, dark, wavy hair, the sexiest curves and big, bright eyes. She smiled at me and I swear my heart stopped beating. I'd never seen a smile quite like it. Well, not since Mairi. My insides began churning and I *hated* that I immediately found her attractive. But... it wasn't the same as the way I'd found the blonde attractive recently.

This was different.

Not good. Not good at all.

Too soon.

I gritted my teeth and took a deep breath. I didn't like

my body's response to her. The hairs at my nape stood to attention, and I could swear I felt my pupils dilate. What a stupid reaction. I didn't know her from Adam, for fuck's sake. Good thing this was a tourist area and there was a good chance she'd be gone quickly and I'd never see her again.

I made my way over to where she'd perched herself on a bar stool, and I leaned on the bar in front of her, my arms rigid and locked. Her eyes were vivid blue and crystal clear. I could've fallen right in and drowned. Instead, I plastered on a surly expression. My aim was to be intimidating. Don't ask me why. I think it was maybe a self-defence mechanism. But let's face it, it wasn't *her* fault I wanted to jump over the bar and ravish the poor woman.

'What can I get you?' Ouch, my voice came out like a growl. She flinched a little. I felt like a complete arse.

'Erm... can I just have a diet cola, please?' she whispered. Yep, I'd scared her.

Well done, McBradden, you bloody moron.

I should've apologised for my shitty attitude but instead I just turned and walked away like the callous bastard I'd become. I could see her watching me in my peripheral vision. Her eyes travelled up and down my body. *That's not helping, lady.*

I walked back over and slammed her drink down. *Idiot.* What was wrong with me? Seriously? 'One sixty.' *Well, I might as well continue being a dick. No point giving up now, eh?* I took the English five-pound note she held out and rolled my eyes. *Again, idiot. They're bloody legal tender, so what's my bloody problem? Poor lass is English, after all. Probably only just arrived and hasn't acquired any Scottish ones yet!* She held out her hand and I gave her the change.

She cleared her throat 'I – erm – that is *we*... are new here.' This time she sounded more confident. Her voice was kind of... musical. *Beautiful.* 'We've bought one of the cottages just by the water.'

Oh great. So it's you, eh? The interloper. Like a true arse, I just shrugged at her. *How to make someone feel welcome in one easy step.* The fact that she was here to stay did not sit well with me at all.

She looked nervous and was fiddling with the glass. 'Yeah, my fiancé and I moved up here from Yorkshire. We might become regulars in here, living so close.'

Oh, so there's a fiancé. Not a husband. But she's definitely with someone. Bollocks. No... no. Good... that's a good thing, definitely.

'Lucky us.' *Fuck! Did I just say that shitty, sarcastic comment out loud?* I caught sight of her horrified expression, which confirmed my fear. *Yes. Yes, I did say it out loud.* I tried to save myself by adding, 'Next drink'll be on the house then, eh?' But I still sounded sarcastic, which hadn't actually been my intention. There was absolutely no need for me to be so cruel. The poor wee girl was just trying to be friendly and as I was the first impression she was getting of the locals it wouldn't surprise me if she was selling up before the week was out. But maybe that was a good thing.

She finished her drink a bit too quickly and made for the door. Ron scowled at me and followed close behind her, muttering under his breath and shaking his head. I heard my name in amongst the expletives and gave him an apologetic look. But his glare told me I was in for it later.

Oh, joy.

*

Deciding I needed some fresh air, I grabbed Rhiannon and went out the back. It wasn't my usual place. I preferred the view of the stone bridge from the front but being out the back was probably safer. The dark-haired beauty's fiancé couldn't come and kick my head in out here. Not that I was scared of him. Or anyone, for that matter. I just didn't feel in the mood for fighting. Least of all when I knew I deserved a good beating for my attitude towards her.

I began to strum away in the hope that my cares would melt into the guitar strings. 'I Don't Want to Know' by Fleetwood Mac came to mind and so that's what I began to play. Admittedly, it was a wee bit cheerier-sounding than my recent choices. I closed my eyes as I often did when I played and when I opened them, Stella was standing in front of me, smiling. She raised her eyebrows.

I turned my mouth up in response and shook my head. 'Caught me again, eh?'

'I love a bit of Fleetwood Mac.'

'Yeah, me too. Look… Rhiannon needs some work. I'm going to drop her into the shop tomorrow but after that… well, I'll give it a go, okay?' As soon as the words fell haphazardly from my mouth, I realised I hadn't *really* thought it through. I'd acted on a bit of a whim; a knee-jerk reaction to being caught red-handed. *Stupid arse!* But it was too late. I'd said it. As the sentence repeated over in my head, my heart pounded and the enormity of what I'd just agreed to do slapped me round the face. *No going back now.*

Stella clapped her hands in front of her face like a kid in a sweetshop. 'Oh, that's wonderful! I'm *so* pleased, Gregory.'

'Yeah, well, I'd reserve judgement until I've done it if I were you. I might scare the customers away yet.'

'I seriously doubt that, hen.'

'We'll see, eh?'

With a face-splitting grin as if she'd won the lottery, she turned and skipped back inside. I followed soon after to get back to work.

*

Ron came back early that evening. As soon as he glowered at me from the doorway, I knew I was in for it.

'Now, Gregory, I know that you have had a terrible, terrible year. But the look on that wee lassie's face when you were so horrid... I have to say, Gregory, I was ashamed of you. I was ashamed to know you. She seems like a lovely, sweet young lassie, and you treated her as if she'd robbed your granny!'

My stomach knotted and twisted with guilt. Of course he was right, and I hadn't been able to get it out my head all day despite the guitar-playing. And I couldn't eat my lunch, which is *not* like me.

'Don't, Ron. I feel like shit about it already. I'll go away over tomorrow and take them some wine or something as a housewarming. I'll apologise... I'll explain.' I rubbed my hand through my hair as the moths in my stomach took flight at the thought of facing her. I'd say butterflies, but they're too pretty to be residing in my guts. There was the distinct possibility that her man would punch me on the nose.

I couldn't blame him if he did, but I had to at least try to make amends for my shitty behaviour. Maybe seeing them together would help to stop the stupid feelings she'd evoked in me. I could only hope.

The rain was hammering down outside. My walk with Angus later was going to be a soggy one. The door opened and some brave soul out walking came in for shelter. The drenched person rubbed a hand over her face and her hood fell off.

It was *her*.

I swallowed hard, waiting for her man to follow her in and look for me. He didn't arrive and I breathed a sigh of relief. When she glanced over at me, I had this ridiculous urge to run over and hug her. She looked so bloody cute. The make-up around her eyes had run all down her face. She could've given Gene Simmons a run for his money. *Bless her*. She began to walk towards me and I had to stifle a laugh.

Something flashed in her eyes. 'Excuse me. I don't know what you're finding so funny. I'm soaked to the skin and bloody freezing, which is in no way amusing to me.' Her Yorkshire accent sounded harsh, broader than it had been earlier, and her tone was venomous.

I felt about two inches tall. Everyone in the place was looking first at her and then at me for my reaction. I couldn't look at her anymore. I dropped my gaze. In all honesty, I felt ashamed. She certainly wasn't a nervous, cute wee girl any more. My earlier response to her had no doubt exacerbated the situation and I felt bad. She was right to be angry; I had treated her badly.

Did I tell her that I found her Kiss tribute make-up amusing? *Possibly better to not use those exact words.* 'It's just that... erm... never mind.' I continued to grin. 'Can I get you a drink?'

She shook her head. 'No,' she snapped. 'That is, no, *thank you*... Sam... my fiancé should be here by now but… he's not and I had no choice other than to come over here, seeing as I can't get a mobile signal and my landline isn't connected yet. If it's not too much trouble can I use your public telephone, please? Assuming you have one. Then I won't be bothering you again.' Her words came out in a rush and she huffed once she'd finished, as if exhausted.

The payphone had been reported broken a couple of days before when someone had tried to cram an old ten-pence piece into the slot, rendering it useless.

I peered around the pub and people awkwardly got back to their conversations.

'Public phone isn't working. You'll have to come through to the back and use the private one,' I told her, and, without making eye contact, I lifted the bar so she could come through. She followed me into the back hallway and I nodded towards the closed door before us, suddenly feeling the urge to reach out and squeeze her shoulder or make some small gesture of kindness. 'There you go. And you might want to look in a mirror before you come back through.' I walked away and left her.

Ron sat with his arms folded across his chest. He didn't need to tell me what he was thinking… but he did anyway. 'You deserved that response, in fact you deserved a proper tongue-lashing, Gregory… You got off lightly there.'

I grimaced in frustration with the old guy. 'Just drop it, Ron, eh?'

He didn't.

Instead he pointed a stubby old finger at me. 'If I were you, I would be waiting for her and apologise properly before she leaves and gets her gentleman friend to knock your spots off.'

I huffed and rubbed my hands over my face. Once again he was irritatingly right. I rolled my eyes like an errant teenager and went back through to wait for her. She came out of the bathroom and I smiled, trying my best to be nice. She'd cleaned the streaks of black from her face and was back to being damned beautiful again.

Still smiling, I plucked up my courage. 'So you're a Yorkshire lass, eh?'

She scowled at me. 'That's what I said.'

Okay... she wasn't going to make it easy for me. 'I have friends in York,' I told her, God only knows why. She smiled... my heart melted and I smiled back. I pushed myself off the wall and stood in front of her. 'Look, I'm sorry for being an arsehole earlier.' *Watch the fucking language, you stupid shit.* 'I've been having a shitty time of it lately but I had no place being like that.' *Fuck... language!* I cringed.

She pursed her lips. 'Don't worry about it. We're not friends. You don't have to explain yourself.' She stood there, arms folded, glaring at me. Still looking hot. I gulped.

'Oh, okay. Yes, I get it. That's fine, then, I'll be getting back to the bar.' I felt like crap. She'd actually *hurt* me. I'd tried but she'd shot me down in flames. This gorgeous, engaged-to-be-married Yorkshire lass had *really* hurt me. How did I come back from that? I didn't think I had a chance.

She watched me expectantly, but when I didn't say anything further, she stormed off through the bar and out of the door into the rainy night. As I watched her retreating form, I was overcome with regret. If I hadn't been such a bastard, she and I could've maybe been friends. Well, I'd ruined that now.

Chapter Eight

The next day I was out with Angus, and I saw Colin and Christine standing outside the shop chatting to Ron. I thought about going over, but it looked like they were having some sort of witches' coven meeting and so I decided to bypass them and get on my way. I was trying to calculate what I would say when I went over to see the Yorkshire lass and her bloke. I owed them an apology.

'Greg!' Christine shouted. I glanced over and she motioned to me to join them. Taking a much-needed deep breath, I plastered a smile on my face and made my way over, wondering if Ron had spread the news about my less than cordial welcome.

'Mornin' all,' I said as breezily as I could manage.

'Have you heard the terrible, terrible news?' Christine asked, wiping at her eyes. Oh shit. What had happened?

I shook my head. 'What terrible news? What's happened?'

Ron shook his head. 'That poor wee girl. The one who's moved into Sealladh-mara Cottage…' Ron paused and lifted his hand to rub at the wrinkled skin around his eyes.

'Aye, what about her?' Shit, had she packed up and left already?

Christine sniffed and Colin put his arm around her. 'Her man... her fiancé... won't be joining her.'

My eyebrows shot up. 'Really? Shit, has he dumped her?'

Ron heaved a deep shaking sigh. 'No, Gregory... he's... he's *dead*.'

As if I were on a roller coaster, my stomach plummeted.

'*Fuck*, no. What happened?' I ran my hands over my head as I was sure the colour was draining from my face. The churning sensation in my stomach increased and flashbacks of hearing about Mairi's death tortured me and mingled in with the words I was hearing from my friends. *This can't be happening. It can't. Not to her too.*

'He was on his way up here and there was an accident. He was hit by another vehicle on the road by Loch Lomond.'

I huffed the air through my puffed cheeks as the news sank in. *That poor girl. Shit, and I was such an arse to her.*

'Oh, God, that poor woman.' I glanced at Ron, expecting him to be giving me the evil eye, but instead he wore a sad expression.

'Poor girl indeed,' he agreed. 'Anyway, I'll be on my way. I might just pop over there and see if I can do anything to help. I saw she had a little dog. Maybe I could take it for a walk. I don't know... I just want to do something useful.'

I completely understood his sentiment but figured I'd be the last person she'd be likely to accept help from, so there was no point offering.

Christine wiped her eyes. 'I was speaking to Aileen from down the road. She thinks there are some friends and family coming to stay.'

'That's good that she's got someone coming,' Ron said. 'It must be terrible being in a new place. Not knowing anyone and being alone.'

I made my excuses to leave. I felt terrible. Out of everyone here I was probably the one who understood her pain the most – but I could be no use to her. After all, we hadn't exactly had the best start. The last thing she needed was some tactless Scotsman making things worse.

*

In the days following the news about the English girl's fiancé, I noticed comings and goings over at the cottage. I was grateful to the complete strangers for being there for the woman. That was something she would need: friends and family. I saw the funeral cortege leave on the day of the service, and I stood with Ron with my head bowed down as the black cars left the village. In a ridiculous way I was envious. At least she was getting to say goodbye properly. I was glad of that for her. I wouldn't wish what I'd been through on anyone.

As the vehicle passed us, I caught sight of the dark-haired woman. She looked so... *lost*. Her face a stoic mask. Emotionless. But lost all the same. My lower lip quivered as I saw the vehicles retreating up the road and my heart ached for the poor young woman.

The pain she must be feeling.

Ron grasped my shoulder. 'Are you all right, Gregory? You've gone pale, son.'

I nodded and pursed my lips for a moment; desperate not to cry in front of the old guy. Eventually I answered, 'Aye. I'm good, thanks.'

I wasn't due at the pub and so I decided to take my boat *Little Blue* out for a wee while. I grabbed my iPod from home and the boat keys along with my big fleece blanket. Angus and I climbed into the Landy and drove the short distance to the village. After dropping Angus off with Stella at the pub, I made my way down to the small marina where the boat was docked.

I pulled on my woolly hat and set out. I sailed for around half an hour, dropped anchor, and then stuck in my earbuds and listened to music for a while. I enjoyed being out in the open water with just my music and my thoughts. It afforded me time to think. Admittedly, I'd been doing rather too much of that in the months after Mairi's death, but I still needed the alone time.

*

Eventually the temperature began to drop and I pulled my coat up around my neck and my hat down around my ears. 'You Found Me' by The Fray bounced around my head as I watched the sun disappear behind the horizon. The vast expanse of water before me had turned black so I switched on the lights, hoisted up the anchor, turned, and made my way back to shore. Once I was docked, I climbed down from the boat.

A blood-curdling scream rent the still night air and I swivelled around to the direction of the noise. I could just make out a figure on the beach. Realising that the person was in distress, I took off running across the shingle. The cold wind whipped at my cheeks as I stumbled a little on the pebbles beneath my feet.

The closer I got, the more clearly I could hear the most heartbreaking noise. It was *her*. The Yorkshire lass – and she was sobbing her heart out. She must've been bloody freezing, kneeling there on the pebbles in her flimsy black top. Her feet were bare. Luckily, I had the blanket in my arms and so I scooped her up and wrapped her in the fleece simultaneously. I lifted her and her head flopped onto my chest. She'd passed out. Heart galloping, I carried her over to my car as quickly as I could and fumbled with the lock to open the passenger door. Once I placed her on the seat, she came round a little, much to my relief. I made my way round to the driver's side and stuck the key in the ignition. Switching on the map light, I whacked the heater on full, opened all the vents, and aimed them directly at the Yorkshire lass.

I reached under the seat where I'd put a flask of coffee. It had a dash of whisky in it to fend off the chills. I wasn't planning on drinking the whole flask. Don't get me wrong. I don't advocate drinking and driving. It's more a case of being there in case I get snowed into my car or break down. Anyway, I handed a half-filled cup over to her as she opened her eyes.

'Here, take this,' I said as I held the cup of steaming liquid towards her. She looked up slightly but didn't seem to be focussing. 'C'mon, Yorkshire lassie, drink it. You need to get warm. You could've caught your death out there.'

She shivered. 'I don't care,' she said in a helpless voice that broke my heart all over again.

I took a deep breath and found some strength. 'Aye, that's as may be, but there are plenty that *do* care. Now drink.'

She took the cup from my hand and hesitantly took a wee sip. She coughed and I couldn't help smiling. The whisky would have come as a surprise and did have a certain kick to it.

'You're not a whisky drinker, I take it?'

She frowned and looked up at me. Her eyes widened. *'You?'*

'Well, I was me last time I checked, but then again I have been known to have a grumpy-arsed side too.' I smiled in the hope that I would allay any fears she might be having about being in my car. 'I didn't catch your name, Yorkshire Lassie, but I'm Gregory. My friends call me Greg.'

'So you mostly get called Gregory, then, on account of having no friends?'

Ouch! She really didn't hold back, this one. But then again, I reminded myself that I hadn't endeared myself to the woman. This was mild compared to what I could've received. I decided to make light of the situation.

Holding my chest, I fell back into my seat. 'Ouch, I think I deserved that, eh?' I smiled again. I really did want to make amends. 'So are you goin' to tell me your name, Miss Yorkshire Lassie?'

'Please don't call me that.' Tears escaped her eyes and trickled down her beautiful but sad face.

Well done. McBradden strikes again. 'Okay, so tell me your name, then?'

'Mallory Westerman,' she said as she wiped her face with the back of her hand.

Remembering some of Mairi's books about one of her heroes, George Leigh Mallory, I raised my eyebrows. 'After the mountaineer, eh?' It was a stupid question and I expected her to scrunch her face and ask what I was talking about, but instead she nodded. *Now* I was intrigued. I guessed her parents must've been into climbing too to name their daughter after such a man. What a small world.

We sat in silence for a while until I had to ask, 'Did he call you that? Miss Yorkshire Lassie, I mean. Is that what *he* called you?'

Her lip trembled as she nodded. 'A version of it, I suppose. Miss Yorkshire... that's what he called me.' She smiled as if remembering him.

'Ah, I see. Sorry. If I'd known, I would've called you something else.'

She snorted. 'What would you have called me? You didn't know my name.'

She had a fair point. I had to think on my feet. Another opportunity to make her smile maybe? 'Probably *Wee Crabbit Lassie*.' I smirked at her to let her know I was kidding in case she knew what I meant. The responding frown told me she didn't.

'And what does *that* mean?' she asked suspiciously.

'Oh-h-h... it means pretty and quiet,' I joked.

Her face brightened as she squinted her eyes at me in mock annoyance. 'It does not! I know you're being mean. Tell me the truth.'

'You sure? Okay, you asked for it. *Wee* as in little and *crabbit* as in bad-tempered.' I shrank away, fully expecting her to clobber me, but instead she just gave me an indignant glare.

'Huh, *you* can talk!'

Yep, fair point. 'Aye, that's true.' I scratched my head and grinned. There was something about her that I couldn't help but like. Even though she clearly wasn't overly keen on me. A little glimmer of hope sparked inside me that maybe she'd actually forgive me.

After another few moments of silence I glanced over at her again. 'You all right now?'

Instead of the affirmative nod I hoped for, she shook her head slowly as more tears spilled down her cheeks. She covered her face with her free hand and began to sob. My heart squeezed in my chest and I felt helpless. I wanted to alleviate her pain somehow. But I didn't know what to do. I didn't know the girl and she clearly wasn't that fond of me. I took the cup from her hand and placed it on the dashboard. Sliding over toward her, I slipped my arm around her and pulled her head into my chest.

'Hey, c'mon, shhhhh, you'll be fine. Shhhh. It gets easier, I promise you that,' I lied. It *didn't* get easier. I was living proof of the sad fact. I swallowed hard to try to free the lump of emotion that had chosen that exact moment to close up my throat. My eyes began to sting and I chewed at the inside of my cheek, trying my best to fend off the tears. When I tasted the copper tang of blood, I released the soft, damaged flesh from between my teeth. I stroked her hair, incapable of speaking for fear of letting my emotions free. This wasn't about *me.* I had to keep my own grief in check.

After she had calmed a little, she raised her head and made eye contact with me. Her bright blue irises were circled with red and the skin around her eyes swollen and puffy. The grief I saw there tugged at my insides. I wanted to hold her again, tell her that I understood. But the words didn't come. Instead I moved back over to my side of the car again.

'Come on. We'd better get you home, eh? They'll all be wondering where you've got to.' I pulled out of the car park and headed down the road towards the cottages.

Chapter Nine

I pulled up the Landy outside Mallory's new home and climbed out. As I reached her side of the car, the door to the house burst open and three terrified-looking people ran out, followed by a little black ball of fluff on legs that was barking its head off and jumping around. The people all shouted at once and were clearly relieved about her safe return.

I opened the car door and Mallory tried to climb out, but I stopped her. 'Whoa there, lassie, you've nothin' on your feet,' I scolded her as I picked her up in my arms and began to carry her towards the cottage and her waiting family.

One of the people, a guy about Mallory's age whom I presumed was her brother or some relative, glared at me, nostrils flared and jaw ticcing as if he was ready to pounce on me.

I couldn't say I blamed him. I would've been the same if someone I didn't know was carrying my sister home looking bedraggled and distressed.

He followed close behind me and I could hear his heavy breathing as I followed the women and carried Mallory into the house. I placed her on the couch and turned to find his stare still fixed on me. His attitude was pissing me off. It was as if he thought I'd had ulterior motives with the woman; he didn't know me yet he was quick to judge and presume shit he had no clue about.

His accusative scowl made my skin prickle and anger flared up within me. After he'd asked who I was and insinuated that I was the reason she was *in* a state I fronted up to him. 'I found her on the beach sobbing her heart out, if you must know. She's nothing on her feet and no coat. Have you any idea how cold it gets out there, *pal*?' I'm pretty sure I bared my teeth at him.

'Whoa, hey! Knock it off, please,' Mallory implored. 'Brad… Greg came to my rescue when I went a bit crazy tonight and, Greg… Brad wasn't responsible for my lack of appropriate clothing. I went out like this of my own accord. So can you please just back up and shake hands?'

We all stared at her. This was the most she'd said all night.

The great lummox and I shook hands, and I told Mallory I was going to go. But Brad invited me to stay for coffee. I glanced uncomfortably at Mallory but she just shrugged. So much for gratitude, eh? The others cleared out of the room and it felt a little too contrived for my liking.

I sat beside her on the couch and nudged her shoulder. 'See, you *have* people who care. Don't go scaring them like that again, okay?'

She glanced up at me with those big blue eyes. 'When we were in your car, you said it gets easier... how do you know that? How can *anyone* say that?' Her voice wavered and my heart ached for her.

I stared straight ahead at the dancing flames in the fireplace. 'Well, only those who've experienced loss and grief and have come out the other side can really know, I suppose.'

'You've been through this?' She sounded surprised and... almost hopeful too. Like perhaps she thought I *could* help her. I knew I couldn't really. No one could. I wished it weren't true.

'Aye.' I sensed she wanted details. But I couldn't say any more.

'Your wife?' she pushed.

I needed to leave. I couldn't do this. Not now. Not with her.

'Na', my—' I scrubbed my hands over my face. No, I *really* couldn't do this. I knew it was cowardly. 'Look, it's late, I'd better go, I've got an early start the morrow. Got to pick Rhiannon up and I can't be late. Tell your family I'm grateful for the offer of a drink, but I really should be off.' I stood, pulled open the front door, and left without looking back.

I climbed back in the Landy and smashed my hands into the steering wheel. *Fuck! You fucking shithead! She needed your help. Some kind of reassurance would've been nice! You fucking prick!* I clenched and unclenched my jaw before ramming the key in the ignition and reversing up the lane like the idiot I'd become.

Pulling to a jerky halt outside the pub, I yanked the handbrake on. Then I flung open my door, climbed out of the Landy, pushed through the double doors, and stalked inside with purpose. Wallet in hand, I walked behind the bar, grabbed a bottle of the cheaper whisky, and thrust a note into the cash register.

'Greg? Everything okay?' Stella asked with a look of grave concern.

'Aye… I'm just a fucking prick, that's all,' I mumbled loud enough for only her to hear.

'Oh, is *that* all?' She smirked.

I gave her a snide curl of my lip.

As I turned to walk out, she grabbed my arm. 'Don't go drinking yourself stupid, Greg, okay?'

Her eyes told me that she knew that was *exactly* what I was going to do. I had to think fast to change her train of thought. 'Oh, erm… hey. How about Friday? For me to play, I mean?'

Her face lit up. 'Really? Oh, Gregory, that would be wonderful!'

'Fine. Getting Rhiannon back tomorrow, so I'll be fine by Friday.'

'Great. Thanks, Greg.' She squeezed my arm. 'It *will* be okay, you know.'

I couldn't decide whether she meant the gig or my life

in general. Maybe she meant both. I smiled tightly and nodded once. She released me and I averted my gaze and called out to Angus. Once he'd trotted up to my side we left the pub quick smart. Shit, I'd gone and confirmed it now. I was *definitely* a brainless idiot.

*

By Friday I'd worked myself up into a frenzy about the gig. What the hell had I suggested it for? I liked to play, obviously, but I liked to play melancholy songs about heartbreak in the privacy of my own home. The thought of singing in front of people scared me shitless. My stomach churned and I pulled almost every shirt I owned out of the wardrobe. *What should I wear? Shirt? T-shirt? Do I need to look a particular way? Fu-u-u-uck!*

After a great deal of toing and froing, I settled on my navy button-up shirt with pale blue flowers on it. I grabbed Rhiannon and made my way to the pub. It was already busy and my heart leapt as I walked over to the bar. Stella was wearing a proud grin. Bless her. She really did care.

When it was time to perform, she gave me a warm smile of encouragement. The knots in my stomach tightened and my mouth went dry. Glancing around the pub, I spotted a fair few familiar local faces. My gaze landed on a head of long, dark, wavy hair. *Mallory. Oh, great.*

I took my place behind the mic stand and cleared my throat. 'Ahem... evening, all.' I coughed. 'Good to see you. Ah-h... for those of you who haven't had the pleasure of being served intoxicating liquor by my good self, I'd better introduce myself, eh?' Trying to get comfy on my seat, I wriggled about a bit. 'My name is Greg McBradden and I'm the local handyman, bartender, boatman and all-round grumpy arse.' I glanced straight over in Mallory's direction and she cringed. I couldn't help sniggering a little at her reaction. 'Anyways, I'm going to do my best to add *entertainer* to my list of talents. Thanks to Stella, the owner here – she seems to have a disliking for all you locals, as she's agreed to let me sing to you.'

The place erupted in laughter and I smiled. Maybe this wouldn't be so bad. The locals heckled and booed me, which made me laugh. *Bloody mad lot.*

I looked over at Mallory again, but her head was down and she was picking at her jeans. I wondered if maybe I'd overstepped the mark... again. Holding my guitar aloft, I carried on talking shite.

'Anyways... I'd like to introduce you to Rhiannon, my guitar, named after a Fleetwood Mac song that got me into playing in the first place. So you can blame them if you don't like ma playing.' Everyone laughed again and I relaxed a little more. 'She's just been repaired at the guitar hospital, also known as a music shop for you heathens, so she sounds grand. If any of yous gets up and leaves, don't forget I know where most of you live.' I chuckled along with the crowd. They were lapping it up, and the tension in my body continued to ebb away.

'Right, well, seeing as this is my first night, I'm not going to scare you away with my own compositions. This first one, you should all know, but don't bloody sing along. I hate that.' I laughed, but I'd said it in all seriousness. There's nothing worse than hearing that inane bloody mumbling that people make when they try to sing along with something they don't really know. It's ridiculous and highly embarrassing; cringeworthy, even. Plus the fact that if there's someone on a stage performing, it's *his* job. So shut the hell up, I say!

'It's a little number I like to call "Trouble" ... because erm... that's the song title.' Another rumble of laughter, but this time I felt like a dick. *Stupid fucking thing to say.* 'It's by a guy called Ray LaMontagne, and I'd like anyone who knows him or follows him on Twitter to tell him I'm sorry.' The place roared with laughter yet again. Get me. I was quite funny really. A smile took up residence on my ugly mug and I felt just a tiny bit happy.

Chapter Ten

The night was going swimmingly. Being applauded sent shivers of excitement down my spine and I decided then and there that I'd be doing it again. I took a long gulp of my beer as I scanned the room. After placing my glass back down, I began to play the introduction to one of my all-time favourite songs. The singular notes played in a staccato rhythm rang out through the room as people fell silent. Clearly it wasn't just me that liked it.

I sang the opening line of 'Chasing Cars' by Snow Patrol. The hush that had fallen on the room was broken by the scraping of a chair and fumbling noises. I glanced up in the direction of the noise just as Mallory shoved her way through the crowd and made a dash for the door. *What the hell?* Maybe the long-haired beauty had drunk a little too much. I couldn't blame her. It wasn't as if I'd been sober since Mairi's death.

As I sang, her friends dashed out after her. Concern etched on their faces as they flung open the door and ran out of the pub. *Shit. Maybe she's sick.* I carried on playing but an uneasy knot returned to my stomach. Maybe she wasn't used to the alcohol and it'd affected her badly. I vowed I would go over tomorrow and check up on her.

At the end of the night the crowd congratulated me and shook my hand. The compliments were flying. *You should have been playing here for ages, Greg... You're a natural, Greg... You have the sexiest voice, Greg.* It was quite an ego boost. But it was all overshadowed by a niggling in my gut. Was Mallory okay? Why did I care so much? Okay, so we shared something in common: grief. But I didn't know her and she didn't like me. It was stupid to feel so concerned about someone I'd only just met. But for some reason I couldn't stop thinking about her.

I arrived home and made myself a cup of coffee. Probably not the best idea, since caffeine so late at night was bound to exacerbate my sleeping issues. But I wasn't tired anyway. Images of Mallory crying came to mind; the way her limp body huddled into me as I carried her to the car; the way she sobbed silently when we shared those few words of conversation; her running out of the pub without looking back. There must've been a valid reason for her speedy retreat from the pub tonight, and I needed to know that she was all right. That got to me though. I didn't simply *want* to know. I *needed* to know.

At around two in the morning I said goodnight to Angus and climbed the stairs to my bedroom. After stripping free of my clothes, I climbed into bed. I should've showered first, but I figured the sooner I got to bed, the sooner I could get up and go round to check on the Yorkshire lassie.

Just as I'd anticipated, sleep didn't grant me the pleasure of its company for quite a while. Instead I tossed and turned. Churning the possibilities around in my mind for Mallory's earlier quick exit, I narrowed it down to five:

1) She was sick.
2) She hated my singing.
3) She was drunk.
4) She was drunk *and* sick.
5) She was drunk, sick and my singing made it *worse*.

Fu-u-u-uck! I slammed my fists back into the mattress. When I did eventually fall into a fitful sleep, I was plagued by the image of Mallory on her knees on the beach again. My heart broke as I ran towards her, pain-filled sobs ringing in the silent night air.

I awoke with a start, a little confused and racked with guilt at the fact that my dreams had, for once, been filled with a virtual stranger instead of the love of my life.

*

Once I'd showered and dressed, I jumped in the Landy with Angus and drove down to the village. I parked across from the pub and dropped Angus in with Stella. She took him out the back and gave him some leftover steak. His tail wagged frantically and no bloody wonder. He was better fed than I was.

'I've just... erm... got something to do, okay? Be back soon,' I informed her. Leaving the pub, I paused and took in a deep breath with my head back, letting the morning sunlight warm my face. *Courage, McBradden. Just walk over, knock on the door, ask how she is, and then leave. Simple.* My feet began to move and before I knew it I was knocking on the door of Sealladh-mara Cottage, Mallory's front door, with a pounding heart and sweating palms.

The door opened and there stood the petite blonde friend who I had gathered was called Josie or Jodie or something like that. In her arms was the small wriggling black dog I'd seen before, wagging its tail frantically.

Before lifting her head, she frowned at the dog. 'Keep still Ruby.' When she set eyes on me she raised her eyebrows. 'Oh, hi. What are you doing here?'

I twisted the Landy keys in my hand. 'I came to check up on Mallory. I saw her run out last night and was worried she was sick or something.' I nervously ran my hand through my hair as the moths in my stomach set about beating their wings.

'Oh, yes, of course. Thanks.' Her expression saddened a little. 'You played "Chasing Cars". That was the song that was played at her engagement. It meant a lot to her and Sam... It was their song.'

As if I were on the world's biggest roller coaster, my stomach fell and my heart tripped over itself. 'Oh my God. No fuckin' wonder she ran out.' I felt like utter shit. The poor wee girl. I covered my face with my free hand and exhaled all the air from my lungs. Words suddenly escaped me and I found myself floundering in front of this total stranger. 'Please... fuck, oh, I'm sorry to swear, but fuck. Please tell her I'm so, so sorry. Fuck. What a fucking idiot!'

She held out her hands towards me in reassurance. A wasted gesture. 'Hey, Greg, you weren't to know. Honestly, don't beat yourself up, eh?'

'Fuck. Fuck. Fuck. Oh, God, sorry, my language.' I covered my mouth as if doing so would stop my verbal diarrhoea.

A voice travelled through from somewhere inside the house. 'Don't worry, mate, Josie has said much worse.'

Brad's attempt at putting me at ease didn't help any either. I shook my head. 'Every time I see that girl, I put ma fuckin' size ten in my mouth. I'm going to go before I do any more damage to the poor wee girl. As if she hasn't been through enough, eh?' I turned to go but looked back over my shoulder to see pity in the blonde's eyes. 'Seriously, please tell her I'm so sorry. I'll be keepin' out of her way, I reckon.'

'That won't be necessary, Greg, honestly. You weren't to know.' Her eyes told me she genuinely didn't blame me. But *I* did. As I walked away swearing at myself, I decided that I really needed to just lay off and stay away from her. Not only had I been a shit to her that first day, but I'd upset her friends *and* broken her heart with a bloody song. Not bad going for a few weeks' work.

Better not walk under any ladders, McBradden. Karma is a bitch.

Chapter Eleven

Thinking about Karma got me thinking back to Alice. I suppose now would be a good time to tell you that delightfully twisted story, eh? I met Alice at university in the nineties.

Alice Gibb was sex on legs. Long blonde hair, killer curves, big brown eyes, lush breasts… Don't judge me, I am a man after all. Anyway, I was only nineteen and she was every teenage bloke's wet dream. Sorry for my crude turn of phrase but… aww, who the hell am I kidding? You've already figured out what I'm like, eh?

I keep digressing… sorry.

So, I was attracted to her instantly, but so was every other guy at university. I thought I was uber cool with my long hair and my grunge attire. I absolutely idolised Eddie Vedder from Pearl Jam, Dave Grohl from Nirvana, and Chris Cornell from Soundgarden. I was a real grunger: checked lumberjack shirts, band tees, and combat boots. I used to walk around campus with my headphones on as some American rock, indie, or suchlike screeched out of my CD Walkman. Jeez, showing my age now, eh?

We were taking completely different subjects. I was

music production, she was textiles. She was going to be the next Vivien Westwood and I was going to be the next Jimmy Page. To say we both had delusions of grandeur would be an understatement. I got chatting to her one lunchtime…

*

'Can you pass me a can of Diet Coke, please?' came a sweet voice from beside me. I looked to my right and met the big brown eyes of the girl I'd been staring at for the past few months. She was even hotter up close. Long blonde waves that fell past her shoulders. Large, perky breasts and big hips. She wasn't fat. Far from it. She was luscious in that Marilyn Monroe way. Every guy in university had been ogling her from day one and I was no different.

'Oh, yeah, sure.' I reached for a can and passed it back to her. She smiled and blushed. Too cute for words.

She scrunched her face. 'You're Gregory, aren't you?'

She knows who I am? I gulped in disbelief and must've looked ridiculous opening and closing my mouth like a goldfish out of water.

'Yeah. That's… that's me.' I nodded emphatically as heat rose in my cheeks.

'You play guitar, don't you?' she asked with her head to one side and a playful look in her eyes. I nodded again. *Come on, stupid mouth, work!* Despite my chastising myself, intelligent words wouldn't form.

Tilting her head to the other side, she bit her lip for a moment. 'I think guitarists are hot.' And with that she turned and walked away, glancing over her shoulder and almost electrocuting me with a killer smile.

'Oy! Are you moving or what?' came an angry voice to the side of where I was apparently superglued to the floor in the lunch line.

My head swivelled round to the pissed-off guy. 'Aye. Sorry, mate. Sorry.' I shuffled on.

Later that same day I was walking back to my digs when someone behind me shouted my name. I stopped and turned around. It was her.

'Wait! God, you walk fast,' she panted.

'Sorry, I was just on my way home.'

'Want some company?'

'Sure. Yeah. You not going home yoursel'?'

'Na'. Not yet. Thought I'd come and see where *you* live first.' She pulled her bottom lip between her teeth again. All the blood in my body rushed south, and I hoped to God she couldn't see what was happening down there.

'So, Gregory—'

'Call me Greg, all my friends do.'

A wide smile spread across her stunning face. 'So, *Greg*, do you have a girlfriend?'

'Girlfriend? Me? Erm… no.'

‘Would you like one?’ *Wow, she certainly isn’t backwards at coming forwards, that’s for sure.*

Feeling a little braver, I smiled back. ‘You offering?’

‘I’d have to get to know you better first,’ she replied.

‘Sounds good to me.’ I couldn’t quell the shit-eating grin that had taken up residence on my ugly mug.

And that was how the thing started.

*

The following January

We were all going out around Oban. There were a few clubs that played great music, and a gang of us decided we’d go out and get pissed, have a laugh, do some dancing, you know?

I called for Alice around seven thirty. She opened the door to her room and there she stood, short, tight black skirt, thick black stockings, muckle clumpy boots – sounds crap but, believe me, she looked hot as hell – and a tie-dyed cropped top. Her black leather jacket finished off the ensemble nicely. My mouth fell open. I wanted to shove her back on the bed and get her out of the silly clothes that were in my way, but as if reading my mind, she shook her head and wagged her finger at me.

‘Not yet, Mr McBradden. You’ll get yours later tonight.’ A sudden rush of blood descended to my favourite organ. By the way, sex with her was amazing. I had nothing to compare it to – her being my first – but oh, wow, I didn't care. She was horny as anything and couldn't get enough. Which was fine with me.

We arrived at Club Zero and met with the rest of our group of friends. Some had been there awhile and were already on their merry way to pissed-up land. I grabbed us a couple of drinks from the bar and we made our way over to the group. 'Fade Into You' by Mazzy Star played over the PA system, and I watched Alice sway to the music with her eyes closed. She was so incredibly sexy in *everything* she did.

And she knew it.

The song ended and we drank a little more. Her eyes were glazing over and she was totally relaxed. The next song was the Cowboy Junkies version of 'Sweet Jane'. It was a song that Alice and I had made love to on more than one occasion. We were on the dance floor together and with her back to me she ground herself into me as we swayed to the music. A guy appeared in front of her and started dancing with her as if I were invisible. I clenched my jaw as I watched her respond to him. She turned her back to him and faced me. I grimaced at him, hoping the words 'Yeah, fuck you, pal' were clear in my face. But to my utter shock, she lifted her arms up, letting them fall behind her head, and draped them around his neck.

With her eyes fixed on mine she ground her arse back into him as I watched. My heart rate picked up and my hands balled into fists by my sides. I clenched my jaw. This was *our* song. What was she playing at? The guy leaned down and began to kiss her neck as she closed her eyes for a moment. I stopped moving my feet and raised my clenched fists, ready to fly at him. When her eyes opened, she licked her lips at me. The bastard lifted his hand and ran it up her top, grabbing her breast. *What the hell?* Confusion and anger washed over me in equal measures. Why was she doing this? She fixed her hooded gaze on me as he fondled her and my nostrils flared.

I was ready to kill him.

Two can play this game, lady. I grabbed the brunette that was dancing beside me and had desperately been trying to get my attention for the last twenty minutes. I put my arms around her, slid my hands down to her arse and squeezed. She gazed up at me and slipped her arms around my shoulders. I glanced over at Alice, who was frowning now. *Ha! Not liking the taste of your own medicine, eh?* She turned round and stuck her tongue down the guy's throat and I just about hit the roof.

Without thinking, I shoved the brunette aside, lunged forward, and punched the bastard in the face; knocked him out cold. After that I stormed out of the place. I'd had enough. I just couldn't figure her out. I thought we *meant* something.

I heard footsteps behind me and someone grabbed my arm. I swung around and was met with an angry stare. ‘What the hell was that in there, Greg?’ she shouted in my face.

‘I could ask you the same question! What were you doing?’ I shouted back, raising my hands in exasperation.

‘I wanted you to watch, Greg. I wanted you to see that other men find me attractive. You’re so into your music that you ignore me! Well, you won’t do that again, will you?’ A manic grin appeared on her face. What the hell was *wrong* with her?

‘I don’t want to watch you with another fucking man. What kind of sick pervert do you think I am, eh?’

Her laughter was filled with derision. ‘Oh, come on, Greg. Don’t be such a prude.’

‘What man *would* want to see that? You’re *my* girlfriend, Al, not his.’

At that her eyes widened. And then out of nowhere she drew her hand back and punched me. A right hook to my left cheek. I staggered backwards, holding my face.

She lurched towards me angrily. ‘You don’t *own* me, Greg. I’m not an object. I’m a person. Don’t ever act like I *belong* to you again. If I want to dance with another man, I’ll do it.’

I stood there open-mouthed as she rubbed her hand and began to cry. For some unknown reason I felt *sorry* for her. She was insecure even though I’d never given her reason to be.

I pulled her into my arms and held her tight. 'Hey, come on. What's all this about, Al? Eh?'

She sobbed into my chest and clung to my shirt. 'I wanted your attention. That's all. You've been spending so much time playing music with the guys that I felt neglected. I wanted to teach you a lesson.'

My face crumpled in confusion and I pulled away to gaze into her bloodshot eyes. 'Alice, you've been at *every* jam session with me when I've been playing. I haven't been ignoring you at all.'

'But... I want you to myself sometimes.' She hiccupped.

I stroked her hair back from her face and kissed her. My cheek was throbbing and I was a little freaked out by what had just happened, but I put it down to the drink.

Sadly, it wasn't the only time she struck me in anger. But for some reason unbeknownst to me, I put up with her temper. I think I kidded myself that I loved her. The next big blow, however, wasn't a physical one.

We'd been together just over a year...

*

There was a knock on the door to my room and I threw down my pen. I'd been trying to compose a song for the band I was setting up with my best mate, Connell, but my head was filled with cotton wool thanks to a serious lack of sleep. I wasn't expecting anyone and almost decided to ignore the intrusion. But the person knocked again, softly this time, and I went and answered it.

Alice stood in the doorway, her eyes were red-rimmed and she twisted a tissue in her hands. I inhaled sharply. 'Hey, what's wrong, babe?'

'Oh, Greg, I'm so sorry.' She flung her arms around my neck and sobbed into my T-shirt. I lifted her from the ground and walked into my small room. Placing her on the bed, I sat beside her, moving my notes out of the way.

I tilted her chin up so that her eyes met mine. 'Please tell me what's wrong, Alice. You're worrying me.'

'I'm sorry… I'm sorry.' Her slurred words were interspersed with body-shaking sobs. Dread filled me. She'd had an affair. I was sure of it. After the way things had gone with us recently, I was beginning to think we weren't meant to be.

I took a deep breath, trying to calm the storm raging beneath my skin as I thought about her being unfaithful. I hated the idea. She should've dumped me first. 'Alice, just tell me.'

'I'm… Greg… I'm four weeks pregnant.'

Chapter Twelve

My mouth fell open and I could swear my heart stopped for a split second. I let go of her and stood up, running my hands through my hair. I peered down at her, sitting there, sobbing. She looked… *broken.* I rubbed my hands over my face and let out a long huff of air. What the hell did we do now?

She gazed up at me. 'You have to know, Greg, that I didn't mean for this to happen.'

'But… you're on the pill. I don't… I don't get it, Alice… How…?'

She shrugged. 'They don't always work. They're only… like… 90-something per cent reliable.'

'Fuck.' The word fell out of my mouth as I closed my eyes. This was my worst nightmare come true. I loved sex. Couldn't get enough of it. But I had *never* expected this. I thought that we were protected. *Fucking idiot.*

I sat beside her again and leaned my elbows on my knees. 'What… erm… what do we do now?'

'I have no idea, Greg. I'm so scared.' I turned to see her lip trembling and my heart broke. This was *my* fault. *I'd* done this. I know they say it takes two to tango, but I should've worn condoms as well. This was a stupid male pride thing. I hated condoms. And she was my first, so I knew I wouldn't give her anything. Pregnancy never entered my thoughts.

Until now.

It was time to step up and be a man. I had some major decisions to make, but I had to be an adult and grow a pair of metaphorical bollocks. Ironic thought pattern, considering the mess my *actual* bollocks had got me into. *Shit… Me… a daddy? No way.*

We sat there in silence for a long while until Alice stood. 'I think I should go, Greg. We both need time to adjust. And then we need to decide the way forward.'

I stood before her and cupped her face in my hands.

'Marry me.' The words fell out of my mouth before I'd really thought them through – and as soon as they had, I clamped my stupid mouth shut.

Her face lit up. 'What? Greg, are you serious?'

No going back now. 'Well… we're going to have a baby and… we need to make a proper commitment. We need to be a family for this little one,' I said, sliding my hand down across her tummy.

Tears spilled over her chocolate-brown eyes and she hugged me hard. 'Oh, Greg, you've made me so happy. I thought I was going to have to get rid of it. I thought we'd be over. But… Oh, Greg.'

'No, no, we'll be fine. We'll be fine.' I said it for my benefit more than for Alice's. What the hell had I done? *Idiot!* I was twenty and not ready to be either a husband *or* a father.

*

We stood outside Oban register office as Connell snapped photos. Alice's friend Anna did the same. I forced smiles and cringed as Alice clung to me and posed for the camera. Her simple wedding band was flashed at the lens in every shot. She was *so* proud of it. We'd gone for silver bands as we couldn't afford gold. Connell and Anna had been our witnesses, and the ceremony had been over in fifteen minutes. We'd decided to get wed before Alice's bump started to show and she couldn't fit into a nice dress.

She wore a white knee-length summer dress with pale blue flowers dotted all over it. She carried a bunch of fake blue flowers and had put one in her hair too. It all felt so contrived... so pretentious. But what could I do? I'd got the girl pregnant; the least I could do was marry her. A table was booked for the four of us to eat at our favourite Chinese restaurant to celebrate the marriage.

The meal was good, but for some reason my stomach was unsettled. I felt as if a thousand tiny elephants were stampeding through my intestines or learning to bloody tap-dance in there. Something was off. I couldn't help the uneasy feeling that had taken hold. I just wished I could explain it.

Later that night when we got back to my room in

digs, Alice stripped down to her white lacy underwear and stood before me. I'd had a bottle and a half of wine to myself and was feeling sleepy.

'Greg,' she whispered into my ear as I lay sprawled on my bed.

'Mmmm?'

'I want to make love with my new husband.' She slid her hand down my body and gripped me through my black trousers. 'Don't you want me anymore? Is it because I'm getting fat?' Her voice was a little whiny, and I opened my eyes to see that she had removed her underwear and her curves were on display for me. *Only* for me. She pouted as she trailed her fingers up and down my torso.

Suddenly I felt wide awake.

We consummated the marriage that night… twice. As I said before, I'm a man. But I felt a little empty inside. I was starting to wonder about things. Alice hadn't been suffering morning sickness at all. She was surprisingly well for someone who was going through early pregnancy for the first time. As she snuggled into my side and fell asleep, I lay awake.

*

Time was passing at a rate of knots but Alice and I had been getting on well. She was very horny… more than normal. She said it was down to her pregnancy hormones. Obviously, I didn't complain; sex between us always had been great. And to top it off, I was getting excited at the prospect of being a daddy. The thought of having a mini version of me and Alice to look after and care for somehow gave purpose to my life.

My daydreams were all about the baby. Who would he or she look like? Would we have a daughter or a son? Would our child love music as much as I did? Would I be able to change a nappy without vomiting? More to the point, would I be able to *change a nappy*? How would I cope on even less sleep? None of it mattered. As long as the baby was healthy, I'd be happy and I'd love him or her unconditionally. The fact that this was all unexpected began to mean less and less until it faded into insignificance and I even began to coo over babies I saw in the street. I was turning into a sap and I just didn't care.

But all that said, something was niggling at the back of my mind. We were four months into the pregnancy and she *still* hadn't been sick. Now, I'm an intelligent man and I know that every pregnancy is different. But my research had told me that Alice was in the minority with her lack of symptoms. I decided at the next opportunity I'd sit her down and ask her if everything was okay.

Maybe she'd been hiding her sickness? I knew she could be insecure and I wondered if perhaps she was scared of showing her vulnerability in front of me. She needed to know that I wasn't like that. I also felt that maybe I needed to attend her appointments with her. Up to that point she had only told me about them *after* the fact. And I was a wee bit disappointed that I hadn't seen a scan but I had no real clue how these things worked. To top it off I had no point of reference; no one to ask. I worried that maybe the baby wasn't growing enough, seeing as her belly was still quite flat. She'd gained a bit of weight admittedly, but she'd been eating more crap, saying that the baby was craving stuff. Was I mug for believing her? That was it. I needed some questions to be answered. I needed to be involved and if we were going to be a proper family she needed to stop shutting me out.

It was a Friday night and we were sitting in our new digs. A room in a shared house that was large enough for a double bed *and* a cot. We hadn't discussed what would happen when the baby arrived. Who would look after the infant whilst we were in our final year at university? Would one of us have to drop out? Every time I broached the subject, she shrugged it off, saying we had plenty of time to think about things like that. But it was *all* I could think about.

I'd just made coffee for me and decaf tea for Alice. I craved a beer, but I was staying off drink out of respect for her. As we watched TV like an old married couple, a show about holidays came on. We watched as beaches appeared and scantily clad, tanned bodies strolled around on the screen.

Alice had a light-bulb moment. 'Oh, I forgot to mention that I'm booked to go to Amsterdam for a weekend with the girls for my birthday.'

I glanced over at her. 'But your birthday is in December. Won't you have other things going on then? When are you actually going?'

'Oh, don't worry, it's not until the new year.'

'Okay.' I mulled over what she'd said. 'Erm... you do know you'll be heavily pregnant and on the verge of giving birth in the new year, don't you?'

Her head swivelled in my direction. 'I... erm... I...' Her face turned beet red.

'Alice?' I glared at her, waiting for some logical explanation as to why she'd forgotten she was carrying my child.

She laughed and shrugged. 'Oh, silly me. I meant in the spring.'

'But by then we'll *have* a new baby, Alice.' Suspicion spiked within me.

'Yeah... yeah, but you'll be fine for a few days, eh?'

I stared at her. What the hell was going on? 'No, Alice. No, I won't be okay being left whilst you go off on a weekend piss-up with your mates.' The volume of my voice rose exponentially.

She huffed sulkily and turned away from me. 'I need a drink. Got any wine?'

'Alice. That's not funny. You know I gave up alcohol

too. Unless... is there something you need to tell me?'

She stood up and put her hands on her hips. 'What the hell is that supposed to mean, Greg?'

Standing to face her, I stared into her eyes, hoping to see something genuine. 'It means, Alice, that something's not right here.'

She folded her arms and snorted. 'What the hell are you talking about?'

'Pardon me for being suspicious, but... you are *four months* pregnant, and you haven't been sick once. I haven't seen a scan picture and you haven't invited me to any of your pre-natal appointments. You're planning a holiday for when you're supposed to be delivering our baby, and you're craving wine when you're nervous.'

She opened and closed her mouth like a dying goldfish. I waited for her explanation. I waited and waited. And waited some more.

She slumped onto the sofa and dropped her head into her hands. 'It... it was a false alarm.'

'What?' My calm voice belied the increasing rate of my heart and the sweating of my clenched palms.

'My period came a week after I told you. But you'd already asked me to marry you. And... I was so happy, so I kept up with the pretence, Greg.' She lifted her eyes up to meet mine, and tears were running down her face.

I tried to swallow but my throat was closing up. I just stared at her. My heart squeezed in my chest. I'd thought I wasn't ready to be a dad, but gradually over the past few months I'd got used to the idea. I'd actually been looking at babies in a whole new light and feeling excited. Yet here she was shattering the illusion and breaking my heart.

I pulled out the desk chair and carefully lowered my shaking body to it. 'You mean you lied to me?'

'No! No, Greg. I wanted it to be true. I tried so hard to make it true.' Her desperation was almost palpable.

'That's why you've wanted sex so much. Not because of pregnancy hormones.'

'No... I *wanted* it to be true, Greg. I *needed* it to be true. I was terrified of losing you.' She came across the room and dropped to her knees before me. 'I *can't* lose you, Greg. You're my world.'

Her empty words meant nothing to me. Although I heard them, the sentiment was devoid of genuine feeling, and in that moment I hated her. My heart was trying to burst through my chest and escape the space I reluctantly shared with her in that moment.

'But there's no baby. You let me think I was going to be a dad. I married you so we could be a proper little family,' I whispered. Having my fears confirmed hurt more than any physical pain I'd ever experienced. I'd hoped, beyond hope, that she'd have some logical explanation. Like pregnancy brain or some other crazy thing that pregnant women went through.

But here she was, taking all of my dreams of fatherhood and stamping all over them in her fake leather stiletto boots, piercing holes in my heart with her words as she admitted her despicable lies and deceit. The fact that she could *justify* what she had done in her sick little mind by telling me how much she *loved* me made me want to vomit.

She sobbed and clung to my hands as I stared blankly at our entwined fingers. 'I did… and I'm so, *so* sorry. But we can *get* pregnant, Greg. We can try. *We* can make it work. We *can* have a baby. As soon as you want to try, we can try.'

I stood and pulled my hands free from hers. 'I need to get out of here. I need… I need time to think.' I grabbed my coat and my Walkman and stormed out.

Chapter Thirteen

It was eleven at night after Alice had dropped her bombshell and I trawled the streets as the lyrics to 'Big Empty' by Stone Temple Pilots resonated deep within me as the singer talked about lies and creating distance. I bit back the threatening tears as I walked, pounding the pavement, trying to clear my head.

It wasn't working.

I called into the off-licence and bought the cheapest bottle of whisky I could find and then, after half an hour of wandering aimlessly, I entered the local park and found a bench. Pulling the bottle of amber liquid out of the brown paper bag, I sat there swigging from the neck like some alcoholic with nowhere to go.

I tried to force down the lump in my throat as I listened to Stevie Nicks singing about changing in 'Landslide'. What had I done to deserve this shit? Really? In the space of four months I'd become a husband, was dreaming about being a father, and then had that dream ripped from me. Everything I had believed in was crumbling around me and I had no clue what to do.

Sorrow pushed down on me like a heavy weight, and

I choked as the emotion I'd been fighting finally broke free. Tears spilled over from my clenched eyes and sobs racked my body. Gulping for air as my shoulders shuddered, I hugged my arms around myself, still clutching the bottle.

'Why? Why does she insist on breaking my fucking heart?' I asked the empty park, wishing someone were there to hold me and take the pain away, tell me it would all be okay. But of course it wouldn't be okay. I knew that already.

Half a bottle of whisky gone; my head was spinning. I looked up at the sky and felt completely insignificant under the magnitude of whirling constellations. What did my problems mean in the great scheme of things? To me? Everything. Eddie Vedder from Pearl Jam sang 'Elderly Woman Behind the Counter in a Small Town' as tears continued to cascade down my face. The chilly evening air hit my damp skin and I shivered.

In the song it was the old lady's memories that were fading but for me it was the love I'd held in my heart for the woman I had thought was carrying my child. It was fading fast; if it had ever really been there at all.

*

Eventually I decided I should head back. I had nowhere else to go and the temperature had dropped substantially. Glancing at my watch, I realised it was almost one in the morning. Alice would no doubt be worried. And I was glad. I wanted her to suffer. I wanted her chest to ache as mine did. I wanted her to know my pain. How the hell could someone do that to the person they supposedly *loved*? It was one thing to lie about small things. That was bad enough. But to lie about being *pregnant*...

I stomped back towards the bedsit we called home as my blood thundered in my temples. At one point I had to stop and take deep breaths to try and calm the rage within. I couldn't return to her feeling this way. I'd no doubt say something I regretted.

I stopped again around the corner from our bedsit and stared up at the bedroom window. The light was on, which meant she was waiting up for me. I wasn't quite as drunk as I wanted to be. *Fuck it.* I discarded the rest of the bottle of whisky and staggered back across the road.

Opening the door, I stepped inside. Alice was curled up in a ball on the sofa. Her eyes were swollen and red. She glanced up as I walked in. As if unsure whether to approach me, she stood on shaking legs and took a few tentative steps.

I held my hands up to stop her. 'I'm going to go stay at Connell's. I... I can't be near you right now,' I informed her without making eye contact. After walking into the bedroom, I grabbed my holdall, stuffed in a few clothes, and zipped it up. She stood at the doorway, twisting her fingers, watching my every move.

'Can't we just talk about this, Greg? I've said I'm sorry. What more can I do to make it right?'

Moving close to her, so that my nose was almost touching hers, I spoke through gritted teeth as my lower lip trembled and my heart ached again. 'There's nothing you can do, Alice. Once again you've broken my heart. How many more times am I expected to put up with it, eh? Do me a favour. Don't contact me. *I* will contact *you*… if and when I feel like it. Now move.'

She flinched and tears escaped her eyes. I felt no sympathy, only pain.

I arrived at Connell's flat and knocked on the door. He opened it and stood there with a sad expression, and I knew she'd called him.

He gestured into the flat. 'Come in, mate.'

*

Around two weeks later, after I'd had time to cool down and think things through, I turned up at Alice's door. Part of me had no idea why I was there, but another part of me loved her and wanted to make things work; thanks to the minor detail that she was actually *my wife*.

I hadn't seen her at university, and her friends were staying loyal to her by not giving me any information. Not that I asked more than once.

So there I stood outside the place we had begun our

married life together. I tentatively knocked on the door and waited. The scrawny creature that answered the door was hardly recognisable.

'Greg?' she whispered before flinging her arms around me and collapsing into my body. We clung to each other for the longest time and I carried her into the room. Pulling away, she kissed me feverishly and began to unbutton my red-and-black checked shirt. Confusion, hurt, and love washed over me in equal measures; and as we tumbled backwards in each other's arms, my mind was screaming at me to stop this from happening. But my heart overruled my head. I loved her. God only knew why, but I did.

We made love slowly with our eyes locked, whispering heartfelt apologies and words of love as we took pleasure from each other's bodies. The climax I experienced was intense to say the least. But afterwards there was still an emptiness inside me that I couldn't shake.

*

After leaving university, Alice and I moved to Oban, where I got work in a music shop and she began a job with an independent fashion designer. Things had been going well and we'd put all of our hardships behind us. I'd learned to forgive her for what she had put me through. We even got to the point where we had discussed the possibility of trying for a baby, but I didn't feel quite ready.

We were renting a little house just outside the town centre but since the death of my parents, we'd been talking about buying somewhere of our own. Alice was getting frustrated with what she said was my lack of ambition. She wanted me to open a recording studio in Oban and begin to make something of myself, but I was enjoying meeting all the musicians that came into the shop to jam. It was like one long recording session at the place, and I loved the vibrancy and electric atmosphere I encountered every day.

My best mate, Connell, had started working as a music teacher at a school in Oban after following us to move there. His girlfriend was a barmaid at a club in town and so weekends were spent drinking and dancing. I was loving life for the most part.

Except for the constant arguments.

Friday came around. It was the second-to-last weekend in August and we were going to a gig over in Inverness. A band made up of our former uni pals, the Mad Batters, were playing at The Ironworks, which was quite an exciting event as far as I was concerned. I arrived home from work about an hour earlier than normal. Alice was still at work and so I jumped straight into the shower.

As I was towelling myself off, the phone rang. I grabbed the receiver and tucked it under my chin.

‘Hello?’ I said as I hopped around drying my feet.

‘Hi, Greg, mate. Look, I’m really sorry but I cannae make it tonight.’

‘No way? Why the hell not, Connell? We’ve been looking forward to this for ages, mate.’ I couldn’t have disguised the disappointment in my voice even if I’d wanted to.

‘It’s Sarah, she’s really sick. A bug or something. Throwing up like something off *The Exorcist*. Can’t leave her, mate. Sorry.’ There was a muffled sound as Connell shouted to Sarah in the background. ‘Look, mate, I’m sorry. I’d better go, okay? Talk to you tomorrow. Have a great night.’ He hung up.

Fucking knobbing fuck! I threw down my towel. Okay, so my night was *semi*-ruined, but at least Alice and I could go. I dressed in my black jeans, black boots, and my favourite Soundgarden T-shirt. Making my way downstairs, I chuntered to myself about the convenience of Sarah’s supposed illness. She never wanted to go anywhere, that wee lassie. Drove me bloody mad.

As I stood in the kitchen making mysel’ a coffee, the front door opened and Alice walked in, looking pale and miserable.

‘Oh, great. Not you as well?’ I know my attitude was selfish, but I could see my eagerly anticipated night rapidly going down the swanny.

Her brow furrowed. ‘What do you mean, not me as well?’

'Connell rang. Sarah's throwing her guts up and so he can't go tonight.'

'Ah. That explains it, then.' She dropped her head and sighed heavily.

'Explains what?'

'The reason I've been throwing up all day. I was going to come home, but we're pushed out trying to get ready for the fashion show in Glasgow next week.'

I walked over to her and helped her off with her coat. Concern came over me. 'Do you think you've got what Sarah has?'

'We were with them last night and the night before. Stands to reason one of us would get it.'

'Aye, I suppose so.'

She stroked my cheek and hugged me. 'I'm so sorry, Greg. I know how much you've been looking forward to tonight, but I feel crappy. I just want to sleep.'

I dropped my gaze to the floor. She couldn't help being ill. I tried really hard not to let my disappointment show through. 'You go on up to bed, babe. I'll bring you a drink.'

She smiled up at me and kissed my cheek. 'Look... why don't you still go, eh?'

I shook my head and hugged her to me. 'No, it's okay. I'll stay and look after you.'

'All I'll be doing is sleeping. The sickness has stopped. You've been looking forward to this for so long. Just go, sweetie. It's fine... honestly.'

I brightened a little. 'Really? But—'

'I insist that you go. If you stay here, I'll feel guilty and you'll be over the top with the nursey thing.' She was right. I couldn't stand someone I cared for being ill. I tended to go a bit far.

I kissed the top of her head. 'Okay. Only if you're sure.'

'I'm sure.'

'Okay. Thank you, babe. Get yoursel' to bed, eh?'

'I'm going.' She made her way upstairs. Around an hour later I checked on her and she was sound asleep. I kissed her head and left her to recuperate.

Climbing in my Landy, a relatively new acquisition – not brand-new, but new to me – I set off for Inverness.

Chapter Fourteen

The journey from Oban to Inverness was going to take me almost three hours, but I'd got a great soundtrack for the trip. I sang along as loud as I liked as I drove the winding roads of the Highlands, surrounded on all sides by bracken-covered outcrops and lofty mountains that appeared to touch the fading azure-blue canopy overhead. The sun began to set as I travelled; the red, orange, and purple glow to the sky behind the mountains was so stunning that I came over quite emotional. I could never tire of Scotland and its beauty. I knew exactly what Dougie MacLean was singing about in 'Caledonia'. Scotland would always be home to me.

An hour into my journey I was busy singing raucously along to 'In The End' by Linkin Park when my mobile phone began to ring. I could barely hear it over the CD blaring out, and so I leaned to turn the volume down a little. I'd left the phone on the seat and nervously glanced over. *Shit, is it Alice?* I swerved as I looked down at it, trying to get a look at the caller ID. Realising it was stupid to try and read the screen on the move, I pulled over, stuck my hazard lights on and grabbed the phone.

Sarah? Confusion washed over me.

I clicked to answer. 'Hi, Sarah. Are you feeling better?' I tried to sound friendly.

'Better? What are you on about? I'm fine. Can you pass the phone to that arsehole of a boyfriend of mine, *please*? He's got his phone switched off, and my mum's asking if we're coming down again in October. I need to check with him.'

I laughed. 'Very funny, Sarah. Tell him to stop arsing around. I've still got a ways to go yet.'

'Greg, what on *earth* are you waffling on about? Just hand him the sodding phone, will you?' *She* was getting *angry*? At *me*? *She* was the one messing about.

'Sarah, come on now. I'm glad you're feeling better, okay? But I'm hanging up now.' I clicked end call and was about to pull out into the traffic when my phone rang again.

'Hi, Sarah. What is it now?' I couldn't hide my annoyance.

'Can I speak to Alice, then? At least I'll get sense out of *her*.'

'Sorry, Alice is in bed ill. She's got the same as you.'

'What? A set of annoying parents who like to plan ahead?'

I scrunched my face. I had no clue what she was talking about and I was getting more pissed off as the seconds passed. 'What?'

'Greg… I will ask you *once more* and then I'm going

to get really angry. Please can you pass the phone to Connell?'

'And I will tell *you* once more. He is at home with *you*, seeing as you've been calling to Huey all day.'

There was a brief silence. 'He really isn't with you?' *Ah, bingo! The penny droppeth!*

'No, Sarah, he's with *you*.' Everything went quiet again. 'Sarah? Are you still there? Look, I've got to go or I'm going to be late.'

'Erm… Greg, he *isn't* with me. I'm down in Manchester with my parents. He stayed home to go to the gig with you.'

Huh? 'Oh… that's odd. He rang me earlier to say that you were ill and he couldn't leave you.'

'I see. I don't get it, Greg.' I could hear the worry in her voice.

'Me neither. Just hang on, I'll call Alice and see if she's heard from him.'

'Don't bother. Her phone's off too.'

'Oh… yeah, that's right. I turned it off before I left. Didn't want her being bothered, with her being ill.'

'Do you think something's wrong?' Sarah asked after another pause.

'I… I really don't know what to tell you, Sarah.'

'Is he having an affair, Greg?'

Anger bristled at my skin. 'What? Why the hell would you ask me that?'

'Because you're his best friend. And you have a

tendency to stick together. But… please tell me if you know he's having an affair. Don't let him make a fool of me.' Her voice wavered.

'He's *not* having an affair, Sarah. He adores you. I'm sure there's some logical explanation for this.'

'Yes… I hope you're right.'

I heaved a long sigh. 'Look, I'll go home and check at yours, see if he's all right. I'll give you a call, okay?'

'But what about your friends' gig?'

'It's no bother. I'd rather make sure Connell's okay.'

'Thanks, Greg. I really appreciate it. I owe you one.'

My laugh was small and rather humourless. 'Aye, you do. Bye, Sarah.'

I hung up the call and turned the car around. Disappointment mixed with apprehension. What the hell was Connell up to? If he was having an affair, I'd fucking kill him. I drove at the top end of the speed limit all the way back to Connell and Sarah's house. The place was in darkness. I hammered on the door and peered in through the window, but there was no one there.

My mind whirred as I tried to figure out where he could be. I decided to head back to my place and check in on Alice, seeing as I was in the area. Then I'd set back off and catch the latter part of the Mad Batters' show.

I pulled up outside the house and switched off the engine. Once I climbed out, I walked to the door and unlocked it as quietly as I could in case Alice was still sleeping. Sleep was the best thing for a sickly person after all.

I heard noises coming from upstairs. *Shit! It's a good job I came back when I did.* Alice was crying out – bastard that I was, I'd left her alone and sick. I jogged up the stairs and burst into our bedroom.

Alice's eyes snapped to mine and she screamed.

Connell lifted his head from between her thighs and simply said, 'Oh, fuck.'

My heart almost stopped dead.

She scrambled up from the bed and gathered up her clothes, hopping around the room as she dressed. My chest heaved and I literally saw red. Lunging forward, I grabbed my naked so-called best friend by the hair and punched him in the face. He cried out in pain and blood spattered everywhere.

Alice screamed and scratched at me. 'No! Greg, please. Leave him alone!'

I drew back my fist again as I stared into Connell's watering, wide eyes but instead of hitting him again I shoved him backwards and he staggered into the wall.

Alice reached out for my arm. 'Greg, this means nothing. I don't love him. It was just a bit of fun. Please, let's just talk, eh?'

I couldn't quite believe her empty words and as my heart shattered yet again, I growled out, 'You're not fucking worth it! Either of you!' Alice stood there sobbing as if *she* were the injured party in all this. I shook my head as I stepped in front of her. 'I *loved* you, Alice. I loved you *in spite* of the shit you've put me through. Well, no more. It's over. It ends *right now. Don't* call me. *Don't* come looking for me. I will *never* forgive you for this.' I could hear the pain and anguish in my own voice, but I was determined not to cave.

Not this time.

I took my mobile phone out of my pocket and dialled Sarah's number whilst I stood in the room, seething, before my wife and her lover who both stood stock-still, evidently afraid to move.

Sarah answered after one ring.

With a raspy voice I said, 'Sarah, darlin', I'm sorry to do this to you, especially over the phone. But your boyfriend is a lying, cheating, scumbag bastard. And he deserves my lying, cheating, scumbag of a wife if you ask me. He's been sleeping with her. I don't know how long it's been going on, but I've just found them in a rather compromising situation. So much for their fucking lies. Now I suggest you stay where you are, with people who actually *give* a shit about you, and have someone remove your stuff from the house as soon as possible. He doesn't fucking deserve you.' I hung up before she could answer.

With a distinct air of déjà vu, I grabbed a bag and shoved all of the possessions that I could carry inside it, zipping it up when it was full to bursting. Picking up my keys, I walked out of the door and didn't look back.

I reached the Landy, threw my heavy bag in the back

seat, and climbed in behind the wheel. Turning the key in the ignition, I was greeted by the words of 'In a Big Country' by the band Big Country, and the music somehow lifted me. Stuart Adamson seemed to be singing just for me about shattered dreams. A sense of serenity came over me and I actually smiled as I listened. He was right. It was time to leave.

Chapter Fifteen

After the debacle that was my visit to Mallory's, the day after the gig where I'd sung the song that broke her, I managed to avoid her for a while. I figured the less I saw her, the less harm I could cause.

It was a Sunday around the second week in May, and I'd just stopped into the pub to pick up my pay from Stella. As I climbed back in the Landy, I saw Josie and Brad's van driving away from Mallory's house. It looked as if the last of her visitors were going home. Poor lass. Now she'd be alone in that new house. My chest twinged at the thought. I leaned forwards and put the cash in my glove compartment and then turned the key in the ignition. I caught sight of Mallory and her little black dog walking away from the cottage. They stopped at the midpoint of the bridge.

I set off and pulled up alongside where they stood. Winding down the passenger-side window, I shouted over, 'Hey, Mallory, how are you doing?'

'Oh, hi, Greg. I'm okay, I think. Having my moments.' She smiled that beautiful smile that made my insides twist.

Deciding to be brave and face up to the mistake I'd

made at the pub that night, I climbed out of the Landy and jogged round to her.

'Look, I wanted to apologise for that night in the pub.' I ran my hand through my hair – a bit of a telltale, but I couldn't prevent myself from doing it when I was nervous. 'If I'd known…'

'Look, don't worry, you had no clue. How could you have? I'd had quite a bit to drink too, which I don't think helped. Really, please don't worry.' Her smile was warm and caring. I knew she was trying to stop me from feeling guilty, but I couldn't help it.

'I just felt so bad. I came round the day after.'

'Yes, Josie said so. You don't need to worry.'

'Aye, but every time I speak to you, I put my foot in it.'

Her eyes sparkled in the sunlight. I was mesmerised. Her smile got wider. 'Well, if it's any consolation, up to that point in the evening I thought you were really good.'

I felt heat rise in my cheeks. Now you have to understand, I don't embarrass easily; but receiving a compliment from this gorgeous girl did something strange to me, and I suddenly felt like a schoolkid with a crush.

'Really? Thanks. I'm hoping to do it again soon. You should come along. Are there any other songs I should avoid?' I asked with a slight hint of a cringe.

'No, just that one.'

'Okay, noted. Keep a lookout for the blackboard at the pub... well, that is, when I've made one. Right, well, I'd better go. I'm off to fix a leaky tap at Colin's. He tried to do it, but I think it's something a bit more serious than he thought.' I rambled on about shite as usual and walked round to climb back in the Landy. 'I'm glad you're okay. Well, as okay as you can be, eh?'

I fastened my seat belt and watched her as she fiddled with her hair, tucking it behind her ear. She was losing weight, and those sexy curves of hers were disappearing. Absent-mindedly I wondered if she was eating.

'Anyway, you should come up to the pub for some food some time. Stella makes the best steak pie and you look like you could use a good meal.' As soon as the words left my stupid mouth I clamped my hand over it.

The ghost of a smile slipped from her lips, and her brow crumpled. Her gaze slowly drifted to the pavement beneath her feet.

Too late, McBradden, you tosser. Removing my hand, I cringed. 'Fuck. I really should just not talk to you, eh?' I shook my head, put the car into gear, and set off at speed, feeling like a complete and utter arse.

Again.

I began to think it was doubtful that I even *had* a brain-to-mouth filter. If I did, it needed new batteries or a good bloody clean-out.

Although Colin and Christine lived just over the way, I drove in the opposite direction. I was mortified at what

I'd just said to the poor wee girl and couldn't think straight. I glanced in my rear-view mirror to see the pained expression on her face. I'd done that. She peered down at her body and pulled at her trousers where they hung from her hips. Then she began walking again and I turned to concentrate on the road.

What an arsehole I was.

As I drove I decided that there was no way she'd set foot in the damn pub again. I turned the car around and headed back to the village to Colin's. Luckily by the time I'd driven off my feelings of mortification, Mallory and Ruby were nowhere to be seen and so I pulled up, grabbing my toolkit, and made my way into the shop.

Colin was a great bloke in his late fifties with greying hair and kind eyes. He was fairly slim and a good few inches shorter than me. 'Hey, have you seen anything of the new lassie recently? Mallory, I mean?'

I scratched the back of my neck and cringed. 'I've seen her, aye.'

'Oh? Why do I detect a hint of negativity, Gregory?'

I hesitated, firm in the knowledge that he'd berate me just as I'd done myself. 'Well, you know the other night at the gig?'

A wide smile appeared on his face. 'Oh, yes. I meant to say to you how well it went. Chrissy and I loved it.'

'Thanks. I wish I could say the same for Mallory.'

His brow crumpled in confusion. 'She seemed to be enjoying it... before she upped and left with her friends.'

'Aye, well... the reason she left was I sang "Chasing Cars". It reminded her of when her boyfriend Sam proposed. It really broke her heart, Col. I felt terrible. And I know I wasn't to know,' I said, forestalling the reassurance. 'But that's not all.'

Colin rolled his eyes. 'Oh, great. What else have you done?'

'I... erm... pretty much told her she's wasting away and needs to eat.'

Colin gaped for a few moments. 'Oh no, you didn't, did you? Gregory, you know how women can be sensitive about that kind of thing. Honestly. Have you not the sense you were born with, man?'

I felt my cheeks burning. 'I'm not known for my tact, am I, Col?'

He shook his head with a look of pity. 'That's true. I heard from Ron about how you greeted her when she first arrived. Goodness me, Greg, put brain in gear before engaging mouth.'

'Don't worry. I've learned my lesson. I just wish... I wish I could do something nice for her. You know? I understand what she's going through.'

As if the wheels were turning in his brain, Colin pursed his lips and stared into space. 'Hmm.' Then he walked away, shouting, 'I'll get the kettle on.'

Nothing more was said and so I set about fixing the tap, drinking coffee, and keeping my feet out of my mouth.

*

Mallory invaded my thoughts continuously and I hated the fact. Mairi should have been on my mind, not some woman who I hardly knew. It irked me that I thought of her at all with anything other than pity and knew I had to deal with it.

As soon as I arrived home, I jumped in the shower, turning the dial to cold, determined to eject Mallory from my mind. The icy stream of water took my breath away as it pounded at my sensitive skin, and for a few moments my focus was drawn away from Yorkshire lasses with chocolate-brown hair and sexy curves. Instead I felt my teeth chattering and wondered if my balls would ever descend again.

Once I had tortured myself enough, I switched off the shower and grabbed a warm towel from the radiator, wrapping it around my body and relishing the heat that radiated through to my bones. When I was dry I went downstairs, poured myself a glass of whisky, and picked up Rhiannon. For some reason Fleetwood Mac always popped into my head when I thought about Mallory; and it turned out the shower had done me no good whatsoever as their well-known song 'Don't Stop' popped into my head. I began strumming.

The lyrics could've been written for her. In fact, *I* could've written them *myself*, for her. That was the thing I'd discovered about music. I couldn't adequately express my own feelings since Alice did the dirty on me. But I could usually find a song by someone else that said exactly what I was feeling.

Perhaps I'd sing 'Don't Stop' next time I played at the pub, and if she was there I'd dedicate it to her... *Soppy swine.* I played a few more songs as Angus lay snoring on the rug in front of me. I stroked his belly with my bare foot, and he smiled. I know they say that dogs can't smile, but Angus did. I could just tell.

When I was beginning to get tired, I made my way up to bed, stripped naked, and climbed in under the covers. As I lay down, I realized I hadn't needed a single malt to take away the usual ache.

*

My eyes fluttered open and I gasped in shock at the figure standing at the end of my bed. Mallory was dressed in the biggest sweater I'd ever seen. I was confused at first as to why she was in my bedroom, but even more so as to why her sweater was getting bigger. I stifled a laugh, remembering that she didn't like me and that I'd laughed at her before and received a tongue-lashing that made me feel two inches tall.

'I don't fit, Greg.' Her voice was so sad and a tear slipped down her cheek. She wiped it away on the huge sleeve.

'What do you mean you don't fit?' I asked.

'I don't fit anywhere. I don't fit here in Clachan Seil… I don't fit back home in Leeds now that Sam has gone… I don't even fit into my clothes anymore.'

My heart broke and I sat up and crawled to the end of the bed, disregarding the fact that I was naked. I cupped her face in my palms. 'You do fit. You do belong. You belong here, Mallory… with me.' I leaned forward, pressing my now prominent arousal into her belly, and was just about to take her in my arms and kiss her—

Chapter Sixteen

I sat at my small kitchen table, drinking a cup of strong coffee. Last night's dream whirred around in my head; and every time I remembered the part where I was about to kiss her, shivers ran down my spine and I had to adjust myself in my boxers. *She was wearing a huge jumper, for fuck's sake! What's sexy about that? And where the hell was Mairi? Why wasn't Mairi the one I dreamed about?* Anger spiked within me and I slammed my cup down; the thud echoed around the silent room and most of the cup's contents spilled out and began a rhythmical drip-dripping onto the tiled floor. Cursing to myself, I wiped up the mess I'd made.

Music.

That was what I needed. Music. I turned on my iPod attached it to its docking station, hit random, and cranked up the volume, figuring I could deafen my thoughts into submission. Soundgarden's 'Black Hole Sun' vibrated around the room as I lay back on my couch, eyes closed. The next track had me sitting up and staring at my sound system as if it were forging some kind of conspiracy against me. 'Ever Fallen in Love' by the Buzzcocks mocked me through the speakers.

'I'm not in fucking love with her!' I shouted at the inanimate object before hitting the off button in a massive huff. I decided to go and do some work on *Little Blue*, seeing as I wasn't due at the pub until later.

The sky was a beautiful cornflower blue. But the trouble was, it reminded me of the eyes of a particular Yorkshire lass I seemed to be unable to forget about. Evermore determined to stop thinking about her, I touched up a bit of paintwork and sanded down the interior of the cabin. It was a job I'd been meaning to do for a while. Angus sat on the dock, watching me work; his tail wagging as always. He was usually reluctant to set paws on the boat on account of the motion of the deck making him sick.

Eventually I realised that a few hours had passed and I hadn't thought about Mallory. But as soon as I realised it, there she was, slap bang in the middle of my head again. She stayed there until it was time for work. I growled at myself and made my way down to the pub for my shift, with Angus following behind. He knew he'd be getting some leftovers. Bright dog.

Thankfully the place was busy and it helped me keep my mind away from erotic thoughts of a girl wearing a huge jumper. Don't judge me. I can't help what gets my motor running.

I was chatting to a nice old guy who was on holiday in the area. He was asking which of the guest beers I would recommend and I was letting him sample some of them. I caught sight of her as she entered the pub, but she scowled in my direction and so I pretended I hadn't seen her. I let her approach the bar, and when I'd finished chatting to the tourist, I walked over. She eyed the logo on my T-shirt as if trying to figure out its meaning, and I guessed she'd never heard of A Perfect Circle. It afforded me time to surreptitiously check her out. Her breasts were smaller now. She wore a fitted red sweater that had my mouth watering. She was still curvy, thankfully; although why I should be particularly thankful for that, I had no clue.

I nodded at her and then stupidly said, 'You came out, then?'

Without smiling she replied, 'I guess so, or else I'm a very realistic hologram.'

I offered to buy her a drink and she made the mistake of ordering a Jack and Coke. She had clearly forgotten where she was – in a pub in the Highlands that served the best Scottish whiskies money could buy. Of course, me being *me*, I wasted no time in pointing the fact out to her and, as always, I immediately wished I hadn't opened my big mouth. Once I'd put her drink in front of her, I passed her a menu and reminded her about the steak pie.

After I'd served a couple more people, I was back before the dark-haired beauty… I mean *Mallory*.

'What are you eating, then?' I growled in my usual charming manner.

'Well, you recommend the pie so I'll go for that, please.' She smiled despite my crappy attitude.

'Mashed tatties or chips?'

'Mash, please.' This time her smile was a little sarcastic in its nature. *Mash, my arse.* I still thought she needed feeding up.

'Chips it is, then.' I grinned and walked away before she could protest.

Stella was beavering away in the kitchen when I took Mallory's order through.

'Oh, she came, then?' she asked with a smile that told me she'd seen inside my head.

'It would appear so, yes.'

'Are you going to chat to her? You know, make her feel welcome in your capacity as bar manager?'

'In my capacity as *bar manager*? There's only me and you. You own the bloody place, so who do I manage? My bloody self?' I laughed.

'Oh, shut up, Greg, and go take her food, will you?' She passed me the plated-up meal and made a face at me.

Once I'd placed the food in front of Mallory, I walked away again. Stella had come through from the kitchen and gestured that I should go back and talk to her. We had a non-verbal conversation of hand signals and raised eyebrows, which ended in me sticking up two fingers at her. She just laughed. Nothing much fazed Stella.

Conceding defeat, I pulled out a chair and sat opposite Mallory where she was tucking into the pie. I'd known she'd like it. When I asked her if she was enjoying it, she just nodded. After a pause where I watched as she chewed and blushed, I had to break the silence, seeing as I felt as if I was imposing and that Stella had got it totally wrong.

'Anyway, have you got that workshop sorted yet?'

'How did you know about that?' she asked with a puzzled expression and a mouth full of pie.

'The guy who lived there before, James McLaughlan. I did a bit of work for him a few years back. A bit of rewiring and stuff. He moved up north to be wi' his family. Nice guy. He used to make wooden toys for the hospital and the hospice in Oban,' I explained.

We chatted a bit about Mallory's craft business and the things that she made. The little Christmas decorations and hanging signs with quotes and phrases on sounded cute and she spoke with a light in her eyes that had been missing since the funeral. It was clear that she loved what she did.

She took a large gulp of her drink. 'Funny you should mention the workshop, actually.'

'Aye? Why's that?' I narrowed my eyes, wondering what was coming next.

She hesitated, as if choosing her words carefully. 'Well, you mentioned earlier that you were fixing Colin's tap, and I wondered if you could come and have a look at the sink in the workshop.' She pulled her bottom lip between her teeth and my attention was momentarily drawn there. To that luscious pink flesh. I gulped and flicked my eyes up to meet hers again; realising there was uncertainty in her gaze. 'If you have the time, obviously, no pressure.'

She wants my help. Huh. 'Oh, right. Aye, I could come and have a wee look. What seems to be wrong with it?'

'I think it may need a new tap altogether. It won't budge.'

I tried to think back to what I was supposed to be doing the day after but decided that, whatever it was, I could move it on.

She watched me as if expecting me to say no. 'If you can, I thought maybe I could make you that chalkboard you mentioned when I saw you earlier. You know, by way of payment and to save you a job.'

So we were going to trade our skills, then? I liked the sound of it. I'd never owned something quite so personal – something made especially for me – and I couldn't help the wide smile that spread across my face.

I held out my hand but Mallory looked puzzled at the gesture, so I clarified my meaning. 'Got yourself a deal, Mallory.' She grasped my hand and smiled. Her skin was soft and smooth, and her hand was swallowed up by my huge shovel. 'I'll come round tomorrow and have a wee look, if you like.'

'Great.'

I released her hand and she blushed bright pink.

Too damn bloody cute.

When I got home after my shift that night, I had the worst set of butterflies known to man. I was a six-foot-plus-tall, thirty-seven-year-old man – but the way my stomach was churning, you'd have been excused for thinking I'd regressed back to my teenage years. I couldn't sleep. Okay, I *usually* couldn't sleep, but this was worse. So there I lay in my bed, all night, wide awake as visions of a chocolate-haired girl in just an oversized sweater danced around my mind, tantalising and torturing me with something I could never have and shouldn't want.

Chapter Seventeen

I dressed in a sleeveless T-shirt and my combats, seeing as the weather was bright outside, and at eight o'clock sharp I knocked on Mallory's door. I waited for a while until she opened it, looking rather bleary-eyed.

I was grinning like an idiot. 'Morning! Am I too early? Just thought I'd call in as I was out and about, so shall I have a look at that tap?' I was lying through my teeth, of course. I'd been up since the crack of dawn, looking forward to it. But she didn't need to know that.

She looked befuddled and I wondered if she'd forgotten I'd said I was stopping by. 'I'm not exactly...' She gestured at her pyjamas.

I looked her up and down and once again was taken by how cute she looked; all rumpled from sleep. 'Oh, no bother, they're very fetching. Get the kettle on, eh? Shall I just go away up there? I know my way.' I realised I was talking at about three hundred miles an hour and blamed the adrenaline coursing through my veins.

She chuntered something sulkily under her breath, but when I explained that I hadn't heard and asked her to repeat what she'd said, she was all smiles. *Funny woman.*

I made my way up to the workshop at the end of Mallory's garden and got out my tools. Getting down on my back under the sink, I set to trying to figure out what was wrong with the bloody thing. After heaving and hammering I surmised that lack of use had caused it to seize up.

Mallory walked in with some coffee and peered down at me with a worried expression. 'How bad is it?'

'Hard to say at the moment, the nuts are all seized... and there's nothing worse than seized nuts!' I couldn't help laughing at my own joke. I killed myself sometimes. Shame no one else really *got* my daft sense of humour. I heard her giggle and it was a really sweet sound. She switched on the CD player that sat on the counter top in the corner and Foo Fighters played in the background as I worked on freeing the nuts. Ha-ha! Still cracks me up now. I smiled as we both sang along. It was strange how I didn't mind really, considering my usual feelings towards audience participation. Although maybe it was just because I wasn't on the stage. Or... maybe it was simply because it was *her* doing the singing.

She went silent and I could see her in my peripheral vision examining my inked bicep. 'That's an interesting tattoo on your arm, Greg. What does it mean?'

I knew it. I *knew* she'd ask. I'd been waiting for it. The trouble was I didn't want to talk about it. When I did, it lowered my mood. And today was a good day.

'Ah, it's just something I had done last year.' I hoped

my short answer would get the message across that the topic wasn't for discussion. But no, she was a bloody tenacious little thing.

'Oh, right. Why *K2*? What's the significance?'

'Maybe it's a story for another time, eh?' I stood, walked over to my coffee, and drained the mug – despite the vile taste – before getting back to work. Absent-mindedly I thought how strange it was that someone so lovely... I mean someone with such good taste bought such crappy coffee. The conversation died and she'd clearly got the point that the tattoo wasn't up for discussion. After standing there in silence for a few minutes, she said she was heading back up to the house.

When she'd gone I sat there for a while staring into space. The tap was buggered and needed replacing. And I was trying to think of ways to spend more time with Mallory, so it was perfect. Only for the purposes of making amends for my shitty behaviour.

That was all.

Nothing else.

Not a thing.

When I was packing my tools away, she appeared again. She was showered and dressed, looking fresh and smelling amazing. As I inhaled through my nose and briefly closed my eyes, my blood rushed south. She asked if I was finished and I explained about the tap needing to be replaced. I said I'd be back the day after to fix it, and she seemed concerned that she was putting me out.

She really wasn't.

'It's fine. I'll squeeze it in. It's not a massive job. I've got to go now 'cause I have a few errands to run before lunch and then I'm working on my boat this afternoon. Plus, I'll need to shower and get something to eat before I go to the marina.'

'Oh. I didn't mean for you to drop everything for me, you know. You could've come later, after your jobs and I could've made you some sandwiches or something to take away. It's the least I could do.'

I glanced up at her and caught another nose full of her fragrance. My body's reaction to her made anger spike within me. It was too soon, and guilt crawled under my skin. 'I'm quite capable of making my own sandwiches, thank you,' I snapped and immediately felt shitty. *Hello, mouth, allow me to reintroduce my foot.* She dropped her gaze, which told me I'd stung her with my words for about the hundredth time. 'I'll show myself out,' I told her as double the guilt descended on me.

As I walked away, my phone rang and I glanced at the caller ID. It was Mairi's father. My stomach dropped and my heart hammered at my ribcage.

'Aye, what is it?' I stood frozen to the spot.

'It's Duncan, can you talk?'

'No, I'm just finishing a job.'

'Okay, I'll make it quick. They found a backpack.

Thought it was Mairi's.'

Fuck! 'Where did they find it?'

'About a mile away from the last find. It wasn't hers, but I wanted to let you know they're still looking.'

'Aye, okay. Thanks for letting me know.' I ended the call and shook my head. Despair washed over me at the whole damned situation and the guilt I'd been feeling over my apparent attraction to Mallory intensified. Once again I was reminded that I should be grieving, not thinking about moving on. But in actual fact I was trapped in some kind of limbo; unable to move forward and just as unable to let go of the past.

Filled with sadness, I turned back to Mallory. 'See you tomorrow.'

*

Once I'd dropped my tools in the Landy, I got in and made my way to the boat. It was a great day for sailing and I felt sure I'd get some tourists along. I had foregone lunch on account of being sick to my stomach over my attitude to Mallory and my guilt over Mairi. Mallory wasn't to blame so I had to stop acting as if she were. One of these days I'd make her smile instead of frown. It was my goal. I just had to figure out how to go about it.

I pulled on my favourite woolly hat to keep my hair out my face and placed the little sign I'd made ages ago on the marina. It was looking a little worse for wear, and I wondered if I should get Mallory to make me a new one. If she'd ever talk to me again, which was doubtful.

A couple of hours passed and I was contemplating going out on my own, but I could feel eyes on me. And when I turned, it was *her*. I couldn't help smiling. 'Hey, you're out again. It's becoming a habit.'

For a minute she seemed pissed off, but I was puzzled as to why. I usually knew what I'd said wrong.

She made her way towards the boat, nodding her head. 'This is you, then, eh? I hadn't twigged that you did excursions when you said you were working on your boat this afternoon.'

'Aye, it's my day job. You up for a trip out?' I really hoped she was.

'Why not? I could do with a bit of fresh air. How many of us will there be?' Her question made me smirk. The day I'd thought would bring in paying passengers hadn't brought in a soul.

'You're it. Bit of a slow day. I was just about to give up and go out by myself.'

'Are you sure you want me to tag along?' She frowned and fidgeted.

'Aye, why not? I get sick o' my own company. Get enough of it, day in, day out.' I held out my hand to her, and her cheeks set on fire. I helped her onto the boat and she immediately thrust a tenner towards me. I wasn't going to take her money so I waved it away, shaking my head defiantly, and she got the message.

She made small talk about the boat's name and I told her about my old dog Little Blue that the boat was named for. He was a smashing dog that I had raised from a pup when I lived with my parents.

When I asked her if she wanted the running commentary that I usually gave to passengers, she gave me another puzzled glance, which made me laugh. 'You know,' I said, gesturing out at the water. 'And on my left we have a seal and on my right, oh, look, there's another seal.'

She laughed too and it was such a lovely sound. 'No, it's okay. I just wanted to get some fresh air, to be honest. Colin in the shop recommended a boat trip. Feel free to pretend I'm not here.'

Pretending she wasn't here was something I knew I couldn't do. It was nice to be with her and not be pissing her off for a change. We set off on the still water with the slight breeze in our faces. The farther out we got, the chillier it became. Once we had travelled out far enough just to see the land in the distance, I cut the engine and dropped the anchor. I reached down and picked up the flask of coffee I'd brought and handed Mallory a tin cup.

'Thought we could sit and chill for a bit here – is that okay? It's usually a good place for seal-spotting.'

She inhaled deeply and looked out at the view. 'Yes, I suppose. Am I not keeping you from anything? Another job perhaps?'

I took a gulp of the coffee in my cup. 'Na', boat trips three days a week, odd jobs two days a week and pub shifts the rest of time... oh, and entertainer at the pub on my nights off now, that's me.'

'Crikey! I'm not sure I could keep up with all that. I think I'll just stick to making stuff, plain and simple.'

She was right. Keeping busy was the thing to do. It was what I'd been doing for the last eight months. 'Aye, you should do that. It's good to have something to focus on at times like this.'

She seemed to drift off and a deep melancholy settled over her. I watched her change before my eyes, and my heart ached for the pain I knew she was feeling. I had the same pain.

Leaning forward, I rested my elbows on my knees. 'It sounds like a cliché, but it does get easier with time.' I wanted her to believe that even if I didn't fully. 'You just need to keep busy.' It suddenly dawned on me that that was exactly what I'd been doing these past months since Mairi's death.

'Is that what you're doing with your gazillion different jobs?' she asked.

I looked up and was met with her beautiful but pained blue eyes. I wanted to comfort her, but as soon as the thought popped into my head, it was followed by guilt. 'Na'. I like the variety. Don't get bored that way.' I didn't feel like owning up to my true feelings. That would require more introspection and I was scared of what else I might find. I took another gulp of my coffee. 'Anyway, it's good that you're getting out and about. No point sitting and wallowing in self-pity, eh?' I knew she'd be angry at my harsh words and I hated that I'd actually said them out loud, but it was a way to keep the barriers in place.

'Thanks for your concern, I think,' she snapped. 'But I'm not wallowing, as you so eloquently put it. I'm grieving; there's a difference.' Yep, I'd pissed her off, all right. Her brow crumpled and her nostrils flared.

'Aye, what I meant is you should nae be on your own all the time. If you were my little sister I'd be keeping an eye on you, is all I'm saying.'

'Well, thankfully I'm not your *little sister*. I'm a twenty-nine-year-old woman with her own life and I'm fine with Ruby for company, thank you. Don't be so bloody patronising.'

There was an edge of irritation to her voice. And no wonder really. It was no business of mine what she did. But I knew what'd happened to me, and I figured I'd try to stop it from happening to her too; although I wasn't too sure why I was so insistent on helping when my input was evidently unwelcome.

I'd really gone and done it, hadn't I? What was it with me and this bloody woman? Could I ever learn to think about what I said before the words actually fell out my mouth like oral incontinence?

My mind whirred with what I could say to break the tension. 'So, you made any other friends in the village yet?' I finally asked.

She snorted. *Okay, so she definitely doesn't count me as a friend.* My stomach knotted at her unspoken yet clearly intended words. I'd actually been trying hard with her, despite how it appeared.

She cringed. 'Sorry. That was mean. I was just surprised to hear you class yourself as my friend,' she explained. 'We haven't exactly got along very well since we met, wouldn't you agree?'

I forced a smile but was sure my sadness was visible on my face.

She sighed and continued, 'Great, now it's my turn to put my foot in it, eh?'

I didn't know what to say so I figured I'd stay quiet in case I said the wrong thing again.

After a long silence I leaned forward once more. 'Look, I know I can be an arse, all right? I've never had a female friend, I suppose. I've two brothers who never dare let me meet their girlfriends for fear I'll speak to them how I speak to you. I spend a lot of time on my own – by choice, I hasten to add – and I feel sorry for you.'

She sat up straight and glared at me. 'You feel *sorry* for me? I don't want you to go out of your way to be *your version of nice* simply because you *pity* me.' The pitch of her voice rose exponentially with its volume.

My version of nice? Oh, for fuck's sake! 'No, you misunderstand me.' I couldn't help getting pissed off at my own choice of words. 'That's not what I meant. See? This is why I don't do... this.' I waved my hand back and forth between us.

She frowned at me. 'What are you on about? You don't do what?'

I placed my cup down on the bench beside me and rubbed my hands over my face. 'Look, that night on the beach, I really felt your pain.' I paused to think my words through carefully for once. 'I felt so terrible for what you were going through. I understood... I under*stand*.' I looked up at the cloudless sky for a moment. 'It's not pity, it's... it's... argh... What's the fuckin' word...? *Empathy!*' Finally, the right word came to me. I felt relieved that I could say what I actually meant for once. When I looked over, her lip was quivering and tears were brimming in her eyes.

Oh no. Not again. I leaned towards her, desperate to hold her in my arms and tell her that everything would be okay. But how could I? She would no doubt take my intended act of kindness completely wrong as she took all of my good intentions completely wrong. So instead I sat back and clenched my fists lest they act of their own accord.

I swallowed the familiar lump in my throat. 'I know how hard it is. You're in a strange place where you hardly know anyone, and you've lost the one person in your life that would've made that whole situation okay.' Needing something to do with my hands, I pulled my hat off and ran my fingers through my hair. 'I get that. I get what you're going through. I wanted to help – no, *needed* to help – but it turns out I keep making it worse.' She turned her face to me as tears spilled over. 'Oh, fuck, and now I've fuckin' made you cry again.'

She sniffed and wiped at her eyes. 'It's fine. I'm not your responsibility! I get that you understand, but every time I try to ask you anything, you go all mean and moody on me. I have no clue how to take you. If you want to be friends, you have to change how you act around me. I can't do with trying to second-guess your mood and wondering if I've overstepped the mark.'

I slid over to sit close to her – against my earlier better judgement, I might add. Her scent filled my nostrils and my stomach flip-flopped as my heart did its best to make an escape through my ribcage. 'Right, this is stupid. Can we please just fuckin' start over, eh?' *Watch the fucking language, McBradden.* 'Fuck, I'm sorry I keep swearing.'

She smirked at me. 'It's fucking fine! Just don't fucking do it again, okay? It's fucking rude!' she shouted. I stared at her in shock but then we both cracked up. It felt good to laugh. No, it felt good to laugh with *her*.

Chapter Eighteen

As we sat there in the boat we both relaxed and the tension between us eased. I began to tell her about Mairi and how we met. In fact I told her everything, and it felt cathartic to talk about it all. Once I'd finished, I sat in silence for a while again, but this time the silence was comfortable.

After a few moments I spoke again. 'You don't need to feel lonely here,' I told her. 'Folk around here are great. They're warm, friendly people. From what I've heard, they all have nice things to say about you. It's funny, you know, some can move here and are here for years but never fit in. Not you, though. People love you already.' It was true. The villagers were already fond of her. And why wouldn't they be? She was a very sweet lassie. I suddenly had a brainwave. A total out-of-left-field idea. 'Hey, you know what you should do?'

She eyed me suspiciously. 'Hmm, you seem rather excited, and that worries me.'

'You need a way to meet people. Stella's looking for an extra bartender for the evening. I could put a word in for you.'

She looked as if she was thinking about it, and I was

quite hopeful but instead she shook her head. 'But I have no clue how to pull a pint and I can't add up in my head.'

'Ah, but I can train you to pull pints. And we have an electronic cash register, you know. We don't live in the Dark Ages up here.'

'Okay, well, have a word with her, then. I could come in for a trial to see if I like it and if Stella likes me.'

'Aye, well, Stella employs *me*, don't forget, so being likeable can't be one of the requirements.' I laughed and Mallory joined in. I was so glad she was considering this. I knew that Stella would think she was great. There was no doubt in my mind.

*

We arrived back on shore a couple of hours later, and I felt as if we'd really cleared the air. I was a little raw, emotionally, but it was no wonder. I'd talked about Mairi openly for the first time since she died. It was difficult but somehow I felt better. Mallory was a good listener and I appreciated her lending her ear when she was grieving herself.

'What are you up to this afternoon, then? More leaking sinks to repair?' She smiled and I could tell she felt the same about things between us.

'Na'... I'm away to pick up Angus, and I think we might go for a long walk.'

Mallory scrunched her nose. 'Angus?'

I realised I hadn't mentioned Angus before. 'Aye, I don't bring him on the boat too often. He can get seasick and sometimes he bothers the customers.'

'Is Angus your son?' she asked.

A laugh erupted from somewhere near my boots.

'What's funny?' she asked with a smile that was tinged with confusion.

'My son! Actually, he *is* rather spoiled, so I suppose in a way he is. He's my dog. Stella looks after him sometimes when I'm out on the boat.'

Her cheeks turned pink and she laughed. 'Ah, right. What type of dog is he?'

'He's a Lab-satian.'

'A what?'

I chuckled. 'Labrador-Alsatian cross. He's bloody huge, greedy, and daft as a brush.'

'Oh, lovely. I'd love to meet him some time. I can't believe you have a seasick dog.' She giggled as I helped her out of the boat. Once I'd moored up I climbed out too and together we walked back to the car park.

'Aye, I wasn't too impressed the first time I took him out, I can tell you.' I opened the car door and climbed inside. 'Look, I'll speak to Stella tonight, okay? See you tomorrow.'

'Bye for now.'

After slamming the door and starting the engine, I pulled away and headed for the pub to collect Angus. I had this warm fuzzy feeling inside me. Thinking on it for a while, I realised it was happiness. *What the hell?* I'd forgotten what it felt like, so no wonder it didn't register. Mallory was a great lass. She made me smile without saying or doing much. Just her company was enough to make me happy. It felt a wee bit strange though. I didn't really know her but we shared something quite deep and special. A kind of mutual grief. We understood what each other was going through and, whilst I wouldn't wish the way I felt on my worst enemy, it felt good to know I wasn't alone.

As always Angus was giddy when he saw me. He brightened up my days and it appeared I did the same for him. He, of course, couldn't call me a grumpy arse and it didn't matter if I put my foot in my mouth with him. His love was unconditional and I was glad of the fact.

Angus and I set out to buy the washers, taps, and sealant to sort out Mallory's workshop sink. I figured the sooner I got it fixed, the sooner she could make me the chalkboard I needed to advertise my gigs at the pub. Every time I thought about her making the board especially for me I felt a twinge of something strange. A bit like excitement crossed with emotion. She was going through shit but was making something for me regardless. So selfless. Quite a woman, eh?

And it was going to be good to make my gigs at the pub official. I just had to be more careful with my song choices. Maybe I could run them by Mallory before I played. I would have to think that through.

Armed with all the necessary bits and pieces from the plumbers' merchant, we made our way back home, and I decided that I'd head down to the pub as a paying customer for an hour. Angus liked the attention he got from the patrons and I loved the atmosphere in the place.

As I sat there with my wee dram of whisky in hand, Stella marched around behind the bar, taking drink orders and then heading in the kitchen to handle the limited food orders she was taking, seeing as she was on alone. I had half a mind to offer my help but figured if I did, it would kind of negate the conversation I was about to have with her.

She headed back over to me and blew her hair from her eyes. 'Don't suppose you fancy helping a poor woman out, do you?' she asked with a smile.

'Nope. It's ma night off, but I know someone who's looking for a job, if you're interested?'

'If *I'm* interested? Gregory, I've been advertising for ages and *no one else* is interested. They either don't live around here or enjoy being a customer too much to stand at this side of the bar. Who could you possibly know who would want a job?'

'Mallory.'

'Mallory? Seriously?' After she thought about it, she put her hands on her hips and glared at me. 'Has this been *her* decision, Greg, or are you interfering more than necessary?'

I held up my hands in surrender. 'I made a suggestion that it might be a good way to get involved and meet people, and she agreed. Don't shoot the messenger.'

Her smile became wide and she laughed. 'Well done, Greg, I like your thinking. How soon can she start?'

'Oh, I don't exactly know. I said I'd ask you, and she said something about coming in for a trial.'

She shook her head and waved a disregarding hand. 'No need for that. Tell her she can start whenever she likes. On *her* terms. No pressure. Whatever hours she likes. It'll just be good to have an extra person however often she can manage.'

'Great!' I was sure I looked like a grinning idiot, but I was in no mind to bother. Finally I was doing something right by Mallory. It felt bloody great and I didn't care who knew it. I couldn't wait to tell her the news. I was very much aware that she didn't need the money, but what she *did* need was occupation and company. Working at the pub would give her both. And the only negative thing was that she'd have to put up with me and my shitty social skills. But, hey, small price to pay!

Chapter Nineteen

Bearing in mind that I'd caught her off guard the day before, I decided to wait a while before heading off to Mallory's house the next day. At around twenty past ten I made my way down to the little cottage by the water. Angus was his usual giddy self. Of course we'd had the conversation about him being on his best behaviour around the new ladies I was going to introduce him to. And yes, I realise he's a dog and not capable of cognitive thought processes, but that didn't stop me from telling him about Mallory and Ruby. As I've said before, don't judge me!

I knocked on the door and waited. And waited. And waited. Eventually a rather bedraggled woman opened the door to me. *Not again?*

'I was beginning to think you'd done a moonlight flit,' I told her as she stood there all squinty-eyed. Angus wagged his tail frantically.

'Sorry, I must have slept really deeply. I've only just woken up.' She yawned and I felt bad for showing up when she was tired again. She looked ready to crawl back into bed, and I couldn't help smiling at her appearance.

'I brought Angus, is that okay? You said you'd like to meet him.' She nodded and Ruby, the little black ball of fluff, came trotting through the house. She must have scented Angus. Her little tail wagged as the two dogs sniffed at each other's backside. I pointed at them and said, 'I hope you don't expect me to greet you like that.'

Mallory burst out laughing. 'No, a simple hello will suffice.' She bent to say hello to my big daft dog, and in true Angus fashion he licked her with his muckle tongue right up the middle of her face.

I laughed. 'I'll not do that either, I promise.'

Wiping her face on her pyjamas sleeve, she eyed me warily. 'Thank goodness!'

Marching into the house, I walked straight through to the kitchen. 'Sit yoursel' down, I'll make us a coffee.' Surprisingly she did so without protest. *Progress.* 'I got that new tap sorted. I just need to fit it and then you're away.'

'Great,' she mumbled from the living room.

I carried the mugs of coffee through to the lounge and handed one to Mallory, who was looking a little more awake despite her attire.

'So, I spoke to Stella last night.' I couldn't hide the glee from my face. 'She says you're very welcome to come and give it a go. See what you think. What do you reckon, eh?'

She pursed her lips at me and looked a little worried. 'Oh... great, yes, thanks.'

I waved my free hand at her. 'No, no, calm down with your mad enthusiasm, you'll do yourself an injury.'

Smiling and cringing at the same time, she shook her head. 'Sorry. I just… I've had second thoughts… I'm not sure I'm ready… It's only been a few weeks, Greg.'

'Hey, no one knows better than I do about this shit. And I say grab the bull by the horns and get out and meet people, make friends. Anyways, I said you'd be there tonight at about six so I can show you the ropes, eh?'

With her resolve a little firmer, she nodded. 'Okay. I'll be there.'

'Great. I'm really glad.' I drained my cup. As the bitterness hit the back of my throat, I fought back a shiver. Her coffee was awful but marginally better, seeing as *I'd* made it. I'd have to introduce her to better bloody coffee, that one thing was certain. 'So, any plans for visitors in the near future?'

'Yes, actually. Josie and Brad are coming up for my birthday next month. I think it'd be hard if they weren't here with it being the first… Well, you know.' She dropped her gaze.

'So, am I right in thinking you'll be the big three-oh this time, eh?' I asked, grinning at her as the cogs began turning in my brain. Big plans were afoot.

Mallory gaped at me with narrowed eyes. 'Don't remind me. I feel old,' she said as she rubbed her face and her shoulders hunched.

Old? Shit! What did that make me, then? 'Ah, rubbish. You're a wee bairn. Wait 'til you're my age, *then* you'll feel old.'

'What age is that, then?'

Ah-h, this could be fun. 'Guess.'

'I may offend you,' she warned.

'Na'. I don't offend that easily. Age is just a number.'

'Okay, you asked for it.' She thought about it for a moment, tapping her chin and looking to the ceiling. 'Erm... fifty-five?'

What? Shit, maybe I didn't look as good as I thought. I opened my mouth to speak but couldn't think of a single thing to say. My heart rate accelerated with panic and I felt the desperate urge to go look in a mirror to see what she was seeing.

Her eyes brightened and she punched me on the arm. 'Ah-h-h, you said you wouldn't get offended. Age is just a number, you said.'

I huffed out a long breath and shook my head. 'You cheeky wee mare.' Now I really needed to know what she thought, if only to soothe my bruised ego. 'Go on, seriously, how old would you say I am?'

'Seriously? About thirty-four... maybe thirty-five?' I could tell that she was being honest this time and my heart soared. *That's more like it.*

Sitting up a little straighter, I smiled. 'Na'. I'm thirty-eight next birthday. I just look bloody good for my age.' We laughed together and my insides did a little flip.

'Yes, it's your modesty I admire the most.'

Like a spoiled child I made a face at her before laughing out loud. She joined in and my heart skipped. Deciding now would be a good time to end the conversation before I ruined things, I got up to leave and made my way up to fit the new tap, leaving Mallory to shower and dress.

My brain ticked over with plans. She was going to be thirty and that only happened once. After what she'd been through her birthday needed to be something she remembered in a good way. I wanted her to smile and have fun. I figured she needed that.

After a while a familiar scent infiltrated my thoughts and I glanced up to see her standing there in the doorway of the workshop. She looked incredibly sexy even in casual gear. The long-sleeved blue top she wore hung loosely over her leggings, leaving far too much to my fertile imagination. She was a fair bit slimmer, which was a shame because she had the most stunning curves before; but she still looked pretty and I wanted to tell her. But fearing I'd say the wrong thing again, I bit my lip and just smiled.

She began to get some wood and paints out, and I hoped it was my chalkboard she was going to make. I got on with my task at hand and sang along to her Pearl Jam CD, but every so often I glanced over surreptitiously and saw her sketching with her tongue out of one side of her mouth. *So bloody cute.* I could've watched her work for hours. The concentration on her face and the way her brow creased was kind of mesmerising. But eventually I was finished fixing the tap.

'All done,' I told her as I wiped my hand on the rag tucked into my belt. I turned on the tap to display my handiwork and thankfully water gushed out and into the Belfast sink below.

'Oh, that's fantastic, Greg, thank you so much.' She looked as if she wanted to hug me, but I froze. She dropped her hands to her sides and blushed bright pink. Was I giving off don't-you-dare vibes? I hadn't meant to.

Internally kicking myself yet again for my reaction, I bid her goodbye and said I'd see her at the pub later. Why could I never seem to do the right thing where she was concerned? I'd have to figure out a way to make amends. I just had no clue how.

Then a light bulb clicked on in my head. What I could do was organise a surprise party! Surely that way she would see that I wasn't a total socially inept arse? Maybe she would see that I was actually a decent, caring bloke worthy of her friendship?

But no sooner had the light bulb illuminated than it extinguished. Why would I arrange a party for her? Surely that was something a real friend would do? She had said before she didn't class me as a friend so it would be weird, wouldn't it? And maybe she wouldn't want all the fuss? I know I wouldn't have. But then again, she wasn't me. She adored her friends and, let's face it, if you're going to cry on your birthday – which she no doubt would under the circumstances – who would you need around you more than your friends?

My brain whirred with ideas but as Angus and I climbed in to the Landy I shook my head as if to dislodge my own stupidity. *You're grieving too, you idiot. Jeez, you're the last person to make a success of arranging anything that involves laughter and fun, you miserable arse. People will think you're stupid. Mallory will think you're creepy. And what about Mairi?*

Alarmed by my train of thought, I stopped in my tracks. Another epiphany hit. For the first time in what seemed like forever, I was actually considering someone else's feelings above my own. What was that all about? Why the hell did it matter so much? I shook my head to rid myself of the errant thoughts and carried on my way.

I knew one thing for certain: I wanted to make Mallory's birthday special and I knew just the people to help me. I would need access to Mallory's phone at some point, but that could wait. First and foremost I needed a venue.

Chapter Twenty

I made sure to arrive at the pub just after five. It gave me a chance to speak to Stella about Mallory's birthday. My plans were deliberately simple; I got the feeling Mallory was the type of woman who didn't go for the expensive, glamorous parties. She seemed quite shy in many ways, and the last thing I wanted to do was embarrass her. But she needed to know she was surrounded by people who cared. The villagers loved her more than she could possibly know.

'Are you sure this is a good idea, Gregory? It's not long since she lost her fiancé. Maybe this would be too much?' Stella's concern was etched all over her face.

She was right of course but I was on a mission. 'I really think I can make it special though, Stella. Just a few close friends and some nice food and… and me.'

Her brow furrowed. *'You?'*

'Aye. I thought I'd… you know… play a few of her favourite songs, maybe.'

She smiled widely. 'Oh, Gregory. That's such a thoughtful thing to do. You clearly think a lot of her.' She patted my arm and I felt my cheeks heating up.

I didn't want anyone getting the wrong impression.

This was me making amends, not advances. 'No, no, it's not that. I just… I just want to do something nice, seeing as I always seem to do the wrong thing around her.'

'I know, love. I know.' But from the glint in her eyes I guessed that what she 'knew' wasn't the same as what I 'knew' about the situation. As I had feared, she clearly was reading too much into things.

At just before six I was standing chatting to Ron when the door opened and in walked Mallory. Stella greeted her with a hug and took her coat. She looked… beautiful; very smartly dressed in trousers that hugged her curves and a top that showed just enough cleavage to tantalise unintentionally. She wasn't the kind to flaunt herself. She was carrying a large, flat package wrapped in brown paper. My heart flipped. Mallory followed Stella behind the bar and Stella left her with me.

A wave of excitement came over me as I eyed the parcel. 'Is that what I think it is?' I asked her.

Tilting her head to one side, she smiled. 'Hmm, depends what you think it is.'

'I think it's my chalkboard,' I said with a smile.

'Then, in that case, you would be correct.'

She handed me the package and I ripped the paper off like an excited kid at Christmas. I could feel her watching me for my reaction. She chewed nervously on a nail. As I stared at the beautiful board with its scrolled writing and smooth painted surface, a lump lodged in my throat. No one had ever made something just for me

– well, not since Mairi anyway. And certainly not someone to whom I'd been a total shit. She'd made this for me. Me, the arsehole who always said the wrong thing. Me, the stupid idiot who'd made her cry. It just confirmed the type of person she was. One of a kind in the best possible way.

Steeling myself and clearing my throat, I was able to speak. 'Mallory, Mallory, Mallory... it's bloody brilliant!' I caught her letting out a breath. Her face relaxed into a beautiful smile. Still grinning, I repeated myself, 'Bloody brilliant! I love it!' I turned it around to show Ron, who beamed from ear to ear.

'Aye, she's a talented lassie, our Mallory.'

Mallory's smile widened and my heart melted. I placed the board down and met her eyes. I had an overwhelming desire to pull her into my arms but wasn't sure if I should. After staring at her and fidgeting awkwardly for a moment, I did it anyway. The softness of her breasts met the muscles of my chest and I closed my eyes, relishing the feeling of her curves against me. It had been so long since I had held a woman in my arms and I'd had no clue how much I'd missed the feeling of closeness. Guilt suddenly pummelled my insides. This wasn't Mairi. *And* this girl was grieving. The last thing she needed was to be pawed at by some arsey stranger. I broke away and ran my hands through my hair, the heat of embarrassment setting my face afire.

'Um... I'd better go and... um... put this somewhere

safe,' I mumbled, picking up the board and walking through to the back. I heard Mallory and Ron chuckling as I left. *Great, now I'm a sodding laughing stock. Just great.* Placing the board down, loosely rewrapped in the scraps of brown paper, I took a few deep breaths and calmed myself. It had felt so good to hold someone again. It wasn't that it was Mallory. No... it was just that feeling of connection... *Oh, fuck it, who am I trying to kid here?* It *was* her. Anger replaced the niggle of guilt and I clenched my fist and my jaw simultaneously; angry that my body had reacted that way towards her. *God, what she does to me! I'm supposed to be trying to be her friend, for goodness' sake.* Once I was back to my normal self again, I went back through to the bar.

I clapped my hands together, making Mallory jump, and I couldn't stop myself from laughing at her startled expression. Plastering as much seriousness on my face as I could, I said, 'Okay, bar school lesson one...'

She picked up how to use the cash register very quickly and before long she was a dab hand at it. Shorts were a doddle too. I was impressed with how easy she was picking things up. Not that bar work is akin to rocket science, but she was a natural. Well, that was until it came to pulling a pint.

Showing Mallory how to pull a pint was not the easiest thing I've ever done. But it did make me laugh. She kept growling at her initial attempts and I had to fight to keep my face straight. Ron kept on shaking his head and rolling his eyes, which didn't really help.

'Arrgh! Too much bloody froth,' she exclaimed at the glass of foam she'd placed on the bar.

'It's called a *head*,' I informed her with a smirk.

Scowling at me, she tried again. This time the glass was filled to the brim with just beer. 'Awww... not *enough* froth this time.'

'*Head*, Mallory.'

She laughed this time and I couldn't help joining in. I showed her once more how to tilt the glass so that enough 'froth' formed on the top. Her next attempt was much improved, and so Ron and I gave her a round of applause, making her blush.

Despite their failure to look like proper pints, Ron eyed up the line of beers Mallory had pulled. I gestured for him to help himself, and his eyes lit up as if he'd won the lottery.

It was time for her to get stuck in and start serving patrons. After dealing with the first lot of customers, she had a huge grin on her face and Ron and I applauded her again. Ron told her she was a natural, and you'd have thought he'd told her she'd won the *Pull*-itzer prize – see what I did there? – with the smile she wore for the rest of the night. Fitting in was clearly very important to her, and I was really pleased that I'd pushed her into the job.

Whilst Mallory served customers, it was time to try and put my plan into action. I went through to the back and spotted her bag. What I was about to do was something that, if I were caught, could get me into shitloads of trouble, but I justified it by telling myself I was doing it *for* Mallory. My heart thundered in my chest and I felt sure the whole bloody pub could hear it. I slipped my hand into her bag and grabbed her phone. Luckily it wasn't locked with a code, and so I rifled through her contacts until I found Josie's number. I quickly entered it into my phone and put hers back. I would ring Josie and get the other numbers I needed from her... hopefully – as long as she didn't think I was some bloody crazed stalker. Shit. I hadn't really thought it through.

At the end of the night I congratulated Mallory on a job well done, and she left the pub with a huge smile that I'd helped to put there. I was so proud of her for taking this step. She was brave to have accepted a new job in a new town with no one to go home and share things with, and I wished I could've told her so without it coming out like patronisation. But I kept my mouth shut just in case.

I was learning.

*

That night when I got home I gulped down a wee dram of Dutch courage, switched on my iPod to some random playlist and grabbed my phone. I sat down on the couch with a huff and hit dial on Josie's number but immediately hung up.

What the hell was I thinking?

People who've just lost loved ones don't want bloody parties, you tit.

I thought back to the day I'd heard the dreaded words that told me my life, as I knew it, was over. Would I have wanted someone to throw a party for me? *Absolutely no bloody way.* As I thought back to that day my heart lurched and the emotions came flooding back. The pain; the anger; the utter desolation tore at my heart all over again and I squeezed my eyes shut trying to calm my breathing as my blood rushed a little too quickly around my body.

I stood and paced the room, passing the framed photos of Mairi on the mantel. I stopped directly in front of one and jabbed a pointed finger at it. '*You* left *me.* You couldn't just be happy here with me, could you? You just had to go off and challenge yourself.' I shook my head and briefly clenched my eyes closed again. 'Jeez, what I would give to have a second chance to talk to you. To tell you no, you can't bloody go. You can't leave me, Mairi.' My lip trembled and my eyes began to sting. 'I wasn't enough for you, was I? Eh?'

I lowered my gaze from her happy, smiling expression. Why was I shouting at a ghost? This was all on me. *I* was the one angry for having feelings for another woman, regardless of how trivial the feelings were. I fancied her. That was *it*, for God's sake. I wasn't about to bloody propose.

Raising my face once more, I reached out and touched the photograph and my throat tightened. 'I just miss you. And I don't know how to move on. Are you up there, somewhere, watching me muck things up? Eh? Are you angry with me for finding someone attractive? I'm just a man, Mairi. A lonely one at that. And I've spent months being a shit to my friends. And that poor wee lassie *needs* friends. I just want to do something kind. I used to be kind. Didn't I?'

I stared at my phone. *Should I sleep on it? Should I just not do it?* I growled out loud and stared up at the ceiling as if the answers would magically appear there; or perhaps some divine inspiration would shine down on me. Right on cue I heard the opening bars to the Beatles' 'With a Little Help from My Friends' and my heart skipped. I gasped and shook my head. *Bloody hell. Shitting, bloody flipping hell.*

I glanced back at the photo of Mairi and laughed out loud, blinking through a fog of tears. 'Okay, I'll do it. But if it all goes wrong I'm blaming you.'

After another wee dram I sat again, phone in hand, and took a deep breath. After dialling Josie's number, I sat there drumming my fingers on my knee, waiting for her to answer.

'Hello?' She sounded confused. And then I realised that my number would have shown up with no name.

Maybe I should've texted first.

'Erm... Hi, Josie?'

'Who is this?' came the terse reply.

'It's... it's Greg, from Scotland. The bloke from the pub?'

'Oh, right. What's up, Greg? Is Mallory okay?' I could hear the panic in her voice.

'Oh, aye. Yeah, she's fine. Look, sorry it's late but I'm ringing to ask you a huge favour.'

'Right.' She paused and I felt sure I could hear the cogs whirring in her brain. 'Okay, go for it.'

I took a deep breath and cleared my throat. 'So... it's Mallory's thirtieth birthday next month, and you and I both know she's had it rough lately. So I wanted to do something nice. I thought maybe a surprise party?'

'Really? You'd do that for Mallory?'

'Yes. She and I didn't get off to the best start and... I really want to make it up to her.'

A sniffling sound came down the line. 'That's so sweet, Greg. Thank you.'

'Are you crying?' Yorkshire women and I were obviously a bad combination.

'A little. But only because I can't quite believe how sweet you're being. If I'm honest, I thought you were a grumpy-arsed sod at first, but... well, I take it all back.'

Charming! Although she did have a point. I'd kind of disappeared up my own arse since Mairi had died, so Josie and Mallory had only met the *me* that presented myself as just that. A grumpy arse.

I forced a laugh. 'I'll take that as a compliment.'

'Sorry if I sounded harsh. So, what do you need from me?'

I went on to ask for a list of Mallory's favourite songs, which Josie duly gave to me. I was thankful that she had such good taste and I wasn't going to have to sit there and sing some bubble-gum boy-band shite. Next she gave me the number for Sam's mother, Renee, in Canada and a list of Mallory's favourite foods. The more we chatted, the giddier she got. But the next thing I had to ask stopped her joviality dead.

'You want me to do *what*?' The sound of incredulity wasn't lost on me.

'I know it sounds like a shitty thing to do. But if she thinks you're not coming, I can muscle in and make some fake arrangements to take her out for her birthday.'

'No way! You can't ask me to call her up and upset her like that. What am I supposed to say? *Oh, hi, Mally, I'm your best friend in the whole world, but I've decided I can't be arsed to come up for your first milestone birthday since Sam died.* Yeah, I'm sure that'll go down really well.'

Okay, I'd really pissed her off.

I cringed. 'I know it seems cruel, but think about it. If she knows you're coming, she'll want to make plans to stay in with wine and a takeaway or something. You'd never get her out of the house.'

She sighed. 'You have a point, I suppose.'

'I do. And I promise she will know that *I* made you do it when this is all done. I promise you that, Josie.'

There was a silent pause, and I was sure she was going to tell me to sod off. 'Okay. I'll do it.' The reluctance in her voice almost deafened me. 'But I'll have to ring her when she'll be out and leave a message. I can't lie to her, Greg. She'll be heartbroken.'

I silently thrust a triumphant fist into the air. 'Like I said, it's all for the right reason and she'll know that it was *all* me.'

'Okay. But if she rings me sobbing, I'll tell her everything,' she warned.

'She won't. I'll make sure you don't have to lie for me.'

'Fine. Let me know if there's anything else you need me to do. You know, kidnap Ruby, set fire to her photos, tell her she's ugly.'

I rolled my eyes in spite of the fact she couldn't see me. 'Funny.'

'Hmm. I'm not amused. Bye, Greg.'

'Bye, Josie.'

'Oh, and, Greg?'

'Yeah?'

'Don't have any expectations of her, okay? She needs *friends* right now. That's all.'

'Josie, I can assure you my intentions are purely

platonic. I just want to make her smile.'

'Okay.' She wasn't convinced – it was clear in her voice. And if I was completely honest with myself, I wasn't either.

Chapter Twenty-one

Armed with a list of Mallory's favourite songs and musicians, I began to practise them as soon as I had some free time. Oasis, Neil Diamond, and Newton Faulkner amongst others. A *very* eclectic list and I loved that. It was fun to be learning new tracks, especially with the end goal in mind. It felt so good to have a purpose that didn't involve alcohol for once.

I'd spoken to Renee and had secretly made arrangements for her Canadian family to come over. I was happy that they thought so highly of her that they would drop everything and jump on a plane like that. Things were going great, and I could hardly contain my excitement.

There was a week to go to Mallory's birthday, and she was working the bar whilst I played my third gig. The second one had gone really well, and Mallory's chalkboard had worked wonders. The third one was no different. The place was buzzing and I was quaking in my boots. Standing at the bar, I nervously guzzled down my drink. Cola. Singing on whisky always dried my throat out.

Mallory watched me intently. 'You look terrified.

What's up?'

'Ah, nothing. I always get like this before I go on. Goodness knows why. I'm a grown man.'

'Age has nothing to do with it. We all get nervous, Greg. You'll be fine.' Her words of encouragement spurred me on and I took my place behind the mic. My nerves were a little calmer and I glanced over at Mallory as she smiled back at me with her thumbs up.

I returned her smile and then focused my attention on the crowd. 'Evening, all, anyone would think something was going on with all of yous turning up tonight. As always, I'll steer clear of my own stuff – but be warned, one of these days I'm going to sneak one in when you're not looking.' The folks in the pub laughed and I relaxed a little more. 'Don't forget, no singing along, it puts me off and yous lot can't sing anyway.' The retorts and heckling made me laugh.

My first song was special. It was for Mallory. She and I somehow had forged a friendship, and it was a beautiful thing. 'Right, this first song is a wee bit obscure, but I love it so tough. It's by a band called Nirvana that takes me back to my younger days. I'd like to dedicate this to someone who I think I can now class as a good mate. This is "About a Girl".'

I began to strum with my eyes closed and when I opened them and glanced over, Mallory was dancing and with a stunning smile on her face, and I felt amazing.

At the end of the night all I wanted to do was talk to Mallory and find out what she thought of my set, but I was swamped. A group of women of all ages caged me in. Asking for my autograph *and* my number. I was shocked. And flattered. Being treated like a rock star made a change from being seen as the grumpy git. When the ladies eventually let me be, I made my way over to the bar.

'Get you with your groupies,' Mallory joked when I stopped in front of her.

'Aye, they cannae resist,' I joked. 'What did you think tonight, matey?'

She smiled but it was rapidly followed by a frown. 'I thought it was a bit rubbish, really.'

Bollocks. That wasn't what I wanted to hear.

A grin pulled at her mouth. 'God, for someone who doesn't get offended easily, you get offended... *easily*!' She threw a bar towel at me. 'You were fab as always, you numpty.' She was the only bloody person who'd ever rattled my cage that way, and it was a little disconcerting.

She said that she especially liked the Nirvana track, and I ribbed her about her young age. When I offered to walk her across home, she ribbed me about my groupies again, joking that they might lynch her if they saw us together. The banter we were sharing was fun. It was good craic, and ours was beginning to feel like a *real* friendship. Knowing this, however, had me worrying that she wouldn't stick around and that I'd miss her terribly if she chose to leave.

When we arrived at Sealladh-mara Cottage we were greeted by an excited little ball of black fluff. Ruby was making a high-pitched yipping noise as if she hadn't seen her owner for weeks. I glanced over to the answering machine, where I noticed there was a message. Mallory had gone through to the kitchen to make coffee, and so I shouted to let her know.

She brought the coffee back through and after placing it down, she hit play on the machine.

'Oh, hi, Mally. It's Josie. Look… I'm really sorry, but we can't make it up for your birthday. Brad has a lot on with his latest job and we just won't get the time to come up. I'm sure you'll understand, babe. I'll ring you later. Love you! Bye-bye.'

I swallowed hard and glanced over at her. She looked broken and I felt like a total bastard. After the fun of the night and how great things had been, I'd inadvertently shit on her from a great height. *Well done, McBradden, you tosser.*

Sitting beside her on the couch, I draped my arm around her shoulders. 'Don't worry. We'll still have a laugh. I'll keep you entertained.' She didn't respond and so I nudged her. 'Look, we'll have drink at the pub and then take a bucket barbie onto the beach and I'll cook a steak, eh?'

She was on the verge of tears but she tried to smile.

My heart broke. After a thoughtful pause, she nodded emphatically. 'Yes, thanks, Greg, I appreciate it.'

I knew I had a hell of a lot of making up to do for the upset I'd caused her, but at least *Operation Make Mallory Smile* was working so far. I would be taking her to the beach, so she thought. I just hoped I hadn't made a huge mistake.

*

Mallory's birthday arrived and thankfully it was a bright June day. Taking that as a good sign, I stood in my garden ready to go down and wish the birthday girl many happy returns of the day when I stopped and glanced up at the sky. I didn't know what I believed in as far as heaven was concerned, but I hoped it existed and that Sam was okay with what I was doing for his woman.

I glanced around my road to make sure no one was within earshot. I didn't want anyone to hear or see what I was about to do. If they saw, chances were they'd think I was a few beer bottles short of a brewery. I had no idea why, but I felt compelled to do it. I cleared my throat, as if it would make a difference.

Looking up into the blue, I began to speak. 'Sam… mate. I know I never met you. But I know for a fact that you'd rather be here right now with your beautiful girl than wherever you are.' I felt my throat tighten and swallowed before I could continue. 'I just wanted to say that... well, I hope it's okay that I've arranged this party for her. I'm not trying to take your place, you know. I just... I know what she's going through. How much she misses you. It's the same way I feel about Mairi. It's a pain so real that it can be all-consuming, but... *because* I understand that... because I lost my Mairi like Mallory lost you... I want to make your girl smile. Even if it only takes her mind off her grief for one night. I hope that's okay. I really care for her, mate. She's one of kind, is Mallory, and I can see why you loved her so much. Not that... not that I *love* her, you understand. Only as a friend. That's all. But... well, I hope I have your blessing today.'

My eyes began to sting as I compared my loss to Mallory's. It hit home yet again how much we had in common. We were a pair of broken souls with pieces missing and neither of us truly knew if the holes inside us would ever heal. I felt a familiar tightening in my chest and cleared my throat again, dropping my gaze back to the road before me.

I wanted so much for this all to be okay. I'd never planned a party for someone else before, and I still didn't know Mallory all that well, but... Well, there was a hell of a lot riding on this. Mainly my friendship with Mallory. Because that was what this was... a friendship. Wasn't it? My train of thought scared me again. Why would I question my feelings? This *was* a friendship. Of *course* it bloody was. Gah! I needed to stop thinking and just get on with it. I climbed in the Landy and set off.

Chapter Twenty-two

A few minutes later I arrived outside Mallory's house and climbed out of the car clutching the bunch of helium balloons I'd bought especially with *Thirty Today* plastered all over them. I hoped she wasn't one of these women who hated everyone knowing her age, but I figured it was a bit late now. Just like me to worry about shutting the stable door after the horse had already done a runner.

I paused a while to take in the view around me of the lush green trees over on the mainland and the sunlight glinting off the water in the Atlantic inlet. Then up the lane towards the bridge; the stonework always glowed warmly at this time of day, its rugged surface taking on the appearance of velvet. Such a beautiful place.

After a calming breath I knocked on the door. I knew she would be in as Stella had given her the day off and insisted she relax and pamper herself. But knowing what a big deal this day was to her, I wasn't sure what kind of mood I'd find her in.

She opened the door and when she saw me she tried to smile. But the smile didn't light up her eyes as I'd seen before. Her eyes were... empty. Distant even. I knew I had to remedy that right away. I began to sing 'Happy Birthday' at the top of my voice in the flattest key I could come up with. I knew that the neighbours would hear me if they were about, but that just spurred me on. It sounded horrendous – and she burst into fits of giggles, grabbed my jacket, and tugged me into the house and almost off my feet. I couldn't help but join in her laughter. It was always contagious when she laughed.

'Come in, you nutter.'

Once inside I let the balloons float up to the low ceiling and handed her the gift bag that I'd brought with me. Her eyes widened for a moment, but she shook her head slightly to rid whatever thought had sprung up. She peered into the bag and pulled out the first parcel. Ripping off the paper eagerly, she smiled at the pack of craft pens I'd bought for her.

'Oh, Greg, that's lovely. Thanks ever so much.' She seemed genuinely touched.

'There's something else in there too,' I told her as I pointed at the bag. She put her hand inside again and brought out the little black velvet box.

'Oh,' she whispered. Her gaze met mine and then dropped to the box. This happened a couple more times and I smiled at her surprised reaction. She opened it and gasped as she took out the silver chain with a Celtic pendant hanging from it.

'It's a Celtic knot,' I informed her. 'It's the symbol for

friendship.' Suddenly my cheeks began to heat and I watched as her eyes became glassy and filled with emotion. *No, no, don't cry. Please don't cry.*

'Oh, Greg, it's beautiful.' Suddenly her arms were around my neck and she was squeezing me so tight that I thought I might pass out. When she pulled away, her cheeks were flushed and she swallowed hard, keeping her gaze on mine. She stepped back and I mourned the loss of her closeness. Holding her had felt so good; *right* somehow. But yet again the guilt struck and I ran my hand through my hair, breaking eye contact and feeling awkward. I just couldn't meet those blue eyes at that moment. I could easily have fallen in and drowned in them.

'Here, put it on me,' she said, holding out the chain to me. I obliged, sweeping her long, dark hair over one shoulder. My fingers grazed the skin at the nape of her neck and she shivered slightly. Her skin was so smooth and flawless and all I could think about was placing one kiss there, on her bare skin. Just *one*. But instead I fastened the necklace in place and pulled her hair around so that it fell in soft waves down her back. I tried to ignore the ache in my chest as she turned to face me.

'Gorgeous,' I whispered.

And she really was.

*

We made arrangements for the barbie that I'd convinced Mallory we were having that evening, and she seemed to have cheered up plenty, which in turn made me happy. I left her with instructions to get dressed up for the ultimate, exclusive beach-dining experience. Of course she had *no clue* that she was going to be walking into a pub filled with her family and friends.

I couldn't wait.

Later on at home, after I'd showered, towelled myself off, and trimmed my beard, I stood in front of my wardrobe in my fitted boxers with my hands on my hips. I wanted to make an effort as I did when I was playing. After all, *I was* playing.

Angus watched me intently.

'What do I wear, fella?' I asked him.

He wagged his tail in response.

'Do I go with a shirt?'

No wag.

'A long-sleeved T-shirt?'

Wag.

Okay, that was that decision made. 'Right... What colour, Angus? Black?

No wag.

'Okay, not black. Actually, you're probably right. Black is depressing and this is a happy occasion. How about white?'

Wag.

'Great stuff. I should do this more often, eh? Let you

make my important decisions for me.'

Wag. He clearly agreed.

'So how about my black jeans?'

Wag, wag, wag.

'Angus, you could give Gok Wan a run for his money, pal.' I scratched his head as his long tongue lolled out of his mouth.

After wardrobe guidance from my canine companion – remember what I keep saying about not judging me – I pulled on a white long-sleeved T-shirt and my favourite leather jacket with my black jeans. I slicked my hair back as best I could and decided I would have to do. She wasn't going to find me attractive, so what did it matter? As long as I felt good, that would do; and Angus clearly approved, so all was well with the world.

*

At half seven I knocked on her door and she opened it as if she'd been eagerly awaiting my arrival. The thought made my insides knot up. I felt like a bloody teenage lad on prom night. I was greeted with the breathtaking sight of Mallory standing there in a long turquoise-and-black skirt and a V-neck T-shirt in the same turquoise. I could see a hint of cleavage and it made my mouth water. She looked very classy and more than a little bit sexy. I forgot how to speak for a few moments – all the blood that should've been in my head had descended south of my waistline. She asked if she looked okay and I just stared at her.

Realising she had in fact asked me a question, I managed to say, 'You look… great.' And, boy, did she. I wanted to run my hand down the side of her just to feel the sweep of the inward curve of her waist. *Shit! Thinking like that's not helping the blood supply to your brain, you dick.* Snapping myself out of the stupor, I suggested we go for a birthday drink over at the pub. Thankfully she agreed. *Phew! So far so good, McBradden. Appears you're not a complete tool after all.*

When we arrived at the pub, I opened the door and gestured for her to go in first. She made some comment about me being the perfect gentleman, but I was too scared to respond. What if she didn't like what was coming? My heart was in my throat and I felt as if I might puke it up at any second.

Chapter Twenty-three

'SURPRISE!' everyone shouted in unison. It was deafening, as the pub was packed with people.

I stood there, leaning on the door frame with my arms folded, and watched as the shock registered on her beautiful face. Cameras flashed and party poppers exploded, covering Mallory in streams of silver, gold, and pastel-coloured paper. Grinning to myself, I took in the sight of her happiness and knew then and there that I'd done the right thing. But I also knew then and there that my heart would never be the same again.

I was falling.

Fuck it, who was I kidding? It was too late. I already had. Past tense.

She turned to meet my eyes, hers narrowed suspiciously, and pointed at me. 'You knew?'

I chuckled as I held up my thumb and finger. 'Little bit.'

Josie appeared and Mallory burst into tears of happiness. I heard her exclaim, 'But… but you rang! You weren't coming!'

A teary-eyed Josie, in true Josie form, shouted back, 'You daft cow! Do you think I'd miss this? Not a chance. We were always going to be here, but we were the first people Greg rang when he decided to plan this thing.'

I saw Mallory cover her mouth but I didn't catch what she said as she was scooped up in a group hug by her adopted Canadian family. Even the new addition to the family, a cute baby boy, had made the journey. More and more people surrounded her, and I took that as my cue to stop staring and grab a drink. The nerves had started jangling, seeing as it was soon time for the next part of my surprise for Mallory.

Stella poured me a whisky without my needing to ask. 'How are you doing, Gregory?'

'I'm bloody terrified. What the hell's wrong with me? I'm a grown man.'

'Nerves can apply to anyone. And it only means that you care.'

'Aye, well, not in the way you think,' I lied.

She gave me a knowing smile and shook her head. 'Are you ready to go on?'

'Just give me a while to calm my nerves and I will be.'

'Well, don't be getting drunk and spoiling it. I know what you get like, remember?'

I grimaced in disgust at her accusation. It didn't matter that it was true. 'As if I would spoil that lassie's birthday. Pah!' Ignoring my own rule of not drinking alcohol before a performance, I drained the glass and edged through the crowd to take my place behind the mic.

'Evening, party people!' I searched the room, looking for the birthday girl, and spotted her giggling away with her best friend. 'Well, we're all here tonight to celebrate the fact that Mallory is, and I quote, "getting old".' Everyone laughed and turned to face her. She went bright red and I couldn't help laughing. *I'll pay for that later, no doubt.* 'I reckon the first number tonight requires a bit of audience participation. Which, as you may know, is not something I usually encourage. You all know the words and this time you *can* sing along!' A cheer erupted around the room as I began to play the opening bars of 'Happy Birthday'.

Mallory's grin told me she was having a whale of a time, and that made me all warm and fuzzy inside – or it could've been the whisky, or maybe both. Anyway, when the raucous rendition of the birthday classic had ended, she turned to me and mouthed the words *thank you* and I responded with a smile and *you're welcome.* The urge to hug her came over me again but I fought it down.

'Right, that's enough of you lot singing! It's my turn now, and you know what I always say?'

'DON'T BLOODY SING ALONG!' Everyone shouted together, and Mallory threw her head back with laughter once more. Mallory laughing was the best sight I'd witnessed in a very long time.

I nodded vigorously at the bar full of people. 'Aye,

that's right, and don't you forget it.'

I serenaded the crowd with songs from the likes of Nirvana, Foo Fighters, Oasis, Fleetwood Mac, Hozier and Pearl Jam to name but a few. Dougie Maclean's 'Caledonia' had a few folks weeping – not surprising, seeing as it had that effect on me sometimes too.

Taking a break, I went over to grab the birthday girl. 'Can I buy you a drink?' I shouted over the noise of the crowd and the jukebox that Stella had switched on.

'I'll have my usual, please.' She smiled knowingly. But I wasn't going to rib her about her drink choice. Not tonight. When I brought her drink back, 'Hi Ho Silver Lining' began to play and Mallory screamed.

'Ooooh, I love this song! We've got to dance!'

I threw my head back and guffawed at her enthusiasm. 'Aye, okay, birthday girl.' Well, I couldn't *not* dance with her on her birthday now, could I? I slipped my arm around her waist and we took the pose of a ballroom dancing couple, except she was singing so loud I could hardly dance for laughing. I spun her round and the whole pub joined us with the chorus. Her blue eyes sparkled. There was life in them again. And the fact that I'd helped to put it there made my eyes sting with unshed tears.

As the song was ending she hugged me fiercely and said, 'Thank you, Greg,' right into my ear.

A shiver travelled down my back and I gazed into her eyes. For a brief moment she gazed back at me, a ghost of a smile on her full lips. But the spell was quickly broken when Josie grabbed her.

'Give her back, Greggy-weggy! Go sing some more!'

I took my place at the mic once more and grabbed Rhiannon. Starting up again, I watched as Mallory was hugged by more people. The folks in the village adored her. And why wouldn't they?

Despite my requests for no bloody singing, every fucker was at it. I laughed despite myself. There was nothing more hilarious than a room full of drunkards trying to sing Neil Diamond's 'I am, I said'. I dedicated a very apt song to Mallory that really grabbed her attention. Fleetwood Mac's 'Don't Stop' seemed to say things to her that I wanted to say myself. But they did it so much better than I ever could. I did my best to put every ounce of sincerity I was feeling into what I was singing, and her responding smile told me I'd done my job.

She was presented with a delicious-looking birthday cake thanks to Colin and Chrissy, and she blew out the single candle with a childish grin on her face. The night was drawing to a close and so I decided to try and calm things down a little. No mean feat, I can tell you.

'Well, I'm hoping the birthday girl has had as wonderful a night as the rest of us, eh? It's been great to have you all here. But I have to say, when it comes to singing, don't go giving up your day jobs. Leave it to the professionals. Know what I'm saying?' The fuckers booed me! They booed and heckled! I shrugged, knowing I was damn right.

'I'll finish tonight with another of Mally's favourites, and I have to say that it's grown on me this week whilst I've been practising it. It's by a bloke with an interesting name, if nothing else. He's a mighty talented guitarist, not unlike myself.' Groans greeted me this time. 'Okay, okay. He's a young guy called Newton Faulkner, and this is a beautiful song for a beautiful… ah… friend, and it goes like this.'

Shit, I nearly slipped up there. I tapped on my guitar and strummed the intro to 'Dream Catch Me'. It wasn't a song I'd been that familiar with until Josie had mentioned it to me, but I have to say that the more I listened to the lyrics, the more they resonated within me. There was one particular line that rang oh, so true; and if you know the song, I bet you can guess. You know, the one where the singer can't quite believe what's happening? Aye… *that* one.

My eyes found Mallory's just as I sang that *one line* and they locked on. I couldn't look away. She stared back at me and swallowed before her lips parted as she kept her gaze fixed on me. *Fuck. What am I doing?* The spell was quickly broken, when her best friend slipped her arms around her shoulders and whispered something into her ear. Whatever it was, Mallory didn't like it, and her gaze dropped to the floor. *Great.*

The pub gradually began to empty and people said

their goodbyes. I made my way over to where Mallory was hugging Ron and thanking him for coming. As he walked past me, he patted my arm and winked. He obviously was proud of me for the successful night, and it felt grand.

Mallory lingered. Looking her up and down, I shook my head. 'Och, shit, Mallory, you're looking old now, you know.' She hit my arm and I pretended to fall. 'Have you had a good time?'

'The best. Thanks so much for doing this for me, Greg. It was so sweet of you.' She blushed, which was really cute. But then again, everything she bloody did was cute.

'No bother. That's what friends do. And like I said, it's my fortieth in a wee while,' I reminded her, wiggling my eyebrows. It was a couple of years away, but no harm in getting in early, eh?

'Well, I'm guessing you won't let me forget that.'

'Am I allowed to hug you?' I asked her with open arms. 'I think I made a total balls-up of the last time I hugged you. You know? The incident I now like to call "Chalkboard-gate". I cringe whenever I think about it. What a complete spanner.' I felt like a total prick, actually, but I was trying to curb my language. She stepped into my embrace and I squeezed her to me for a moment. Not wanting to hold on too long for obvious reasons – i.e. my growing bloody feelings – I let her go.

'Thanks again, Greg. You are a really good friend,'

she said, staring right into my eyes. *Okay, message received loud and clear.*

My heart sank a little but I forced a smile. 'Aye, you're not so bad yourself, matey.' She reached up and kissed my cheek, pausing a little, and I could have sworn she smelled me. I mean, she inhaled as her nose was by my face, but I got the distinct impression it was deliberate.

A tiny seed of hope began to grow inside me.

Chapter Twenty-four

When I arrived home after the party, I was buzzing. There was no way I was going to sleep right away. The whole thing had been a massive success, and I couldn't have been happier. Mallory had laughed, danced, and sung. She'd practically glowed all night and as I sat there replaying the evening over in my mind, I couldn't help the smile that crept over my face. Lying back on the couch with Angus at my feet, I closed my eyes and was taken back to the party.

I caught sight of the sequins on her skirt and shoes sparkling in the dim, atmospheric lighting of the pub. The fabric billowed out as she spun around and I was mesmerised. The T-shirt she wore hugged her breasts beautifully, and I wondered if they were as gorgeous in the flesh as they looked under the taut turquoise fabric.

I'm pretty sure I was caught watching her on more than one occasion by Josie, Brad, *and* Sam's mother, Renee. I wondered if she thought me a lecherous old prick. Not that someone as classy as *she* was would've used such language, but the sentiment would have been the same. My thoughts about Mallory weren't lecherous though. I'm not saying they were *pure* – I'm not gonna lie. But there was just... something about her. As I've said before, she was one of a kind.

I took myself off to bed and as I was brushing my teeth I took a long hard look in the mirror. Who was I kidding? I was almost eight years her senior and she didn't *see* me in *that* way. She'd made that blaringly obvious with her *such-a-good-friend* comment. And to top it off, what the *fuck* was I doing getting attached to someone when *I* was still grieving? It was pointless. Rebounds never worked out.

But as I eventually climbed into bed and waited for sleep, deep down I knew that this was no rebound.

*

When I opened my eyes, Mallory was standing at the end of my bed in her turquoise T-shirt and skirt from the party. This time I knew it was a dream but I didn't fight it. I lay there, just gazing up at her as she slowly removed her skirt, kicking it to one side of the room. Her cropped denim jacket followed. Her eyes didn't leave mine and she didn't speak. Her hands reached for the hem of her T-shirt and she was slowly lifting it up... up... up. I sat up as the anticipation grew, but the sudden movement made me dizzy and when I looked down I had hold of Mairi's hand. We were on a freezing-cold mountainside. I wasn't sure how I'd got there and for a moment I was disorientated and confused. But then I remembered I'd been dreaming and fought myself to wake up. I observed my surroundings with a pounding in my chest and I could hear the blood rushing in my ears. Why wasn't I waking up? I glanced down again and realised my grip was slipping and Mairi's terror-filled stare chilled me to the bone. Her hand slid from mine and she fell—

I sat with a violent jerk and opened my eyes wide. My chest heaved and like every occasion before I was covered in sweat and gasping for breath. *What the hell?* I wanted… no, I *needed* the nightmares to stop. I was losing my grip on my fucking sanity and I had no idea how to stop it from happening. This one was worse than the others. The sense of panic had my heart beating so fast, I clutched my chest and considered calling the paramedics in case I was on the verge of a heart attack.

This was because of my feelings for Mallory. It had to stop. I had to apologise for staring at her when I sang that bloody song. God, what must she be thinking? She was grieving and I threw myself at the poor woman vicariously through someone else's words. Again, what was I thinking?

With my resolve set firm, I climbed out of bed and turned the shower on. I decided I would wash, dress, have a coffee, and set out for some much-needed fresh air. I had to clear my head of the cobwebs that had taken up residence, clouding my mind and making me forget what I'd lost. Well, that fucking nightmare had reminded me. I wouldn't forget it again in a hurry.

Once I was suitably caffeinated I grabbed my coat and went to the door, Angus at my heels. The sky was dark and I was betting I'd get soaked during our walk, but Angus didn't care about the rain. Closing the front door but not bothering to lock it – I rarely did – I pulled the refreshing chilled air into my lungs and we set off towards the village.

As we got to the village something caught Angus's attention and he went shooting off towards the bridge.

I began to jog after him. 'Angus, you bloody mad hound! Come back here,' I shouted. But then I realised what had been the distraction that made him run. Mallory and Ruby were standing in the middle of the bridge. She turned and looked at me. *Awww, no.* I really didn't want to face her, but if I didn't want to appear the fucking tube I really was, I had no choice. Shaking my head at myself, I waved and began to jog over to join her.

When I arrived on the bridge I forced a smile. 'I obviously didn't do my job right last night, eh?' She raised her eyebrows and asked what I meant. 'Well, you don't look in the least bit bloody hung over. What were you drinking at your birthday bash? Earl Grey?'

We joked about the fact that Mallory had been so caught up in the events of the night that drinking hadn't really been her top priority. The glow on her face had been pure happiness. Despite the nightmare, my heart warmed at the memory.

Feeling more relaxed in her presence than I'd expected, I invited her and Ruby to join Angus and I on our walk. She hesitated and I thought she'd turn me down. But surprisingly enough, she accepted. We set off together towards the beach. The four of us.

Once we were on the sand, the two doggy friends went off together, frolicking and barking. Watching them made me smile. If only being human were so simple.

After a few minutes of silence, I spoke. 'So… it was a good party last night, eh?' I kept my eyes focused on the dogs skipping around each other.

'It was wonderful, Greg. I can't believe you did all that for me.'

I glanced out of the corner of my eye, and she too had her eyes fixed firmly front and centre. I shrugged. 'Well, I figured that's the kind of thing Josie would do if you were down Yorkshire way.'

She made a snorting noise and laughed. 'Maybe not with so much gusto though. Josie would have done the pub and the friends, but they would have been their own entertainment.'

I put my arm around her shoulders and gripped her roughly in what I considered a friendly kind of… well… *man* hug. 'Well, I'm just glad I did you proud.'

When I released her from my grasp, I watched what looked like confusion take over her features. *Huh?*

What's up now? Her brow pulled in and she chewed her lip, avoiding eye contact. Great! I couldn't do right for doing wrong!

Once again we were back to silence and watching our two mad canines dashing around the beach, flicking sand up in their wake. The first drop of rain hit my forehead and I glanced skyward. Here came the deluge. Mallory pulled up her hood and told me she was going to go away up to the rental cottage to see Sam's family. I said I'd walk with her, seeing as I had a free day. It had been my intention to relax and maybe catch up on doing nothing. I figured I was overdue.

We headed back up the beach towards the road. Big, fat raindrops began to splatter us, and it wasn't long before we were completely soaked. Stupidly I decided that right then would be a good time to apologise for my stupid puppy dog eyes the night before. I was pretty sure I'd made her feel uncomfortable, but how did I broach the subject without making it worse?

I stopped and took her arm. The wet hair stuck to my forehead with the weight of the rain, and I swiped it away. She turned to me with a look of confusion.

Taking a deep breath, I told her, 'I have to say something. Please just let me speak and don't say anything, okay?'

She narrowed her eyes. 'Oooh-kay.'

I could see the worry etched on her face, but I carried on regardless. It needed to be said no matter how much it irked me to utter the words. They were, after all, a lie. I took a deep breath, hoping to inhale some courage from the Scottish air. 'Mallory, you and I didn't get off to the best start, we both know that. I feel that now, though, we're friends, good friends?' I waited for her to agree and she nodded. *Phew! Okay, it's a start.* 'Seeing you look so happy last night made me feel amazing. Knowing I had a part in it. You know? But I think I may have given you the wrong impression. I know for a fact you felt uncomfortable at one point when I caught your eye… in the last song?'

I saw the light of acknowledgement in her eyes. I'd been bang on with my assumption. 'Now, I want you to know that I put your friendship above anything… I would never want to jeopardise that. If I made you feel uncomfortable by the way I looked at you, then I am so, so sorry. I just… you know… I sometimes get caught up in the meaning of a song. It didn't mean anything,' I lied. 'Like I said before, I'm crap at this friends business. And if I'm completely honest, and I think I should be, I *do* find you attractive. But there are *so many* reasons I can't and won't even bother to dwell on that fact. So please don't worry. Do you understand what I'm waffling on about?'

Her brow creased and she seemed to be thinking my words through. I wasn't sure if that was a good or bad thing. 'Basically, what I'm trying to say is that, if we'd met under different circumstances, if we were closer in age, if we both weren't so broken, if I was braver, if you even remotely found me attractive, then maybe things would be different. But I know that things are how they are. We're friends and that's enough. Please promise me that you won't start to withdraw and avoid me for fear of hurting me or doing... saying the wrong thing. I'm a big boy. I can handle it. I'm happy to be just friends.'

She gazed up at me and I felt sure that the water around her eyes was no longer *just* rain. She lowered her head for a moment and the moisture trickled down her cheeks and off the end of her pink-tinged nose. Her cheeks were rosy now too and the blue of her irises appeared more vivid. *So beautiful.* The urge to tell her to forget everything I'd said and just kiss her was almost impossible to fight. But fight it I did. And as if I'd just given her the best gift ever, she threw her arms around me and pulled me against her body. I slipped one arm around her back and cupped her soaking-wet head with the other, returning the embrace.

Fighting back my emotions, I pulled away and swallowed as I gazed into her bright blue eyes. I needed space. I hated that I wanted her *so much*. Smiling, I said my goodbyes and headed towards home. At least I'd made *her* feel better, even if in doing so a piece of my own heart had broken.

Chapter Twenty-five

After our chat on Sunday it seemed as if I was getting myself together again and the relief was immense. Although I *had* found myself inadvertently listening to a few tracks that made me think of Mallory, which I told myself was a minor setback. As I sat there listening to Pearl Jam the phone rang.

'Hello?'

'Oh, hi, is this Gregory?' a female voice asked.

'Yeah. Who's this?'

'Hi, dear, this is Renee. I'm Mallory's... well... mother-in-law for want of a more suitable term. I'm calling to ask you a huge favour that involves her dog.'

'Ruby? Okay, what can I do for you?'

'Well, the thing is, we've bought tickets for Mallory to come out to Canada for a while. We think the break will do her good. And to be in Sam's home again might be a good way for her to say goodbye. I was wondering... Would you be able to look after Ruby while she's away?'

She's going away? Okay... I'm not sure how I feel about this. 'Erm... y-yeah, sure. H-how long will she be gone?'

'That's the thing. She'll be away for around three weeks. But if there's a problem—'

'No... no problem. I'm happy to help. Just let me know when to pick her up.'

'Okay. Or we may drop her off at your house.'

'Yeah... yeah, whatever's easiest.'

'Thank you so much, Gregory. It'll be a weight off her mind knowing little Ruby will be cared for.'

'No worries. Bye, Renee.'

'Bye, dear. And thank you.'

I hung up and slumped onto the couch, dropping my head into my hands.

*

On the Monday morning, the day after I'd given Mallory the get-out she needed from her guilt, and the day after I found out that she'd be leaving for three weeks, I suddenly realised I was sitting there in my lounge with tear tracks down my face as A Perfect Circle's Maynard Keenan sang '3 Libras'. He was talking about feeling invisible and expecting too much from people who are broken, and regardless how the lyrics seemed to fit my situation I also realised in that moment it was time to get out of the house. What the hell was I doing with my life? Mourning in one breath and going doe-eyed over someone who I couldn't have was the resounding answer. I needed to stop wallowing.

I spent most of Monday and part of Tuesday working out on the boat. An influx of tourists had arrived with the improved temperatures, and being out there on the water had a calming effect on me. I'd watched the comings and goings over at Mallory's house from a distance but I'd left her alone. It hadn't been easy, seeing as I seemed to be bloody drawn to the woman. And I was thankful that she hadn't had any shifts with me at the pub. The time apart, however short, had done me good. Or so I kept repeating over and over in my head, like a mantra.

The tourists had been mainly Americans on a coaching holiday in Scotland. The majority of them were over sixty-five, and I think most of the women wanted to adopt me. I lost count of the number of times I was called 'sugar' or 'handsome' and found myself laughing along with the old dears on more than one occasion. Thankfully the seals were on top form and so the cameras were out in force, snapping away whilst I waxed lyrical about the location and its natural beauty. A new vista lay around every corner and each season brought its own colours and changes. How could anyone want to live elsewhere?

I just bloody loved the place and couldn't hide the fact. Or at least I *had* before Mallory had showed up and stolen what was left of my smashed-up heart. I was torn between running away and staying put to see what happened. And besides, the thought of not being near her was not one I contemplated with ease. Although for the next few weeks it was going to be something I had to face.

On Tuesday evening I left the boat after a successful day and went for a walk. The weather was lovely and I was making my way to the bridge to catch the stunning view as the sunlight danced on the surface of the Atlantic Ocean in the distance. It was one of my favourite views.

I spotted Mallory struggling with bags and bags of shopping, and before I could think or stop myself I was making my way towards her.

'Hi, matey. You seem to have been busy today.'

'Yes, I have. I think I've bought most of Oban. I only went for essentials.' She cringed and her cheeks turned pink.

'Are they for your trip?' I asked, trying to sound happy but failing miserably.

'Yes, they are.' Her face brightened and she smiled widely. 'Oh, by the way, thanks so much for agreeing to have Rubes. She and Angus will have fun. You coming in for a coffee?'

'Aye, why not – as long as I can make it? You can do me a fashion show if you like.' *What the hell am I doing?*

'Oh, I don't think that's necessary. You'd be bored. I only got jeans and tops. Apart from one dress that I couldn't resist.'

Following her into the house, I didn't give up. 'Tell you what, you go put that lot somewhere and try your dress on. Maybe you need a second opinion, eh? I'll make the coffee. Your coffee's not as good as mine anyway.'

'Cheeky. Okay, if you're sure.' She picked up the bags and headed for the stairs.

'Oh. I'm positive. It's the worst coffee I've tasted.'

She smirked at me but tried to hide her amusement. 'I meant about the dress, you cheeky sod.' Sticking out her tongue at me, she took her bags away to her room.

Chuckling to myself, I went into the kitchen and filled the kettle. Opening the coffee canister, I gagged at the smell of the powdery shit inside. I really needed to educate the girl. But for now, I'd put up with the ghastly stuff. Pulling down a couple of mugs, I spooned in the greyish-brown granules that looked more like instant gravy powder than coffee.

I heard, 'Tadaaaaaa!' and I swung round. My heart leapt and my eyes bugged out of my head. She stood there in a fitted red dress that hugged her every curve the way I wanted to. Suddenly I was envious of the thing. She looked stunning. There was no other word for her.

Stunning.

Without speaking a word, I trailed my gaze down her body to the black strappy sandals adorning her pretty feet and I swallowed hard. A familiar surge of blood southwards had hampered my thinking process, and I realised she had drawn her arms around her body self-consciously.

'Oh, God, I look ridiculous, don't I? I knew I shouldn't have shopped alone. I always make stupid decisions.'

My eyes snapped up to meet hers, which were now filled with regret. *Say something, you tit. Anything. Use your fucking words, McBradden!* 'Ah, no, no… ah… Mallory… you look… I mean… you're… um… wow.' *Well done, you arse.*

'Is that good wow or wow I can't believe you were so stupid?'

My brain fought to respond to her question. 'Erm, I'd say it's a good wow… definitely good.' *Oh God, I have to leave. This was a bad idea. I can't be here.* I backed away from the kitchen and began to walk towards the front door. 'Anyway, I should go. I've remembered I need to… ah… goodnight.' I slammed the door behind me and took a very deep breath, running my hands through my hair.

Looking down at the bulge in my pants, I hissed, 'And you didn't bloody help, did you? One track mind, you've got. Well, of course you have, you're a penis, but that's not the point!'

I stormed across to the pub and straight into the men's room. Closing the door on a cubicle, I sat on the toilet lid and rested my head in my hands. Images of Mallory sprang to mind to torture me, and I smacked myself in the forehead to try and get them out. I was acting like a sodding lunatic!

I groaned as I remembered the way the slinky red fabric had grazed her full breasts and swept over the curves of her hips. She had the perfect hourglass figure and all I could think about was running my hands down her body as she lay naked in my arms. To see her gaze up at me longingly and lovingly… *Argh! Stop it!*

I have no clue how long I sat there, but after splashing my face with cold water and making my second brain calm down, I went and sat at the bar. I was due to start at 7.30 p.m. but she was going to be there too. Shit! I needed to get away. In some way I knew I was overreacting but it didn't matter. Seeing her was something I couldn't face right now, and putting miles between us seemed the most logical thing to do. Irrational maybe, but still a logical solution in my head. If I couldn't see her, I couldn't feel things I didn't want to feel… Okay, so that wasn't strictly true… I could still *think* – but at least I wouldn't have to see her as well.

'Are you okay, Gregory? Your cheeks are flushed. Are you coming down with something, hon?' Stella asked, concern lacing her voice.

'No… no, I'm not. Look, Stella, I need some time off. Is that okay? Just a few days. I need to clear my head.'

She crumpled her brow in concern. 'If you need it, Greg, then take it. But please be back for when Mallory goes, eh?'

'Sure. Of course.'

She placed a glass with two fingers of amber liquid before me. 'Looks like you need this.'

I lifted the glass to my lips and stared into it for a moment. Deciding not to resort to my usual method of escape, and knowing it would limit how soon I could leave, I lowered it again.

Chapter Twenty-six

The door to the pub burst open and I heard heavy, stomping footsteps coming towards me. That familiar flowery scent hit me.

Mallory.

'What the hell happened to you back there?' she demanded.

I closed my eyes, unable to look into hers. 'Mallory, not now, okay?'

'Yes, now. What did I do?'

With as much venom as I could muster, I snapped back at her, 'Oh yes, 'cause the world revolves around you, now, doesn't it, eh?'

She gasped and I felt like shit. I made the mistake of glancing in her direction and meeting her pain-filled eyes. 'That's unfair, Greg. All I want to do is understand. You said I should show you the dress, so I did. Then you went all Weirdsville and beggared off.'

I couldn't answer. What could I say?

'Okay, have it your way. I'll just keep out of your way tonight, okay?'

I continued to stare into my glass, swirling the liquid around; I still hadn't touched the whisky. 'No need. I've got the rest of the week off, so I'm leaving for a while.'

'Oh. Right... what am I to do about Ruby, then, for my holiday? Do you know of a boarding kennel?'

I glared at her as my stomach twisted into knots and my fists clenched. 'Don't fuckin' worry, I'll be back by Friday. God forbid I should let you down and disappoint you again, eh?'

She threw up her hands in exasperation. I couldn't blame her. 'Oh, whatever, Greg. I can take her somewhere else.'

I almost growled my next words. 'I said I'd have her and I will. Bring her to mine at five Friday. I'll be there.' And without saying anything further I stood, slammed my glass of untouched single malt down, and walked out.

*

I needed to get away and there was no time like the present. When I arrived home, Angus followed me around the house as I grabbed clothes and shoved them into my duffle bag. I had no idea where I would go; the Buckle didn't feel like the right place. Wherever I ended up, I wanted to be outdoors, so I pulled my tent out of the under-stairs cupboard and carried it and my bag out to the car. After selecting a few CDs to take with me, I called to Angus and we climbed into the Landy.

There were so many emotions swirling around my

head that I didn't know how to handle them. I chewed on the inside of my cheek as tears stung my eyes. What the hell was I playing at? She was infuriating! And I hated that she affected me this way. I just wanted it to stop. I needed to grieve and then get on with my life. Mallory was a complication I couldn't cope with. Even though it wasn't her fault I was falling – had fallen – for her.

Slipping a CD into the slot, I turned the key in the ignition then cranked up the sound and inhaled a calming breath. The heartbreaking lyrics of '3 Libras' filled the car and I set off. Unsure of where I was going but desperately needing to get there.

*

Night fell and after a couple of hours of driving, I was seeing signs for Mallaig. It seemed like as good a place as any. I located a small but crowded campsite on the edge of the town and drove in.

I was greeted by a pretty woman with bright blue eyes. Her long black hair was streaked with a blue similar to her eyes, and she smiled widely when I stepped inside the reception cabin. It struck me how similar her eyes were to Mallory's, and I shook my head to dislodge the errant thought. I was here to get away from her, not to compare every woman I saw to her.

'Look, I know it's late, but I was wondering if you

had a small pitch available for a few days. I know it's short notice.' I cringed, expecting her to say no, judging by how busy the small site was.

'One sec… I think we had a cancellation earlier on. I heard my dad on the phone, so let me just check the system.'

She tip-tapped on the computer in front of her and smiled again. 'You're in luck! Just one spot. It's a large pitch in the quiet area, if that's okay? At least that means you can set up right in the middle and have some privacy, eh?'

'Oh, that's great. Thank you…' I glanced at her name badge. 'Thank you, Trina.'

'No problem. The thing is, it's a bit late to be hammering in pegs just now so you'll have to keep the noise down.' It was her turn to cringe now.

'Would it be easier if I maybe slept in the car tonight and set up tomorrow? So I don't upset the neighbours?' I asked with a smile.

'Well, that's entirely up to you.'

I'd slept in the Landy before so it was no big deal. 'Yeah, sure. No worries.'

'Great. Can I get you to fill in a registration form, please?' She handed me the form and a pen and then stepped around the counter. 'Aww, who's this handsome chap?' she asked.

Feeling playful, I didn't look up, but instead I answered, 'Oh, my name's Greg, nice to meet you.' I glanced up and I smiled.

She laughed at me. 'I think you know I meant the dog, Greg.'

'A fella can try though, eh? He's Angus and he's a lot more trouble than I am.' I winked at her. What the hell was I doing? Bloody moron.

She bent and scratched Angus's head before straightening up and fiddling with her blue-streaked locks and biting her lip. 'So, what brings you to Mallaig, Greg?'

'Ah, just needed a wee break. You know how it is.'

'I do, yes. What are your plans while you're here?'

'No idea. I thought I might do the local pubs tomorrow, you know, sample the local beer. Although it'll be a bit like a busman's holiday, considering I work in a pub myself.'

She looked thoughtful. 'Have you eaten? There's a great burger place up the road if you fancy it. They're open late.'

Fuck me, she's not backwards at coming forward... reminds me of someone I'd rather forget. Oh, well, in for a penny, as they say. 'That'd be great, Trina. I could eat a horse.'

She giggled. 'Will a beef burger do?'

I shrugged and chuckled. 'I suppose. Are you heading up that way now?'

'I am. I just need to lock up. You can leave your car out front.'

She went about closing up the place and removed her name badge, placing it on the counter. We stepped out of the building and locked the door.

'Are you sure you want to escort me for a burger? You don't exactly know me,' I said, suddenly wondering if this was a mistake.

She stopped and put her hands on my shoulders. 'Okay, Greg. I'm a black belt in karate and I teach self-defence at a women's centre. So don't try anything funny and you'll be fine.'

I widened my eyes. 'Shit, maybe it's me that should be worried. Don't take advantage of me, will you?' I joked in a feminine tone. She slapped my arm playfully and we set off.

It was strangely comfortable walking along the road with Trina. She seemed sweet and had a sexy figure, so it was no hardship chatting to her.

We arrived at the burger joint and I ordered food for both of us and a couple of patties without bread for Angus, who was waiting patiently outside. I was pretty sure I shouldn't have done that, but as soon as we'd got near the place and he smelled food, he was drooling and staring at me with his big brown eyes so I couldn't resist.

After handing over the money we stepped outside and walked over to a wooden bench to eat.

'So, what did you need a break from back at home?' she asked as we sat there.

'Long story,' I replied through a mouthful of burger.

She nudged me. 'I don't have to be anywhere. I'm a bit old for a curfew.'

I heaved out a long breath. 'I needed some space from… someone. A woman. Mallory. We're friends but… well, things have been a bit tricky recently.'

'Ah. I see. Friendships between men and women can be difficult. I hope you get it sorted when you get back.'

'Me too. Anyway, I don't really feel like talking about her.'

'Look, I don't normally do this… but… I live on the site in a caravan. My folks own the place and I run it most of the time, although today was my last day for a few, so… Look, what I'm trying to say is, do you want to come back to my caravan for a drink or something?'

'Or something?'

'You know… a drink, and we'll see where things go?'

'Trina, I've known you for an hour. You don't know me from Adam. This isn't exactly a safe situation for you to be in.'

She laughed. 'The fact that you're saying that tells me you're not dangerous. And like I said, I'm a martial artist who knows how to take a man down. And who says a woman can't be forward these days? I'm all for equality.'

I sat there listening to her, thinking that this was crazy. But then again, I was single. I had no ties. And I was looking for a total break for a while. She seemed nice and I didn't have to have sex with the woman unless I wanted to.

'If you're sure. That'd be great. Warmer than going straight back to the car, that's for sure, thanks.'

'Come on, then.' She held out her hand and pulled me up to my feet.

Chapter Twenty-seven

Back at Trina's home, she opened the door and flicked on the light. It wasn't like any caravan I'd ever seen. It was far more luxurious, rather like a small apartment. The décor was neutral and she had pretty much everything she would've had in a one-bedroom flat.

'What can I get you to drink?' she asked as I glanced around my new surroundings.

'Whatever you've got.'

'A glass of single malt?'

'Really? I wouldn't have taken you for a whisky drinker.'

She smiled and bit her lip again. 'It's my dad's, actually. I'm not keen. I think I'll have a glass of red wine.'

'Oh, right.' I suddenly felt old. 'Wine will be fine for me too.'

She poured two glasses of Shiraz and handed one to me. We both sat in silence on the coffee-coloured sofa at one end of the caravan. I felt out of place.

'Can I ask… how old are you, Trina?'

She laughed at my question. 'Don't fret. I'm thirty. I just look young, which can be a blessing and a curse really. Can you believe I still have to show my driving licence before I can buy wine? It makes me laugh.'

I relaxed a little. 'So what are you doing on your days off? Any big plans?'

'Well… there's this guy who's new to the area and I thought… maybe he might like a tour guide?' She stared at me expectantly.

'Oh, right. Right.'

'I mean, I don't have to, obviously—'

'Oh, no, that's fine. That'd be nice, thanks.' I glanced at the clock and it was already heading for one in the morning. 'Look, I should go really. I've a date with ma hairy friend Angus, a sleeping bag and a car seat.' I chuckled.

'Look, sleep on the couch. Set up your tent tomorrow morning when you've had a decent night's sleep, eh? I'm sure Angus will appreciate the carpet too.'

I scrunched my brow. 'Are you sure?'

'Positive. It's fine. I've taken pity on you. Not all women are trying to drive you mad, you see?'

I laughed and shook my head as she went into what I presumed to be her bedroom and returned with a fleece blanket and a pillow.

She held them out towards me. 'Here you go, Greg. Bathroom is through there and if you need anything in the night my room is through here. Help yourself to tea and coffee and anything you fancy to eat.'

I cringed. 'Trina, this just doesn't—'

'I've said it's fine. Don't worry. Goodnight.'

'Goodnight. And thanks again.'

I lay awake for quite a while, knowing that being in the home of some woman I'd only just met was not the best idea I'd ever had. But eventually I drifted off.

*

My eyes fluttered open and I was surrounded by an expanse of white. Completely disorientated, I sat up and peered at my surroundings until my eyes finally settled on a red figure in the distance. Scrambling to my feet, I squinted at the figure, trying my best to focus on it. It was then that I heard her screaming my name. Horror washed over me and I began to run towards her as quick as I could, but my legs felt weighted down, making it difficult to move. Cold seeped into my bones and when I glanced down, I realised I was shirtless and wearing only my boxers. Why was I outside in the snow in only my underwear? Confusion took over for a moment until the screaming stopped.

When I returned my focus to the girl again, she'd gone and panic rose within me. Who was it and why was she screaming? I'd let her down. She was gone and it was my fault for losing concentration. My eyes darted around me as my heart pounded at the inside of my ribcage. I could hear her calling my name again, over and over, but I couldn't see her. My breathing had become erratic and I suddenly couldn't move my feet at all. I flailed my arms madly, trying to make myself move, but I was cemented to the spot in the freezing white landscape.

'Greg... Greg... wake up.' Someone was shaking me lightly as I opened my eyes.

I glanced around, trying to get my bearings. 'Oh... h-hi. I'm... sorry... I...'

'It's okay. That was some nightmare. Are you okay?' she asked, pushing my hair out of my eyes. She had switched on a lamp and was sitting beside me on the sofa, concern etched on her face.

I pulled myself up to a sitting position. 'Yeah. I'm fine. Did I wake you?'

She shrugged and smiled. 'Yes, but it's fine.' She cupped my cheek and ran her thumb over my bottom lip.

I stared into her blue eyes and was suddenly transported somewhere else entirely. Without thinking, I slipped my hand into the black and blue strands of her silky hair and pulled her towards me with urgency, crushing my mouth into hers. She gasped as my tongue slid past her lips and then moaned as she smoothed her hands up my bare chest. Her hands travelled up again and fisted in my hair as the kiss gained fervour. My heart pounded and our heavy breaths sounded loud in the silence of the room. Our tongues tangled and I hardened in my boxers. With her mouth still on mine, she moved so that she straddled my waist and ground her pelvis into me.

God, I needed this. I needed to feel; to be connected to someone physically again; to let passion and adrenaline course through my veins and to just lose myself in a woman once more. But the heated exchange felt wrong and the only person in my mind was... Mallory.

I pulled away. My chest was heaving and I ran my hands through my hair just so that I had an excuse to take them from her body. 'Shit... sorry, T-Trina. I... I can't do this.' I closed my eyes as guilt and self-loathing took over. Opening them again, I was met by the understanding gaze of the stranger I'd tried to pretend was Mallory only moments before. But she didn't come close to Mallory in *any* way, and I hated myself for almost getting carried away with her.

She stroked her fingers down my face. 'Hey, it's okay. We can get to know each other first. I'm not really that kind of girl anyway. But... I find you *very* attractive and I really like you... so I would've slept with you. Just so you know.'

I caught her smiling at me, her plumps lips swollen and red. She was very pretty. But she wasn't Mallory... or Mairi for that matter. Climbing off me, she pulled down the hem of her vest top and adjusted her sleep shorts where they had got twisted in our body collision.

'Do you fancy a coffee and a bacon sandwich

maybe?' she asked as she walked towards the kitchen area.

'Just coffee, thanks. It's getting light out and I should go and get my tent set up.'

'Okay. But… well, you'd be welcome to stay here if you'd like?'

'Na', it's okay. I like camping. And besides, you need your personal space, so…'

She nodded sadly and went to turn on the kettle. 'You can use the shower if you'd like.'

'I'll grab one after I've put the tent up. I'll use the shower block though. I don't want to put you out any more than I have.'

'Well, you haven't, so don't worry.'

I went into the bathroom to get dressed, but first I stood before the mirror to examine my reflection. Who the hell was I kidding? There was no way someone like Mallory would be in the slightest bit interested in someone like me. Trina, on the other hand… She was different. And she was available. She was definitely attracted to me; the incident earlier had proved that. And for a split second I'd really wanted her. Maybe moving on with Trina was the right thing to do? Maybe I should've just given in to my baser desires and done the deed. Moving away from whatever the hell I was feeling for the Yorkshire lass was what was needed. And Trina was sexy in a blue-haired, quirky kind of way. Okay, so she didn't have Mallory's curves and her smile didn't make my insides flip-flop, but her personality was... was... *nice*. But Mallory had the ability to turn me to mush with just a look or a baggy sweater.

Ugh! I was doing myself no good at all. I dressed quickly and went back out to the living area, where Trina handed me a coffee. We drank in silence and, once we were done, I went out to the Landy, climbed in, and drove round to my pitch. She wasn't wrong when she said it was a large plot. It was screened on three sides by trees, and there was a little picnic bench to one end. My tent was usually a doddle to set up, but the rocky ground meant a bit of elbow grease and heavy hammering was necessary. I took out my pent-up sexual and emotional frustration on the poor tent pegs, bending some in the process, and I realised it was a good thing I hadn't attempted this the night before.

When my camp was all set up I sat on the grass to admire my handiwork whilst Angus rolled on his back with his legs in the air for me to scratch his belly.

Trina arrived and dropped beside me on the grass. 'So, are you up for a walk into town? There's a heritage centre if you're interested in that kind of stuff.'

I was beginning to wish she'd leave me alone, but it was clear she was trying to be nice and so I smiled up at her. 'Yeah, sounds good. I just need to shower. Can you watch Angus for me?'

'Absolutely.'

I grabbed my toilet bag and walked over to the small

shower block. As I scrubbed my sweaty skin, I thought things through. I came to the conclusion that maybe having a female companion would be quite good. Maybe I'd be able to clear Mallory out of my head easier this way.

Twenty minutes later Trina and I were meandering around the Mallaig Heritage Centre and I was learning about the fishing industry and the famous railway. The whole time we were in there Trina followed close behind me and I could feel her eyes on me. Every so often I glanced over and smiled at her and her eyes lit up. Call me conceited, but I could tell she was smitten.

Later on we sat outside a nice little pub, getting to know each other better as she'd recommended previously. She was an only child and her parents had handed over the running of the campsite to her so that they could take retirement. I told her about my divorce but didn't go into detail. She didn't need to know. Trina was quite a touchy-feely girl and she made her attraction clear in the way she kept sliding her fingers down my arm. I wanted to feel something. I really did. And I was determined to keep trying.

All in all it was a really nice day. I loved the Scottish countryside anyway but it was nice to see an area I hadn't experienced before. The harbour was small and quaint with different-coloured fishing and leisure vessels dotted around the moorings and white-painted houses lining the tiered mountainside. In the opposite direction was the lush, green island of Skye against the cornflower-blue backdrop.

After spending the day together, we picked up a bottle of wine and went back to sit outside my tent on a blanket to share it. It should've been very romantic. As the sun went down, the temperature dropped and Trina snuggled up to me. Out of courtesy I slipped my arm around her shoulder to warm her up. Glancing up at me, she leaned in and kissed my lips gently but I didn't reciprocate. I couldn't.

She pulled away. 'You're not attracted to me, are you?'

I frowned at her words. 'What? I... you're a very attractive girl. I just... I don't know... Maybe I need more time. This past year has been difficult and I'm not sure what I want right now.' *Liar. You want Mallory.*

'I see. Well, I can give you time.' She snuggled back into my side. 'I know it's very soon, but I really like you, Greg. I'd like to see where this goes. If anywhere. No pressure.'

Now, when someone you have known for only twenty four hours or so tells you she really likes you, wants to sleep with you within the first few hours, and is prepared to 'see where this goes', you can guarantee that pressure *is* involved. Alarm bells were already ringing, but for some reason I ignored them.

Chapter Twenty-eight

Trina had ended up working on Thursday and so Angus and I had the time to explore the area without her. We sat on a beach for a few hours just looking out to sea and sharing a haggis baguette. I'm pretty sure Angus thought it was his birthday.

My time in Mallaig was coming to a close and I wasn't sure how I felt about returning to Clachan.

When Friday morning came around I fluttered my eyes open to adjust to the light coming in through the fabric of the tent canopy. Yawning wide, I tried to stretch my arms over my head, but one was weighed down. With the not-quite-irrational fear of finding a severed horse head beside me, I turned my head in slow motion and my eyes widened at what I saw.

Snuggled into my side was Trina.

Although she was wrapped in a fleece blanket and lying *outside* my sleeping bag, I had my arm around her and was a little puzzled as to how she got in without Angus barking – or, more to the point, without waking me.

Her eyes opened and she reached up and kissed me. For some reason, things sprang to life below my waistline – or my morning erection was happy to feel her squashed up against me. Either way I was aroused, and the urge to take her was burgeoning as she peered into my eyes with longing.

Biting her lip, she slipped her hand down my chest, into my sleeping bag and gripped me firmly. I inhaled through my nose as she covered my mouth with hers and pushed her tongue between my lips. She moaned as her hand moved, clearly delighted to find my body willing, and I couldn't help the groan of pleasure that erupted from my throat as the sensation radiated throughout my extremities.

Suddenly Angus leapt to his feet and began barking. The ear-splitting noise in the close confines of the tent had Trina and I wincing. She stopped her ministrations and I raised my head to find my daft dog staring at me as he made his presence known.

'Oh… I think he might need to pee,' I told her.

She giggled and covered her eyes. 'Great timing, Angus.'

I scrambled from my sleeping bag and relief washed over me. Being with Trina wasn't something I really wanted, if I was honest, and maybe Angus somehow knew this. Anyway, it was a bit creepy doing that stuff with him in the tent. I let him out and he immediately dashed off to relieve his doggy bladder.

Trina crawled out of the small tent and winked at me. She skipped off in the direction of her caravan and returned quite quickly with two steaming mugs of coffee. It tasted really good and for a split second I wondered if maybe she *would* be worth getting to know. Realising I was on the verge of making a relationship decision based on *coffee*, I cursed at myself and began to take down the tent with her help.

Whilst we were loading up the Landy, she peered over at me, biting her lip again. It was starting to irritate me. 'Look... I was wondering... and I know it's a bit cheeky, but... I wondered if I could come back to Clachan with you? I've never seen the bridge and would love to. I'd just stay for the weekend and then I could get the train home. What do you think?'

What the...? 'Oh... erm...' I cringed.

She blushed and dropped her gaze. 'Sorry, that was really rude of me. Forget it.'

I went silent for a while as I thought her request through. *It would be a great way to show Mallory that I'm serious about being friends. She could see that I'm moving on. Even if technically I'm not.*

Taking a deep breath and wondering if I was about to make another colossal mistake, I leaned and tilted her chin up so her eyes would meet mine. 'I'd like it if you came back with me for a few days. But... you have to understand that I'm *not* promising you a relationship. As long as we're clear on that. Like I said, my head is a bit fucked at the minute.'

Her face lit up and she flung her arms around me.

'Yay! That's fantastic,' she gushed as though my head being fucked were something to celebrate. 'I'll go and grab some clothes. I won't get in your way, I promise.'

'Hurry though, eh? I've got to be home by five and I need to call at the supermarket to pick up some groceries on the way. My friend is dropping her dog off for me to look after while she goes away.'

'No problem,' she called as she jogged back towards her caravan.

'Oh, no, Angus. Did I just do something stupid?'

He grumbled, wagged his tail, and lay down beside me.

'I'll take that as a yes, then.'

*

Just over a couple of hours later we arrived at my house. Trina helped me carry the tent in, and Angus insisted on getting under our feet.

'Make yourself at home, Trina. I'm going to go jump in the shower.'

'No worries at all. Maybe I'll explore.'

I showed her the guest room and noticed the disappointment on her face as I left her to settle in. It felt weird having a woman in the house again. And *not* in a good way. I couldn't quite believe I'd allowed a complete stranger into my home. *To stay.* And if you're sitting there thinking I'm stupid, I reckon you're right.

Once out of the shower I checked the time. *Shit! Five to five.* Mallory would arrive any second. As I stood there with a towel around my waist and drying my hair on another, Trina appeared at the door. 'Greg, can I borrow an old T-shirt to lounge around in, please? I thought I could cook for you, but I don't want to splash tomato sauce down my clothes. I haven't brought much.' She trailed her eyes down my body, making me feel a little uncomfortable.

'Oh, yeah. Hang on.' I grabbed a T-shirt from the drawer and handed it to her. She went back to the guest room to change just as someone knocked on the front door.

'I'll get it while you get dressed,' Trina shouted as she headed down the stairs. I heard her open the door and say, 'Hello, can I help you?'

I faintly heard Mallory's voice and hopped around the room, pulling on my jeans in a panic. Without bothering to grab a T-shirt, I made my way downstairs as quickly as I could. Hoping to prove to Mallory that I was cool with being her friend, I slipped my arms around Trina's waist and greeted my friend at the door.

'Oh, hi, Mally, have you brought Rubes for me?'

I watched her expression change as she glanced at my arms where they sat around Trina.

She scowled at me. 'Erm, yes, but if it's not convenient anymore, Ron said—'

Oh, hell. Maybe this was a bit much. 'No, no, don't

be daft! We're happy to have her, aren't we, Trina?' Trina nodded and beamed at me. I plastered a big fake smile on my face. 'We'll take good care of her, don't you worry. She'll have great fun with Angus, won't you, girl?' I glanced down at Ruby, and she was wagging her tail – but I felt a little sick. Mallory let go of Ruby's lead and began to walk away. I thought I saw tears in her eyes.

'I'm just going to go say goodbye, Trina. Will you take Ruby's lead off?'

'Sure.' She picked up Ruby and cuddled the little ball of fluff.

I jogged out after Mallory. "Hey, Mally, are you okay? She *will* be fine, you know,' I told her as she stopped at her car.

She didn't turn round but I heard her sniff. 'I know that. I'm just going to miss her.'

'Look, I wanted to apologise.' I walked closer and she turned around slightly. Placing my finger lightly under her chin, I tilted her face to make her look at me. Her blue eyes seared into me and I caught my breath. 'I was an arse, yet again, last week. I don't know what was wrong. But...' I swallowed hard, as if doing so would give me the time I needed to muster up more lies '...I had a few days away and met Trina. She's nice, eh?' I tried hard to keep an enthusiastic smile on my face, but I was dying a little inside with every word.

'Oh, yes, she seems delightful.' I sensed a little

sarcasm in her voice and didn't quite understand why. I was doing her a favour by showing I'd moved on.

'Aye, I had a lot of thinking to do, but it's done and I'm over it now.' I held my arms out for some reason that I don't really understand myself. Her eyes trailed to the tattooed phrase on my chest and I shivered. Well, I was shirtless and shoeless after all.

'Good for you.' She smiled but her eyes didn't light up.

'Aye, well, there's no point wanting what you can't have, eh?' I too tried to smile but sadness washed over me as I uttered the words that declared a stark reality.

'No, no point at all,' she agreed. 'I'll be off, then. I'm staying at a hotel near the airport with the Buchannans tonight and then we fly out early morning.'

I nodded, sensing sadness in her too. 'Well, have a brilliant time, eh? And don't worry about this place. We'll all still be here when you get back.'

Another forced smile graced her features. 'Great... see you in three weeks, then.' She bent to climb into her little car and I suddenly panicked.

I desperately wanted to hold her. 'Don't you have a hug for your bestie, eh?'

She hesitated but then stepped into my open arms. Feeling her softness press against me brought back the longing I still harboured deep within, and so I thumped her back as I would a male friend's. *Bloody idiot.* She pulled away and climbed into her car. When she gazed up at me for a few moments, as she turned the key in the ignition, I saw something in her eyes that said she felt something more for me than she was prepared to admit. I swallowed hard and a frown pulled at my brow. Raising my hand to wave, I was overcome with anguish and fear as she drove away and out of my life for at least three weeks.

What if she didn't come back?

Chapter Twenty-nine

I walked back into the house and Trina was nowhere to be seen. Ruby and Angus were chasing each other around the back garden, having a whale of a time. The door was ajar and so I poked my head out to see if Trina was outside enjoying the sunshine, but there was no sign of her. I made my way upstairs to see if she was ready for something to eat, but she wasn't in the guest room either. Feeling a little befuddled, I decided to go to my room and grab a T-shirt.

I opened the door and got the shock of my fucking life.

Trina was lying on my bed, completely stark naked! My eyes widened so much that I felt sure they were going to fall out of the sockets. My cakehole opened and closed as my gaze trailed down her body, and the involuntary reaction happened in my boxers... but words wouldn't form.

Eventually my brain reconnected with my mouth and there was a second surge of blood, this time northwards – my cheeks could've spontaneously combusted at any minute – but it meant my tongue worked again.

I swallowed hard. 'Trina... what the fuck?' *Oh, very*

subtle, as always, McBradden.

She leaned up on her elbows with her knees together and her ankles apart. Her head tilted to one side as she smiled at me sexily. 'I was tired of waiting for you to make the move, so I thought I'd give you a little push.'

My feet were frozen to the spot and I glanced over the tattoo that reached from the curve at the top of one breast, down between both, towards her navel and wrapped around the indentation. It was a vine of Japanese flowers and was extremely well done. Why the hell I was thinking about the quality of the tattoo when there was a starkers wee woman on my bed, God only knows. My eyes trailed down the winding foliage and rested just above her neatly trimmed... erm... lady parts. My head – the one on my shoulders, that was – was suddenly a little fuzzy and I was willing my other eager body part to calm the hell down. I had no intention of letting him out to play. Had I? *Shit.* The fact that I was actually considering my options scared the crap out of me.

She smiled up at me, and when I didn't return the smile, she began to chew on the inside of her cheek. Instead of the sexiness she was trying to project mere moments ago, she now oozed vulnerability. My heart squeezed in my chest and I took a step towards her, suddenly feeling the urge to protect her; save her from herself even. She shouldn't be throwing herself at men... least of all me. I was an ass of prize proportions and didn't deserve for her to offer her body to me so readily. It was flattering to have such a pretty young woman willing to give herself to me, and in some small way I wished I weren't about to let her down. I rubbed my palms over my face. Now that I'd made the decision, my hormones began to calm.

Running my hands through my hair and breathing out heavily, I told her, 'Trina, I'm sorry but... Look, I'm just not in the market for a fling right now.'

She clambered to the end of the bed and kneeled before me. Grasping my waistband, she pulled me forward and unfastened the button, slipping her hand inside. The sharp intake of breath that echoed around the room sounded as if it came from someone else. It was like some weird kind of out-of-body experience. I gulped and peered down into her blue eyes.

She bit her lip and leaned up to kiss my bare chest. 'Who said anything about a *fling*?'

Huh? What's that supposed to mean? 'Trina, sweetheart, I've literally *just* met you. What else *would* it be?'

She pulled away from my chest and frowned up at me. 'But... we have a connection, Greg. We really do.'

On some level she was right. There must have been some kind of connection for me to bring her to my home. What the hell was I expecting? She and I had a lot in common – superficially at least. Music, tattoos, and a sense of wanting what we couldn't have. But nonetheless

I was beginning to worry about her feelings for me. This was all a bit much and it was a little disconcerting to have a woman I'd only known a few days insinuating that we were... *something*. The thought crossed my mind that perhaps... if I allowed it... we *could* be something. Being with her might be easy. She was nice to look at and clearly had a fantastic body. I would really be moving on... wouldn't I?

Mallory's face appeared in my mind's eye and all thoughts of moving on dissipated into the thick atmosphere in the room. Snapping myself back to reality, I realised I'd been staring at Trina. Sensibility took over and I stepped back, freeing myself from her grip and shaking my head. 'Erm, Trina. I don't mean to hurt your feelings, but... well... if you and I *were* to sleep together, it would just be sex to me. And I think you seem like a really sweet woman. But... well, the truth is, you and I won't ever be anything more than friends. I'm... I'm sorry.'

It was her turn to have the wide eyes. But they weren't just wide, they were brimming with tears. She slumped back onto her bottom, and her lip began trembling. I was a prize bastard.

'Oh,' she whispered. 'But I thought we connected. We get on so well. You let me come to stay with you.' She lifted her chin, and hopeful glistening blue eyes gazed up at me as her words echoed the exact thoughts I'd had seconds before.

I sat on the bed and pulled the throw from the end, wrapping it around her to try and rescue her dignity. 'Aye, I did, and I see now that it wasn't the best thing to do. We *do* get on. But I have to be honest with you. I'm kind of getting over losing someone, and I can't imagine ever feeling for someone else what I felt for *her*.' *Okay, so that's a lie.*

'But how do you know if you don't try?' she whined, like a kid who'd just been told there was no dessert for after dinner. Raising her hands, she rubbed at her eyes and smudged the mascara around them until she resembled a very sad panda.

'I just *know*, Trina. I'm sorry. I *really* am. I would love not to feel this way.' *And ain't that the truth!*

She turned away and wiped her running nose on my bed throw. *Nice.* And then, grabbing her scattered clothing, she pulled the throw around herself and left the room. The bathroom door slammed a few seconds later. I grabbed a T-shirt and pulled it over my head. Flopping down onto the edge of the bed, I leaned forward, dropped my head into my hands, and closed my eyes. I was pretty sure I'd have reacted very differently if it'd been Mallory offering her body to me so readily.

Awww, fuck, Mallory.

I hadn't thought about the hole in my heart that she'd left when she'd driven away earlier, on account of the naked drama that had unfolded when I'd come back into the house. I knew she couldn't be that far away by now and part of me hoped that she'd turn around, come back, and tell me she didn't want to go all the way to Canada after all.

No such luck.

The black-and-blue-haired virtual stranger came out of my bathroom fully dressed; the mascara from around her eyes all cleaned up.

She smiled awkwardly at me. 'Well. I feel like a complete and utter fool. So I think I'm going to go back home. Could you call me a cab to take me to the train station, please?'

I stood and stuck my hands in my pockets. 'I can take you back home if you like.'

She shook her head and dropped her gaze. 'I'd rather not be around you any more than I have to, Greg. No offence. I'll go grab my bag.'

I cringed. 'I can understand that.' She stepped aside so I could pass her on the landing, and as I glanced back I saw her disappear into the guest room.

Once I'd called Billy at the local taxi company, I made coffee just for something to do. I didn't even want it. A few minutes later Trina arrived back in the kitchen, looking rather sheepish.

I placed my steaming mug down and stepped towards her. 'Hey, are you okay?'

She rolled her eyes. 'What do *you* think?'

'Okay, daft question. Look, I really didn't mean to hurt your feelings. And I'm sure you really are a lovely girl—'

She held her hands up. 'Please stop before you say something really fucking glib like "It's not you… blah, fucking blah." I'm a big girl, Greg. I'll be perfectly fine, all right?'

I pulled both my lips in and nodded, unsure what I could say to make amends for embarrassing her. Instead of saying anything that would end up making her feel worse, I simply said, 'Taxi's on its way.'

'Great. Thanks.' Just as she ended her sentence, Billy pulled his white saloon car up in front of my house and honked his horn. 'Bye, Greg,' she said with a sad smile. 'Have a nice life, eh?'

I nodded again. 'Aye. You too, Trina. Be happy.'

And with that she rolled her eyes again and walked out of the door. I waited at the window in case she waved, but of course she didn't. She thought I was an arsehole of the most humongous proportions. And *I* felt the same about me too. I couldn't seem to do the right thing by anyone. Women in particular. Look how I'd treated Mallory from the start. There was no hope really. None. I was doomed to remain alone with no one to annoy but myself.

Chapter Thirty

The first week without Mallory dragged by at such a bloody snail's pace, I expected everyone to be walking in slow motion when I went outside. And every time someone spoke to me, I anticipated that ridiculous, slurry, deep voice that you get when you reduce the speed of a film. But of course, everyone else's lives were going on as normal. It was just *me* that was as miserable as sin. Not that anyone really noticed. I'm guessing that this was how they viewed me anyway.

It was Saturday night and Stella had finally told me to bugger off home, seeing as my miserable face was putting the customers off and turning the beer sour too. Angus and Ruby were fast asleep upstairs in Stella's place after both eating a belly full of leftover steak pie so I let them be. I grabbed Rhiannon and jumped in the Landy, deciding on impulse where I would go. There was a place in Oban that held an open mic night every so often and I had nothing better to do, so I thought I'd take my guitar and maybe consider getting up to sing if the mood struck me.

When I arrived the place was buzzing. I grabbed a pint of Coke and sat down at a small table in the middle of the room. There was a young lad on stage performing a ballad at a keyboard. He had a good voice but the song was dull as shit. When he finished and only a few people clapped, I felt a bit sorry for him. Most of them probably hadn't even realised he was up there.

The next act was a girl with long, dark, wavy hair. I couldn't see the colour of her eyes, but if I squinted *my* eyes so they were a little out of focus and peered up at her, it could've been Mallory. Okay, so I was missing her more than I really cared to acknowledge. So much so that there I was sitting in the middle of a dark pub, scrunching my face up at the poor woman onstage like some complete and utter weirdo.

And it was true that every time I saw a girl with long, dark hair I had to check to see if it was Mallory like the desperate man does in the movies where he's running down the street, searching for the love of his life and grabbing every similar-looking woman he sees. Bloody stupid, considering I had her dog at my house and *she* was in Canada.

The girl sang 'Stay With Me Till Dawn' by Judy Tzuke and shivers travelled down my spine. She sang with such feeling that it was as if she really meant *every single word*. It's such a beautiful song, and when applause rang out around the room and I caught myself wiping at my eyes, I realised a few tears had escaped. Okay, so for some reason the lyrics affected me deeply, I admit it. And I also admit that I was turning soft. I slammed my palms together with force and even stuck my fingers in my mouth to whistle. I wasn't alone. The crowd loved her and it didn't surprise me in the slightest.

After watching the response she got, I decided I'd put my name down and do a number. I was feeling more confident these days. My performances had been going well at the pub back home and singing was a great method of distraction. Much healthier than whisky, that was for sure.

When it was my turn to get up I took my seat on the small stage and looked out at the crowd. I could only make out fuzzy shapes due to the bright spotlight shining down on me, but most of the people I *could* make out were chatting amongst themselves. Some, however, seemed to be waiting to hear what I was about to deliver.

'Um... good evening, folks. My name is Greg McBradden and I stay up by the bridge over the Atlantic. Anyways I thought I'd play a song for you tonight that I happen to love. It's an acoustic version of quite an old one by a band called Chicago and it's called "Hard Habit to Break".' The room fell into silent anticipation as I started to strum my guitar with the opening chords of my own unique version of the 1980s classic love song.

As I sang the words with my eyes closed, I replayed some of the moments I'd shared with Mallory since I'd met her. I realised that this song was in no way the distraction I'd hoped for. Quite the opposite, in fact. Images of the sweet Yorkshire lass floated through my mind. The way her face lit up at her party as she stared over at me where I leaned against the door, watching her being engulfed in a group hug. How her hair fluttered across her face when we sat out on *Little Blue* and she gazed out at the mountains that led up and away from the water. Her sad eyes as she pulled away from me the day she left for Canada. I wish I'd known what she was thinking. What she felt.

All of a sudden it became difficult for me to sing due to the lump in my tightened throat. What the hell was *wrong* with me? I shouldn't be feeling this way. What was the point? She'd never allow herself to feel the same, even if she wanted to. Her pain from losing Sam was still so raw, like an open, bleeding wound. And what about my own grief? How the hell could I switch it off so easily? Guilt twisted my insides into a tight ball and I hated myself.

Thankfully I made it to the end of the song. And the place erupted. I opened my eyes and gulped down a knot of emotion as I peered out at the crowd, many of whom were on their feet applauding. I spotted a couple of women dabbing their eyes and once again realised my own face was damp. So much for escaping. Maybe whisky was the right distraction after all.

Ugh, I've got it bad. Very, very bad.

Sitting back at the table I'd left earlier, I watched and

listened as act after act performed to the revved-up crowd. Later on I got back on stage and sang the classic Proclaimers song 'I'm Gonna Be (500 Miles)' and the whole place sang along at the chorus. Although I hated that under normal circumstances, the majority of the audience were performers in their own right and so it didn't sound half bad. I had no reason to complain. Well… not much anyway.

As the night unfolded I began to relax more as I chatted to some of the other musicians. One of the guys told me about an agency, Class Act Talent, which was looking for acts to represent. It sounded interesting and he seemed to think that I would be right up their street. Being a full-time performer was an idea that had never really occurred to me, but talking about it made it seem like a possibility.

At the end of the night I set off home, and for the first half an hour I fought with the music on my car stereo. Every song seemed hell-bent on making me think about Mallory. Even songs that weren't bloody love songs. There was something in everything I listened to that brought her to mind. Or rather she was there already and apparently had no intention of shifting. I eventually gave up and drove the rest of the journey in silence.

The buzz of the night had subsided, and I arrived home in the wee hours feeling shattered. As I walked through the front door I was struck with how empty the house felt. I'd felt that after Mairi died, but it had left my mind for a while until I stood there with the words to John Waite's 'Missing You' spinning around my head. I was turning into a wuss. Some teenage spotty kid with a crush on someone he shouldn't be crushing on.

There was definitely only one thing for it.

Whisky.

Chapter Thirty-one

After I'd survived three weeks of being virtually alone, it was the day Mallory was due to arrive home. I'd spent time working out, walking, jogging, and working; anything to try and free my mind from all things to do with the Yorkshire lass. But now she was due home, I was a nervous wreck. I was eager to see her but dreading it at the same time. Could I do it? Could I be her friend? I hoped so. I would just have to squash the feelings I was having and put them down to something pathetic like loneliness.

I stood at the kitchen window as the rain spattered on the glass, making everything beyond blurry and obscured. I loved rain. But of course, I began to think about the awkward conversation I'd had with Mallory when we were out with the dogs. I must've looked like a drowned rat that day, with my hair slicked back and droplets hanging from my nose end. Not a pretty picture.

I'd been meaning to fix an oil leak on the car for a few days, but the weather hadn't been ideal for mechanics, and so I'd put it off and put it off. Glancing at the clock, I realised there were a couple of hours before Mallory would be home and then she probably wouldn't come around for Ruby straight away. No time like the present, then. I changed into some work clothes and grabbed the tools I needed.

Aside from Angus and Rhiannon, my Landy was my pride and joy. It had done me proud for many years and I always made sure I looked after it. Funny how it was an *it*, and my guitar was a female with a name. I'm quirky, all right? Sue me! Actually, don't bother. I'm pretty skint.

Anyway, I digress. The bonnet of the car shielded my head from the rain for the most part, but the rest of me was soaked. After half an hour I was covered in oil too. *Great.* And as they say oil and water… Do. Not. Mix!

I was just finishing up when something touched my shoulder and I nearly jumped out of my skin. I reared up and smacked my head on the bonnet. I winced and inhaled sharply as a throbbing pain registered in my nerves. But as I dizzily turned round, trying my best not to swear but blinking rapidly in the hope that the pain would recede quickly, there she was. As beautiful as ever.

Mallory.

'You're actually home.' Brilliant, wasn't I? I wiped my oily hands down my already grimy shirt. 'Come in, I'll make us a coffee.'

She followed me towards the house. My heart was making its best attempt to burst through my chest by that point, and I opened the door with shaking hands.

Ruby came scuttling up making a yipping noise. She was clearly excited to see her human again. I glanced over as I filled the kettle and smiled as I watched Mallory kneeling down and cuddling the dog. Her gorgeous round arse in the air. I swallowed and gave myself an internal talking-to.

She turned to face me and I realised I'd been staring. At her arse. My cheeks increased in temperature by what must have been a few hundred degrees and I turned away.

'So, where's Trina?' she asked. *What the fuck? How do I answer that?* Do *I answer that?*

Running my dirty hands through my hair, I mumbled something deliberately incoherent. She must have sensed my discomfort as she held up her hands in surrender. 'Sorry, it's none of my business. Rude of me to ask.'

My eyes widened. I didn't want her to feel bad for asking. 'Na', it's okay. We just weren't compatible, let's say.'

'Oh. Right.'

'Truth be told, she was ready for moving in permanently and getting engaged. I mean, for fuck's sake, I'd only known her a few days.' Remembering what a sight I must look and realising it would be a good excuse to avoid having this particular conversation right now, I glanced down at my oil-spattered clothes and cringed. 'I'll be back in a minute.'

I took the stairs two at a time, leaving her standing in my kitchen – probably wondering why I'd just bolted. I entered the bathroom and closed the door behind me. Standing before the mirror, I rolled my eyes at my reflection, which confirmed that I was indeed wearing an oil stripe across my nose and under both eyes à la Adam Ant from the eighties. I emptied half a tub of face wash into my hand and scrubbed at the oil marks, turning my face pink in the process. Once I'd dried my face, I hurried into the bedroom, hopping around on one leg to remove the soggy jeans that were plastered in place. I quickly ran the towel around my thighs so that getting dry jeans on would be easier and grabbed a clean T-shirt from the drawer. I made my way back down the stairs, rubbing at my hair as I walked.

'So, good time?' I asked her as I pulled my shirt on.

'Brilliant,' she replied.

'Make any new friends out there?' *Translation: Meet any men out there who you fancied?*

'Yes, quite a few, actually. I even got asked out.' Her cheeks turned pink and she looked embarrassed. My heart jumped in my chest like a bloody excited puppy. Of course other men found her attractive. Who wouldn't?

I watched as she fiddled with her fingernails. 'Why do you sound surprised?'

Her brow creased. 'Oh, I don't know. It was nice. I'd forgotten what it was like to be asked out.'

'So, did you go?' I didn't really want to know the answer and realised my frown was mirroring hers. I turned and walked back through to the kitchen to reboil the kettle.

'No, he wasn't my type.'

I turned to face her again. 'Oh, right. Do you have a type, then?' Now this answer was one I *did* want to hear.

She shrugged and tucked her hair behind her ear. 'I didn't think so. But anyway, he wasn't it, that's for sure. Too… oh, I don't know. I just didn't fancy him.'

I shook my head. *So that's how to avoid giving a real answer, eh?* I decided to change the subject. 'I've something to ask you, anyways.' I poured boiling water into the mugs in front of me and added milk, handing one to her.

'Oh yeah? What's that, then?' She took a sip and yelped.

'Too eager! I made it with hot water and everything, you know.' I couldn't help teasing.

She rolled her eyes. 'Ha-ha.'

'Anyway. It's my birthday next weekend and I thought we could maybe have that beach barbie we'd talked about for your birthday.' *Please say yes.* 'I know that was just a ruse to get you to cheer up whilst I was planning your *actual* birthday, but I do quite fancy it.'

She pursed her lips for a second and then smiled. 'Oooh, thirty-eight, then, eh? Barbeque sounds good.

Who shall we invite to come along?'

Yes! I mentally fist-bumped the air then shrugged off her question about guests and told her I'd sort it out. We chatted a bit more about general shit – she enquired about my car and I asked about her time away. She lit up as she spoke and I could see that she'd benefitted from her break in Canada.

Then she told me about a memorial service they'd had at Sam's parents' home.

'All his friends were there. They said some amazing things about him. We all wore bright colours and released lanterns. It was really beautiful.'

It sounded like a very touching experience and I suddenly acknowledged a sadness bubbling up from within along with a touch of envy; it was more than evident how much she still loved Sam.

Trying to push my selfish feelings down, I smiled. 'Sounds great. Did it help you? You know, to be around his friends and family?'

The sparkle to her blue eyes gave me my answer. 'Definitely.' She paused and took a deep breath. 'I felt like I said a proper goodbye. Not like at the cremation where I was so numb I couldn't even cry.' She dropped her gaze to the contents of her mug as sadness pulled at her features.

'Must have been lovely.' My voice came out as a whisper and I realised I had a stinging sensation behind my eyes.

After another brief silence she lifted her gaze to meet mine. 'Hey, how would you feel about doing something similar for Mairi?'

I narrowed my eyes. 'What do you mean?'

'Well, we could get a few friends together and say a few words and maybe release balloons or lanterns for her?'

I really wasn't keen on having people around me. Despite keeping in touch with Mairi's parents by phone, we didn't really get along. I told her this, and the fact that Mairi's friends had done a climb in memory of her already. There really wasn't anyone to invite, even if I'd wanted to, and in all honesty it was strange and potentially hypocritical to consider doing such a thing with the thoughts I'd had about Mallory lately; although I couldn't say *that* out loud.

She took a step towards me, and her expression told me she was fighting with her emotions but I didn't want her pity and I bristled a little.

She shrugged. 'Well, okay, you and I could do it.'

Huh? Wow. I'd got her all wrong. *Again.* 'You'd do that… for me?'

A sweet smile arched her full lips. 'I would… of course.'

Regardless of my inner conflict I knew that a proper goodbye might help me. Perhaps that was why I was in this state of limbo: because the goodbye I'd said hadn't felt complete. There was no real closure. And Mallory was trying to be the friend I was failing to be. Add to all of that the fact that I *had* to get my head on straight where Mallory was concerned, maybe this was an opportunity to draw that much-needed line in the sand? Perhaps if I did this with Mallory our friendship would be cemented and I could stop fantasising about things that would never happen?

'When could we do it? You and me? And where?' The words fell from my mouth as if I had no control over them. Okay, so it appeared my subconscious was on board. The two of us. Candle lanterns. A proper goodbye for Mairi. And this time it would mean something for *me*. Unlike the one her friends held.

'Whenever and wherever you feel ready,' she said.

'How about on my birthday?' I smiled, filled with hope. It was a lovely idea and I wanted to hug her. But I didn't dare move.

'That's fine by me.'

I was now grinning like an idiot and I didn't care. I hadn't had a friend to suggest something like this until now, and for some reason the little ceremony sounded perfect. Cathartic somehow. Maybe the nightmares would stop? 'Great. I'll just write a few words and we'll get some lanterns to release. Leave it with me. You can speak too if you like.'

Mallory shook her head. 'Hang on, though. Wouldn't you prefer to have your friends at your birthday? Maybe the memorial should wait until after you've celebrated.'

Stepping towards her, I placed my hand on her shoulder and gazed into her mesmerising, clear blue eyes. 'Mallory, you *are* my friends. The only friend who understands and the only friend I'm that bothered about spending my birthday with, anyway. It's fine.'

'Okay. Lovely. I'll start planning when I get home.' She took a long pull of her coffee. 'So what have you been up to whilst I've been away?'

I shrugged and shook my head. 'Not much. Been working mostly.' *And thinking about you. Oh, and having sex dreams about you too. And crying... yeah, I've even cried over you.* Thankfully those thoughts didn't become words, but I glanced up at Mallory, whose head was cocked to one side quizzically. She'd obviously been watching my expression change as my train of thought veered off the tracks and plummeted down a ravine. I shook my head to dislodge the thoughts and smiled.

She breathed in loudly and returned the smile before fumbling around in her pocket and pulling out a little white bag. 'Right. Well, I'll get Ruby home, then. Thanks again for looking after her. I really appreciate it. Oh... I bought you this. It's not much. But I saw it and... well... thought of you.'

I reached out and took the bag from her hand. Opening it, I pulled out a plaited leather wristband with a little silver tree charm hanging from it. *There's that stinging sensation again. Wimp.*

I swallowed and cleared my throat. 'Thank you, Mallory. It's… it's beautiful.'

Her cheeks coloured and she chewed the inside of her lower lip. 'It's not much. Just a little thank-you. It's the tree of life. I figured we'd both had enough death in our lives.'

She tugged at her sleeve and I noticed she was wearing an identical bracelet, but hers was purple leather. I know it probably sounds very girly and silly, but the fact that we owned matching bracelets made me feel a little warm and fuzzy. What can I say? She obviously brought the romantic out in me regardless of how pointless it was to feel that way.

We shared an awkward silence and I gave her a stiff hug before she said goodbye and led Ruby out to her car.

Chapter Thirty-two

A couple of days later I was due to play at the pub again. Mallory was working and I'd decided to wear a new shirt I'd bought on a trip to Oban. It was white with a squiggly pattern that Stella later told me was called paisley. Look, I'm no fashion... wotsit... guru... expert thingy, all right? Anyway, I wanted to look nice. Not for Mallory, obviously. Okay, not *just* for Mallory.

Okay, *for* Mallory.

Speaking of the Yorkshire lass, she was behind the bar when I arrived and so I went over to say hi. She was wearing a grey dress that wrapped around her body and enhanced her cleavage but without looking slutty. She *never* looked slutty. Always very classy and sexy and never over the top.

She placed a pint of Coke in front of me and smiled. 'Looking very smart this evening, Mr McBradden.'

'Why thank you, lassie. You don't look too shabby yourself,' I replied in my best Sean Connery voice and it made her giggle.

She glanced down at the dress that hugged each curve delectably and I almost moaned as I watched her smooth it down her body as she smiled. 'What, this old thing?'

I shook my head and took a swig of my drink. 'Actually, now you come to mention it, maybe you *do* look a bit shabby.' I winked and she threw a damp bar towel at me. Luckily it narrowly missed my chest. 'Oy! New shirt, Westerman!'

She stuck out her tongue at me and of course it made me laugh. 'So, what are you singing tonight?'

I crumpled my nose. 'Aw, nothing you'll have heard of. You're only a wee one.'

Placing her hands on her hips, she pursed her lips for a moment. 'An eight-year age gap does not make me less of an expert in music. Try me.'

I loved her feisty side. 'Okay… I'm going to do a little number by a guy called Jeff Buckley. 'The song is "Hallelujah",' I told her, folding my arms across my chest and feeling sure she wouldn't have a clue who he was.

'Funny that. *Grace* is one of my favourite CDs of all time,' she said with raised eyebrows.

Could she get any more perfect? 'Okay. I'm also doing "Is This Love" by Whitesnake.' *Surely she won't know them.*

'Hmm, I used to have a poster of David Coverdale. My dad liked them *and* Deep Purple. And Rainbow, actually.'

Oh. My. God. See… perfect.

I opened and closed my mouth like the goldfish I seemed to impersonate regularly lately, and she smiled smugly.

'Yeah... well... *whatever*,' I retorted like a pathetic schoolboy.

Throwing her head back, she roared with laughter, clearly knowing she'd won and that I'd given up trying to best her. I couldn't help laughing too. She had the best laugh, after all, and it just happened to be bloody contagious.

I walked over and took my place behind the mic. I began my set and for once the crowd in the pub was very well behaved and *not* singing along... much. Every so often I glanced over and saw Mallory jigging up and down and mouthing the words as she dried glasses or pulled pints. Why did such a simple thing give me the warm and fuzzies?

I began to play the opening chords of "Is This Love" and closed my eyes. Some might not have liked eighties rock with the hairspray and lip gloss that went with it, but some of the songs were *really* good. I'd been a sucker for Bon Jovi and Def Leppard in my younger days; my tastes had expanded, but there was always room in my heart for a bit of gravel and guitar. I opened my eyes and made an effort not to look over at Mallory in case she thought I was aiming the lyrics at her again.

Call me paranoid.

But when I sneaked a glance, I caught her out of the corner of my eye, leaning on the bar, staring in my direction with a faraway look in her eyes. When the song ended and the room erupted in applause, she almost jumped out of her skin. I smiled over at her and she joined the crowd, clapping her hands above her head.

Beautiful, talented, great taste in music, and the sexiest curves I'd ever seen. I really was *not* helping myself.

At the end of the gig I walked her over to her cottage and we chatted about the night and which songs were her favourites.

When we reached her front door, she jangled the keys in her hand. 'Want to come in for coffee?' she asked.

My heart screamed, *Yes, yes, I want to come in, scoop you up in my arms, and kiss every inch of you.*

Where the hell did that come from?

But thankfully my head was in charge – the one on my shoulders, that was – and so I shook my head, mock shivered, and pulled a face. 'Eww! No, thanks. Did you not know you make the *worst* coffee *ever*?'

She gasped, scrunched her brow, and slapped my arm. Hard. 'Cheeky sod!' she squeaked.

I rubbed the sore patch on my bicep. 'Ow! Look, friends should be *honest* with each other,' I told her with a playful smirk.

'Yeah? Well, *you* can't sing.'

I grabbed my chest as if she'd shot me and staggered back. Then I righted myself and shook my head.

Wagging my finger at her, I said, 'Now you know

that's a lie, Miss Westerman.' She stuck her tongue out at me as usual and turned to open her door. Whilst she had her back to me I leaned in close and whispered in her ear, 'You know it's rude to stick out your tongue, don't you? And *you* do it rather a lot. You're so bad, I should take you over my knee.' I was kidding around, but as soon as the words left my mouth, my first thought was, *oh, shit that was stupid.*

She shivered and turned to face me. Her eyes widened when she realised how close I was. I immediately stepped back and rubbed the back of my neck with my hand, chewing my lip at the same time. 'Sorry. I… I was just messing about.'

Her lips turned up into a smile. 'I'll let you off. See you Saturday?'

'Absolutely. See you Saturday. Night, Mallory.' I turned and headed back up the lane and it took all my willpower not to punch myself in the face for such an idiotic move. *How to fucking ruin a friendship in one easy step. Make a sweet girl like Mallory think you're into fucking kinky shit like spanking. Clever.*

'Greg!' Her voice echoed through the night air and I flinched. She was going to cancel Saturday. *Shitty, shit fuck!*

I stopped and turned around. 'Yeah?'

'It *was* a lie. You *can* sing, and you were brilliant tonight,' she called.

A huge grin made its way slowly across my face and I

shook my head, turned, and carried on walking, lifting my hand in a salute as I strode away. My heart skipped and my stomach twisted.

Bang went any hopes of not dreaming about her now.

Chapter Thirty-three

By Saturday afternoon I was a nervous wreck. Of course I was looking forward to seeing Mallory, but the prospect of being upset in front of her didn't fill me with glee. And there was no doubt that I'd get emotional, seeing as this was supposed to be both my birthday celebration *and* my official goodbye to Mairi.

I questioned my sanity over agreeing to do such a thing:

a) on my birthday, and
b) with Mallory – the woman I clearly was in *lust* with.

As I brushed my teeth I stared at the man in the mirror who had a distinct glint in his eye. I wanted to shout at him and tell him he had *no right* to be thinking about another woman in such a way. My heart was Mairi's. I was betraying her by being so distracted. But as I rinsed my toothbrush a niggling voice from my subconscious told me, *Mairi's gone. You can't live forever in the past. Life has to go on. You can't stay still in an ever-changing world. Mairi wouldn't want that.*

A shiver travelled the length of my spine and I leaned on the sink, gripping at the cool porcelain as my chest tightened and I lost my breath; just as I did whenever Mairi's passing came back to me. She *was* gone and someday… *someday*, I would have to accept the fact that I was still a relatively young man in the great scheme of things and the rest of my life was hopefully going to be a long time – too long to spend it alone. And there was the fact that I'd always had dreams of becoming a father. That was something that *couldn't* happen if I stayed so weighed down under a blanket of guilt *and* rooted in place. With a deep breath and a nod to the man in the mirror I summoned up the courage I needed and carried on getting myself ready.

The weather was being kind and I was almost pissed off at the fact. At least if it'd been pissing down rain, I would've had a good excuse for backing out. But instead I donned my khakis and a shirt, grabbed my sunnies, and headed out of the door to call on my friend.

Mallory opened the door with a wide smile on her face, and my breath caught in my throat. I cursed myself inwardly as my whole body reacted to the sight of her standing there in black trousers that apparently loved her curves as much as I did, judging by the way they caressed her. On top she wore a bluey-green long-sleeved top that accentuated the curve of her full breasts. *I really will have to stop thinking like this.*

'Hi,' she said as she slipped into a black denim jacket.

'I've been thinking about this all morning, Greg. I wasn't sure you'd show up, to be honest.'

Is she a bloody mind-reader now? 'Oh? Why's that?'

She shrugged. 'I wondered if you'd think maybe I was overstepping a mark wanting to be involved when I never met Mairi. I thought perhaps I had been a little too intrusive.'

I sighed. 'Not intrusive. Thoughtful.'

The expression on her face changed and a line appeared between her brows. 'Are you sure you want to do this… with me?'

I smiled, suddenly wanting this more than anything. 'I'm sure.'

She nodded decisively. 'Come on, then. Let's get going whilst the weather's nice. You never can tell around here. It seems it can turn at a moment's notice.' She seemed giddy and my mood began calming too, the nerves dissipating.

We loaded up the Landy and climbed in. I drove us the short distance to the beach and parked up. We carried the barbeque and supplies down onto the sand, which thankfully was empty apart from the two of us, and Mallory laid out the blanket whilst I lit the coals. I plonked myself down beside her and frowned as she handed me a small package wrapped in brown paper that had gold stars printed on it. I was absolutely bloody floored by the amount of thought she put into gifts *and* the fact that she was creative enough to make her own wrapping.

'Awww, Mallory, what's this, eh? You didn't have to go and get me a gift, you daft lassie.' I smiled though, secretly excited; I'd thought birthday gifts were a thing of the past now that Mairi was gone. I tore off the paper to find a sweet little painted wooden sign, complete with a tartan hanging ribbon. She'd made it especially for me. And just like the chalkboard, seeing it made me a tad emotional. Her thoughtfulness knew no bounds.

Lifting up the plaque, I read aloud the wording, '"True friends are hard to find, thank goodness I found you."' My eyes became blurry as saltwater began to well in them. Another familiar occurrence lately. My lip trembled and I kind of lurched forward at her, grappling her into my arms, holding on for dear life. My heart hammered in my chest, and her perfume infiltrated my nostrils, transporting me into a brief fantasy of her gazing up from beneath my body. The scent of her made me think crazy shit like that. I pulled my face away from her neck and searched her eyes for *any* spark that said she felt the same way I did – although I didn't fully understand the way *I* felt. Her eyes sparkled as she smiled up at me.

I cleared my mind *and* my throat before I spoke. 'I couldn't have dreamt of anything better, Mallory, it's beautiful… thank you.' She frowned for a split second and I *swear* I could feel her heart beating against mine as I held her close to me. I swallowed hard, desperate to kiss her. Knowing the feeling couldn't be acted upon, I pulled away. 'I... think the temperature should be about right now. Better get the food on, eh?'

She seemed relieved that I had let her go and it saddened me. *Friends, Greg. That's all you are.*

As I placed the burgers on the rack and turned them, she began to quiz me about the lack of friends invited to our little gathering. I tried to explain that I didn't really *have* friends on account of the ones like Connell, who had betrayed me by sleeping with my wife in my own fucking bed. Who needed friends like that? I told her that I'd rather keep myself to myself. But she was like a dog with a bone and didn't give up digging.

'But what about me?' she asked with her head cocked to one side. *Good question. What about her?*

I thought for a moment about how best to respond. After huffing out a breath I explained, 'You're different. Don't ask me why, but I trust you. I don't think you'd ever let me down. I get the feeling I would only ever lose you if *I* was the one who did the wrong thing.' I gazed into her bright blue eyes, hoping that what I had said came across right.

She smiled cheekily. 'Hmm, better be on your best behaviour, then.'

We chatted easily as we ate our food, and I was glad it all had turned out bloody delicious. I was impressed with myself and kept telling Mallory so. She muttered something about my modesty being endearing – sarcastic woman.

As night fell, the stars came out, dotted across the dark canvas of the sky in their clustered constellations. I glanced over at Mallory sitting next to me. Her eyes were focused up at the darkening sky too. A serene smile played on her lips and I thought to myself how good it felt to see her happy.

She must have sensed me watching her, as she met my gaze and her smile faded. 'Shall we go set the lanterns free?'

I chewed on my lip. The thought of saying goodbye to Mairi once and for all made my heart ache. I wasn't sure if I was ready yet. But knowing I had to move on I pushed myself up from the blanket and held my hand out to Mallory.

I'd never done anything like this before so I was reluctant to speak in case I made an utter tit of myself. Mallory knew what she was doing and how these things went so, clearing my throat, I spoke. 'Would you… you know… speak first? Please?' She nodded and relief washed over me. We collected the lanterns and the tags we'd written and made our way down to the water's edge. My heart began to pound again and a familiar lump in my throat made itself known to me. I blinked rapidly to try and stop the stinging sensation in my eyes and took a deep breath, preparing myself for what she was about to say.

She lit her lantern and began to speak. 'Mairi, you

were a bright light in Greg's life. You were a brave and adventurous woman and you made my friend very happy...' her voice was quiet and sincere as she turned to me and smiled warmly before continuing '...and I'm sure, had I met you, we would have been the best of friends too. Now you've left this world, you're a bright star in the night sky. You are missed and will always be loved.'

I closed my eyes as she spoke and pictured Mairi jogging with me along this very beach, holding my hand as we laughed and chased each other across the sand. Her titian hair trailing across her face and her big green eyes sparkling with a mischievousness I loved so very much. Remembering I wasn't alone, I opened my eyes and turned towards Mallory as she released her lantern.

Reaching out, I squeezed her hand. 'That was beautiful. Thank you.' The tears in my eyes were ready to spill over but I took yet another calming breath as Mallory nodded her encouragement.

As I began to speak, my voice wavered. 'Mairi, my heart and my love, you were a vivacious, stunningly beautiful woman, both inside and out. I was so proud of you for all you achieved at such a young age. Your courage knew no bounds. When you walked into a room, all heads turned and you made everyone smile, especially me. Since you left, my world has got a little darker. I've spent the last year feeling a type of pain that no one else could understand. But Mallory came along and changed that. She helped me to come to terms with losing you. She helped me to come here today to say goodbye in a way I wasn't able to do before. I miss you so much that sometimes I still feel physical pain, but I know that you can't return and I have to try and let you go.' I couldn't fight the sob that burst from my throat. This was harder than I ever could've imagined. My heart was breaking all over again but I fought to carry on. 'Please know that wherever you are, I will always, *always* love you.'

I released my lantern and watched for a moment as it soared towards the heavens to join the other. Towards Mairi. I felt a part of my heart leaving with the glowing paper and I hoped that I could begin to move on. But knowing that the anniversary of her death was coming up, I was guessing it would be easier said than done.

I blew out a shaking breath and rubbed my face before turning to Mallory. 'Thank you for suggesting this. It's been really cathartic.' At that moment having Mallory here seeing me cry was insignificant. What she'd done for me, on the other hand, was the most significant experience I'd had since Mairi had died.

I reached out and touched her cheek. 'You need to know that I would never have let go of all this if it wasn't for… your help.' I could hardly get my words out and my voice broke, but I didn't care. What she'd given me was so much more than *anyone* had since I lost the love of my life.

Mallory shivered and so I slipped my arm around her shoulder as if it were the most natural thing in the world. A weight had been lifted from my shoulders. And even though I knew it was more than likely a temporary feeling, I grasped it with all my might, determined to hold onto it for as long as possible. Mairi was never coming back and I *had* to move on. Life kept sprinting forward and I had been struggling to keep up until now.

After collecting some pieces of driftwood – out of which Mallory was bound to create something spectacular – we sat on the blanket under the stars for a while and I poured hot chocolate out of the flask I'd prepared. You see, I think of everything. This could have been the most romantic evening, but instead we sat there as friends sharing a common grief, gazing up at the stars and wondering if we were being observed from on high by our loved ones. I think it was one of the most profound evenings I'd ever spent.

Chapter Thirty-four

Monday evening Mallory and I were working behind the bar at the pub like a well-oiled machine. It was like a scene from *Cocktail* with Tom Cruise, only without the bottle tossing. I *had* suggested it, but Mallory had scowled at me, and I think I heard her swear too. Her reaction made me howl with laughter and call her a cowardy-custard, and she flicked me with a bar towel.

A while later I caught her watching me. It was as if there was something she wanted to say. So after waiting for her to speak up I thought, *fuck it,* and stood before her.

'Out with it, Westerman. I can see you're desperate to say something,' I said, arms crossed over my chest.

She chewed on her lip. 'I've... erm... had an idea.'

I rolled my eyes. 'How many times do I need to tell you that thinking is *bad* for you?'

She pursed her lips and scowled again. I know it may sound incredibly desperate, but I had begun to love that scowl. 'I'm being serious, McBradden.'

'Okay... hit me with it.'

'What, a brick? Tempting.'

'Ha-ha. What's the *idea* you've had?'

She fell silent again as if trying to pluck up courage. 'You know Sam's ashes?'

I scrunched my brow. My stomach dropped. I didn't know what I'd been expecting, but it wasn't anything to do with Sam's ashes. 'Yeah?' I asked hesitantly.

'Well… it's nearly the end of July and I figure I need to scatter them at some point. And I think I have an idea as to how to go about it.'

'Okay. What's the idea?'

'Well… Sam and I used to love travelling around the Highlands and…' She closed her eyes for a moment, and when she opened them again, I could see the glisten of tears forming. 'I thought…' She took a deep breath. 'I thought maybe I could travel around and scatter the ashes in all the places we visited. Is that silly?' Her lower lip quivered and I wanted to wrap my arms around her.

'I think it's a *wonderful* idea. And I know for a fact, if Sam could tell you himself, he would say the same.'

'The thing is…'

I turned my mouth up at one side. 'What's the thing?'

'I wondered if you would mind driving me.' She cringed but I don't know why.

A feeling I couldn't really understand overtook me. 'Mallory, I would be *honoured* to go with you. Thank you for asking me to be a part of it.'

She huffed the air from her lungs as if she'd been terrified to ask. 'Thank you. It… it means a lot that you'll go with me. You understand. I do appreciate it.'

‘Hey, that’s what friends do, eh? So, do you know the places you want to go?’

‘Yes, I have a list that I’ve drawn up. It might take quite a while… is that okay?’

‘We’ll take as long as you need, Mally.’ I liked the familiarity of shortening her name. It made me feel as if we were *close* friends. And I suppose after the things we’d shared, we were.

She nodded but seemed unable to speak. She walked by me and squeezed my arm as she headed for the ladies’ toilets.

*

Once we left work that night I didn’t see Mallory for the rest of the week. I was tied up in doing odd jobs, taking *Little Blue* out and practising new songs. I compiled a CD of music that I thought she might like to listen to on our journey and I hoped I hadn’t overstepped the mark in doing so.

As agreed I called for Mallory at seven on Saturday morning. She looked as if she hadn’t slept, and when I mentioned the CD I’d made, she burst into tears. At first I thought she was upset with me and that we were having a repeat of the ‘Chasing Cars’ incident in the pub. But then she put her arms around me and hugged me, resting her head on my chest. I had to chew the inside of my cheek to try and get a hold on my own emotions. Seeing me bawling my eyes out was the last thing she needed. But she had such a profound effect on me *every single time* she cried or became upset.

I was turning into a bloody hormonal woman.

We set out on the journey that I knew would be painful for her. I was glad I was there to help pick up the pieces if she needed me to. And I guessed she *would* need me to. We travelled in silence for much of the journey and I didn't mind. Mallory needed time to think and I respected that. I wasn't about to push her into talking inane crap as I usually did. Silence in company was always something I struggled with. But with Mallory silence was a little more comfortable.

As we travelled I caught sight of the Buckle rising proudly from the moorland with the sun highlighting its summit. I could feel Mallory's eyes on me when she realised where we were, but I stayed silent. This wasn't about me. I felt sure that she was willing me to speak, but my eyes stayed firmly on the road ahead and I kept my trap shut.

The second stop we made was at Glencoe Visitor Centre. I stayed with the Landy whilst Mallory went off and did what she needed to do. When I next caught sight of her, she was all red eyed and puffy; I was leaning with my arms folded, soaking up the early August sun.

She lifted her hands and rubbed them over her eyes. 'C'mon, breakfast is on me. The café should be open by now,' she called to me from the edge of the car park.

Deciding I could definitely eat, I jogged over to her and we made our way into the little café. I ordered bacon sandwiches and coffee, and we sat at a table by the window. We had a fantastic view of the mountains where they rose in their rugged splendour from the mossy ground and stretched towards the clouds like long-lost lovers, yearning to touch but unable to reach far enough.

As I sat there I began to compare my relationship with Mairi to the one Mallory had with Sam. I realised I'd been silent for a while and glanced up to find Mallory studying me with concern etched on her face.

Moving my gaze away from the view, I lifted my coffee cup but placed it down again with a sigh. 'You know, I'm kind of jealous of the relationship you had with Sam. And I don't mean because I have feelings for you or anything. I mean because of how intensely you loved each other.' Why I'd said the thing about feelings, God only knows. But it was out there so I waited to see what she'd say, if anything.

Her brow furrowed. 'It's clear to me that your love for Mairi was intense.'

Was it one-sided, though? Why was I suddenly thinking this way?

I heaved a sigh. 'The thing with Mairi was… she was adventurous. She was always looking for that next natural high. I supported her, of course I did, but since I lost her, I've often wondered how long it would have taken for her to move on anyway.' *Why am I saying this out loud? Why am I saying it* now?

'Greg, you can't think that way. I'm sure she loved you just the same.'

I was filled with doubt. 'It's just... The more I've looked back, since meeting you and witnessing how strong things were for you guys, the more I got to analysing my relationship. You see, Mairi was a good deal younger than me and, if I'm honest, I worry that maybe things were one-sided.'

The waitress chose that moment to bring our food and it gave me a chance to think about what I was saying. 'I think that all along I feared she'd leave. Her being killed like that almost suspends her in time. It makes me look at how wonderful things were. I'm happy in the Highlands. It's where I belong, where I feel safe and at home. Mairi was always looking to the horizon. I think it was niggling at the back of my mind all along that she might meet someone else on one of her trips. You know... someone who was a bit more adventurous, like her.' Sadness washed over me and Mallory just sat there listening intently.

She eventually reached across the table and grabbed my wrist. 'Greg, what you've suffered, what *we've* suffered is the worst possible thing that could happen to anyone in love. But... If you dwell on things you can never possibly know you'll drive yourself mad. At the end of the day no one truly knows what goes on in someone's mind. All you can do is focus on the wonderful times you shared and how you felt when you were with her. *That's* what's real. She chose *you*. Out of all the people she met on her travels and climbs, *you* were the one she came home to. *You* were the one she made plans with. That's the important thing. Everything else is... is conjecture. So stop trying to figure out who loved who more. It's not healthy. And it won't help you. Wondering what if never does, believe me.'

Of course she was totally right and I felt like a shit. 'Sorry. This day isn't about me. I'm waffling on.'

'No... no, it's fine. It helps to talk. But from the things you've said she loved you madly, Greg. Hold onto that.'

'You're right. What we had *was* real. I don't know why the insecurity's surfaced now. I think I'm... *scared*. I'm scared I'll never find it again, you know? What Mairi and I had, what you and Sam had... I *want* that again. I want to be a father and get married and all the usual stuff but I'm not exactly in my twenties anymore.' I forced a laugh, trying to lighten the mood.

The problem was, I'd recently made the terrible discovery that I wanted those things with *her*. With Mallory. It was a pointless hope and ridiculous considering how long I'd known her *and* what I knew of her situation. And I *had* loved Mairi with all of my broken, cynical, damaged heart.

Realising I'd poured a little too much of my heart

out, I added, 'Don't get me wrong, I would have married her after the first date. And all the emotions I felt... *feel*... are still real. Nothing can change that.'

She smiled warmly and squeezed my arm again. 'I know that. And you *can* still have all of that again. Don't give up hope. You know what they say... Love conquers all.'

My breath caught in my throat as she uttered the words that—unbeknownst to her—I had inked in Gaelic script on my chest. I was momentarily dumbstruck but eventually I recovered my composure. She was right yet again. But the fact remained, I felt torn in two, sitting here talking about my past with Mairi but desperately, and unreasonably, hoping for a future with the woman before me. Guilt at my renewed emotional betrayal began to needle at me from within as I was ever drawn to the stunning, compassionate blue gaze belonging to my friend across the table.

My *friend*.

Chapter Thirty-five

The Ardnamurchan peninsula had always been a favourite place of mine, and with the amber hues of the summer day glistening across it, the place came to life. After crossing the calm, mirror-like water of Loch Linnhe on the Corran car ferry, we drove on a little farther through the shadows that danced on the road, made by the sun casting its glow through the Douglas fir trees. We parked up and walked towards the water's edge at Loch Shiel where the Glenfinnan monument stood proudly peering out towards the famous viaduct.

Mallory asked to be alone and so I respected her wishes. I waited at the base of the monument as she walked over and sat on a huge, gnarled tree stump and hugged the urn close to her body. She delved into the pot and raised her hand in the air, letting the cloud of ashes fly free on the warm, gentle breeze. Her head dropped and her shoulders shuddered. I stood by feeling helpless and wishing I had the strength or supernatural ability to take away her pain but also knowing that she needed this time to be alone with her memories.

Eventually, with a tear-streaked face, she arrived by my side and we set off back towards the car. I silently slipped my arm around her shoulder in what I hoped was a comforting gesture. She nestled into my side, clearly needing the closeness of human contact. She was doing so well, and in a way, I admired her.

We spent lunchtime in a little pub by Fort Augustus. I was absolutely starving and ordered the steak pie. Mallory was distant throughout lunch and getting her to open up was difficult. I guessed the stop off at Glenfinnan had been emotionally draining.

The next stop was Fort Augustus itself, but we didn't stay long. Mallory was heartbroken when we strolled over the lock bridge stretching across the Caledonian canal to the ice-cream parlour that she had been to with Sam, only to discover it had changed use and in its place was a standard café. It was as if she couldn't get away fast enough.

After a quiet journey just listening to the music I had brought, Mallory gazed out of the window. I couldn't see her eyes but I was sure they were filled with sadness. I parked the Landy up at Eilean Donan Castle, which was perched on a spit of land stretching out into Loch Duich. The imposing structure fascinated me, and as Mallory walked up onto the footbridge, I took out my camera and began snapping away.

Trying to be as discreet as possible, I zoomed in on Mallory's face as her gaze trailed over the view beyond the loch. Watching her through the lens, I could see the pain in her eyes and the crease in her brow as the tears left glistening trails down her flushed cheeks. I clicked the shutter release without really thinking. Even in her grief she was beautiful. She had a warm heart that was filled with anguish, and in that moment, I knew I would do *anything* to help her find happiness. Even if it wasn't with me. Which it most likely wouldn't be. A fact I would have to get used to.

She began to walk away from the castle with her head down, and I made my way towards her. 'Hey, are you all right?'

'I'm okay. I found that bit so hard.' Her trembling lower lip and swollen eyes told me she was anything but okay.

I wrapped my arms around her and pulled her close. 'Hey, shhhh, it's okay. You've done so well. You've been so brave. I'm proud of you.' I kissed the top of her head and ran my hand over the waves of her thick, dark hair.

Poor wee girl.

We walked back to the car with our arms around each other. *Just friends.* I racked my brain for the right words but as usual nothing came to mind and so I stayed silent. We climbed back into the car and began the three-and-a-half-hour journey back to Clachan Seil. Mallory leaned against the window again, her eyes sometimes closed and sometimes trained on the heather-covered moors and rugged mountains beyond the glass.

'So, it's been a nice day, weather-wise, eh?' I said, keeping my eyes focused on the road ahead. Small talk was never my forte and here I was proving that fact by talking about the sodding weather. *Smooth as always, McBradden.*

Without moving her head, she replied, 'I really appreciate you bringing me, Greg. I think I would have hated to make the journey alone.'

'Aye, well, Josie would've come, surely?' I glanced across but she was still staring out of the window.

'She offered. I just thought that... well, *you* know how I feel about it all. You've lost someone you were in love with.' She raised her hand and swiped at a tear that had dared to escape.

Sadness washed over me and my heart squeezed for her... for us both. 'Well, that's true. I loved her more than anything.'

She turned in her seat and looked right at me with a determined gaze. 'And, Greg, all that stuff you said before about being unsure of her feelings for you... there's no point torturing yourself over that. You loved her. You maybe will never know the true depth of her feelings. So you just go with how *you* feel about *her*. What's the point in dwelling on whether she did or didn't love you the *same*?' Turning away again, she rested her head back against the glass.

She had a point.

Mallory eventually became very quiet, and I could tell by the steady rhythm of her breathing that she had fallen asleep. Every so often I glanced over at her and I became very much aware of the sense of protectiveness that was continuing to surface from deep within me. I was going to have to be extremely careful. I was already losing what was left of my heart to her.

*

I pulled up outside her cottage and switched off the engine. Leaning over, I gently squeezed her shoulder to rouse her from slumber and her eyelids fluttered open.

'Hey, sleepyhead. We're home,' I whispered.

Sitting up, she smoothed her hair and sheepishly lifted her eyes to meet mine. She smiled and opened the car door.

As she climbed down from the vehicle, she inhaled a lungful of the evening air. 'I won't invite you in, if you don't mind. I hope that's not unfair of me. I have a job to do before I go in. Then I just want to go to bed and cry myself to sleep.'

'Hey, no bother. You take care and give me a call if you need me, okay?' I hoped she knew that I sincerely meant that. I would be there for her no matter what time of day or night. The connection I felt to her, even if it was one-sided, was deepening with every passing day; and although the thought of unrequited love terrified me, it was a price I was willing to pay just to help her.

'Thanks again, Greg. I can't express how much today has meant to me.'

'You're very welcome. I'm glad I was able to help. Goodnight, sweet Mallory. Sleep well, eh?' She smiled and I started the engine, turned, and pulled away. As I drove, I saw her walking towards the bridge. Another of her special places.

In my heart I held onto the wish that someday the bridge could become more than a sad memory. More than somewhere to cry. I wanted, more than anything, for it to become her bridge of hope.

Chapter Thirty-six

During the following week Mallory and I shared a shift at the pub and she announced she was going down to Yorkshire to visit with Josie and Brad. My stomach knotted at the prospect of her deciding to stay there and not return, but I couldn't voice my worries. It would've been completely inappropriate in light of our recent journey. It was already August and I was dreading the following weeks. It was probably best that Mallory was going away. She didn't need to cope with her friend falling apart on her. I wished her a safe journey and kept my mouth shut about everything else.

I walked around in a daze for a few days. There were photos of Mairi strewn over every surface of my house, and I'd taken to drinking whisky again. Although I was no alcoholic, I knew I was walking a fine line and vowed that as soon as the anniversary was out of the way, things would change. I had hoped that the little beach memorial Mallory and I had shared would've made the anniversary of losing Mairi easier to deal with, but of course it didn't.

Then Mallory was due back in Clachan and I couldn't bear to see her. I was a mess. I'd worked one shift at the pub but Stella watched me with eagle eyes the whole time. Every so often I'd pull my brow in and say, 'Stella, I'm fine.' Of course, it was a blatant lie and she knew it.

To say I was confused was a total understatement. Here I was a year on from the death of the woman I loved, still grieving, but having all these intense feelings for someone who was incapable of loving me back. She just couldn't *see* me that way. And I couldn't blame her for that. I felt so guilty, as if I was betraying Mairi's memory by feeling *anything* for anybody else, let alone someone who was going through the *exact same thing* as me. How stupid could I be?

The answer? *Plenty* more fucking stupid.

*

I was due in at the pub and Mallory was going to be there too. But instead of rocking up for my shift, I grabbed a couple of bottles of whisky, my tent, and a sleeping bag and shoved it all in the car as quickly as I could before I could think about changing my mind. I put food and water down for Angus—this wasn't a trip he could take with me as I knew I wouldn't be able to keep an eye on him. I'd message Stella and get her to collect him—she wouldn't mind. Once the boot was secured, I climbed into the Landy, switched on the engine, and pulled out of my driveway.

August twentieth. Exactly a year since Mairi was declared dead.

One year of my life had passed since I lost her. One fucking year of pain, sorrow, and heartache. And all for what? All the rage I'd originally felt at her passing came back with a vengeance. I was angry at her for being so desperate to climb K2 that she would leave and never return. Did I mean so *little* to her? There was no real surprise that I doubted her feelings for me. Sam never would have abandoned Mallory to go off and do something like that. He would've put Mallory first.

As I drove I flicked through my music to find something to listen to – I needed something angry that I could scream along to. Something that would help me to express the pain of agonising and unnecessary loss. 'Without You', a song about lost love and mistakes by Hinder, echoed around the car and my heart ached as I tried to sing along and release the tension in my body. But as I continued on my journey, anger was replaced by sadness. Tension became a deep knot of despair that I felt right down to my bones. My stomach twisted as I focused on where I was driving to and why. Seether's 'Broken' became the anthem to my lonely journey because that was what I was... broken.

After a couple of hours, I pulled down the lane that led to the Buckle. The sun was beginning to set and the colours all around were changing from green to grey right before me. My heart ached as it always did when I saw the place where I met Mairi.

Pulling into the usual layby, I grabbed my sleeping bag and the whisky and dragged them under the bridge. Once I had left my sleeping bag there, I took the bottle of Lagavulin and walked down to the little rock that gave me the best view of the mountain, and there I sat watching the sunset cast shadows that mirrored the one hanging over me and my wounded heart.

The temperature dropped but thanks to the whisky I didn't really care. I kept on drinking in the hope that my pain would be numbed.

She was gone.

My beautiful, fearless, red-haired beauty with the musical laugh and big heart was gone. Lost on the snow-covered face of a giant monolith that most people would be incapable of taming. Mairi too had fallen foul of the beast that had claimed so many lives before hers. Her light had been snuffed out far too soon. Would we have lasted? Who can possibly know? All I *did* know, sitting there as the evening air chilled my damp cheeks, was that losing her was the hardest thing I'd ever endured. My unfaithful wife betraying me had stung, but the pain I had felt at losing the woman I had dared to give my fragile heart to was a physical pain like nothing else.

As the alcohol continued to reach every nerve ending, my thoughts became disjointed and fuzzy.

'I miss you, Mallory,' I slurred. 'I miss you so *fucking* much.' Even in my drunken stupor I realised my mistake and fresh anger broke free from within. 'Fuck! Mairi. I mean *Mairi*. Fuck, fuck, *FUCK*!' The scream ripped from my chest as I picked up the empty bottle beside me and launched it across the road, hearing it shatter into a million tiny pieces and along with it went my last shred of hope.

Leaning forward, I picked up the second bottle and broke the seal; swigging down the amber liquid and feeling it burn as it made the fast journey to my rolling, empty stomach. My sobs rent the night air and I was past caring. If there were others around, they'd be unlikely to approach me and I doubted that anyone would care enough to call the police.

'Why?' was the next question to be thrown out into the universe as loud as my raw throat would allow. It was a clichéd question, but I wished I knew the answer nevertheless. I became silent again and noticed a set of headlights slowly travelling towards me. *Oh, fuck. Police.*

I heard a door slam but I was too far gone to worry. Everything echoed and seemed unreal now. When I moved my head, the scenery followed on a split second after. It took lots of effort to open my eyes again once I blinked them shut.

I was suitably numb.

I thought I heard someone calling out my name but decided it was just a dream and so I stayed silent. I didn't want or *need* to be rescued. I just wanted to be alone.

Alone.

A word I no doubt would have to become accustomed to, seeing as my past relationships had always rendered me that way. Perhaps it was my destiny.

'Greg!' came the voice again. I chuckled to myself, thinking my ability to conjure up Mallory's voice was amazing considering the state of my mind. Something very bright stung at my eyes, making me flinch. *What the fuck?* I dropped my head forward and closed my eyes again as footsteps approached me.

'Greg. Are you okay?' a worried voice asked.

I didn't speak, still unsure whether she was a figment of my warped, alcohol-addled mind.

Something touched my chin, and my head tilted back involuntarily. 'Greg, it's me, Mallory.'

I made the effort to open my eyes a little and stared up into the bright blue eyes of a beautiful Yorkshire lass.

With her face highlighted by a torch, I could see the worry in her eyes, and I frowned. 'Mallory?' Was it really her? 'Oh, aye, Mallory, my bestest friend in the world, Mallory, Mallory.'

She tugged the bottle from my hand. 'Oh, Greg, you silly, *silly* sod. What have you done?'

Smiling up at her as innocent as could be, I told her, 'Ahhhhad a wee drinky. In memory of my wee lassie. She's dead, you know.'

She sighed. 'Yes, Greg, I know. Come on, let's get

you home. We'll collect your car tomorrow, eh?'

What? No way. I was staying put. 'Fuck off!' I flapped my arms around aimlessly. I must've looked a complete arse. 'You just fuck the fuck away. I'm stayin' here with my Mairi.'

'Oy, don't swear at me.' She grabbed my arm and wrapped it around her neck. Struggling to lift my heavy frame, she eventually dragged me to a standing position. 'You can't stay here, not in this state.'

Swaying rather a lot, I somehow managed to feel guilty for my use of colourful language. 'Aham shorry, Mallilly. I don't mean to swear at you. You're my best friend, you know that?'

'Yes, Greg, so you said. Now come on. You're going to feel like shit in the morning and I need to get you home. You've had me worried sick,' she snapped through gritted teeth as her nostrils flared. I'd never seen her this angry before. There was no doubt about it; I'd *really* pissed her off. That and the fact that she too had sworn suddenly made me laugh, and I told her of her misdemeanour.

'Sorry for swearing, Greg, now come on. You can't stay here. It's a car park, not a campsite.'

We staggered – well, *I* staggered as Mallory tried to stop me from falling – back towards the Landy. Suddenly overcome with a deep sense of loss again, I turned to face the mountain. The moon now highlighted the crevices and striations of its surface.

‘I met her there on that wee path. I’d been out walking and I was on my way back to the car. She dropped her map and tripped over her laces trying to pick it up… I caught her.’ It was a lucid moment where the alcohol in my system evidently ceased to affect me briefly, and I turned to gaze into Mallory’s eyes. ‘She was so beautiful, Mally, so beautiful. Long, red hair, green eyes.’ I felt a tear spill over and crawl down my cheek but I didn’t wipe it away. With a trembling lip I continued. ‘I miss her so much. I don’t want to be alone. I hate it.’

In that moment all the sorrow I was feeling erupted and another sob broke free. This time I was aware that I sounded lost and helpless. My body shuddered with grief as Mallory pulled me into her arms and let me cry. I nestled my damp face into her neck and inhaled the comforting floral scent of her hair as my tears subsided.

Pulling away, I met her eyes. They glinted in the moonlight. Unreadable emotions crossed her features and I felt sure there was something there; something *more* than friendship. My gaze trailed down her face and landed upon her lips. I needed to taste her. To feel her mouth on mine. And so I lowered my face and kissed her.

For a split second it felt as though she was going to open her mouth and let me in, but she pulled away and glared at me with confusion. ‘Greg, no! What are you *doing*?’ She stepped away and my heart sank.

Realising what I'd just done, I touched my lips. I could still feel her there. 'Shit. I'm sorry, Mallory, I – I don't know why I did that.'

She responded in a less-than-cordial tone. 'No, neither do I. Let's just forget about it. Come on. You need to get home to bed.' She helped me over to the car and opened the door.

I bent myself almost double climbing into the tiny space and peered up at her through my blurry eyes. 'You're mad with me. *Please* don't be mad with me. I couldn't help myself, I really couldn't. I'm sorry. I know you don't see me that way.'

I *was* sorry. But I was only sorry *because* she didn't see me that way.

Chapter Thirty-seven

The car rolled along and so did my fragile, alcohol-filled stomach. I couldn't appreciate the way the silver of the moonlight danced on the streams and lochs as we passed them by. My head was already thumping, giving me a wee glimpse of the way I would feel after I'd slept. *Fucking idiotic knobhead.*

After about two hours Mallory pulled onto the driveway of my house. I seemed to have lost all cognitive thought process and muscle function by this point, and Mallory virtually had to carry me up the stairs to my room, which – considering my height and weight – was no mean feat.

She helped me onto the bed and I wanted to pull her down with me, but thankfully my brain functioned sufficiently to remind me that she wouldn't like it and would more than likely slap me. She tugged at my boots and flung them under the bed before pulling the duvet over my fully clothed body.

'Mallory?' I whispered through my croaky, dry throat.

Mallory sat beside me on the bed. 'Yes?'

'I'm not sorry.'

She frowned. 'Not sorry about what?'

'For kissing you.' I watched through bleary eyes as she stood, shook her head, and switched off the light before leaving me there.

*

The next thing I was completely aware of was my bedroom door opening. I was sprawled across the bed on my stomach, and the room did a funny sideways jolt when I opened my eyes. I felt someone stroking my hair and thought to myself how nice it felt. But when the scent of Mallory's perfume drifted into my nose, I sat bolt upright – then glanced down and saw my dick on full display. I covered myself quickly as she blushed bright pink.

'Shit-fuck! Mallory!' My head swam and my heart pounded. I felt like death on a stick. I covered my eyes as the room swivelled.

'Are you okay? I was so worried when you took off yesterday. You were in a state when I found you.'

I opened my eyes and met her concerned gaze. 'I'm okay... I think. Sorry to worry you. I don't know what happened. I remember bits of it. Did I... did I... *kiss* you?' I cringed as I waited for the answer I knew was coming. Once she confirmed that I had, in fact, gone *there*, I felt ten times worse and apologised profusely.

She then went on to tell me that I had told her I

wasn't sorry for what I'd done. God, I was an arsehole when I was pissed. I glanced down at my naked form and then it hit me. *She bloody undressed me, didn't she?*

'Did you...?' I gestured down at my privates. 'Did you... take my clothes—?'

'God no!' she snapped. 'I took your boots off and pulled the covers over you. You must have got up and done the rest.'

Fucking knobbing idiot. I mentally slapped myself around the head. 'Regardless of what I said last night, I *am* sorry. Please forgive me.'

She pursed her lips and did her best to keep her eyes fixed above my waistline. 'Look, Greg, it's difficult for me to sit here talking to you when you're naked. I'll go and put the kettle on. You get a quick shower and come down when you're ready.'

She walked out of the room and I slammed my fists into the mattress, muttering expletives at myself. I got out of bed and took my naked self into the shower. As the hot water cascaded over my tender body, I thought things through to see how much more I could remember of the night before. The answer was not a whole lot.

The problem was, as I ran my hands down my body, I closed my eyes and imagined she was there with me and that *her* fingers were the ones lathering my chest, biceps, and stomach. I could still smell her perfume and see her face as her eyes locked on mine. If only she wanted me. If only I could let go of Mairi and tell

Mallory that I wanted *her*. But it would do no good.

My body ached for her and I leaned on the wall with one hand as my other drifted down my body and I wished I could take her to my bed and make love to her; feel her soft curves beneath me safe in the knowledge that she felt the same way I did. But of course she didn't and the fantasy was all I would ever have.

Why the hell was I feeling this way? It was too soon and I knew it, really. Why couldn't I let it go? Maybe it was just mixed-up feelings of grief and loneliness? I turned the stream of water around to the cold setting to douse the flames burning within me and jerked my hand away from my body, slapping my palm hard against the tiled wall.

Once I'd dried off I pulled on some lounge pants and dragged the towel through my wet hair. Nervously I made my way downstairs and found Mallory in the kitchen making coffee. Guilt washed over me as I remembered the thoughts I'd been having in the shower. I smiled but she turned away.

I walked over, came to a stop right behind her, and kissed the top of her head. Maybe I should fucking go for it. What did I have to lose? Her friendship? Well, being friends wasn't all it was cracked up to be when one of you felt something more.

She turned to face me with her lips slightly parted, in surprise at my intimate gesture, no doubt. *What am I doing?* Her eyes left mine and trailed down to my damp chest, and she licked her lips, sparking a new flicker of hope within me.

'I *am* sorry I kissed you,' I whispered.

'Y-yes, you said.' Confusion clouded her eyes.

I didn't know what the hell I was doing as I stood there, gazing down at her. Willing her to see me. *Really* see me.

With a wave of sadness, I stroked my fingers tenderly down her cheek. 'But... I'm only sorry because I know you don't feel the way I do. If I thought for a second you felt the same...'

A crease appeared in her brow again and she shook her head. 'I – I don't understand.'

Why don't you fucking understand? Why? I felt my jaw clenching over and over. 'Mallory, do I have to spell it out for you? I've wanted you since the first time I laid eyes on you in the pub. That's why I was so angry and unpleasant. I was still grieving. I shouldn't have felt that way, but I couldn't help it.' *Oh, God, it's out there now. No going back. Shit.*

With a voice laced with sadness, she reminded me that I'd told her I was happy being just friends. *She's right. I did say that. I'm a lying arsehole.* Her cheeks had flushed bright pink and I wanted nothing more than to wrap my arms around her and kiss her; but instead I tucked a stray lock of dark hair behind her ear.

'I tolerate being only friends. If I'm completely honest, I want more. *Much* more. I'm sorry, but it's the truth. Can't you find room for me in your heart?' *Please say yes. Please.*

Her hands clenched and flexed beside her as if she was fighting with her feelings for me.

I *willed* her to just give in. I could see it... or something... in her eyes. I know she wanted me then. I *know* she did.

But in a small, fragile voice she said, 'I can't, Greg, it's not right.' Her eyes closed and her chin tilted upwards. Her body was betraying the words she'd spoken. She was silently asking to be kissed – but I wouldn't do it. Not like this. Not when she'd said no. I'm a man, not a monster. Mixed in amongst the desire she clearly felt was fear.

Fear.

I'd made her afraid and it made me want to throw up. So much for not being a fucking monster. In that moment I hated myself.

Her eyes sprang open and she gazed up at me in confusion.

Through gritted teeth I told her, 'I know... You don't have to worry. I won't say anything again.' I was physically shaking with anger at myself and regret at my reckless actions. I stepped away. 'You'd maybe better go.' I could hear the edge in my voice and I knew she'd think I was angry at *her*, but I did nothing to stop it. It was maybe better this way.

'Greg, please, I'm still grieving. It's too soon. Please

don't be upset with me. I couldn't bear to lose you.' Her voice was wavering as she pleaded with me, and a sob broke free as she covered her mouth.

But like a heartless bastard I glared at her coldly and with menace. 'I'm clearly not yours to lose, now, am I? And you're not mine. Just go.'

With a trembling lip and tears streaming down her face, she dashed to the door. But before she opened it, she turned to face me again. 'Greg, you are my closest friend here. If I don't have you, then I may as well go home, back to Yorkshire.'

'I don't do ultimatums.'

She sobbed as she pleaded with me, 'Please don't be like this.'

With an aching inside me that mirrored the expression on her face, I shook my head. 'Mallory. We've reached an impasse. I want what you can't give. Enough said. It's over. I can't pretend to be just friends with you anymore. Now for fuck's sake just go!'

Chapter Thirty-eight

I could hear Mallory sobbing as she ran to her car. It was as if she couldn't get away from me fast enough, and I couldn't blame her. I slammed my fist into the wall, causing pain to radiate up my arm and tears to spring from my eyes. *What the hell have I done? She was pretty much my only real friend and now she hates me and I deserve it.*

Hand throbbing, I glanced out of the window again and realised she hadn't left. *Shit! Do I go out to her? Maybe if I explain... Explain what, you fucking prick?* But as I deliberated, the engine of her little car roared to life and she sped off, spewing up a cloud of dust behind her. *Oh, God, please let her drive carefully. I couldn't bear it if... if what? If I lost her?* I'd already managed to do that.

After everything she'd been through and after everything *she'd* done for *me*, how could I have been so cruel? Maybe I was the bastard people usually took me for. Maybe eventually we become our reputations. Well, I was living up to mine now.

My mind began to torture me with memories of the selfless and thoughtful things she had done for me. The memorial, the chalkboard, the birthday gift, hell, just being a friend. God, the way she had looked that night at the beach. All I'd wanted to do was hold and kiss her, and at the time I'd felt guilty because I was there to say goodbye to Mairi. But the more I thought about it, the more I realised I couldn't do anything to bring Mairi back. She was *gone*. I wanted Mallory to be my future, but I spoiled things at every possible opportunity.

Pacing up and down the room, I knew I had to do something. There was no way I could leave things as they were. She was special to me and I *had* to make her see that. I'd lied when I said I didn't want to be friends. If that was all she had to offer me, then I'd take it. I'd grab it with both hands and cling on with all my might to whatever it was that meant she was still in my life. I couldn't quite believe I'd been so idiotic. What had I expected her to say really? She was faithful to Sam to the last, and it would be so very difficult for her to let anyone else in after suffering such a blow. How could I not accept that?

Anger boiled beneath my skin and I wanted to smash things. I wanted to beat myself up. But there was no point in that. Doing that wouldn't make things right. I stomped over to the stereo and hit the random selection. Maybe music would help me to calm down. Maynard Keenan's voice floated through the air and into my auditory senses as he sang '3 Libras'. No two people interpreted lyrics the same, and I was pretty sure his rendition while he was part of 'A Perfect Circle' was the most intriguing. But as I listened I was struck again by the way song spoke to me. And a light bulb flicked on in my mind.

Music.

I would explain to her using music. Okay, it was possibly the most clichéd thing I could think of doing but it worked for teenagers back in the eighties when mix tapes were all the rage. And the 'A Perfect Circle' track was the perfect one to begin with.

Grabbing a blank CD from the pile on the floor, I set up the system to transfer my selection onto a disc for Mallory. There were so many songs I could choose to express my feelings, but I had the perfect list in my mind and so, as all those teenagers had once done, I began to tell her how I felt. The whole truth.

'Walking After You' by the Foo Fighters came after '3 Libras'. I wanted her to know that I wouldn't give up on her despite my stupid words. I would do everything I could to make up for my mistakes – and I'd made so many. But she needed to know I was sorry and that I wouldn't let her go from my life so readily.

'How to Save a Life' by The Fray was the third track. Although I knew the story behind the lyrics for the track, I hoped she would read into them something more relevant to us. Something that let her know I wished I could go back in time and stop her suffering. Even if it meant her still being with Sam. All I wanted was her happiness. She had come along and saved *me*. I wanted to save *her* too.

Nickelback was a band that always managed to express deep emotions in its poetry, and 'Far Away' was no different. I chose it as the fourth track. The song told her exactly how I felt in words that I could never find the courage to say myself. I was terrified she'd run away back to Yorkshire as she had threatened. I didn't want the distance between us. I wanted her to stay here. Where her smile could brighten my day and where we could laugh and joke behind the bar as we used to. I chewed on the inside of my cheek as I listened to the words. I'd stopped worrying about wiping away the tears that came. I was alone and so what did it matter? I'd never been so fucking emotional. What she did to me…

Finally, it had to be 'The Reason' by Hoobastank. Honestly, the words could've been written by me for her. She couldn't fail to understand what I was trying to communicate. I desperately hoped she would listen to the CD to the end. This track sent shivers down my spine. If there was a reason for me to change, *she* was it.

Once the CD was finished, I scribbled on it and stuck it in an envelope along with a note that read:

Mallory

Once again, I have proved myself

unworthy of your friendship and most definitely of anything else. Since meeting you I appear to have lost the ability to communicate my feelings like an adult. In fact, I'm not sure I ever could. I made you cry again, which makes me sick to my stomach. Please listen to the tracks on the CD. Hopefully they will explain a lot better than I can. Your friend, always, Greg.

I grabbed my car keys and climbed into the Landy. I was debating whether to knock and hand it to her or just stick it through the letterbox. I decided on the latter, feeling that it was unlikely she would want to see me, let alone converse with me.

Pulling up outside her cottage, I took deep breaths to try and calm my jangling nerves. *I'm doing the right thing here, aren't I? Yes... yes, definitely.* My heart thundered in my chest and I could hear the blood thrumming in my ears. I was pretty much on the verge of a heart attack. I climbed out of the car and then stumbled over my own feet as I walked the short distance to the front door. As I stood there shaking, the hand holding the envelope hovering by the slot in the door, the rain began to fall. Glancing up at the sky, I allowed the cooling droplets to cover my skin. And with one final reaffirming breath I pushed the envelope inside and released it from my grip.

The deed was done. Now I had to wait. I returned home to Angus, who wagged his tail lazily as I walked in. Poor wee lad. I'd been a blubbering wreck all morning and we hadn't even been out for a walk. I called to him and we set out.

He covered twice my distance, running back and forth with his tongue lolling out of the side of his mouth. Such an easy, carefree life.

When we arrived at the bridge over the Atlantic, I stopped and glanced towards Mallory's cottage. I wondered what she was doing. Was she listening to the CD? The rain was getting faster now and I pictured her sitting there, listening and getting angrier and angrier at me for telling her how I felt through other people's words. But I had no other choice.

Angus and I carried on walking for over an hour until we returned back home soaked to the skin. It was gone two and so I made myself a sandwich and proceeded to stare at it lying there on the plate. I couldn't bring myself to eat. My stomach was in knots.

Why hadn't she called? Even if it was to tell me to fuck off. Had she gone already? Maybe the CD had pushed her over the edge and she'd gone back to Yorkshire after all.

Oh, God, I couldn't bear it.

At least Angus enjoyed the beef sandwich I'd made. He licked his lips and drooled all over the kitchen floor as I broke it up and fed it to him. Once he'd finished, I scratched his head and he followed me through to the lounge, where I switched on the TV. There was some chat show on about unrequited love... switched that off... a news report about emigration... switched that off... a romantic film where you just *knew* the guy would get the girl. *Fuck!* The TV was *not* an option. I drummed my fingers on the sofa and glanced at the clock.

Almost four and no word.

I stood with determination and walked over and hit play on my own copy of the CD I had made. I had to check that I hadn't given her the wrong impression in my choices. But as I listened, more tears spilled over my sore eyes, trailing damp lines down my face that leaked into my mouth. I could taste the salt where it rested.

I had to go to her.

Chapter Thirty-nine

The rain was really hammering down and even though I'd dried out in the house from my earlier jaunt, as soon as I walked to my car again I was completely soaked. The water felt soothing as it seeped through my clothing and I stood there, head towards the heavens, and let myself be cleansed.

After I had parked the car outside the pub I made a quick detour inside to drop Angus with Stella. I gave a brief explanation that I needed to be somewhere and she gave me a knowing roll of her eyes before disappearing through to the back with my furry pal. Once outside the pub again I took a deep calming breath, gathered my scattered thoughts and jogged down to Mallory's cottage. I hammered on the door, stepped back, and waited. I could hear music coming from inside.

Shit. She's listening to the CD now.

The door flung open and there she stood, my beautiful friend, her red-rimmed eyes brimming with tears ready to join the ones already leaving damp trails down her face. My God, even in a state of raw emotion she was stunning.

I breathlessly told her, 'I couldn't wait any longer. It's

been hours. I was scared you'd packed up and gone.' Without giving her time to protest, I stepped into the cottage and swept her up into my arms as 'The Reason' played in the background. She *had* listened all the way to the end. *Thank you, God.*

Pulling away slightly, I kissed her forehead. 'I'm sorry. I'm so sorry,' I murmured expecting her to push me away; but instead she pulled me closer despite my sodden clothing.

She eventually pulled away and gazed up into my eyes. 'Don't hurt me like that again, Greg, please.' She said I looked at her with hate. But she was so wrong.

Taking her face in my trembling hands, I stared deeply into her glistening blue eyes. 'I could *never* hate you. It's *me* that I hate. I'll never, *ever* be so stupid again, I promise. I'm such an idiot. I care about you so much. I would never want to hurt you, *ever*. I just don't know what else to do, Mallory. I... I love you *so much*... I don't *care* anymore if it's wrong... All I care about is you. If friends are what we are, then that's what we are. I'll get used to it, I promise I will.' *Oh, God help me, I'm rambling like an idiot.* I pulled her into my arms again. 'I can't be without you in my life. I said some *terrible* things. Can you forgive me? The songs were meant to make you understand, not make you cry.' Taking her face between my hands once again, I paused for breath, my chest heaving. I caught her tears and wiped them away. 'I want to kiss you so badly right now...' *Whoops.* 'Oh, God, I just said that out loud, didn't I?' I closed my eyes and waited for the fallout.

She pulled me down so that my forehead rested on hers. 'So do it.'

Huh? Great, now my mind's playing tricks on me. 'What?'

'Kiss me, Greg.'

With a strangled sound releasing from my throat, I crushed my lips against hers, slipped my hands into her hair, and grasped at her, not quite believing this was happening. She tasted so good. *This has to be a cruel dream. It has to be.* But I didn't dare break the spell as my tongue wrapped around hers in a magical, sensual dance of love. Because despite trying to fight it, that was what it was for me.

Love.

She gripped my shoulders and tugged at my hair as if she couldn't get close enough. I wanted her. Desperately. But I was terrified of ruining things, so I pulled away and we both gasped for breath. My gaze flicked from her eyes down to her swollen lips.

She placed a hand on either side of my face and peered into my eyes and into my soul. 'Greg... I *do* see you.' My heart skipped when I heard her chosen words. The meaning was loud and clear to me and I knew she was referring to a line in '3 Libras'. Knowing that she had listened so intently and heard exactly what I was trying to convey, I couldn't resist taking her mouth in another delicious, deep kiss.

*

We eventually moved over to the couch and sat snuggled together. Just the feel of her so close to me filled me with something I can only describe as elation.

This was it. This was *us*.

Well, we were close to becoming an *us*. But I wasn't going to rush it. I had to make sure things were going at *her* pace. And there was no rush needed anyway. If I had my way, we'd have all the time in the world to discover each other. Right at that very moment all's I wanted to do was to kiss and hold her and relish in the closeness of her body to mine. Every so often she gazed up at me and I kissed her head or her nose. I could hardly believe this was happening, and the tiny seed of useless hope I'd had all along began to grow inside me as the possibility of a future with this amazing woman became tangible.

We mostly sat in silence and I stroked my fingers up and down her arm, loving how her skin quivered beneath my touch. Admittedly there was nothing I wanted more than to carry her up the stairs to her bedroom, lay her down, and make love to her all night, but I had to keep calm and know that those things *would* happen. I just had to be patient.

But, my God, patience was something I would struggle with. I knew this just by the way my body reacted to her every sigh or movement where our bodies touched so innocently. Thinking back, I tried to remember when I'd last had this feeling of desperation to claim someone as my own. To make the most of every single second. Had I felt this way with Mairi? Maybe I had, but I couldn't bring it to mind. This all felt so new. So necessary. It wasn't just a feeling of lust. As I trailed my gaze over her relaxed features, I was overcome by a sense of need.

I *needed* her.

Fuck.

The realisation both excited and terrified me. I was a fiercely independent man. In fact my independence verged on the antisocial but here I was desperate to not be alone for once, with this gorgeous, caring, sexy woman in my arms; and I was having to fight my masculine, caveman-like urges to make her mine, waiting be damned. What if she suddenly realised she'd made a mistake? Shit, I'd fall apart, I just knew it. I tenderly stroked my hand down her cheek, and she closed her eyes as she nuzzled even closer.

She dozed off in my arms and I watched her sleeping for about an hour, taking the time to study her face and neck, the curve of her breasts and the sweep of her waist. I wasn't helping myself on the taking-it-slow front and I was relieved when she awoke. She apologised for being asleep but I told her I'd enjoyed looking at her. It was true.

Her gaze flicked around the room and she knotted her fingers in her lap. 'So… what happens now?'

Pulling her close, I cupped her cheek. 'Well, that's up to you. We take things at your pace. When you feel you want to move forward, we do, until then it's whatever you want it to be.'

Biting her lip, she confessed, 'I… I'm scared of making huge mistakes… I'm scared of being judged… I'm scared of judging myself and being disappointed that I didn't give myself time.'

'Then time is what you'll have. Mallory, earlier today was… I felt so happy just being *with* you. Kissing you was… wow… not what I expected. I'm so terrified you'll regret it and that's why I didn't try to…' I hoped she knew what I meant when my words trailed off.

Her lips turned up in a sweet smile. 'I know, and I can't tell you how much I appreciated that.' She sat upright, trailing her gaze over my face, and her cheeks flushed.

Oh, no. She's regretting it already. 'What? What's wrong?' I couldn't hide the panic from my voice.

'N-nothing… I was just thinking… never mind.' The colour of her cheeks intensified and she twisted her hands together.

I gently placed my finger under her chin and lifted her face so that her eyes would meet mine. 'If you need to say something, please just say it. Don't leave me wondering. I'm terrified here.' I smiled, trying to make light of the situation.

'It's silly really... I was just seeing you through fresh eyes, I guess. You're an incredibly good-looking man, you know?' She smiled nervously and relief flooded my body. *Thank goodness.* I felt my own cheeks heat at her words. It was wonderful that she found me attractive because I really, *really* found *her* attractive. It was like a magnetic pull for me.

I knew she was scared of what the people around us would think about our budding romance, but I also knew that the people in the village had really taken to her. All they wanted was for her to be happy and for her to stay. We chatted about her fears and I hoped she believed what I was saying. People really *wouldn't* judge her at all. They'd be shocked she'd chosen a grumpy arse like *me* and would be more likely to judge her on her *choice* of man rather than the fact that she had *chosen* to be with *someone.*

I felt her body relax and the tension leave her. She climbed onto my lap and rested her forehead on mine. The sensation where our bodies touched was one of intense pleasure and I groaned. She began to kiss me and as she leaned even closer, she ground herself into me. I don't think she was doing it on purpose – it was just her natural movements as we kissed – but I hardened beneath her and the contact and friction were sending my heart into frenzy. I grasped her arse, pulling her even closer, and as the kisses became more and more urgent I could feel my desire taking over.

I had to stop it.

Lifting her from my lap, I placed her down on the couch and moved away. Glancing back at her, I saw the hurt in her eyes. She thought I'd rejected her. *Oh, no, no, you've got it wrong, sweetheart.*

'What... what's wrong, Greg?' Her voice was a strangled whisper. I stood and walked over to the fireplace and rested my hands there, dropping my head. Breathing deeply, I willed my thudding heart to calm and my prominent arousal to subside.

'I... I have to stop now; before we go too far. You're not ready... We need to be careful not to rush things. I don't want to lose you... I can't lose *you* too.' I knew it was the right thing to do. For *her*. I heard her get up and held my breath, wondering what she was going to do. Ask me to leave? Instead she slipped her arms around me and rested her head on my back. I released the breath steadily.

Turning around, I enveloped her in my embrace once again, and she tilted her face up to mine. I gazed into her mesmerizing azure eyes and inhaled deeply for courage. 'Just promise me one thing.'

She reached up and kissed my chin. 'Anything.'

'If you have second thoughts about us, or if I'm taking things at the wrong speed, even if I'm going too slowly, please talk to me. Don't shut me out. I couldn't cope with that, Mallory. I'm afraid I'm in love with you… deeply in love with you. I'm not sure how you feel about me right now. I'm not asking you to tell me. I just hope that we have a chance at a future.' Inwardly I cringed. There I was on one hand saying we'd take things slow and on the other telling her my innermost feelings. *Sheesh!*

Her brow creased and I feared the worst again. 'I… Can you give me some time? I have so many feelings whizzing around my head right now that I just can't make sense of them. But please know that I *do* have feelings.'

As I smiled down at her, my heart melted. I felt a small crack appear in the façade of my burgeoning hope but did my best to ignore it. *Give her time, McBradden. Just give her time.* I forced a warm expression and told her, 'That will tide me over.'

Chapter Forty

We went back to snuggling on the couch and sharing a bottle of wine. We talked about all sorts of stuff: our childhoods, our friends – or lack thereof, in my case. Watching her delicious mouth as she spoke had me wanting her lips on mine again and again and every time we made eye contact I felt a jolt of excitement that had desire unfurling low in my abdomen. The fact that she smiled so often throughout our conversation gave me a warm glow. Or it could've been the alcohol... No, who was I trying to kid? It was *definitely* Mallory.

Glancing over at the clock, I realised it was almost the middle of the night. Placing my glass down on the floor, I said the words that I knew would make my heart sink. 'I really should go.'

She slid her body closer to mine and stroked her fingers down my stubbled face. 'You could stay.' My body was screaming, *Yes, yes! Hell, yes!* But I reminded her that we had agreed to take things slowly. And if I stayed, there was no guarantee that I could stick to that promise.

'We could just hold each other and stay clothed,' she suggested.

My will was weakening, but I had to make one last attempt to do the right thing. 'I'll stay, but why don't I sleep in the spare room?'

She grasped my hands in hers and pleaded with me with her eyes. 'Look, I don't want to be alone. Today… in fact this last month has been a whirlwind. I don't want you to go. Why don't we just sleep in the same bed and stay clothed?'

So much for my firm resolve. I let her take my hand and lead me up the stairs. She disappeared into the bathroom and closed the door. Running my hands over my face, I inhaled and exhaled a shaking breath. Removing my T-shirt and socks, I awaited her return with a pounding heart. I had *no clue* how this whole thing would pan out, but what my head and my heart wanted were two *completely* different things; both led by my feelings for her. I was standing by the bed when she returned looking so damn cute in a pair of white pyjamas – all virginal and innocent. I knew she wasn't a virgin, but there was a definite air of innocence around her.

With her eyes fixed on mine, she walked around the bed and pulled the covers back. Taking it as an invite, I climbed in and lay down, holding my arm out to her. She climbed in beside me and snuggled into me for a moment before we rolled to face each other. I stroked her cheek gently and whispered a heartfelt, 'I love you.' A tear slipped from her eye and trailed down her flushed face into her hair as she traced my tattoo with her fingertips. Leaning forward, she kissed me there on my chest, and I inhaled the scent of her shampoo as my heart rate increased and my body sprang to life once more.

'Can I kiss you one last time before you go to sleep?' I would have to get a handle on my body's reaction to her. Otherwise I'd be constantly walking around with my hands in front of my jeans. The muscles of my thighs tightened as I imagined her tongue caressing mine. God, what she did to me.

She didn't answer. Instead she pulled me towards her and took my mouth with hers. She kissed me with such passion and I found it hard to resist taking things further as she pressed her soft body into my hardness. I could feel her heart pounding against my own and her breathing accelerating too. She pulled away and gazed into my eyes one last time before snuggling into me and falling asleep. I inhaled deeply and closed my eyes, willing my own heart to calm. Being so close to her was hard… pardon the pun… and not acting on my instincts was damn near killing me; but I had so much to lose if I rushed her.

Think of anything else, McBradden… anything but how close she is and the fact that all there is between you is a thin layer of white cotton…

*

I was woken by a vibrating sensation around my groin, which was rather alarming to say the least. Realising I hadn't taken my phone out of my jeans pocket, I struggled to retrieve it, determined not to wake the sleeping beauty beside me. I slipped out from under the duvet and she murmured and rolled over. Her buttons had popped open, giving me a wonderful view of her stomach and part of her breast. My mouth watered a little and I fought the urge to climb back in beside her to free her from her pyjamas altogether, seeing as the vibrations had stopped.

My fantasy was rudely interrupted as no sooner had they stopped than the vibrations started again. I pulled on my T-shirt and tiptoed out of the bedroom and down the stairs. It wasn't a number I recognised, so I figured it might have been something to do with Mairi.

I reached the kitchen and answered. 'Hello?'

'Greg?'

Scrunching my brow, I replied, 'Who is this?'

'Aww, forgotten me already, have you? Maybe your new *girlfriend* is taking up too much space in your brain.'

Alice. Fuck.

'What do you know about my new girlfriend?' I asked in a harsh whisper.

She giggled and it sent a shiver of displeasure down my spine. 'I didn't, but you've just confirmed you *have* one. You still living in the arsehole of the world?'

Bitch. 'I *love* this place and I'd rather you didn't call it that,' I informed her in a less-than-cordial tone.

'Sorry, I was only kidding around. You're so easy to wind up. Listen, I've been thinking about you. I wondered if we could get together and... you know... talk?'

'Alice, I have nothing to say to you.'

'Really? We *are* still married, you know. I'm your *wife*, Greg. Don't you think it might be worth talking about *that* fact? Or is your *girlfriend* completely *fine* that she's seeing a married man?'

I fell silent. *Oh, great.*

'Oooh, she doesn't *know*, does she?' Her voice was now tinged with mischief.

'Look, Alice. Can't you just leave me to get on with my life? Haven't you done enough to ruin things for me already?'

'I don't want to ruin your life, Greg. I just think we have unresolved issues that we need to discuss, and I think you need to tell your girlfriend that you're married.'

I could feel my future with Mallory slipping away from me. 'What do you suggest we do?'

'I suggest I come to see you. We need to talk things through and decide a way forward.'

I snorted derisively at her choice of words. 'The only way forward, Alice, is *divorce*.'

There was a silent pause for a few moments. 'I can't

say I'm surprised to hear you say that, but I do think we need to talk. Things were left on such a bad note.'

'You *think*?' God, she was good at stating the fucking obvious. 'We won't be friends, Alice. That ship sailed many years ago.'

She sighed down the line. 'I'd like you to forgive me. And I hope that if we can talk, we can work towards that.'

'Whatever.' My jaw automatically clenched and I flared my nostrils. 'When are you thinking of coming?'

'Soon. Very soon, in fact. I'll sort the arrangements and let you know.'

'Well, I can't say I'm looking forward to seeing you, Alice.'

'Let's just talk, okay? At least give me a chance?'

'A chance to make up more lies?'

'No. No, I won't do that. Look... you were the best thing that ever happened to me. I went about things all wrong, but I never stopped loving you. I have so many regrets, Greg. I just want the chance to make it up to you.'

'That's not possible. Look, we'll talk when you get here.'

'Okay. And, Greg?'

'What?'

'You need to tell your girlfriend about us.'

'There *is* no *us*,' I informed her before hanging up and throwing my phone onto the table, where it landed with a thud.

Chapter Forty-one

Mallory almost floated into the room with a heart-stopping smile on her face. 'Hey, you.'

She sashayed towards me where I sat at her kitchen table. Her cheeks had a pink glow and seeing her so happy made a deep sadness settle over me. 'Hey, yourself. Sleep well?'

She slipped her arms around my neck. 'Wonderfully well, you?'

I gently touched her face, feeling as if it might be one of the last times I got to be so intimate with her. 'I did too.'

She kissed me and asked me what was wrong. Damn, it was *that* obvious? A lump lodged in my throat and I looked at the floor. I was about to break her heart and I didn't want to watch.

I heaved out a long, shaking breath. 'I've been thinking… I… I'm not sure this is a good idea… you and me,' I lied, and then I had to swallow down the nausea that had suddenly crept up on me.

She dropped her arms from around me and pulled out a chair. She lowered herself down and with a panicked expression she stuttered, 'What? Why? What's happened? Did I say something wrong?' The only thing she'd done wrong was presuming this shitty situation was *her* fault. There was only one person to blame, and that was me.

I shook my head and smiled at her. 'You were... you *are* perfect.' I believed that with all my heart. And losing her would be just as painful as losing Mairi had been.

But it was inevitable.

'Then what's the problem? Is it... is it because I didn't sleep with you?'

What?

Anger at the whole fucking situation bubbled to the surface and I jumped to my feet, knocking over the chair. 'How could you even *think* that? Let alone *say* it out loud?'

She stood and held her hands up in surrender. 'Okay, okay. It was uncalled for, I'm sorry. You've been the perfect gentleman. I didn't mean it, but please tell me what made you change your mind.' Pain was evident in her voice, and I realised I was the biggest bastard that ever lived.

My stomach knotted. 'There are things you don't know about me. Things about my past.' Well, in truth there was *one huge* thing she didn't know about me.

'Greg, we have time to get to know about each other's past.' She sounded panicked and her hands were shaking. I wanted to comfort her but couldn't bring myself to touch her again. It would be more than I could bear. I shook my head and glanced into her widened eyes.

Her chest heaved. 'Why now? Why go through all that shit yesterday and then do this now?' she shouted angrily, her voice breaking. She had every right to be angry.

Time to tell your sordid little secret. 'I had a call this morning. While you were sleeping.'

'And this call made you not want me anymore?' Her voice wavered.

'No, it's not that at all, please don't think that, Mallory. My feelings for you haven't changed. They will *never* change.' Fuck, my heart was breaking. I had to fight to keep my composure, but I was rapidly losing the battle.

She inhaled deeply as if to calm herself. 'You said to me yesterday that if I had second thoughts I was to tell you. Why does that not apply to you?'

She was right. I at least should offer her the same courtesy.

'Okay, okay, fair point. But I'm warning you. When I tell you, it'll be the end of any future we had. Are you ready to lose that before it even begins?' After picking up the chair, I sat down again and dropped my head into my hands.

'Well, *you're* ending this anyway, so just tell me!' she shouted, and I flinched at the anger in her voice, my eyes snapping up to hers.

I gestured that she should sit down, and she did so shakily. I started at the beginning and told her about Alice and me. The fake pregnancy and our marriage, and then about finding her in bed with Connell and me walking out. She sat silently, absorbing my words open-mouthed.

When I finished speaking, Mallory threw her hands up. 'So what's the problem? You got divorced and met Mairi and the rest is history, right?' The hope in her voice almost crippled me.

Okay, here comes the final blow. The last nail in the coffin of our fledgling relationship. 'Mallory… I never got divorced.'

'What?' She stood quickly and the colour drained from her face.

'We just never got divorced. I didn't want to *speak* to her, let alone spend time discussing the finer points of our relationship in front of lawyers. I left her with the rental of the house and all our belongings. I thought that would be the last I would ever see of her. Until…'

Her eyes widened as realisation dawned. 'Until *she* called you this morning asking to see you?'

'Yes. I'm so sorry.'

Her lip trembled and she briefly closed her eyes. 'I think you had better go now, Greg.'

My heart sank. The inevitable had come to pass. Without fighting back, I went to the door and pulled my boots on, trying to focus through blurred vision caused by the tears welling in my eyes. I wasn't good enough for her. I had far too much emotional baggage, and she had enough of her own to contend with.

But for *one night* everything had been perfect. And it was *that* night I would remember for the rest of my lonely, miserable fucking life. My one night where I felt hope for a wonderful future with a truly amazing woman.

I closed my eyes, causing a couple of stray tears to escape. The last thing I wanted to do was cry in front of her, but I couldn't help it. 'I never told you because I don't think of her as my wife.'

She snorted as tears spilled down her cheeks too. 'No, but she *is* your wife, regardless. It's a pretty huge thing to keep from someone you are *supposedly* in love with, don't you think? What else haven't you told me? How many *more* lies will I uncover? I nearly *slept* with you! How can I trust you now?'

She was right again. How *could* she trust me? *I* wouldn't. 'I don't love her, Mallory, I love *you*. I don't feel *anything* for her. Not even hate any more. I'm apathetic when it comes to Alice. If I could go back in time and tell you *everything*, I would.' I couldn't rein in my anguish any longer and a strangled sob left my throat.

My stomach knotted and my heart cracked. 'The sad thing is that yesterday I had a glimpse of you and me together; the whole nine yards, a proper future. And I loved it. I hope that maybe someday you'll forgive me for keeping the truth from you. Please don't move away. Not because of me.'

I didn't say goodbye. I hated the word and it was something I never wanted to say again. I'd said it too many times as it was. But I *couldn't* say it to Mallory. Instead I turned and left her standing there in her kitchen, sobbing with my shattered heart beneath her feet.

*

I called at the pub for Angus and by the way Stella looked at me but kept silent I guessed my pain was visible on my face. I drove home in a daze and eventually walked through my front door and closed it behind me. Sliding down it, I slumped to the floor with my head in my hands. It was over. I was alone. Perhaps I just needed to get used to the fact. My eyes stung and my shoulders shuddered as my sadness and emptiness got the better of me. All I had ever wanted was to make her happy, and instead I'd broken her fragile heart with lies of omission. She would never trust me again; and the physical plain I felt at knowing that rendered me immobile.

Angus never left my side. He sat beside me and licked my face—sensitive wee soul. I nuzzled his fur, inhaling his familiar doggy smell. After fussing with my canine friend for a while I managed to drag my lead-like body from the floor and went to the kitchen to drown my sorrows.

*

Mallory swapped shifts to avoid me for the next week. Stella apologised, but of course it wasn't her fault. I didn't go into detail, but I think she must've guessed what had happened, seeing as she wasn't her usual interfering self. Stella liked to fix things but this was one thing that couldn't be fixed. I saw Mallory briefly when we did our shift changeover, but we were reduced to business transactions only. *This barrel needs changing... We need to order more of that,* etc. Seeing her always saddened me and continually reminded me of what I'd lost through my own stupidity. But it was better than not seeing her at all. The breakdown of my other relationships had been out of my hands. With this one – if you could even call it a relationship – the onus was completely on me.

When the For Sale board went up outside Mallory's house, I went home after my evening shift at the pub and cried myself to sleep like a bloody teenage girl.

Pathetic.

But I couldn't help how I felt. It was a dull, nagging pain that knotted my insides with regret and shame. I knew I'd lost her for good. She'd be moving back to

Yorkshire, no doubt, and I'd never see her again.

Chapter Forty-two

During early September my unwanted guest arrived. Alice breezed back into my life as if we'd never been apart. She took great delight in hugging me at every given opportunity and linking arms with me any time we stepped out of the front door. I had no fight in me. I was still apathetic to her presence. She was staying at the pub at my request but insisted on cooking me breakfast at home every morning so we could 'talk'; except her idea of *talking* consisted mainly of her flirting with and touching me. At first I was so depressed about Mallory and how things had ended that I couldn't be arsed to argue with her for being in my space, but a week into her visit and I was getting more and more pissed off with her as the days passed.

Yet another breakfast conversation began with me trying to sort out the important matters. 'Alice, we need to talk about this divorce.'

'Oh... yes... yes, we do. Anyway, there's more bacon if you'd like some. Then we could maybe go for a walk.'

'And figure out what we need to do to end our marriage,' I almost snarled.

She laughed, shrugging off my comment. 'Oh, come

on, Mr Grumpy. I think you should show me around. Let me see what it is about this place that you love so much.'

'What I *love* so much is that *you* live so far away,' I chuntered loudly enough for her to hear. 'And the fact that I finally have genuine people around me who don't stab me in the back.'

She ignored my direct jab and breezily asked, 'Should I make more toast?'

I slid my plate away. Suddenly bereft of appetite. 'Alice, I don't want you to come here anymore. Let's just agree on the divorce proceedings and then we can both move on, eh?' I was just about at the end of my tether and had lost count of the numerous times in the past week that I had told her I wasn't interested. What made things worse was that I was angry with myself for allowing her to wheedle her way into my life again so easily.

I had to get out of the house.

I grabbed my hoody. 'I'm going out. I don't know how long I'll be.'

When I said I was going for a walk, you'd have thought I'd asked her to renew our vows. The excitement on her face pissed me off. 'Yes! Just what I wanted to do. Lovely. I'll grab my jacket.'

I had meant to just take Angus. But of course that wasn't an option. Alice didn't seem to understand the concept of *no*. She never had.

She skipped down the driveway like a giddy teenager, her arm linked in mine as my daft dog trotted back and forth before us, but I stayed silent and uninterested. Whatever I said she ignored, so I resigned myself to the fact that arguing with her was futile. I hadn't the energy for it. As we approached the village I told her I wanted to call into the pub and speak to Stella about my shifts and maybe doing some more gigs.

But as the bridge came into sight my heart almost stopped. Mallory was there with Ruby in her favourite spot. The little dog's tail wagged frantically when she spotted us. Mallory, on the other hand, was staring at us with a furrowed brow. I guessed she was wondering why I was walking along with the blonde woman who was staying at the pub.

As we approached her I was taken aback by how beautiful she looked. But then she always did. Even way back when we first met and she was inadvertently doing her Gene Simmons impersonation. The memory of our early encounter made me smile.

I swallowed hard but didn't clear my throat and so my voice came out croaky. 'Hi, Mallory.'

'Greg.' Her fake smile was brief.

Oh great, I'm going to have to introduce them. 'Mallory... erm... this is Alice, Alice this is Mallory.'

Mallory's eyes widened in horror and I felt sick.

Alice chimed in, 'Hi, Mallory, I've heard a lot about you.' The lies fell easily from her lips as she held out her hand. I hadn't told her anything. She was just good at reading people. And it was probably obvious who Mallory was by our reaction to each other.

'I'm sure you have,' Mallory replied with an acidic tone as she extracted her hand.

'We were just taking a walk, you know, clearing the cobwebs,' I told her.

I could see sadness in her eyes as she stepped away. 'Lovely. Well, enjoy yourselves. I need to get going.' She dashed away, taking my heart with her.

Once she'd gone I turned to Alice. 'Look, I'm going to wait for Mallory. She and I need to talk.'

Alice folded her arms across her chest and scowled. 'I think *our* talk is more important than the one you want to have with your bit on the side.'

Her snide comment made my blood boil and I gritted my teeth. 'Don't *ever* call her that again. You and I are married on paper only. And the sooner you realise that, the better.'

She huffed and stormed off, which was a relief as it gave me the opportunity to speak to Mallory alone. I knew she'd have to walk by me when she left the shop so I plonked myself down at one of the tables outside the pub and waited.

A few minutes later and she appeared. My heart began to race. 'Mallory, can you talk?'

With evident reluctance she sat down opposite me and there began a very awkward and strained conversation. She was angry; it was clear by her harsh tone of voice, folded arms and furrowed brow. *I* had done this to her.

But after a few moments of trying to be pleasant, her attitude got to me. 'Why do you have to be so hostile, Mallory? Nothing has changed for me. I wish you'd realise that.'

'It's of no consequence to me how you feel. How is your *wife* liking it here?'

Ouch. That was meant to sting and it really did. 'Okay, we're being like that, are we? She's just here to finalise things. That's all. And I really thought we had something a little more mature, Mallory. I thought there were feelings on both sides of this. Clearly I was wrong.' And it was apparent she wasn't prepared to forgive and forget. But what did I really expect her to do?

She cocked her head to one side and snarled at me. 'Greg, you're married. You kept that fact from me just as I was about to give myself to you. Whilst I was still grieving for the *real* love of my life. Excuse me if I'm a little indignant.'

Okay, I deserved that too. 'Can we at least be civil? Or maybe even friends? We got along so well, Mallory. Don't you miss that? I know I do.'

'It's irrelevant. I can't trust you. How can we possibly be friends?'

'Okay, well, it was worth a try.' At that point I felt the familiar, physical pain return to my stomach and my chest. I looked down at the table; the three feet of gnarled and splintered wood that created an impenetrable barrier between us might as well have been three miles. The scars on its surface evidence of the battering it had taken, just like the invisible but ever-present scars on mine and Mallory's relationship.

I longed to reach out and touch her but clenched my fists instead. 'Will you do me one thing? Will you tell me if you do sell the house? I would at least like a chance to say goodbye.'

She stood from the table and I gazed up at her. But she returned my gaze with regret in her eyes. 'Greg, we said goodbye that day in August.' And with that final nail in the coffin, she walked away from me.

*

When I returned home Alice was waiting, arms folded. I heaved a defeated sigh. 'Look, Alice, I'm not in the mood to fight, okay? I'm playing tonight and I want to run through a couple of songs before I go in, so can we… just… *not*?'

Her eyes softened and she walked towards me. Stopping a couple of steps away, she reached out and stroked my arm. 'It didn't go well, then?'

'That's a fucking understatement. The fact that I told her I'm in love with her and then the morning after finished things off with, "*Oh, and by the way, I forgot to mention that I'm still married"* was the fucking final straw. I can't blame her. Can you?'

She closed the gap between us and slipped her arms around my neck. 'She doesn't deserve you, Greg.' Her voice was a soft whisper filled with longing.

'And *you* do?' I asked incredulously as I grasped her wrists firmly and removed her arms from my body. Shock registered on her face at my actions, and so, to further drive my point home, I moved my hands to the tops of her arms and physically removed her from my path.

I took the stairs two at a time, entered my bedroom, and slammed the door behind me. Grabbing Rhiannon from the stand, I walked over and sat on the edge of my bed.

Music. I needed music.

*

Later that evening I arrived at the pub to prepare for my gig. Alice had followed me like some lost puppy dog and pulled a chair up beside me as I checked the tuning on my guitar. She began to talk to me about people she was still in contact with back home – people that I knew too. It was nice to hear about old friends, I suppose, but that was as far as it went. I had no interest in keeping in contact with anyone from my past. Least of all Alice. We were over. She needed to understand that. I'd tried the softly, softly approach but I was really going to have to get nasty if she didn't piss off soon.

Mallory had arrived and gone straight behind the bar without even saying hello. Alice leaned in and whispered, 'Greg, that Melanie is staring at us.'

I glanced over and then hissed at Alice, 'Her name is *Mallory*.' As I finished speaking, the glass Mallory was drying slipped from her hand and shattered on the floor. Before Alice could protest I was beside Mallory. 'Hey, are you okay?'

She huffed. 'Greg, it's just broken glass. I'm fine.'

I grabbed the dustpan and brush from on top of the dishwasher. 'Let me help you.'

She snatched them from my hands. 'Greg, just go. You're supposed to be singing, aren't you?' It was clear my presence wasn't appreciated.

'Look, I've said sorry about everything. What else am I meant to do?' I asked in exasperation.

'Nothing. There is *nothing* you can do. Just go!' She was on the verge of angry tears and so I stepped away with a heavy heart and left her to it.

When the time came I took my usual position, ready to play. The pub was crowded and I was aware that many people had come out especially to see me, which was a bit surreal to be honest. Greeting the patrons as I always did, I reminded them that singing along wasn't appreciated; but this time I didn't feel the humour in the comment. I continued on with my introduction. Having chosen the first song specifically for the most important person in the room, I hoped she listened to the words as she had done when I sent her the CD. I desperately wanted her to understand how I felt.

'I know you all are gradually discovering how eclectic ma taste in music is. Well, just to prove the point even further, I'm going to kick off with a little bit of Chicago. The band, not the musical.' I managed a chuckle and the crowd laughed along. 'This is a beautiful song called "Hard to Say I'm Sorry".'

I began to sing with my eyes closed and tried very hard to rein my emotions in, but even *I* could hear the rawness of my voice. Opening my eyes, I fixed them on Mallory behind the bar and willed her with all my might to look at me. To *see* me as she said she did before, when we came so close. But she completely avoided my gaze and eventually, just after the middle of the song, she walked out of the bar towards the ladies' toilets.

When my song finished she still wasn't back. I leaned down to take a swig of my drink in the hope that it would dislodge the lump of knotted sadness from my throat. When she appeared again I could see that she'd been crying. I wanted to hold her in my arms and kiss her tears away. But it wasn't an option.

Alice appeared beside me and kissed the top of my head before I could dodge her. I flinched and my train of vision settled on Stella at the bar— Shit, she'd seen her kiss me. I hoped Mallory hadn't noticed, as I didn't want her getting the wrong impression regardless of what she felt about me.

'Anyway, onto my next number... ahem... Now unrequited love is a bitch, eh? I know, I've been there – anyone else?' A rumble of agreement travelled the room. Clearly I was not alone then. 'Aye, some of you should relate well to this next one. It's by one of my favourite bands, Fleetwood Mac and it's called "Go Your Own Way". Oh, and remember, don't sing along, eh?' The audience laughed at the catchphrase I'd become known for. I forced a smile before I began.

I played the song with a semblance of anger even though I was breaking up inside, and I glared over at Mallory, willing her to look at me. But as before she kept her eyes firmly focused elsewhere.

My next song was bound to get a reaction. Or so I hoped. But I realised that maybe this was all a very self-centred night. The audience hadn't come to hear me pouring my heart out to someone who didn't want to listen. But I thought, *fuck it, I'm the one with the microphone. They can leave if they don't like it.*

Realising that my selfish attitude could end up in Stella losing paying customers, I decided to make a token apology to the crowd. 'Sorry, folks, it's all a bit melancholy tonight. I'm feeling that way out. Must be my hormones. Anyway, this next one is a sad, sad song by a wonderful songwriter called John Waite. It's about a guy who's in love with a girl. She left him and moved away. He really doesn't know why she's gone and he misses her desperately, but he's trying to convince himself that he isn't... He's failing miserably. She's all he can think about. She's all he sees. He wants her to realise and come back to him... It's called "Missing You".'

I began to play and the lyrics flowed from my lips like a prayer that I hoped she would hear and answer. I didn't want to say goodbye. I didn't want her to go back to Yorkshire. How would I cope? What would I do if I didn't get to see her bright blue eyes and warm smile? The thought brought back the tightening sensation to my throat. I caught sight of her in my peripheral vision. She'd stopped what she was doing and was listening intently. I made eye contact with her for a moment but she turned away and walked through to the back.

She didn't return.

Chapter Forty-three

I awoke early the next morning and decided I was going to confront Mallory about why she walked out during my gig. I knew the answer deep down. She still felt something for me and had a hard time hearing my feelings expressed like that. But I *needed* to hear her say it. Maybe if she could admit that to me, we had a chance. So with renewed hope, I left the house and made my way down to the village.

To my horror she was just pulling away from home. I ran in front of the car like some crazed lunatic with a death wish and held my hands up. Luckily she had her wits about her and slammed on the brakes.

I jogged around to the driver's window and noticed her belongings piled on the back seat and Ruby's bed in the passenger foot well.

Fuck!

She wound the window down and I panted, 'Mallory… are you leaving?'

'What business is it of yours?' she snapped in that acidic tone she'd been using towards me lately.

'The case in the back. Ruby… Are you going for good?'

With a sneer she bitterly retorted, 'Why don't you ask your *wife*, Greg?' And with that she sped away, tyres screeching, across the bridge and out of sight. All I could do was stand and watch her retreating vehicle with my hands in my hair.

I flopped down onto one of the benches outside the pub and rested my head on my folded arms on the table. I didn't know what else to do. As if she had been listening in, Alice appeared from out of nowhere to offer comfort. Or her *version* of it.

'Hey, are you okay, honey?' Her sickly sweet voice made me nauseated. Or was it the way Mallory left me with her venom in my veins? Whatever it was, I felt sick as a dog.

'Don't call me honey,' I growled.

She sighed. 'Oh, Greg, it's just a term of endearment.'

I lifted my head and glared at her. 'Yeah? Well *nothing* is going to endear *you* to me so fuck off home.'

'Oooh, touchy. Did she kick you to the kerb, then?' She sniggered and I wanted to slap her but I would *never* hit a woman – even one like Alice with all her sly, nasty deviousness.

'Drop it, Alice, if you know what's good for you.'

She rolled her eyes. 'Oh, let me guess... She told you about our little conversation in the ladies.'

I clenched my jaw. 'What little conversation?'

Alice smiled sweetly. 'I just told her that she'd hurt you and she'd better not do it again. She knows to keep away now so you can move on with your life. I did you a favour.' That was the straw that broke the camel's back and I knew she could tell from the way my eyes widened that I was raging. She huffed. 'And there's no need to *threaten* me, Greg. I'm trying to be a friend.'

I laughed derisively. 'A *friend*? *You?* Is that what you were doing with Connell when you *fucked* him in our marital bed, eh, being a *friend*?'

She rolled her eyes. 'Oh, for goodness' sake, Greg. Why can't you just let that go?'

I stood up, anger boiling beneath my skin, and spoke through clenched teeth. 'I *have* let it fucking go. And I've let *you* go, Alice.' I spat as I jabbed a pointed finger towards her. 'But you *still* turned up and hung around like the smell of rotting veg under a cupboard. Now I suggest you go home and get a lawyer because *this* time I'm divorcing your arse right out of my life for good!' I stormed away towards home, hoping that she wouldn't follow me for round two.

No such luck.

I heard her feet crunching against the gravel as I increased the pace at which I was trying to escape her.

'Greg!' she called in that pained voice she had mastered to try and manipulate me. 'Greg, please slow down. Let's talk about this like adults, eh?'

I stopped in my tracks and turned to her with a bitter laugh. 'Like adults? Okay... here we go... this is me talking to you like an adult. I don't *like* you, Alice. I don't *want* you and I sure as hell don't fucking *love* you. I feel nothing but disdain where you're concerned. Is that adult enough for you?'

Her lip began to quiver and I somehow felt exhilarated at *finally* getting through to her. Revenge had never been my intent, but seeing her in emotional pain had no effect on me, because in threatening the woman I loved, she'd gone too far.

She shook her head. 'You don't mean that. I know you don't mean that.'

'Alice, I've never meant anything more in my fucking life except for the time I told Mallory I love her with all my heart. Now *there* is a woman worth fighting for. There is a woman capable of genuine love and I don't deserve her. But do you know what? I'm gonna fight for her anyway. Because that's what you do when you love someone. You want their happiness above anything. And that's what I want for Mallory. I want to see her happy, not cut up over my mistakes. And, yes, *you* are one hell of a mistake, Alice. One I will *never* repeat again. Am I making myself clear enough?'

She nodded as tears spilled from her eyes. 'I… I'll go home.'

'Yes, go home and call your solicitor. And do me a favour, okay? Don't come back again.'

*

Alice left the following day after one last-ditch attempt at getting me back. As she stood at the door with her bag, she asked me to at least think about us, but I just shook my head and closed the door in her face. I sat on my couch after she'd gone and stared at my phone. I was desperate to contact Mallory. I needed to know that she was okay. But, of course, if I called she'd more than likely hang up. In the end I resorted to cowardly tactics. It was unlikely she would ignore a text message – even if it was blind curiosity that made her read it. Picking up my phone, I began to type.

> Hey, how r u? Am worried u will not come back. I miss u so much. Please just let me know u r ok.

I hit send and then reread what I'd written. *Great, I sound like a pathetic loser. Way to get the girl, McBradden.* My phone vibrated almost instantly and I dropped it through the sheer shock. After fumbling around on the floor and picking up the phone, I opened the reply.

> Greg, I'm fine. Please just let me be for a while. I need some space, okay? Concentrate on your own life for a while and let me deal with mine.

Yikes, that's harsh. But at least she replied, I suppose. I relaxed a tiny bit, knowing that she was okay and had arrived in Yorkshire safe and sound. All I had to do now was get her to come home so we could try and sort this mess out.

*

Pressuring her probably wasn't the best thing to do, so I left her to it after that. But I did resolve to bloody go down there if she actually *didn't* come home. I'd told her as much in the Foo Fighters song I'd put on her CD.

Working at the pub wasn't the same without Mallory. Even after Alice turned up I'd see her briefly at shift changeovers. Now, being here without her was making me dread going in to work. I played a gig whilst she was away, and as I placed the chalkboard that she made for me outside the door of the pub, my heart sank.

I traced the lettering painted by her fair hand. 'Just come home, eh? Please, come home.'

Once I'd walked back inside, my phone rang. Fumbling it out of my pocket in the hope that it was her, I answered in a rush. 'Hello? Yes?'

'Hi there, is this Greg McBradden?' It was a female voice but it didn't belong to Mallory.

'Yes, this is Greg. Who's calling?'

'Great, my name is Cassandra Carlton. I'm one of the agents with Class Act Talent, or CAT as we like to say for short. My business partner and I have been informed about your shows by another of our artistes, and we've watched a clip of you online too, which impressed us. We'd like to come along and check you out with a view to contracting you for the venues we cover.'

Huh? What? Contract me? I suddenly realised that the conversation I was having was thankfully happening in my head.

'Greg?'

'Um... sorry... sorry. Yes, that'd be great. Thank you,' I finally replied with a pounding heart and a head full of disbelief.

*

A couple of days later and the call from the agent still hadn't really sunk in. I kept replaying it over and over in my mind. As I stood drying glasses behind the bar, the door opened and I got a wonderful surprise.

'Mallory, you're back!' My eyes widened and I wanted to dash out and hug her – but then the thought crossed my mind that she probably wouldn't want that, and the joy of seeing her suddenly evaporated. 'How long are you here for?'

'I'm not sure, Greg. Not yet. Can I speak to you in private, please?'

We stepped outside and I was dreading what she was going to say to me. 'Is everything okay, Mallory?' *Please don't tell me you're leaving now. Please.*

'Greg, I've done a lot of thinking whilst I've been away.'

Okay, brace yourself, McBradden, here comes the

blow. 'I'm not going to like this, am I?' I cringed in readiness.

But she smiled. 'I think maybe I was... too hard on you about the whole marriage thing. I don't feel able to be anything more at the moment, and I doubt that I ever will now... but I think we can maybe be friends... if you want to?'

What? Really? Jeez, take what you can get, arsehole. 'Mallory, I love you. I probably always will. It will be hard to be just friends, but I would rather have that than the icy chill between us.' I absent-mindedly stroked her arm but she flinched. *Why the hell did she flinch? Did I really scare her that day at my house? Shit.* Guilt shredded my heart and I wanted to apologise, but it felt too little too late; and she was offering me an olive branch.

'Well, as I said, friendship is all I can offer.' She went on to ask where Alice was and so I told her that Alice had gone home and that she begged to make a go of things with me again.

'I'm fully aware of that.' Mallory seemed a little pissed off. 'Did she not tell you about our cosy little chat in the ladies that last time you played? She accused me of breaking your heart worse than *she* had and pretty much warned me off you.'

What. The. Fuck? So there was more to the little chat than she let on. It was good that Alice had gone home, because at that very second, I was so angry I wasn't sure what I would've done. 'Shit! Really? Is that why you went—?'

'Ha! Greg, I won't be scared off by her or by anyone. I've become quite tough lately. I just needed a break. That's all,' she said sternly.

The rest of the conversation was a little fuzzy in my head afterwards, as I was seeing red. Mallory told me she was worried I would get hurt if Alice and I gave things another go, but there was absolutely no chance of that happening. I sincerely hoped at that point that Alice had given up on her stupid plot to win me back after the tongue-lashing and home truths I dished her. But with Alice you never did know. The fact that she tried to warn off the woman I loved was enough to convince me that she wouldn't give up easily. Mallory's concern touched me, but she did stress the fact that it was out of concern for me as her *friend*.

*

Later that day I was standing at the bar, a total nervous wreck. The agents from CAT were coming to see me, and I'd resorted to whisky to calm my jagged nerves.

'I thought that stuff dried your vocal cords out,' Mallory said from beside me.

'Aye, but I'm a tad nervous tonight. Some guy put a clip of me on the Internet and some folks from an entertainment agency are coming to see me play.'

‘Wow, Greg. That’s brilliant.’ She gasped. ‘What’ll happen if he likes what he sees?’

I pursed my lips, suddenly feeling a little embarrassed. She was reading more into this than necessary. ‘Ah… I won’t be famous or anything quite so crazy, but it could mean I get gigs farther afield. He has a list of places all over Highland that I could be booked for.’

Mallory’s gaze travelled to the door and I turned to see what she was looking at. The couple who had just walked in looked like undercover coppers, but I guessed they were from the talent agency.

‘Shit, that must be them.’ I took a large gulp of my drink and went over to say hello.

Chapter Forty-four

After introducing myself to the agency reps, I took my place behind the microphone. My mouth was dry and my hands were clammy, making playing a little tricky. Every so often I had to wipe my palms on my jeans, which, I'm guessing, didn't look all that great.

'Evening, all. Good to be here again and to see the place packed. I'm sure Stella is grateful, and I know I am. I'd like to start tonight off with a dedication to someone. She knows who she is. The words have to be said and I can think of no better way to say them… It's a song by a band you may think obscure for a weeknight in a village pub, but the sentiment is important because it's about friendship and putting up with each other's good and bad points in equal measure and it's about having each other's back. It's by Incubus and it's called "Dig".'

I gazed at Mallory as I sang and she smiled back at me in acknowledgement of what I was trying to say. It was like a secret message shared between the two of us, and although there were people present who had figured out what I meant, it didn't matter. We shared the moment and that was all I cared about. The song told her how much I valued her friendship and that I would always be there for her as she was for me. And even though I was determined to have her in my life no matter how that presented itself, I still felt the pang of sadness that we would never be anything more; that we would never share any kind of intimacy again.

The rest of the night went by fast, but the crowd in the pub was appreciative and clapped in all the right places. The only bloody problem was *every time* I sang something they knew, they bloody sang along. I've *always* hated that, and I've told them so on many occasions, but their out-of-tune warbling made me laugh so I eventually forgave them.

Once the gig was over, I made my way back over to the agents from CAT. Cassandra was the first to speak. 'That was fantastic, Greg. The crowd here clearly loves you.'

I felt my cheeks become warm and I rubbed the back of my neck. 'Right… thanks. That's great. Thanks – oh, I already said that.'

Cassandra laughed at my embarrassment. 'We'd like to take you on. However, we understand about your boat business, so we can work around you.'

'Yes,' Hayden, the male rep, said. 'There are lots of our venues that would appreciate your type of music and, forgive me for saying so, we think the *female* clientele will just adore you.'

I shook my head, not really understanding why he

thought that. 'Really? But I'm thirty-eight. Hardly a spring chicken.'

Hayden shook his head and waved his hands up and down my body. 'Believe me, I'm talking from experience here, you have that dark-and-mysterious charisma that women love. And I'm told that the whole rugged-good-looks thing is very *in* at the moment as far as female patrons are concerned, so I think you'll do *very* well.' He raised his eyebrows as if to emphasise his point.

'Oookay. If you say so.'

'Oh, we *know* so, Greg. So what do you say?'

I lifted my hands out from my sides and grinned. 'I say why the fuck not?' *Whoops.* I cringed. 'Erm... sorry about my language.'

Cassandra stifled a giggle and blushed. 'Oh, don't worry about it. We noticed you like your expletives. The places you'll be playing are strictly adults only, so it shouldn't be a *major* problem. Obviously try *not* to swear quite so much when you're representing us, but the odd naughty word can be forgiven.'

Hayden held out his hand. 'Welcome aboard, Greg. I can see great success in your future.'

I shook both of their hands and they left. I was a little shell-shocked to say the least. This whole thing was surreal and taking me well out of my comfort zone, but what the heck, eh? Nothing ventured and all that bollocks.

I went back over to put Rhiannon away and Mallory

appeared at my side. 'Well?' She sounded excited, and when I looked up at her wide eyes I melted inside... *again*.

'They've taken me on!' I flung my arms around her and hugged her, lifting her off the ground. I couldn't help myself, I was so damned excited. She didn't pull away, so I took that as a good sign. In fact she hugged me back with just as much enthusiasm. It felt so bloody good.

'I'm so happy for you, Greg. How amazing.'

When we broke apart, I scratched my chin and pondered my next words carefully. 'Look, I've something to ask you. Feel free to say no if it's too soon to socialise with me again, but... I'm going to an open mic night at the beginning of October in Oban and I wondered if you'd like to come along. I've been before and there are some great performers on.'

Tilting her head to the side, she smiled widely. 'I think I can safely say I'll be there.'

My heart almost stopped. I thought, *fuck it,* and hugged her tight again with a racing heart.

*

October in Scotland is a funny month. One year it can be gloriously sunny and the next bitterly cold. The start of *this* particular October was wet and dull. The only light at the end of the miserable tunnel was my night out in Oban with Mallory and I could. Not. Wait.

Mallory had been showing prospective buyers around her house, and I was selfishly hoping that none of them liked it. If I could prove to her that we could be friends, then there would be no reason she would have to go back to Yorkshire.

Friday the ninth was the long-anticipated night of our trip, and I called to collect her at seven that evening. The two of us had been getting on well. We were back to… hmm… I was going to say *normal*, but I don't think there was such a thing where we were concerned.

As I drove through the rain to Oban, we chatted about music. It turned out that Mallory used to sing in a choir, and I was intrigued by that fact. The trouble was, it only made me love her more. Stupid images of us doing a duet in the pub played in my mind like some sappy teen movie where we'd fall in love across the stage. It was all in soft focus as she gazed lovingly at me from her place beside me.

To top all of that off, she mentioned that she once sang 'Martha's Harbour' by eighties folk rock band, All About Eve, and it was a song that I absolutely loved; it sent shivers down my spine every time I heard it. I decided right then, I had to manufacture a way to get her to sing it. I simply *had* to. Even if she did insist that I did nothing of the sort. My mind was working overtime.

Just like the last time I'd been to the open-mic place, it was heaving busy and the atmosphere was alive with music and voices. This was something I loved. I got such a buzz from being around musos with a penchant for performing. It made me feel alive. Being here with Mallory just iced the cake and put the cherry on the top.

We grabbed a table and got some drinks. We listened to a few of the acts performing, and I slyly watched Mallory smiling up at the stage. Some young guy was singing 'Yellow' by Coldplay, and her eyes were filled with tears as she listened. *She's just too bloody cute.*

The next singer was a girl with long titian hair and vivid green eyes. Her resemblance to Mairi was staggering and I was suddenly mesmerised. Mairi couldn't sing for toffee, but if she could have, I imagined that this was how she'd have sounded. I felt someone squeeze my arm and I glanced to the side to find Mallory watching me with a knowing expression.

I wiped at the moisture around my eyes and smiled. 'I'm… erm… just nipping to the gents'. Won't be long,' I told her as I stood and backed away, feeling a little silly for my outward expression of emotion over the complete stranger on the stage.

Once inside the men's room I went to the sink and stared at my reflection. Being with Mallory just did something good for me. I looked so much more vital. Gone were the dark circles I'd been plagued with and now I looked like *me* again. She had well and truly saved me. I just wished she would let me do the same for her.

I splashed cold water on my face and took some

calming breaths. I was about to put my plan into action, and I was scared she'd slap me or be so angry that our fragile friendship would once again be on the rocks. On the way back to the table, I chatted to the guy taking names of performers and gave him the information he needed. He told me I was up next and so I dashed back to Mallory and grabbed her arm. She followed me with a frown on her face but didn't ask questions, although I saw that she had plenty.

'You know you sang "Martha's Harbour" as a solo in your choir that time?'

She frowned. 'Yes, yes, of course I remember. We were *just* talking about it.'

'Aye, well, I hope you remember the words, 'cause it just so happens it's one of my favourites, and we're just about to perform it live on stage.' I, of course, knew it like the back of my hand.

She pulled her arm to try and free herself from my grip, but I just grinned and held on tighter. *Yep, she's gonna kill me.*

Her eyes widened. 'You must be mad! There's no way I'm—'

Too late. The announcer's voice came over the sound system. 'Ladies, gentleman, it's time for a duet now. Next up this evening we have Greg McBradden accompanying Mallory Westerman as she sings "Martha's Harbour".'

She sat down on the stool beside mine and gawped

open-mouthed in the direction of the audience. The stage lights were bright and so she would be able to make out only shadows as I could. I began to strum the opening chords of the song and gazed at her encouragingly, hoping she wouldn't freeze.

She closed her eyes and began to sing. She had an *amazing* voice. My heart and stomach flipped simultaneously and I almost fell backwards off my perch. I tried my best to focus on my playing so as not to let her down, but honestly, I just wanted to stop and listen instead. My insides turned to mush. *My God, can this woman get any more perfect? Seriously, God, you're having a laugh now with your bloody tormenting.* I glanced skyward for a moment and then back to the angel beside me as she sang the song with such feeling that my stupid eyes began to sting again. This woman turned me into a bloody emotional wreck in the *best* possible way.

When the song ended, I placed my guitar down carefully and banged my hands together with the rest of the crowd. She was fucking *awesome*! My palms were red raw when I stopped clapping but I didn't care. I'd just fulfilled a dream I had only just realised I had and if God had struck me down there and then I would've died a happy man. We stepped down from the stage and I placed Rhiannon against the wall. Scooping Mallory into my arms, I swung her around, kissing her cheeks and head. When I placed her down again, her eyes met mine and the chemistry between us literally took my breath from my body.

I leaned down and gently placed a kiss on her lips. There was nothing I wanted more in that moment than to deepen the kiss and slip my hands into her hair. The way she returned my stare told me she wanted that too, but instead she pulled away.

I huffed out a breath and shook my head. 'You were amazing up there; do you know that?' I told her as I ran my hands roughly through my *own* hair. 'You're a bloody good singer. You've been holding out on me, you sod.'

Her responding smile was wide. 'I have to admit it felt pretty amazing too.'

'Come on, let's go get you a drink. I bet you need one after what I just sprang on you.'

She laughed. 'You say that almost as if you're sorry.'

'Nope, can't say that I am. How else would I have discovered your hidden talent?'

She hit my arm lightly. 'Stop it, you're making me blush.'

'Aye, so I see. Pink suits you,' I teased and she stuck out her tongue like old times, making me chuckle.

After I'd delivered Mallory's much-needed Jack and Coke – I was very diplomatic this time and didn't complain – I went and put my name down again to do a solo number or two. I chose my songs carefully and made sure to connect with Mallory's eyes at key points in each song. I played my own rendition of Cyndi Lauper's 'True Colours' but couldn't make eye contact during that one. I knew my heart would break again if I did. Later I sang 'Ever Fallen in Love' by the Buzzcocks and gave her a cheeky grin, making her blush again.

I figured if she continued to read between the lines as she had done with the CD I'd made her, then maybe... just maybe, there was still a tiny flame of hope to be fanned.

Chapter Forty-five

As we drove home after our night out, we chatted about some of the acts we'd really enjoyed. The quality of performers had been especially good, and we both agreed that it was great to see so many talented people all in one place. I was doing my best to encourage Mallory to join me there again sometime, but she was taking some convincing. Every time I glanced over at her throughout our journey, the twinge of sadness returned – which was in total conflict with the happiness I felt just being with her and talking to her. My life was going to be such a double-edged sword and there appeared to be little I could do to change that.

Eventually we pulled up outside her cottage and I switched off the engine. Turning to face her, I bit the bullet. 'Can I ask you something, Mallory?' I took her hand.

She turned her face away and removed her hand from mine. 'I'm not sure that's a good idea.'

'I'm going to ask anyway. I think I'll be able to tell the real answer by your body language.'

She turned to face me once more. 'Greg, don't, okay? We've had a lovely evening. Please don't spoil it.'

I pushed on regardless of her protest. 'Mallory, can you look me in the eye and tell me honestly that you don't want to be more than friends?'

She sighed. 'Greg, you lied about being married. It doesn't matter *how* I feel. You broke the trust we had. It will take a long time to get that back. I would always be wondering if there was more to come.' Her eyes filled with tears, and I wished so hard that Michael J. Fox were here with his time machine. *What I wouldn't give to go back and change this whole damned situation.*

I spoke again, but the emotion I was trying to keep in check did its best to betray me through my croaky voice. 'Mallory, I don't love her. I still love you. It's always been you.' I took her hand once more. 'I *know* you feel something for me. I *know* you do. Why deny it?'

'Greg, stop. I'm not going there again. It doesn't matter how I feel.'

I was way past the safe zone now. The ice beneath my feet was cracking and I was about to plummet into the deep, dark chilling depths of loneliness again when she told me to get the fuck out of her life, but I continued on my suicide mission because I couldn't stop myself from at least trying to make her change her mind. 'Just let me kiss you. It'll all melt away; all your doubt.' I leaned forward and ran my hand through her hair, grazing her cheek with my thumb.

Her lip trembled and a tear escaped her eye. 'I can't,' she whispered as she pulled her hand away. Without any further words she climbed out of the car and closed the door behind her.

I swallowed hard and closed my eyes briefly. *Okay. Enough now, McBradden. Time to move on.* I started the engine and pulled away from her cottage with a resigned feeling of failure.

*

I had a call from CAT with details of my first gig a few days after the open mic night. And I made my way to a club over by Oban the following Friday night. Once I was set up, I went to the bar to get myself a drink. The woman behind the bar came over to take my order; she smelled like Mallory, and my eyes drifted to meet hers. She was very pretty. Not stunning like Mallory, but attractive. She had friendly, warm brown eyes and full lips. In the back of my mind I wondered if maybe this would present itself as an opportunity to get Mallory out of my head even if she was firmly rooted in my heart.

'Hi there, what can I get you?' she asked as she came to a halt before me.

'Just a pint of cola, please.'

'So I'm guessing you're Greg?' She placed my drink on the mat before me with a sultry smile.

I turned up one side of my mouth even though I didn't feel the smile internally. 'Aye, guilty as charged.'

'My dad showed me the clip online of you playing

"Fields of Gold" by Sting. I have to be honest and tell you it made me cry.'

I laughed. 'Was it that bad?'

She smiled back. 'No, silly, it was beautiful.'

'Why, thank you… erm?'

'Kate. My name's Kate Walker.' She held out her hand and I took it.

'It's a pleasure to meet you, Kate.'

'And you too, Greg.'

Unsure really as to why, I suddenly felt that things were maybe getting too flirty, and a sense of betrayal niggled at the back of my mind only this time it related to Mallory rather than Mairi.

I changed the subject. 'So, you mentioned your dad?'

'Yes, he owns the place. I just help out every so often. I'm actually training to be a nurse.'

'Hmm, very admirable.' I nodded as I took a swig of my drink.

'Very tiring.'

When it was time to perform I smiled out at the audience and introduced myself to the gathered crowd. 'Evening, all. So, my name's Greg and I'm a muso-holic.' A chuckle travelled the room and relief washed over me. They weren't as lively as my usual crowd but maybe they would grow to love me. Who knew?

The night went really well and I played 'Fields of Gold' especially for Kate. I'd liked her instantly and it was evident that she liked me too by the way she touched her hair and fluttered her eyelashes when I addressed her. She seemed very warm and she was curvy in all the right places… rather like Mallory. *Urgh! Will I spend every waking hour comparing every woman to Mallory?* We chatted after the gig before I set off back home, and she accompanied me to the car. Once I loaded my guitar into the Landy, I turned to where she stood beside me, arms folded.

'So… you're here again next week, aren't you?' she asked with hope in her voice.

'I am, Kate, aye. I'll look forward to it.'

'Me too. And thanks for playing that song for me. That was really sweet.'

'You're very welcome. It was a pleasure to meet you.' I shook her hand and she squeezed mine before I climbed into the Landy and rolled the window down. 'Will you be here next time too?'

She bit her lip and smiled shyly. 'I wouldn't miss it for the world.'

Okay… she's flirting again, so why don't I feel anything? 'Great. See you then.' I wound the window back up and drove away, waving as I left.

I let the smile fall from my face like a stiff mask. Mallory didn't want me; she'd made it abundantly clear. So why did trying to move on feel… wrong? Maybe I was trying too hard? Or maybe it was too soon?

My journey home was one of introspection. I wondered if I ever actually would move on. I'd clearly moved on from losing Mairi. Although the pain of losing her was still there, it wasn't as strong as the agony I felt inside at all the mistakes I'd made with Mallory. Why was that? As I drove, the lyrics of 'Better than Me' by Hinder floated around the car, and my heart clenched as Austin Winkler's emotion-filled voice spoke the words that expressed exactly how I felt. Mallory could definitely do better than some grumpy barman with a penchant for sad songs and making mistakes.

Mallory was worth ten of me. And I wanted her to be happy, but the thought of her being with someone else knotted my insides and took my breath away. I pulled over and stopped the car for a moment to calm myself down and fight the tears stinging my eyes.

Resting my head forward on the steering wheel, I remembered my words to Mallory, uttered in a lucid moment when I was drunk and she had rescued me from myself. *'I don't want to be alone. I hate it.'* And I did hate it. But I was torn between being alone for the right reasons and forcing myself to be with someone for the wrong ones.

The more I tossed the thoughts around my mind like papers on the wind, the more I decided that maybe my moving on would help Mallory to do the same. She deserved to be loved by someone worthy. So maybe I should do this... maybe I should find someone else. Maybe I should do it... for her.

*

The night after my gig, Mallory and I had a shift together at the pub. I left my car at home and walked down to the village in the crisp October evening air, enjoying the starry canopy overhead. When I arrived, Mallory was already there behind the bar and she smiled as I walked in.

As the night progressed and things quietened down, I decided to ask Mallory's advice about Kate. I really liked her and seeing as I was *single* – kind of... aside from the small matter of my marriage still being legal – and seeing as Mallory didn't want me, I was thinking of asking Kate out for a drink or meal or something. But this time I would be honest from the start. See, I do learn from my mistakes.

I hoped that Mallory would see I was doing what she had asked of me and after I'd rambled on about Kate for a while, Mallory simply said, 'Well, maybe you should just go for it.' Her voice was devoid of enthusiasm and emotion. I'd clearly bored the head off her.

'Aye, maybe I will.'

*

The following week I arrived again at the club owned by Kate's father. The place was buzzing and quite a crowd had gathered. Adrenaline coursed through my veins for more than one reason. I was excited about the gig, obviously, but I'd also decided to ask Kate out on a date – something I hadn't done in a very long time. She hadn't been wearing a ring on her left hand when we met, and she had flirted with me, so I figured why the fuck not?

She was sitting at the bar rather than standing behind it, and I went over to say hello. She looked lovely in a royal-blue dress that dipped low in the front but not in a tasteless way. As I approached her, she turned and smiled.

'Well, hello there, Greg. Looking very handsome again, I see.'

I'd made a special effort and worn a new shirt with my black jeans, so I was glad she'd noticed. 'Thank you. You're looking rather stunning yourself, Kate.' She blushed, which was really sweet. 'So, not working tonight, eh?'

'No, I decided I wanted to give you my full attention tonight.'

She was *definitely* interested. 'Look, Kate, I was wondering… would you maybe like to go out for a bite to eat with me sometime?'

A wide smile appeared on her face and she pulled her bottom lip into her mouth, something she seemed to do when she was flirting. 'I'd love to. I was hoping you'd ask.'

That was it. It was easier than I'd expected. We

arranged a night out and I went to play. She watched me and sang along when she knew the words, but I didn't mind really. She had a lovely smile and it stayed in place for the whole evening.

At the end of the gig I asked how she was getting home. I wasn't sure if she lived locally or even if she maybe lived above the venue with her father.

'I was going to get a cab, why?'

'I could always drop you at home. That way I know where to pick you up from on our date.'

'Good idea. Come on, then,' she called over her shoulder as she headed towards the exit.

I followed and opened the door for her to climb in.

Chapter Forty-six

After following Kate's directions, we arrived at a small block of flats on the outskirts of Oban and I switched off the engine.

'Do you mind if I don't invite you in?' Her question gave me a flashback of Mallory, and I had to shake my head slightly to dislodge the thought of her from my mind.

'Erm, no, I wasn't expecting you to. We've only just met, after all.'

She leaned across to me and kissed my cheek gently. When she pulled away, she smiled and said, 'Until we meet again, Greg.'

'Y-yes. See you soon, Kate. Have a great week, eh? Don't study too hard.'

She huffed. 'Sorry, I can't promise that. I always have my head stuck in a book. Our lovely date will be a welcome distraction.'

We said goodnight and once I saw she was safely inside, I pulled away from her home. As I drove back to Clachan I analysed the kiss she had bestowed upon me. It wasn't passionate. There were no fireworks. Maybe I just needed to get Mallory out my head? Maybe I needed to give myself time? I hoped that was all it was, seeing as Mallory and I clearly had no future and I didn't want to spend the rest of my life alone. When subjected to my own company for too long I drove mysel' mad, so there was no wonder people felt the same. Oh, God, listen to me on a bloody downer. Right... shut up, McBradden, and get on with the story...

*

Mallory disappeared down to Yorkshire again; a fact that I tried not to get too worked up about. She hadn't agreed to sell the house as such. There had been more interest and I knew the inevitable was coming, but at least *for now* she was sticking around. Kate and I had our second date the last weekend in October whilst Mallory was away. We went to a Halloween fun fair for the evening which was great... well... *fun*!

I'd never been too keen on spinning things, and so when she suggested the Waltzer I gave a firm warning. 'You do know that I may throw up if I go on there, Kate?'

She laughed and pulled me along behind her. 'Oh, come on! Don't be such a big girl. I'll hold your hand if you like.'

We stopped in front of the huge, brightly painted contraption with its ornately decorated cars and I cringed. She was loving this. Loving teasing me.

'Well, don't say I didn't warn you,' I said as I wagged my finger in her face and flicked her nose. 'On your head be it... and I mean that in the very *literal* sense of the phrase. Just remember that hot dogs don't look the same on the way back up.'

She burst into fits of laughter. 'Oh, that's disgusting! Come on, I'm even more determined now.'

We took our place in the carriage and the security bar lowered. My heart pounded and I felt the colour drain from my face. *Oooh, shit.* The spotty teenage attendant took my money and went on his way and Kate gripped my left hand in her right one and squeezed.

'Look at me,' she instructed and so I turned to face her. We hadn't really taken the next step towards any type of intimacy as yet; ending our first date with another chaste kiss on the cheek. But as she sat there beside me I could see the longing in her eyes. 'Just focus on me and you'll be fine.' The smile slipped from her lips as she leaned in and took my mouth with hers and I reciprocated the kiss. Our first kiss. Her lips were soft and her free hand snaked up into the hair at the nape of my neck. But it wasn't anything like my first kiss with Mallory.

She tried to deepen the kiss as the carriage began to move, but I pulled away, instead gazing into her caramel-brown eyes. I *wanted* to want her. I *really* did. But I didn't return the passion she clearly had for me and that made guilt bubble to the surface.

As we spun and she kept her eyes fixed on mine, a wave of nausea came over me. I swallowed it down, closing my eyes briefly and trying to gain my equilibrium as the ride took us round and round, making my head spin.

I just needed time. Didn't I?

I couldn't jump in with both feet as I'd been prepared to do with Mallory. That was different. It was my *heart* that had been in complete control. This time I would use my head and think logically. My heart had steered me wrong too many times in the past.

'Are you okay?' Kate asked over the noise of the engine and loud eighties music. Duran Duran's 'Hungry Like the Wolf' blaring out at far too many decibels didn't help my unsettled feeling. Not that I hated the song. I quite *liked* it, for eighties music, but the volume was a little more brain-shattering than I could take – and I couldn't help comparing Kate to the lyrics, which was maybe a little unnecessary.

'Think so,' I replied. She rested her forehead on mine and smiled. When the ride finished we climbed down, and as I stepped onto terra firma once again, I resembled something akin to Bambi trying to walk on ice. At least I didn't do the splits, I suppose. Not a great way to impress a prospective girlfriend really, but in my opinion, she only had herself to blame. She couldn't stop giggling at me and her laughter was contagious. I must've looked a complete tool.

We laughed all the way to the darts stand, where I attempted, in my dizzy state, to win her a cuddly Disney character. After my failed attempts to impress her with my darts throwing – I reckon they were rigged... well, that's my excuse anyway – we went to buy candy floss.

As we sat munching on the melt-in-the-mouth pink fluff, I fessed up about being married. Subtlety was never my strong suit and she seemed a little shocked at my bluntness at first, but I told her I would *always* be honest with her and she seemed to appreciate that. She said that as long as things were really *over* with me and Alice, then she didn't see any reason why it would be an obstacle.

'People make mistakes,' was her answer to the whole thing. How right she was. Maybe she and I had a chance at a future after all? Maybe.

This time when we arrived at her home she invited me in for coffee, but, seeing the glint in her eye, I declined. I explained my refusal in terms of Angus needing a pee, which she couldn't really argue about. What she didn't know was that he was staying at the pub with Stella that night. Guilt reared its head again, but I managed to batter it down by convincing myself I was doing the right thing for both of us. I actually believed I was.

*

Halloween was going to be a fun event at the pub and I was as giddy as a kid off trick-or-treating. Stella had asked me to play and I'd come up with some monster-related songs to get the party going. The poster on the door said *Fancy Dress Required for Entry.* And I'd gone all out on my – rather hairy – Dracula costume. I could've shaved but there was *no way* I was giving up my fuzz! I was going to look the business if you asked me.

Kate came by to help put up the decorations and we started pinning up pumpkin streamers and bats everywhere. I did the usual teenager stunt of chasing her around with a plastic spider, which resulted in us kissing in the back corridor. I waited for the tingling in my gut, but, alas, it didn't materialise and that saddened me.

Mallory's arrival was a shock. Apparently, Stella had texted her and asked her to come in and help decorate the place. I didn't see her come in at first, but when I spotted her I couldn't read the expression she wore. She was an enigma, that woman.

Later on, when Mallory came back through to the bar, I called to her. She glanced between me and Kate, and I wondered for a moment if she was going to avoid coming over. After fiddling about with some streamers, she walked over to where we were.

'Hey, Mally, remember me telling you about Kate? Well, this is she.' I gestured towards the woman beside me with a stupid flourish.

Mallory held out her hand and her cheeks turned pale. 'Erm... h-hi, Kate. It's lovely to meet you.'

Kate eyed me suspiciously before turning back to Mallory and hesitantly holding out her hand. 'Hi, Mallory. Nice to meet you too.' Silence descended. *Shit.*

I watched the exchange with a hammering heart. What would they think of each other? They stared at one another without words for a few more moments until Mallory cleared her throat. 'Um... I... I should go. Stuff to do, you know.' The colour had returned to her cheeks with a vengeance, and I could swear her eyes had welled with tears, but she turned and dashed off before I could see if my eyes were deceiving me. My gaze followed her retreating form as she disappeared through to the back.

Kate's voice broke me from my reverie. 'She seems... um... nice.'

I nodded. 'Yeah... yeah, she is.' Fuck, that had been awkward. But, as I kept reminding myself, I was moving on – just as Mallory wanted.

By the time we had all finished, the place looked amazing. Cobwebs hung from the beams. A skeleton stood in one corner, and the pub was glowing orange in the light of the carved pumpkins Stella had brought in – her nieces and nephews had been hard at work, by the look of their spooky creations.

When night fell, Kate and I arrived back at the pub. She was dressed as Morticia with a white streak in her long, dark hair and heavy, black make-up around her eyes. My hair was slicked back and made to a point on my forehead with gel. The fangs were a little uncomfortable and I knew they'd have to come out when I sang.

My head was filled with thoughts of Mallory and I hated myself for it, but her surprise arrival earlier had thrown me for a loop. She looked *stunning*. Her curves were returning to the way they were when she first arrived in the village and *every* part of my anatomy appreciated that.

'Are you okay, Greg? You've been a little distant since we left here earlier.'

I took a deep breath, knowing I had promised to be honest with her. Puffing the air out of my mouth, I looked her right in the eyes. 'I'm not sure, to be honest. I – I have something to tell you.'

Her smile disappeared and she looked at her hands. 'That sounds ominous.'

'Come and sit down, eh?'

We walked over to the seats near the fireplace and I took her hand. 'Kate, I really do like you but—'

She cringed. 'Oh, heck. I *knew* this was coming.'

'No, no, you misunderstand. I'm not breaking up with you. Well… maybe I am. I just… Look, I promised to be honest with you and I want to keep that promise.'

She inhaled deeply and sat up, straightening her spine as if bracing herself for a physical blow. 'Okay. What is it?'

'Mallory and I. We had this… connection. I thought we had a future but I ruined things.'

'I see. I thought there was something unspoken between you earlier. How long ago was this?'

'Not long at all. But she made it quite clear when she found out I was married that we're not going anywhere. I'd lied by omission, and she's in a fragile place so she took it badly. I hurt her deeply and I know I have no life with her now so I decided I needed to try and move on.'

Her brow furrowed and she chewed on her lip for a moment. 'Okay… so I'm a rebound?'

Yep. I'm a bastard. 'Not intentionally, Kate. I don't mean you to feel that way. I really like you. But…'

'Your feelings for her are still strong?'

I nodded slowly, daring to meet her sad eyes.

'I see… I see. So where do we go from here?'

'Honestly? I really don't know. I want to move on *so much*. Believe me. I don't *want* to feel this way but… I love her. And I'll take a while to get over it. I should never have strung you along and I feel like shit. I just… I think maybe it's not the right time for you and me to be together. But I *do* like you. Like I said, I think I just need time.' I'm pretty sure I was trying to convince myself as well as Kate.

She nodded and her eyes were pained. 'Okay… I need to think. This is a lot to process. But… I like you too, Greg. I hoped we had the beginnings of something special. And this… this is quite hurtful. Can you understand that?'

'Of course I can. Absolutely. Maybe I could call you? Maybe we could stay friends and see what happens?' Friends. Yeah, 'cause I was such an expert at that concept. Look what I'd done to my other friend. I remembered how shitty it had felt when Mallory had said she'd wanted us to be *just friends*, and yet here I was doing the same thing to Kate. My bastardly ways clearly knew no bounds.

I expected a, 'Hell, no, pal,' but instead Kate said, 'I'd like to say yes, but I can't make that promise. I appreciate you being honest though. I understand about unrequited love and I know how painful it is. But… I don't want to be in *that* position myself. Not again.'

I smiled and stroked her cheek. 'Okay, I totally understand. And I'm sorry for dragging you into this.'

Her eyes were glassy and I wondered how slim the chances of her being able to stay friends with me *were*. My guess was very, *very* slim to the point of being intangible. I expected her to leave immediately, but she stuck around, to my surprise. I wasn't really sure why. I know *I* would've got the hell out of Dodge if things had been the other way around.

*

Mallory walked in shortly after and removed her coat,

revealing her cat outfit. My jaw almost hit the floor. The phrase *hamana-hamana-hamana* sprang to mind. *Rein yourself in, you tit. Kate's here, remember.* Luckily Kate was in the back collecting the food for the buffet, and so she missed my reaction. When she came through, the women greeted each other civilly. But I couldn't help noticing the icy chill that seemed to fall between them. Talk about confused.

Eventually it was time for me to take my familiar spot behind the mic. I started playing and included suitably spooky tracks like 'The Monster Mash' and 'Thriller', which got people dancing. The night was going well, and every so often, in my peripheral vision, I caught sight of Kate and Mallory watching me simultaneously or watching each other when the other wasn't looking. I made eye contact with Mallory for the first time all night, and the look in her eyes was giving very mixed messages, considering it didn't correlate with the words she had uttered to me about being *just friends*.

I decided to throw caution to the wind and send Mallory yet another message through music. It was a last-ditch attempt to make her rethink her decision and it was admittedly a crappy thing to do when Kate was still there, but I was past the point of caring. Announcing the next song as a smoochy number, I encouraged the crowd to pair off in their ghoulish couples.

I have to say that the romance of the moment was

somewhat killed by the amount of fake blood in the room and I had to fight to keep a straight face as I sang 'Wherever You Will Go' by The Calling. I closed my eyes and imagined the look I *wanted* to see on Mallory's face. In my dream world she would be standing there with tears in her eyes, her hands over her mouth as she realised she *was* in love with me after all. It was easier with my eyes closed and I knew that when I opened them she would simply be serving yet another Frankenstein or werewolf with a pint of beer.

At the end of the night I couldn't see Kate. I guessed she had left after all and I resolved to send her a text to check she got home okay. I doubted she would answer a call from me, so there was no point trying that.

I was about to go speak to Mallory when I was surrounded by a group of young women. There was a combination of slutty witches, pumpkins, and axe-wielding, blood-spattered ghouls in skimpy costumes. There was a whole lot of cleavage on show and they were brandishing camera phones and asking for selfies with me. It was hilarious really, but I seemed to have acquired groupies.

I packed away my gear and waved to Mallory as she left. I would have to catch up with her at work on Tuesday, maybe. Monday was going to be a busy one. I had some work to do on *Little Blue* before the really bad weather hit.

After I arrived home I went to bed, wishing Mallory

were there with me. Sometime later I remembered I should text Kate. I received a brief and to-the-point reply letting me know she was fine, and so I went back to bed, still alone and feeling like a complete shit. But where was the change in that?

Chapter Forty-seven

A couple of days later the weather began to turn nasty. It was the beginning of November; torrential rain and storms were a regular occurrence, making any outside work unpleasant and cold. Tuesday afternoon wasn't bad to start with, and I set out to see Tom Carrick Snr in the village about fixing his kitchen sink. When I arrived, their two sons were out somewhere and so Annie was making the most of the fact and cleaning their typical teenage boys' bedrooms.

Every so often she brought down another pile of dirty dishes, mumbling under her breath that she was raising animals. It made me chuckle; I remembered my mum saying the same about me and my brothers. Eventually, when I switched the water back on briefly, Annie made me a cup of coffee – the proper stuff – and I turned the water off again so that I could continue work, changing the seized nuts and making the thing fully functional again.

It was a longer job than anticipated and at around half four I heard Tom on the phone sounding panicked. I placed my empty cup in the newly fixed sink and walked to the door to find him pacing round the lounge and speaking loudly into the phone.

'I can't believe you went out there when I said the weather was going to turn, Tom. I'm going to ring the coastguard. Hang on, son. We'll get to you somehow. Just... hang on.'

Once he'd ended his call his face was white as alabaster and he was shaking violently. Annie was standing beside him, gripping his arm and waiting for his explanation. The sky suddenly lit up outside and the subsequent clap of thunder shook the foundations of the house, making us all jump.

'What on earth has happened, Tom?' Annie asked with a wavering voice.

'Tom Junior and James are out on their dinghy, Annie. They're in trouble and they've lost their paddles. Thank the Lord they got a mobile signal. I need to ring the coastguard.'

A look of confusion washed over Annie's pale features and she gripped the wall for support. 'But... they can't be. You told them not to go.'

'I know darling, I know. But they're teenage boys who think they're invincible. We just need to get them home safe.'

Shit, no! I had to act fast. I was well aware that my boat still needed essential repairs, but time was of the essence so I decided it would have to do. Kids' lives were at risk. 'Right, I'm off to take *Little Blue* out. Did they leave from the marina, Tom?'

He nodded. 'Aye, Greg. Oh, God, if anything happens to them—' He gripped his greying hair.

'No, don't think that way. I'll get out there. You call the coastguard and wait here for news.'

'Please be careful, Greg, and thank you,' Annie called after me as I bolted out to the Landy.

I drove as fast as I could to the marina through the sheet of rain that battered my windscreen. By the time I reached *Little Blue* the torrent was hammering down even harder and I was soaked to the skin. I jumped on board, started the engine and untied the line on the mooring.

The water was choppy and the boat was tossed around like a rag doll as I made my way out into open water past the jagged rocks that edged the small harbour. My damned bucket was thrown overboard by the bouncing and crashing of the boat as a fifteen-foot wave hit. The sky was almost black except for the flashes of lightning that lit up the area like the midday sun. Those poor lads were out there somewhere, terrified, soaking wet, and freezing cold. My determination to find them alive drove me forward.

I caught sight of their orange dinghy about half a mile off shore. How the hell they had drifted out there I didn't know, but it scared the hell out of me watching them being thrown over every wave that hit. My heart drummed at my ribcage and my pulse quickened. *Little Blue* wasn't equipped for rough seas, especially in her current condition. And I had no idea if I would even get out there, but I had to try.

I *had* to.

I pushed on ahead going as fast as I possibly could, but the waters were so very rough and the boat was beginning to take in water. I had nothing with me to bail it out and so I had no other choice but to forge ahead. Lightning flashed again, striking a distant point, and I swiped the rain from my face, scrunching my eyes to try and make out the dinghy. I'd lost sight of it and dread washed over me.

After what felt like hours but was probably more like minutes, I could hear the coastguard's helicopter overhead, but I couldn't make out much thanks to the rain battering my face and body. Suddenly a huge wave crashed into the boat and we hit a rock to the starboard side. I was thrown into the sea, managing to suck in a deep breath before I was pulled under. I had no idea which way was up and I flailed my arms, desperately trying to make it to the surface before my lungs emptied. Filled with panic, I broke into the cold evening air and gasped, trying my best to pull much-needed oxygen into my lungs. I grappled for the hull of the boat and felt splinters pierce my skin. The wet wood was slimy and slipped under my hands, making holding on even more difficult. I wouldn't be able to hold on for long.

Lightning lit up the heavens and the words *Little Blue* were illuminated for a split second before I was thrown back into darkness.

I fought to clamber back on board but *Little Blue* capsized with the next wave, pulling me under a second time. I opened my eyes and the freezing-cold water stung like a thousand needles. The water was black and I could see nothing at all. I moved my arms frantically through the water as my lungs burned, hoping once more that I was going in the right direction. Flailing, I made it to the surface and gasped for air but pulled in water as well this time. I began to choke and tried to cough out the saltwater I'd inhaled. My throat stung and the pain in my lungs was excruciating.

Grasping the sharp pieces of wood that were floating on the surface, I frantically looked around again. As I clung on I thought about those poor boys. I was a grown man, but they were youngsters with their whole lives ahead of them. Okay, I'd made enough mistakes for ten men, but at least I'd had the opportunity to live and to love. My heart ached at the thought of my rescue attempt failing. Yet again, I'd let down someone I cared about. And now I'd be lost at sea and people would have to deal with my mistakes and my failings... as they always did. Anger at my own weakness tugged at me and I gripped what was left of *Little Blue* harder until more splinters pierced my skin and I could see trails of blood, garish in the flickers of lightning, seeping from the puncture wounds.

I thought of Mallory, back at the pub, her blue eyes

sparkling as she served the customers, making them feel important in that special way she had. They all loved her, just as I did. What was there not to love? She would be *distraught* when she heard I'd gone. I know we were nothing more than friends, but I could imagine her heart breaking all over again as it did when she lost Sam. How could I be so stupid? Why did I have to play the hero? I should've let the *real* heroes do their job, but instead I went gung-ho as I always do and I was facing the prospect of losing my life.

Images of Mallory's beautiful face flashed through my mind as I imagined her crying over my death. I didn't want to put her through that. She didn't deserve to go through that *again*. Not for *me*. I wasn't worth it. And I had caused her so much pain as it was. But in a small way I wanted her to think of me as a hero. *Her* hero. From the beginning I'd wanted to save *her,* but instead she'd saved *me*. And now I was going to die without being able to say thank you.

Without seeing her face again.

Without holding her again.

An angry cry ripped from my chest and my heart shattered as another wave crashed into me and *Little Blue*, tossing us around like feathers on a breeze. Bits of wood flew through the air and hit me on my head, face and arms. My legs were beginning to go numb where they were submerged under the icy torrent.

As I waited there and thought about what could have

been, my eyes blurred. Fear wasn't something I'd ever really felt before. But now I was scared. Not about dying but about never getting the chance to say sorry to Mallory properly. I didn't want to be lost at sea, broken apart like an old boat. I wanted to see her again. I wanted the possibility of trying to convince her to forgive me. The last thing I wanted was to make her cry again. But I knew she would. I knew that, in spite of what we'd been through, she would grieve all over again, and it would be for me this time.

An ominous roar rushed towards me. When I looked up, a wall of black water was looming above me. There was nothing I could do except snatch a breath before the sea crashed around me, tearing me away from the boat and tossing and tumbling me in its depths until I couldn't hold my breath any longer.

Chapter Forty-eight

My eyelids fluttered open and my head hurt like hell. Where the hell was I? I wasn't in the water anymore. Was I dead? Confusion clouded my mind and I called out, 'Mallory.' But when my voice left my body it was nothing more than a strangled whisper.

I must have drifted off because the next time I opened my eyes there was a woman hovering over me. I tried to touch her face, but I couldn't raise my hand. I was so very weak. 'Mallory… Mallory,' I whispered again.

'Who's Mallory, love? Can we call her for you?'

'Mallory…' Everything went black once again.

*

I had no idea how much time had passed or whether I was in fact awake at the time, but I heard voices. My eyes wouldn't open and everything echoed as if I were at the end of a very long tunnel. Maybe I was dreaming? Maybe I *was* dead? The cruelty of my imagination ripped at my heart as I heard her voice in my head.

'Greg, I want you to know that I'm sorry for how I reacted when you told me about Alice. You said you don't love her and I should've accepted that. It doesn't matter that you're still married if you don't love her. It's just a piece of paper that can be dealt with... You said you love me. I should have just been happy and now I'm scared I'm going to lose you, too. You need to get better, Greg. You need to come home.'

The voice faded, and when I opened my eyes again, I was standing on the bridge over the Atlantic at night. The crescent moon was high in the sky and the stars dotted the dark canvas around it like tiny jewels. Glancing to my left, I gazed into the sparkling eyes of my true love.

She leaned in and stroked my hair. Her touch was soft and I felt myself relaxing as I gazed at her. God, she was beautiful.

'It's strange how it's taken something like this to kick me up the arse and make me realise exactly how I feel. I was intent on talking things through with you tonight to see if we could get past what happened between us. But when I found out that you had gone missing, I thought through everything we've been through. The arguments, the kisses, the laughs. And it dawned on me. Nothing else matters.'

I opened my mouth to reply to Mallory, but no words would form. I crumpled my brow and tried again as panic washed over me. Why couldn't I answer her? She would think I didn't care.

She continued, 'The thing that matters most is that I

love you, Greg.' The moonlight glistened on her cheeks, betraying her tears, and I tried to reach out but again I couldn't will my body to act. 'Greg, can you hear me?' I tried to reply. I could hear the panic in her voice. *Why can't I speak? I need to answer her.* 'Greg, I'm in love with you. Please don't leave me. I'm stupid and I'm stubborn and self-righteous. I judged you and made assumptions about you and I was so, so wrong. You told me *exactly* how you felt and I threw it back in your face. And now I realise that I love you and don't want to be without you. It doesn't matter how soon this has happened. It's no one's fault. It doesn't make it wrong. Please just wake up and tell me you still love me.' *Wake up? I don't...*

Mallory faded away and once again my mind disconnected with cognitive thought.

*

I opened my eyes and stared up at a white ceiling. A strange-smelling clear mask covered my face tightly and a cold stream of air was being forced into my nose and mouth. Something gripped my hand and I squeezed it back. It felt warm, like soft skin. I turned my face towards the direction of my right hand to find Mallory staring at me, wide-eyed and very pale.

I lifted my left hand and removed the mask from my face. 'Hey, Mally. You came.' My words were filled with disbelief and my throat was very dry and sore.

She let out a sob. 'Of course I came, Greg.' I begged her not to cry and enquired about the boys, Tom and James. Hearing that they were safe and well filled me with relief, and my own eyes stung with unshed tears.

My mind drifted back to the vivid dream I'd had about Mallory and me on the bridge. I told her she had woken me from a really good dream, and she apologised. Should I tell her about it? My mouth took over where my head couldn't decide.

'The dream was strange. You were in it, crying and stroking my hair... and you told me you were in love with me and it made me so happy.' Tears escaped my eyes and I closed them. I could feel my lip trembling. How could I look at her now? I covered my eyes with my free hand. 'But then I woke up.'

She begged me to open my eyes and look at her, but I couldn't possibly do that. I held my hand up to stop her and apologised for what I'd put her through. The shit with Alice. The attempt at moving on with Kate. I'd ruined any chance I had at happiness with her. Every time I realised this, it was like a new pain that I was experiencing for the first time. My heart ached and suddenly I wanted to be left alone. I was exhausted and couldn't deal with the barrage of emotions I was experiencing.

'Greg, look at me, *please*,' she demanded. And so taking a deep breath through my sore nose, I made eye contact with her. Tears trailed down her cheeks but she smiled through them. 'Greg, it wasn't a dream. I said and did those things. I stroked your hair and squeezed your hand. And… and I told you I'm in love with you and that I never want to be without you again.' More saltwater fell from her eyes, and I tried to process what she was saying. Had I drifted off again? Was my subconscious torturing me?

I closed my eyes and replayed what I *thought* I'd just heard. When I opened them, I stared deep into her eyes, looking for any sign that this was real. She smiled back at me and gave a little laugh that melted my heart.

My face relaxed and I asked, 'You did? You *love* me?' I searched her eyes further. This wasn't really happening, was it?

She nodded. 'I love you. Greg, I want to be with you, always.' She leaned into me and kissed my lips gently as if afraid to cause me more pain. 'Do you still… want me though, Greg?'

A wide smile took over my face. I could feel it pulling at the taut, grazed skin around my eyes. 'Do you really need to ask me that?'

Huffing out a long breath, she stroked my hair. 'That's so good to hear. Now please get well so we can get you out of here and decide where the heck I'm going to live… seeing as I think I may have sold my house.'

I reached up to touch her hair as I looked up at her, longing for her to *really* hear me. 'Mallory?'

'Yes, Greg?'

'I love you. More than *anything* in this world.'

Chapter Forty-nine

Mallory stayed with me in hospital for as long as she could and when she left she visited regularly until I was able to leave. And even then, she hardly ever left my side. I was plagued by a fresh set of nightmares. I would wake up screaming and flailing my arms. The images of being surrounded by water and blackness tormented me whenever I closed my eyes. It was a kind of post-traumatic stress according to the psychologist I'd been seeing in hospital. And it would pass eventually but would need time.

Every single time she walked in, the first thing we did was kiss and hold each other. Sometimes our exchanges got a little out of hand, but we didn't care. Even when I was moved to the general ward, I needed to feel her mouth on mine and her hands in my hair just to remind myself that this was real. She was mine and there was no way I was letting her go now.

No. Way.

One particularly heated exchange had Mallory blushing and panting. God, I wanted her so badly and I couldn't wait until I was fitter. I told her the truth straight from my heart. 'If being out there in that icy water, fearing for my life, has taught me anything, it's that from now on I'm not going to hide my emotions any more. I love you and I want you and I don't care who sees or who knows it.' The way she gazed back at me through hooded eyes told me she felt exactly the same and my heart was full to bursting with love for her.

*

I was so relieved to hear that she had rejected the offers made on Sealladh-mara Cottage and had decided to stay in Clachan, and on the day I was released, she picked me up in the Landy to take me back to her house. I was suitably impressed at her driving such a huge vehicle after her tiny one. But that was Mallory. She liked to surprise me.

I expressed how proud of her I was and she laughed. 'Yes, and, boy, that was a fun experience. It put a smile on my face, that's for sure.'

'See, I knew I could convert you. We'll need to get you one instead of that pocket-sized, pretend car you drive around in now.' I loved to tease her. 'Winters around here are a sight to behold but my, oh, my, will you know about it if you try to go out in your toy car.' She pursed her lips at me and I could tell that my comment was being added to her mental list of things to get me back for at a later date. I couldn't wait for her to take her revenge.

As soon as we were back at her house, I pulled her down onto the couch with me and took her mouth in a deep, passionate kiss, stealing the breath from her body as she melted into me. I slipped my tongue over hers as my hand grasped her hair. I wanted to be inside her. My whole body wanted her.

When the kiss was over I met her crystal-clear blue eyes. 'God, I've wanted to do that properly for so long. And I'm willing my ribs to get better quickly. I'm not sure where we are on the taking-it-slow thing, but I'd appreciate a heads-up 'cause I'm just about going to go crazy here.'

'Please, just get well, Greg; quickly.' The kiss that followed her fevered words told me all I needed to know. She was desperate for me too.

As the evening wore on I became more and more exhausted. I was struggling to keep my eyes open, and Mallory helped me up the stairs to bed. We laughed as she tried to get me out of my clothes and I couldn't help the odd cheeky remark.

As I stood before her, bruised and battered in my boxers, she traced the tattoo on my chest with her fingertips. The contact stirred up the longing deep within me again and I closed my eyes.

Eyeing my marks with intrigue, she asked in a whisper, 'What does your tattoo mean? This one on your chest.'

Trying to focus on her question and not on the fact

that my blood was making a speedy journey southwards, I answered, 'It's Gaelic. I studied it at school and it's always been special to me. The tattoo translates, roughly, as "Love conquers all". I got it to remind myself that no matter what life throws at me, whether it's my wife and best friend betraying me; Mairi being killed on a mountain; or me ballsing anything up in a big way… for example with the woman I'm in love with now… Whatever it is, love will still find a way and I've not to give up on it. And you see…' I leaned in and placed a gentle kiss on her forehead '… I was right.'

We climbed into bed and she turned out the light. I slipped my arm around her and she nuzzled into my chest. 'Hmm, feels good to be next to you again,' I whispered.

'It really does.' She stroked my chest until I fell into a peaceful, nightmare-free sleep.

*

At the end of November Mallory was still cautious about us and it worried me a little. When it came down to her telling Sam's family about us, she faltered and I became scared that maybe she hadn't quite put her trust in us. But I discovered her worries lay more around what Sam's family would think of her for betraying Sam's memory. Of course I knew they would think nothing of the sort, but I could understand her trepidation. We talked it all through and she decided to make the call.

I sat beside her as she sobbed down the line to Renee. Her pseudo-mother-in-law was wonderful about the whole thing. It turned out that she'd known from the moment she met me that Mallory and I were destined to be together. Knowing that fact settled my mind and I felt a kind of acceptance that I had never experienced before. I was part of a loving family once more and it felt amazing.

The relief was evident throughout Mallory's whole demeanour once her call to Canada had ended, and I think we both knew at that point that we could move forward.

We spent as much time together as possible from then. We took walks along the beach with Angus and Ruby, the two of us wrapped around each other against the cold. We visited *Little Blue* where she had been moored again ready for repair. Seeing the mangled and splintered pieces of the hull made my insides knot and brought back terrifying memories; but as they say, if you fall off the horse it's best to get right back on, and I would as soon as I was able.

Even mundane tasks like supermarket shopping were fun. I made her laugh hysterically by singing along to the music purposefully out of tune.

'Ever thought of being a singer?' she asked me as we stood in the canned-goods aisle.

'Why? Do you think I should?' I had just finished a

terrible rendition of 'Pour Some Sugar on Me'. I actually should have been suitably impressed that the store was playing decent music instead of ruining it with my caterwauling, but it made my girl laugh so what the heck?

'Well, you do have the voice of an angel,' she teased.

Slipping my arms around her waist, I kissed her right by the baked beans – and no, that's not a euphemism. Everything we did together was new and exciting. I wanted to experience *everything* with her.

I began to get funny looks as I walked through the village, whistling to myself and smiling. I guess people thought Grumpy Greg had been abducted by aliens or something. But I really *had* changed. I had to admit to myself that I was happier right then than I'd ever been. I think I found myself when I found Mallory. Or when she found me. Or when Mairi and Sam brought us together.

My favourite times were when we stood on the bridge over the Atlantic, looking out at the ocean and holding hands or kissing. It was becoming *our* special place and I loved that.

Chapter Fifty

By December my healing process was almost complete, and I was getting about much easier. My fractured ribs had meant my relationship with Mallory had to be taken slow. We had agreed to wait before taking things further, and, my God, it was slowly killing me to lie beside her and be unable to make love to her. It was all I wanted, to connect with her completely, but I kept reminding myself that when it did happen, it would be worth the wait. It was like a daily mantra. Who am I kidding? It was a fucking *hourly* mantra.

I was still plagued with a few other aches and pains, but nothing that a strapping six-foot-two bloke like me couldn't handle. Christmas was on the horizon and I was excited to be sharing it with Mallory. My last Christmas hadn't been that great, so this one was under pressure to be perfect.

The first weekend in December was tree-buying time. I had always thought *I* was a big kid when it came to Christmas, but it turned out Mallory was just as bad – if not worse! She hummed and hawed about which tree to get and we stood there in the tree sales yard for ages.

'That one looks a bit spindly, don't you think?' she

asked as I hugged my arms around my body to keep warm.

'Just pick one so we can bloody go home, woman,' I said, nudging her with my shoulder.

She turned to me, slipped her arms around my neck, and pouted. 'It's got to be just right though, Greg. This is for *us*.'

And there went my heart, melted into a puddle of mush on the floor beneath her furry boots. I leaned in and kissed her tenderly with a smile. 'Whatever you choose it *will* be just right. *Because* it's for us.'

Eventually we went back to the *first* tree we'd looked at – but I now understand this to be a typical female trait. We loaded it into the Landy and climbed in. I glanced over and she looked a little sad.

Reaching over, I stroked her cheek. 'Hey, what's wrong, gorgeous?'

'Oh… nothing. I was just wondering…'

After a pause I became inquisitive. 'Wondering what?'

'Nothing, it's silly. You'll think I'm daft.'

I chuckled. 'I already think you're daft. You're *my* girl, remember?'

She smiled and rolled her eyes. 'I was just wondering… if there *is* a heaven… and Mairi and Sam are up there, do you think…? Do you think they're friends?'

She broke my heart with the way she thought. God,

she was so cute sometimes.

Tilting her chin round so she faced me, I placed a kiss on her nose. 'I *know* they are.' A peaceful smile played on her lips. I'd apparently satisfied her with my answer, and so we set off for home.

Getting the tree into Mallory's cottage was interesting. You don't realise the quirkiness of cottages until you have to manoeuvre something like a hunk of trunk with spiky branches through two doors. Mallory was as much use as a bloody chocolate fire grate. As I struggled with the bloody thing, she giggled uncontrollably, which, of course, in turn, had me laughing too. Two laughing adults plus one large, spiky pine tree equalled a bad combination.

Once the tree was situated in the living room, I poured us a wee dram of sherry and we started going through our decorations. I have to admit at this point to having *very little* taste when it comes to such things. My ornaments were... how do I put it? Well, *tacky* and brightly coloured, whereas hers were classical and showed an understated elegance that my childish ones could never aspire to in a million years.

Whilst I hung fat-bellied, red-nosed Santa Clauses and goggle-eyed snowmen at the front, she surreptitiously removed them and placed them towards the back, replacing them with her own handmade, wooden Christmas trees and gold-sprayed pine cones. I watched her doing this for a while, trying not to give the game away, but eventually I wrestled her to the ground.

Tickling her ribs, I sat astride her torso. 'Admit it, Westerman, admit that you're ashamed of my plastic snowmen.'

Giggling and struggling, she shouted, 'Never! I don't know what you mean.'

'You're taking them off and moving them, you cheeky wee mare.'

'Not a clue what you mean,' she squealed. 'Stop it or I'll pee!' We rolled around laughing hysterically and eventually, even if a little begrudgingly, my plastic snowmen and Santa ornaments took pride of place amongst her grown-up ones. Greg one… Mallory nil.

As we sat there admiring our stunning, if a little bizarrely decorated tree – it really was having an identity crisis – we chatted about Hogmanay, and Brad and Josie's visit. It would be good to see them, but that wasn't what I was looking forward to the most.

Turning to Mallory, I stroked my hand down her cheek. 'Do you know what *I'm* looking forward to?' I moved in closer and could feel her warm breath on my face.

'What?' she whispered, no doubt reading my mind.

'I'm looking forward to unwrapping *you* on Christmas morning and kissing you all over.'

She gasped and her pupils dilated. Leaning in, she took my mouth, slipping her tongue inside and breathing in deeply through her nose. When she pulled away, I locked my eyes on hers through a heady fog of lust.

Swallowing, she smoothed her hand down my chest. 'Why wait until Christmas morning?'

Oh. Fucking. Yes. I needed no further encouragement as I smiled, stood, and took her hand. This was it. It was *finally* happening. I fought back the doubts trying to seep into my mind about whether I would satisfy her and focused on the fact that this was *us* and we were *meant* to be.

I led the way upstairs and once inside the bedroom I pulled her against me, slipping my hands down to her rounded bottom. 'I've waited for this moment since the day I met you.' My voice was almost unrecognisable as lust and emotion had taken me over. I could hardly speak but I wanted to convey my feelings this time using my *own* words instead of those belonging to another. 'I want to savour this. I want to savour *you,* Mallory. I love you with all my heart, but I want you with every inch of my being.'

I'd never spoken a truer word. I was *hers*. *All* of me. I trailed my hand up her body and into her hair. Lowering my mouth so that it almost touched hers, I relished the feeling of her warm breath increasing in speed on my lips as I gazed at her, knowing my longing was clearly evident. I closed my eyes as she slid her hands up over my chest; the feel of her fingers caressing me this way sent pleasure shooting to my very core. I clenched my jaw, determined to keep my cool and fighting the urge to throw her back onto the bed and climb on top of her.

No, I would take this slowly.

As her hands found my hair, I touched my lips to hers, gently at first but I was grasping onto to my self-control by a hair's breadth. The kiss deepened and the taste of her overtook my senses. I heard a groan escape from my throat and felt slightly embarrassed, but she didn't pull away. Her breathing quickened as she grasped at my hair and I at hers.

She tugged at the hem of my T-shirt, dragging it from my body in one swift motion as I stooped to make the process easier. Once my chest was fully exposed to her hungry eyes, she leaned in and kissed my tattoo, grazing my nipple with her tongue. I inhaled sharply and my head rolled back as I relished the feel of her lips on my skin.

I pulled her sweater from her body. My eyes were drawn to her full breasts in their blue lace bra, and I swallowed hard. Tracing my fingers along her collarbone, I kept my eyes on hers, watching her every reaction to my touch. Her hands found my waistband, and before I knew it, I was stepping out of my jeans and kicking them to one side. Then it was her turn. Unclasping the button of her jeans, I slipped my hands inside and squeezed her bottom before sliding the denim down her legs.

We finally stood before each other in just our underwear. The butterflies took flight in my stomach.

This was *really* happening. A wide smile took over my face and I shook my head.

'Why are you smiling?' she asked in a quiet, nervous voice.

'I'm just looking at you and thinking that I must be the luckiest man on the planet right now.' She peered up at me in disbelief, a frown creasing her brow. Taking her face in my hands, I smoothed my thumbs over her lips. 'You truly are beautiful, Mallory. So very sexy. And you just don't seem to realise that. Your curves, your skin… I mean you're just… *so beautiful.* I can't put into words how much I want you.'

'You did a pretty good job with words right there. But if you can't… can't find words… just show me?'

There was nothing I wanted more. I kissed her again as I unfastened the blue lace bra from around her ribs. Dropping it to the floor, I caressed her breasts first with my hands and then with my mouth. Her nipples tightened and she sighed, allowing her eyes to fall closed. She had the most beautiful breasts I had ever seen, and the taste of her skin was like some intoxicating elixir. I couldn't get enough of her and felt sure that I never would.

Dropping to my knees before her, I gazed up into her half-closed eyes and slipped the blue lace panties down her smooth thighs. Kissing her soft belly and hips, I circled the skin there gently with my thumbs. I loved the noises she made; they told me she was enjoying what I was doing to her as much as I was enjoying *doing* it. I nuzzled the soft hair at the junction of her thighs and inhaled her scent. I was already addicted and needed to taste her there too. I slipped my tongue into her damp flesh and her legs almost buckled. Gripping her hips to steady her, I caressed her with my tongue as she massaged my scalp with her deft fingers, sending shivers down my spine.

I watched as her breasts heaved and her mouth fell open. That look of sheer ecstasy had me mesmerised. She was on the verge of release but I wanted more. I stood, removed my boxers, and turned her around. When I pulled her to my chest, my arousal pressed into her lower back, sending delicious tingles down my body to where we connected.

I took her breast into my hand and squeezed the tight bud between my finger and thumb, making her gasp and lean her head back into my shoulder. I kissed and sucked at the soft flesh of her neck and smoothed my hands up and down the curve of her waist; another of my favourite areas of her curvaceous body. Stepping away to take in the vision of her naked body again, I skimmed my eyes down her back to her luscious bottom. I couldn't believe this was happening. I couldn't believe she was finally mine. I'd been hers for so long. The emotion of it all overwhelmed me and I dropped to my knees in disbelief again.

'Mallory.' Her name left my throat as a strangled sob

as I took in the image of her before me. 'Is this real?'

She reached down and took my hands. She pulled to me my feet and cupped my face in her hands. 'Greg, I realised how I felt about you when I was in Yorkshire, the last time. I was so angry with myself for how I handled things. I figured I'd probably ruined everything

I shook my head. I couldn't believe she'd thought that *she'd* ruined things after all the crap *I'd* put her through.

She stepped closer to me, her soft breasts connecting with my skin. 'I love you, Greg, so much. I was so scared to even acknowledge my feelings until I went away. I was terrified that you'd fallen for Kate. I'm so glad you hadn't stopped loving me. This is one hundred percent real. There's no going back for me now.'

'I love you so much, Mallory. So, *so* much.' I placed kisses over her cheeks, eyes, and lips, and as our mouths reconnected and our tongues tangled, I relished the taste of her once again. We tumbled onto the bed, wrapped around each other.

I reached down to my jeans where they had fallen and pulled out a small foil packet, opened it, and stretched the sheath down over myself. I began to caress her again and her soft moans were like the best music I'd ever heard, sending shivers down my body and making me desperate for her. She began to tighten around my fingers, and when she cried out I kissed her deeply, swallowing her noises of desire and bliss as if they were necessary for me to live. Moving my body between her thighs, I gazed down at her as she breathed heavily, her eyes filled with adoration. She pulled at my shoulders in a silent instruction and I sank myself inside her body, closing my eyes as the pleasure of our joining filled every fibre of my being.

Never had making love felt the same as it did with Mallory. In that moment I knew I'd found the other half of my soul; the other half of *me*. As I moved my body within hers, we locked eyes – and fear took over me. What if she changed her mind? What if she realised that I wasn't the man for her? *Oh, God, if I lost her now—*

'Greg.' She tangled the fingers of one hand in my hair. 'I love you and I want you… and I mean *forever*.' She had read my mind or seen the worry in my eyes. Either way, she spoke and my fears melted away as she gasped and pulled me into her hard with her other hand.

I fell into the abyss, calling out her name, and she joined me as she fell once more too.

Chapter Fifty-one

After we made love that first time, Mallory asked me to move in with her. To say I was shocked would be the understatement of the year, but I jumped at the chance. I was so glad she had rejected the offer she'd received on the house she loved. We'd pretty much been living together anyway and making it official was the best feeling. It meant she believed in us. It meant we were a couple with a future, and I simply can't express how that made me feel. There are just no words that come close to describing the happiness.

I loaded up the Landy with all my crap and made my way over to my new home. Angus wagged his tail frantically as if he knew. And when I pulled up outside the cottage, I climbed out, ran over to Mallory, scooped her up, and spun her round.

We carried all the boxes from the car into the house until the living room looked like a warehouse. We vowed to start unpacking them as soon as possible, but Mallory enticed me to take a shower. Because I took a lot of encouraging… ha!

As she led me out of the room and we passed the window, she gasped. 'Greg! It's snowing.' I slipped my arms around her waist as she watched the shimmering flakes float to the ground. 'It's perfect,' she sighed. And it really was.

After gazing out at the picture-perfect view, we made our way up the stairs and into the bathroom. We undressed each other slowly and stepped under the cascading hot water, where we washed and caressed each other and made love languorously until the water ran cold.

*

Christmas morning arrived and I regressed to childhood. After making bacon sandwiches, I made my way upstairs to wake my gorgeous girl. Mallory didn't appear to share my enthusiasm for arising early on our first Christmas Day, and I had to resort to underhanded tactics to get her out of bed. After tickling her, I scooped her up and wrestled her over my shoulder, exposing her bare bottom from under the old T-shirt of mine that she slept in and giving it a little playful slap for good measure. Her protests made me laugh, and even though she slapped at my arse as I carried her, I didn't put her back on the ground until we reached the living room.

We ate our bacon sarnies and drank Buck's Fizz by the Christmas tree with its twinkling white lights and garish display of trinkets, and I couldn't help staring at my Mallory in her just-woken-up, half-naked state. I wanted to have her again right then and there, but we had gifts to open so I decided to hold back, determined that I would make this morning special for her – and then make the most of her body again later.

She handed me a little rectangular parcel and I just stared at it. It looked so beautiful wrapped in her handmade wrapping paper with its gold hearts and snowflakes that I just didn't want to spoil it. She encouraged me, clearly eager to see what I thought of her gift.

Carefully I opened the wrapping and took out the hand-painted sign. She had *made* me a gift, and it was the most beautiful thing I'd ever received. So simple, but the meaning behind it made my lip tremble as I read the sign aloud, '"Welcome to Greg and Mallory's Home". Mallory, this is the best Christmas gift I've ever been given.'

She laughed. 'What? Did you never get a bike or a Scalextric?' she teased.

'Aye, yes, course I did. But *this* means so much more because *you* made it for me and it makes our moving in together official. Best gift ever, just like I said.' We shared a tender kiss before I handed her the gift I'd got for her.

She frowned and the puzzled look on her face at the flat rectangular parcel had me jumping in to explain. 'Now, before you open it and go all apeshit on me, I just want to defend myself and say that it's something for us *both*. But I think you'll be happy and that's what matters.'

She eyed me suspiciously and opened it. 'Bloody hell, Greg! Two first-class return flights to *Canada*?' Before I knew what was happening, she launched herself into my arms and covered my face in kisses.

'Whoa! That's not the reaction I was prepared for!' I slipped my arms around her and pulled her to my chest.

Leaning away from me, she met my eyes. 'I know and I should be angry with you. But how can I be when it's just so perfect?' Her lips met mine again in a less vigorous assault – not that I was complaining about the passion she showed the first time.

'Well, I spoke to Renee and she says we can either stay with her, or, if we don't feel comfortable doing that, she'll book us into the hotel in Kingston, her treat.'

'How wonderful! I love you, Greg McBradden.' We tumbled to the rug, and all thoughts of waiting until later to savour her body again went out of the window and joined the falling snow.

*

On December twenty-eighth Brad and Josie, Mallory's best friends from Yorkshire, arrived to stay in time for Hogmanay. As Brad and I made coffee for our women in the kitchen – giving the girls time to catch up and talk each other's head off – I decided to put my next plan into action.

'So, Brad, mate. How are you fixed for a wee bit of New Year shopping?'

'Yeah, sure. Looking for summat in particular?' His Yorkshire accent was much stronger than Mallory's and sometimes I had to *really* listen to get what he was on about.

'Yeah. I need you to be my smokescreen.'

He raised his eyebrows and grinned. 'Oooh, that sounds intriguing.'

'Not a word to Josie though, eh?'

'You what? Do you think I'm daft or summat? She can't hold her own water, that one.' Brad laughed.

'Great, so you and I will go in one direction and the girls can go off in another, eh? Or better still, they can go in Mally's car and we'll take the Landy. That way I can get sorted without distractions.'

'Good plan, mate.'

My magnificent plan was in motion. Mallory would be getting several surprises come Hogmanay.

*

New Year's Eve – Hogmanay

I dressed in my kilt, knowing Mallory loved a man in Highland dress… well, knowing she loved *me* in Highland dress, actually. Brad and I waited in the living room for the girls to come down the stairs in their finery. I was playing at the pub for the Hogmanay celebrations, and my nerves were jangling for several reasons; the *least* of which was performing.

Suddenly my eyes were drawn to the doorway where Mallory stood in a sexy, fitted silver dress and heels. My mouth fell open and I just stared at her voluptuous curves, thinking to myself that I wanted to fling her over my shoulder, carry her back upstairs, and rip it off. I trailed my eyes down her body and back up again, meeting her blue orbs with a smile. She, too, was staring hungrily at me. *Think sensible thoughts, think sensible thoughts,* I repeated over and over in my head, willing my blood to return northwards. Sheesh, the effect she had on me with just one sultry look of longing.

'Get a bloody room, you two.' Brad chuckled as he punched me on the arm, releasing me from my lust-filled stupor.

We made our way over to the pub in the chilled December air, and I made some joke about wishing I were from Eskimo heritage, considering my crown jewels were turning to ice under my bloody kilt. *So much for looking good for Mallory. It'll be a wonder if my package functions after this bloody weather.*

Thankfully the pub was nice and cosy when we arrived, and the whisky that was handed to me by Stella certainly helped. I wasn't drinking as much of it anymore. I had no sorrows to drown. Just memories to keep in my heart.

I took up my place behind the mic stand and grabbed the attention of the crowd. 'Right, now, guys, as you know, this roller-coaster year is drawing to a close and I'm happy to be sharing this special evening with yous all tonight. I won't be doing much blathering. So enjoy the music, and dance if you have the room around you, but remember…'

'DON'T SING ALONG!' the crowd shouted in unison, and I laughed heartily but I knew for a fact they bloody would.

Chapter Fifty-two

I was right. They bloody sang along at every given opportunity. Having said that, it was my own fault for singing such bouncy bloody songs. I slotted the odd smooch number in there too, especially for my gorgeous girl. And her eyes filled with tears when I brought her to sit by me as I sang 'Just the Way You Are' by Bruno Mars. When the song ended, we kissed, and the place erupted into applause and whistles. There wasn't a dry eye in the pub, and I knew I'd pay later but I didn't care. I wanted the whole world to know how I felt about her.

At the end of the night I sang 'I'm Gonna Be (500 Miles)' by The Proclaimers, and the roof nearly flew off the place as the crowd got rather carried away. I gave up singing in the end and just played as everyone knew the words and I was past caring what they sounded like. I sat there with a huge grin on my face and when I caught Mallory's gaze fixed on me, I playfully rolled my eyes.

I finished at five minutes to midnight and announced the time over the PA system, and the excitement in the place ramped up another notch. I *had* to get to Mallory. It was like swimming upstream against the tide, trying to get through the horde of people telling me what a great night it'd been. But I was on a mission. I wanted to kiss Mallory as the new year came in.

Eventually I reached her, grabbed her hand, and pulled her towards the door. Stella announced four minutes to New Year, and, with a grin fixed on my face, I tugged my beautiful girl behind me as I forged ahead and pulled her out of the door.

She teetered along on her silver heels and giggled uncontrollably. 'Greg! Where are we going? We're going to miss the countdown.'

I didn't answer until we reached the midpoint of the bridge and then I stopped, a little out of breath. 'I think we should celebrate here, Mallory,' I told her before taking her face in my hands and kissing her deeply. She melted into me and I could have kissed her there until sunrise, but there were things I wanted to say. I pulled away and gazed into her eyes as an announcement that it was two minutes to midnight could be heard from inside.

Taking a deep breath, I began to speak. 'Mallory... I love you more than anything in this world, do you know that?' She smiled and stroked my cheek. 'I love your laugh, I love your body, and I love how you make me feel. I want to feel that way for the rest of my life.' I knew I was rambling but I had to get the words out. Her smile faded and her expression became serious.

'One minute to midnight!' came the announcement in the background.

My chest began to heave as the enormity of what I was about to do sank in, but I had never wanted any*thing* or any*one* more. 'Please, would you make me the happiest man alive? Mallory' – I struggled for the words and finally posed the most important question of my life in Gaelic – *'am pos thu mi*?'

Mallory frowned and my heart began to try and make its escape through my dress shirt. I pulled the little velvet box out of my jacket pocket and held it out.

She just stared.

'Ten, nine, eight, seven,' they chanted from the pub.

Dropping to one knee before her, I opened the box to show her the diamond engagement ring enclosed inside and held it aloft. From where I kneeled I gazed up at her widened eyes, which were now glassy with tears and I tried to fight my own emotions, but several tears escaped anyway as I peered up at her. 'Mallory, will you marry me?'

'Four, three, two…'

Her mouth fell open and she touched her fingertips to her lips. 'Oh, Greg. Yes!'

'Happy New Year!' Loud cheers and whoops came from the pub as people began to spill outside to celebrate.

Relief and happiness sprinted throughout my body, and when I stood again I felt ten feet tall. I pulled her into my arms and we kissed as people began singing 'Auld Lang Syne'.

*

Once everyone realised what I'd just done, the joyous crowd made its way over to us and we were engulfed in hugs and congratulations. But the whole time we kept our eyes fixed on each other. The happiness I saw in her made me feel complete. We belonged to each other and now we were going to make it official.

Stella announced that she had champagne back in the pub, and so eventually everyone wandered back inside.

Mallory turned to follow them, but I held her back and took her into my arms. 'I hope you didn't mind me proposing here on the bridge,' I told her as I tucked a strand of her chocolate-brown hair behind her ear. I kissed her tenderly and stroked her cheek. 'I want this to be *our* place too.'

A tear escaped her eye but I caught it with my thumb. She smiled up at me. 'It *is* our place. I have more memories of you and me here now. This is *our* bridge over the Atlantic. It's our bridge of hope.'

Wrapping her in my arms, I began to lead her back to the pub. 'Come on, you're freezing and I've an icy breeze blowing around places I would rather I didn't have it blowing. Let's go have champagne before it's all gone.'

She smiled. 'Champagne… who would have thought it? Didn't realise Stella stocked it.'

I cringed as the truth was about to come out. 'Erm, she *doesn't* usually. I went out with Brad and bought a boot load just in case you said yes. Stella knew all along.'

'Oh, yeah? What if I'd said no?' She dug me in the ribs playfully with her elbow.

'Don't joke. I've been terrified and wondering if they did sale or return.'

*

Josie and Brad decided to stay in the pub that night so that Mallory and I could have the house to ourselves to celebrate our engagement. When we arrived at home I lit the log burner and Mallory let the dogs out before putting them to bed. I grabbed the bottle of champers that I'd hidden by the back door and opened it.

Handing a glass to my gorgeous girl, I held my glass aloft. 'A toast… to my beautiful fiancée, you have made me happy beyond words. I will love you forever.' We clinked our glasses and kissed.

'May I make a toast too?' I nodded. 'To my wonderful husband-to-be. We've had some pretty steep ups and downs, but at least that proves we can handle *anything*. I hope I can continue to make you as happy as you make me. I love you, Greg.'

I took her glass and placed it beside mine on the hearth. I wanted to be closer to her. Pulling her into my lap, I reached up and slipped my hand into her hair as I took her mouth with my own in a sensual, luscious kiss.

She gazed down at me as I slipped my hand around her back and pulled down the zipper of her silver dress. Once her lace-covered breasts were freed, she pulled me into the soft mounds and I inhaled her scent as her warmth radiated into me. Leaning back, I began to unbutton my shirt under her watchful eyes.

With a smile I told her, 'I have a surprise for you.'

'Really? Another one? What is it?' she asked with excitement in her eyes. I reached out to the hearth and pulled out a red velvet box from behind the stack of kindling. I handed the box to her and she opened it and gasped. Inside the box was a silver chain with a pendant hanging from it. It was similar to the friendship necklace I had bought for her birthday, only this was two of the symbols linked together.

She gasped. 'Oh, it's beautiful.'

'The first necklace I bought you, for your birthday, was the symbol for friendship. But this one... the Serch Bythol... this is for everlasting love,' I told her as I fastened the chain around her neck.

Tears welled in her eyes as she looked down at the intertwined knots.

But my surprises didn't end there. 'You know how I disappeared with Brad earlier today?'

She nodded. 'To buy the champagne?'

'No, I already had that. No, I went with Brad into Oban. And I had a little ink done, especially for you.'

Once my shirt was completely removed, I pulled off

the white dressing that was covering my new tattoo.

When she saw what I'd had done, she gasped and covered her mouth as more tears welled in her eyes. I'd had an exact copy of her necklace tattooed on my chest above the Gaelic script there.

'Now you'll always be near my heart and I'll always be close to yours.'

No words were spoken; her eyes told me everything I needed to know. She loved what I'd had done and so did I. Once all of our clothes were relinquished, we lay back on the rug.

I needed to be inside her and she grasped at me too. Neither of us could get close enough. We made love quickly and urgently and found our release together. It was magical.

Sheer bliss.

Chapter Fifty-three

Seeing as I was desperate to marry Mallory, the wheels were set in motion right away. Alice made yet another last-ditch attempt to 'win me back' when she found out about my impending nuptials, but, as I told her, giving her a *second* chance had been stupid, a third would have been plain crazy.

Mallory was sitting beside me when Alice made her last phone call to me. There were no secrets between us anymore. Only honesty. When I ended the call, I glanced over and she was eyeing me with concern.

'Was she okay?'

She had no reason to be concerned about that nasty piece of work, but that's just Mallory. All bloody heart. 'Oh, yeah, she was fine. Faked a few sobs, but she'll get over it. She has no choice. I am utterly yours, gorgeous.'

Lowering her eyes, she fiddled with the hem of her top. 'And are *you* okay about it all?'

'Me? *Of course* I am.' I kissed her in between each word I uttered. 'I have never... ever... been... happier... than... I am... now that... I'm... with you.'

Laying her back on the couch, I tugged her top from her body, delighted to find her braless, and she gazed up at me with longing. 'I can't wait to marry you,' I told her as I removed her yoga pants and panties. 'And I can't wait for you to have my name.' Shrugging off my own clothing as quickly as I could, I settled myself between her silky thighs. 'You are going to make the most stunning bride a man has ever seen... and you'll be all mine.'

She didn't speak. She just pulled me down on top of her and kissed me deeply. I smoothed my hands up over the inward curves of her waist and further on until I caressed her breasts as she gripped my shoulders. Seeing her lost in pleasure was one of my favourite sights; better than any erotic painting or photograph I'd ever laid eyes on. The way her eyes closed and her back arched made me desperate to take her and so I did. As our bodies connected, a low groan left my chest and a hint of a smile appeared on her lips.

'I love hearing you like that,' she gasped. 'I love that I make you feel good.' *Good?* Fuck, was *that* an understatement. 'In fact, I just love you. All of you.' Her breathing accelerated and I could feel the pulse in her neck throbbing when I leaned more fully into her. Nothing compared to the feeling of being immersed in her; body and soul. Sex with her was transcendent. It went way beyond any experience I'd ever had, and I loved her so much, I just couldn't get enough.

Pulling back, I watched our bodies where we were connected so intimately. I couldn't believe that it was possible to fall deeper for her each time we made love, but seeing her there beneath me, giving herself to me and holding nothing back, I fell further and further. The way she fitted me so perfectly and the way her soft curves moulded against me had me on the verge of tears over and over again. Tingles of sheer pleasure began where we were joined and radiated like a starburst throughout my body. Bending forward again, I took one tightened nipple into my mouth and sucked it deep. Her cries of ecstasy were my undoing and we both ascended into outer space.

*

The divorce between Alice and me was finalised in February and that meant all systems were go. Mallory visited Leeds to go wedding-dress shopping with a rather overexcited Josie in tow, and I booked Kilbrandon Church for our service. Everyone who meant anything was invited. Mallory's adopted family from Canada said they wouldn't miss it, and as Mallory's parents had passed many years before, Colin from the shop offered to give the bride away.

The night before the wedding I gave the girls their space and I stayed at the pub. Stella made my favourite meal, her steak pie, and once I'd eaten we sat chatting together.

She cocked her head to one side and eyed me with a

smile. 'You know, I think it's testament to this place that you two got together.'

'How do you mean?' I asked.

'Well, if you think about it, if she and Sam had looked elsewhere, you may never have met. This is the place *you* gravitated to after you and your wife split too. I think there may have been a little divine intervention. Don't you?'

I smiled but didn't reply and she took away the dishes. I retired up to my room with Rhiannon to put the finishing touches to the song I'd been writing for Mallory. We were writing our own vows; and of course I wasn't known for using my own words, but this time it was important that I did.

Working 'til the early hours, I finally finished the song and lay awake replaying the last year and memories of Mallory over in my mind. The first time I saw her walk into the pub. That same day when she arrived looking like a member of a KISS tribute band. Finding her distraught on the beach. Kissing her for the first time even though it was wrong to do it. Waking up beside her that first time before everything fell apart so spectacularly. Her curves, her smile, her radiance. Every little thing about her that I adored. She was so kind, beautiful, warm, loving. And above all else she *got* me. She understood what I'd been through.

We connected.

*

I had made sure to think of everything to make this day as special as it could be, from the red carpet leading up to the church entrance to the white roses – for my very own Yorkshire rose – inside the church, filling the space with their sweet scent. The music was ready, the congregation was ready. *I* was *more* than ready.

Brad stood beside me as my best man and nudged me as the doors opened. 'She's here, mate. It's time to rock 'n' roll, bud.'

'The Reason' by Hoobastank resonated throughout the church, and I slowly raised my eyes to meet hers. I think I stopped breathing for a while when I saw her. She looked more beautiful than ever standing there in that ivory dress, and *that* was saying something. My heart lurched into action and my lip began to tremble. She'd arrived. She hadn't got cold feet and run away.

This was it.

Brad thrust a clean hanky into my hand and I dabbed at my eyes. As she made her way slowly down the aisle towards me, the fitted bodice of her dress sparkled in the sunlight coming in through the stained-glass windows. I shook my head, not quite ready to believe it. But she smiled and my heart melted. I loved her more than anything and it was clear from the tears glistening in her eyes that she felt the same. Her satiny chocolate-brown hair was pinned up, but loose tendrils fell about her shoulders, just touching her skin.

Wow. Just beautiful.

When she arrived before me, I took a deep breath to calm my raging emotions and leaned in to her and whispered, 'Thank you for marrying me. I know this must be a hard day for you. But I've never loved or admired you more than I do right now.' I took her hand in mine and the kind-faced vicar began…

Eventually it was time for us to say the words we'd prepared. My heart pounded at my ribs as I turned to face Mallory and listen to her.

'Greg, since the moment I met you I've been on a roller-coaster ride. We've supported each other through grief and our own individual issues, and it's been difficult at times. But I cannot imagine my life without you in it. And I don't *want* to. Whatever life throws at us, we'll get through it. We've proved that we can… I think my guardian angel was watching over me when he brought me to you.'

I knew the guardian angel she was referring to and I swallowed hard. Her voice had cracked and I was teetering on the edge of a breakdown.

She smiled and gazed lovingly into my eyes. 'There's a saying that's very close to the heart of someone I love that goes… "Love Conquers All", and I never believed that to be true until I met you, but now I believe it irrevocably. I love you with all my heart.'

Her choice of words had me thinking my own

guardian angel had been at work when inspiring me to write Mallory's song. With shaking hands, I took the guitar from Brad and began to play. The song I had written was called 'Love Conquers All' and it told her exactly how she made me feel and what she meant to me.

I want to hold you forever
And that's what I'll do
Whatever life throws our way
It'll be me and you
And we'll both stand tall
Because love conquers all
Yeah we'll both stand tall
Because love conquers all

I fought my way through the words, and at the end there was barely a dry eye in the place, including my own.

I handed my guitar back to Brad, and Mallory flung her arms around me, whispering into my ear, 'Greg, I love you so much. Thank you for such a beautiful gift.'

Feeling her pressed against me and seeing the adoration in her eyes made my heart thump and my stomach flip for joy. The woman in my arms was everything to me. Everything and more. 'There was no other way for me to tell you how I feel. I can't be without you ever again, Mallory. This is it. This is forever.'

'Well, I'm going nowhere unless you come too.'

The vicar announced us as husband and wife, and the place erupted in applause as I took her into my arms and kissed her once more.

My wife.

My love.

My Mallory.

Epilogue

So, here I sit in hospital beside my gorgeous sleeping wife, holding my infant daughter in my arms. We had quite an exhausting time bringing her into the world, I can tell you. *Mairi Samantha.* So very beautiful. I keep having to pinch myself to believe that this is all real. The last couple of years have been a whirlwind to say the least. And as I gaze down at the precious little bundle as she sleeps in her daddy's embrace, I have to blink the tears away. I can't move as I don't want to disturb her. I just want to gaze down at the best thing I've ever made and keep focusing on how *bloomin' lucky* I am.

Hey, notice the lack of swears? Are you proud of me?

She was named after the two people who inadvertently brought me and her mummy together. Little did they know back then that they would play a part in the creation of the most beautiful creature I've ever laid eyes on – aside from her mother, that is. The wee bairn has a mop of wayward dark hair that sticks out at all angles, and when I look at her cute little face I see a combination of myself and Mallory, which makes my chest ache with so much love I think I might just burst. When her eyes were open earlier I couldn't believe how *blue* they were. Now, I know they say that all babies have blue eyes and that eventually they may change colour, but I don't think Mairi Samantha's will. I think she'll have her mother's eyes. Crystal clear, azure blue and full of emotion. And I will do *all* I can to ensure that the only emotion she *ever* feels is happiness.

As I stroke her tiny soft cheek with my finger, I know in my heart that I would do *anything* for her. Slay dragons, fight the monsters under the bed, walk over burning coals… you name it. I'll protect her until my dying day. No matter how old she is. She'll always be my little girl.

Mallory looks so peaceful with a serene smile on her lips, and I have never been more proud of another human being. *Ever.* What she endured to bring our daughter into the world… wow… I will *never* be able to repay her for that.

The words to 'I'm Yours' by The Script roll around my head, and I make a mental note to learn it and play it for her when we take our daughter home. Because although I tell her I love her every day, she still loves it when I play my guitar for her. The way she looks at me… I feel I could do anything. And those lyrics just express my feelings so perfectly.

And I *am* hers.

Forever.

What she and I have together came at a price. We had to fight our own grief *and* guilt to be together. But when you know something's meant to be, there's no stopping it. No amount of rough seas could ever tear me away from my two girls now.

And it's funny to think that not so long ago I stood on that wee stone structure in the village, looking out to sea and wishing that someday it could symbolise something more than grief and sadness. That it would be our special place to build new and happy memories.

Well, I got my wish.

Because from now on when I stand there on the bridge over the Atlantic, with my wife and daughter, looking out at the ocean, I'll know that it was *that bridge* that brought my future. After all the heartache I've suffered and the pain Mallory went through to be here, it was *that bridge* that brought us true love. And it was *that bridge* that brought us both the most precious gift a person could ask for.

It brought us hope.

Acknowledgements

As always there are so many people I want to thank but I'll try and keep it brief. First and foremost, thank you to my family and friends for your continued support and for plying me with cups of tea, biscuits and the odd glass of wine whilst I've been editing. Every writer needs fuel!

Thank you to the many bloggers and readers who continue to share my posts and help me to publicise my books. You're such a huge help and I appreciate your friendship and eagerness to share.

Muckle thanks to the fictional Greg for being a loveable rogue that my readers couldn't let go of. I'm pretty sure they'll adore you even more in your own book.

I owe so much to Rich, aka 'Not Greg', my hubby for accompanying me to signing events and being a sounding board, supporter and fun companion on my writing journey.

I must say a huge thank you to my agent Tracy Brennan of Trace Literary Agency for working so hard on my behalf. I'm so very grateful for all that you do.

Finally, massive thanks and hugs to the whole team at Aria. Authors, editors, publicity—absolutely everyone. Thank you for making this dream a reality.

A Letter from the Author

To my readers,

I began writing this book following the response I received to a short blog post that I had written from Greg's POV. The number of requests for me to write the whole book was overwhelming. It was wonderful to know that people had fallen for Greg so much that they wanted to know more about him and so I willingly obliged. It made me so very happy to write this story as it meant I got to spend more time in Greg's head. I think it's become one of my favourite places!

I have the best, most supportive readers and love that so many of you have been with me since before *my first book* was even published. You've been there, reading snippets and giving me feedback and encouragement every step of the way and I appreciate each and every one of you. In all honesty I can tell you that it felt amazing to be asked to write this story and I can only hope that you love Greg even more when you've taken this journey with him; my potty-mouthed Scotsman.

So with a song in my heart readers, this one's for you.

Lisa

HELLO FROM ARIA

We hope you enjoyed this book! Let us know, we'd love to hear from you.

We are Aria, a dynamic digital-first fiction imprint from award-winning independent publishers Head of Zeus. At heart, we're avid readers committed to publishing exactly the kind of books we love to read — from romance and sagas to crime, thrillers and historical adventures. Visit us online and discover a community of like-minded fiction fans!

We're also on the look out for tomorrow's superstar authors. So, if you're a budding writer looking for a publisher, we'd love to hear from you. You can submit your book online at ariafiction.com/we-want-read-your-book

You can find us at:
Email: aria@headofzeus.com
Website: www.ariafiction.com
Submissions: www.ariafiction.com/we-want-read-your-book
Facebook: @ariafiction
Twitter: @Aria_Fiction
Instagram: @ariafiction